Alan Savage is the pseudonym of a [...] and remarkable storyteller, with a deep personal interest in history and military affairs. His previous bestsellers as Alan Savage are *Ottoman*, *Moghul*, *The Eight Banners*, *Queen of Night* and *The Last Bannerman*.

To Carol
Merry Christmas
Dear
Hope you will enjoy
the bk.
With Love
Bet.

Also by Alan Savage:

OTTOMAN
MOGHUL
THE EIGHT BANNERS
QUEEN OF NIGHT
THE LAST BANNERMAN

QUEEN OF LIONS

Alan Savage

WARNER BOOKS

A *Warner* Book

First published in Great Britain in 1994
by Little, Brown and Company

This edition published in 1994 by Warner Books

Copyright © Alan Savage 1994

The moral right of the author has been asserted.

A CIP catalogue record for this book is
available from the British Library.

ISBN 0 7515 0495 5

Typeset in Times by Solidus (Bristol) Limited
Printed and bound in Great Britain by
Clays Ltd, St. Ives plc

Warner Books
A Division of
Little, Brown and Company (UK) Limited
Brettenham House
Lancaster Place
London WC2 7EN

COMMON ANCESTORY OF HENRY VI AND
MARGARET OF ANJOU

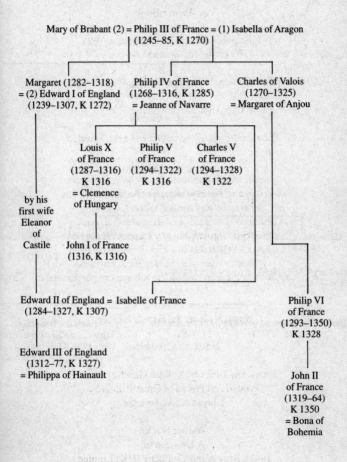

RELATIONSHIP OF HENRY VI OF ENGLAND
TO MARGARET OF ANJOU AND TO DUKES OF BURGUNDY

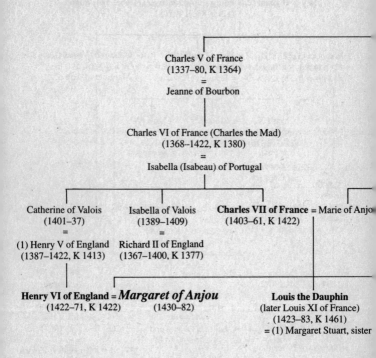

Charles V of France
(1337–80, K 1364)
=
Jeanne of Bourbon

Charles VI of France (Charles the Mad)
(1368–1422, K 1380)
=
Isabella (Isabeau) of Portugal

Catherine of Valois
(1401–37)
=
(1) Henry V of England
(1387–1422, K 1413)

Isabella of Valois
(1389–1409)
=
Richard II of England
(1367–1400, K 1377)

Charles VII of France = Marie of Anjou
(1403–61, K 1422)

Henry VI of England = *Margaret of Anjou*
(1422–71, K 1422)   (1430–82)

Louis the Dauphin
(later Louis XI of France)
(1423–83, K 1461)
= (1) Margaret Stuart, sister

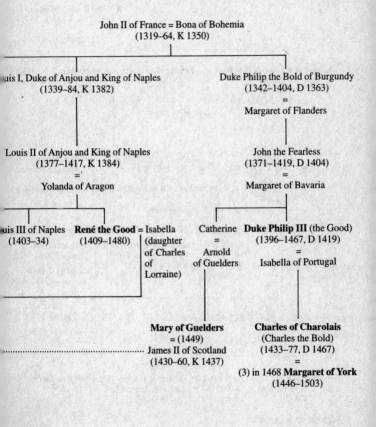

John II of France = Bona of Bohemia
(1319–64, K 1350)

Louis I, Duke of Anjou and King of Naples
(1339–84, K 1382)

Duke Philip the Bold of Burgundy
(1342–1404, D 1363)
=
Margaret of Flanders

Louis II of Anjou and King of Naples
(1377–1417, K 1384)
='
Yolanda of Aragon

John the Fearless
(1371–1419, D 1404)
=
Margaret of Bavaria

Louis III of Naples
(1403–34)

René the Good = Isabella
(1409–1480)   (daughter
               of Charles
               of
               Lorraine)

Catherine
=
Arnold
of Guelders

Duke Philip III (the Good)
(1396–1467, D 1419)
=
Isabella of Portugal

Mary of Guelders
= (1449)
James II of Scotland
(1430–60, K 1437)

Charles of Charolais
(Charles the Bold)
(1433–77, D 1467)
=
(3) in 1468 Margaret of York
(1446–1503)

HOUSE OF LANCASTER

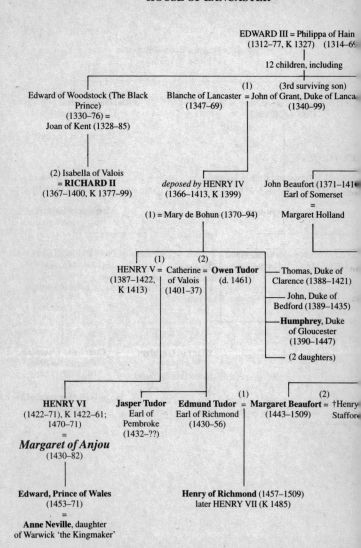

EDWARD III = Philippa of Hain
(1312–77, K 1327)   (1314–69

12 children, including

Edward of Woodstock (The Black
Prince)
(1330–76) =
Joan of Kent (1328–85)

(1)   (3rd surviving son)
Blanche of Lancaster = John of Grant, Duke of Lanca
(1347–69)   (1340–99)

(2) Isabella of Valois
= RICHARD II
(1367–1400, K 1377–99)

deposed by HENRY IV
(1366–1413, K 1399)

(1) = Mary de Bohun (1370–94)

John Beaufort (1371–141
Earl of Somerset
=
Margaret Holland

(1)   (2)
HENRY V = Catherine = **Owen Tudor**
(1387–1422,   of Valois   (d. 1461)
K 1413)   (1401–37)

— Thomas, Duke of
Clarence (1388–1421)

— John, Duke of
Bedford (1389–1435)

— **Humphrey, Duke
of Gloucester**
(1390–1447)

— (2 daughters)

HENRY VI
(1422–71), K 1422–61;
1470–71)
=
Margaret of Anjou
(1430–82)

Jasper Tudor
Earl of
Pembroke
(1432–??)

Edmund Tudor
Earl of Richmond
(1430–56)

(1)
= **Margaret Beaufort**
(1443–1509)

(2)
= †Henry
Stafford

Edward, Prince of Wales
(1453–71)
=
Anne Neville, daughter
of Warwick 'the Kingmaker'

Henry of Richmond (1457–1509)
later HENRY VII (K 1485)

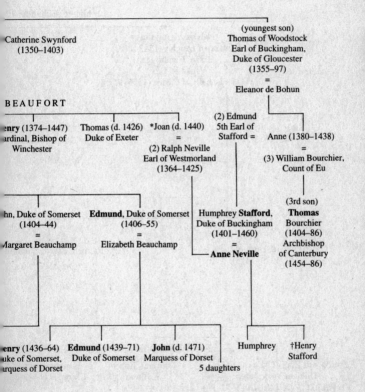

Catherine Swynford
(1350–1403)

(youngest son)
Thomas of Woodstock
Earl of Buckingham,
Duke of Gloucester
(1355–97)
=
Eleanor de Bohun

BEAUFORT

Henry (1374–1447)
Cardinal, Bishop of
Winchester

Thomas (d. 1426)
Duke of Exeter

*Joan (d. 1440)
=
(2) Ralph Neville
Earl of Westmorland
(1364–1425)

(2) Edmund
5th Earl of
Stafford =   Anne (1380–1438)
=
(3) William Bourchier,
Count of Eu

John, Duke of Somerset
(1404–44)
=
Margaret Beauchamp

Edmund, Duke of Somerset
(1406–55)
=
Elizabeth Beauchamp

Humphrey Stafford,
Duke of Buckingham
(1401–1460)
=
Anne Neville

(3rd son)
Thomas
Bourchier
(1404–86)
Archbishop
of Canterbury
(1454–86)

Henry (1436–64)
Duke of Somerset,
Marquess of Dorset

Edmund (1439–71)
Duke of Somerset

John (d. 1471)
Marquess of Dorset
5 daughters

Humphrey

†Henry
Stafford

*see Neville family tree, p xii–xiii

HOUSE OF YORK

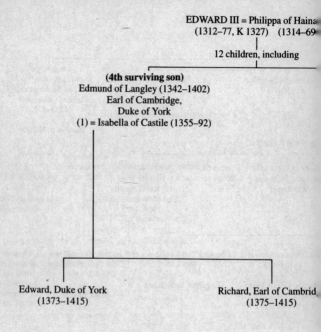

EDWARD III = Philippa of Haina
(1312–77, K 1327)   (1314–69

12 children, including

(4th surviving son)
Edmund of Langley (1342–1402)
Earl of Cambridge,
Duke of York
(1) = Isabella of Castile (1355–92)

Edward, Duke of York
(1373–1415)

Richard, Earl of Cambrid
(1375–1415)

Edward, 6th Earl of March (1442–83)
Duke of York; later
EDWARD IV (K 1461–70; 1471–83)
=
Elizabeth Woodville
(1437–92), the daughter
of Jacquetta the widow of John, Duke of
Bedford (see House of Lancaster)

Edmund, Earl of
Rutland
(1443–60)

George, Duke of
Clarence (1449–78)
=
Isabelle Neville
(1451–76)
daughter of
Warwick 'the
Kingmaker'

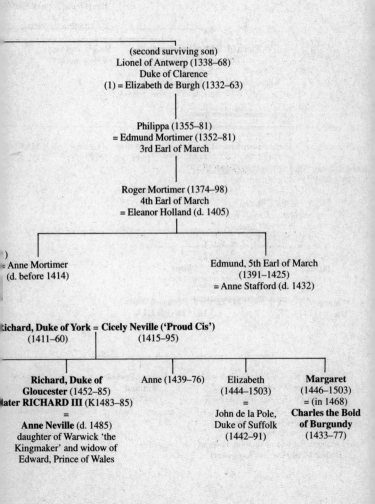

(second surviving son)
Lionel of Antwerp (1338–68)
Duke of Clarence
(1) = Elizabeth de Burgh (1332–63)

Philippa (1355–81)
= Edmund Mortimer (1352–81)
3rd Earl of March

Roger Mortimer (1374–98)
4th Earl of March
= Eleanor Holland (d. 1405)

)
= Anne Mortimer
(d. before 1414)

Edmund, 5th Earl of March
(1391–1425)
= Anne Stafford (d. 1432)

Richard, Duke of York = Cicely Neville ('Proud Cis')
(1411–60)   (1415–95)

**Richard, Duke of
Gloucester** (1452–85)
later **RICHARD III** (K1483–85)
=
Anne Neville (d. 1485)
daughter of Warwick 'the
Kingmaker' and widow of
Edward, Prince of Wales

Anne (1439–76)

Elizabeth
(1444–1503)
=
John de la Pole,
Duke of Suffolk
(1442–91)

Margaret
(1446–1503)
= (in 1468)
**Charles the Bold
of Burgundy**
(1433–77)

THE NEVILLES

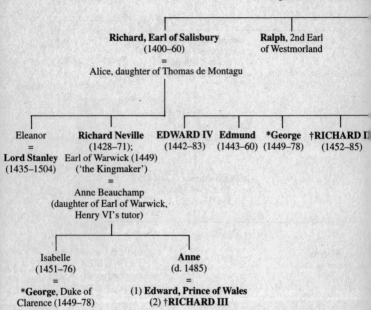

Joan Beaufort (d. 1440)
daughter of John of Gaunt

Richard, Earl of Salisbury   **Ralph**, 2nd Earl
(1400–60)   of Westmorland
=
Alice, daughter of Thomas de Montagu

Eleanor   **Richard Neville**   **EDWARD IV**   **Edmund**   ***George**   **†RICHARD I**
=   (1428–71);   (1442–83)   (1443–60)   (1449–78)   (1452–85)
Lord Stanley   Earl of Warwick (1449)
(1435–1504)   ('the Kingmaker')
=
Anne Beauchamp
(daughter of Earl of Warwick,
Henry VI's tutor)

Isabelle   **Anne**
(1451–76)   (d. 1485)
=   =
*George, Duke of   (1) **Edward, Prince of Wales**
Clarence (1449–78)   (2) **†RICHARD III**

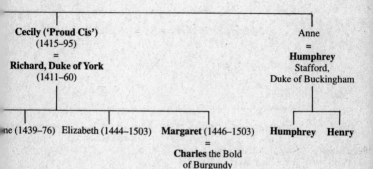

ph Neville (1364–1425)
t Earl of Westmorland

Cecily ('Proud Cis')
(1415–95)
=
Richard, Duke of York
(1411–60)

Anne
=
Humphrey
Stafford,
Duke of Buckingham

ne (1439–76)   Elizabeth (1444–1503)   **Margaret** (1446–1503)
=
Charles the Bold
of Burgundy
(1433–77)

Humphrey   **Henry**

I was a queen. Thus I am still a queen, for how may mere misfortune affect my rank?

Had I but a single wish, it would be that I had married my husband's father. Would we not have conquered the world?

I shall set it all down, if only for my own gratification. I shall spare no one, not even myself.

They called me she-wolf. But they were lions who flocked to my banner.

1

'Come quickly,' my mother said. 'The Earl awaits you.'

'And should an earl not wait upon a princess, Mama?' I asked. 'Especially an upstart earl?'

'This is no ordinary upstart,' Mama declared. 'He is King Henry's favourite. And the match is recommended by Uncle Charles. He takes a great interest in it.'

Undoubtedly my Uncle Charles – he was married to my mother's sister – was interested, and not only in the match. Uncle Charles was interested in everything to do with his 'little Meg'. Sometimes the interest grew irksome. One never knew when he would behave oddly. It was a family weakness.

But I myself was more interested in the proposed match than I had allowed even Mama to suspect. I was fourteen years old, and I was being put forward as the wife of the greatest king in Christendom. Or so it was said. A proposal which, it seemed, must wait upon the approval of this grandson of a merchant! But I have never been negative in my approach to life. If greatness was to come to me through the good offices of a merchant, even so would I accept it.

I waved my ladies aside, and led them through the door, Mama at my elbow, my sister Yolanda behind. And so entered the reception chamber, where this William de la Pole, Earl of Suffolk, awaited me.

*

I knew not what to expect; in my upbringing Englishmen were all represented as scoundrels who burned French manor houses and raped their female occupants. That I should be required to marry their king – perhaps – was a matter of politics, and I had equally been brought up to understand that my own feelings when it came to the marriage bed were to be entirely subjected to affairs of state.

Nor, I will admit, was I even terribly interested in the ambassador. I had been informed that in this May of 1444, the Earl of Suffolk was forty-four years old; that is, he was just old enough to be my grandfather, had he made an early start. Young girls do not take a great interest in grandfathers, even their own.

Thus I was quite taken aback. The Earl made a leg and a flourish at my entrance. He was in any event a blaze of colour in his rose madder robe with its brown fur trim, his grey-blue doublet sleeves which matched his pointed shoes, and his golden coronet. But it was the man himself who took my breath away. He was tall and powerfully built, so unlike the courtiers at Uncle Charles's court, with red-gold hair and beard and flashing blue eyes. His face was somewhat aquiline, at once noble and haughty, his bearing far more regal than my uncle's, who although a king was inclined to mince and stoop his shoulders as if about to receive some bad news. Well, he had received enough bad news in his time. But the Earl of Suffolk had clearly never received other than good.

In a word, here was the most handsome man I had ever beheld, or ever would behold – with one exception, and that exception, may God rot his vitals, was and remains my most implacable foe.

I anticipate. My reaction to seeing the Earl of Suffolk was to reflect that if he was a typical Englishman – and why should he not be? – then was I the most fortunate of women. Had I not been told often enough that Henry VI of England was a true son of his famous father: Henry V, the most splendid man of his time?

I do not boast when I claim that the Earl was hardly less taken with me. Indeed, in an aside to one of his aides, clearly presuming that I understood no English, he remarked, 'Goddam, sirrah, but she is quite beautiful.'

As it happened, I had been taught the English tongue, but I did not take offence, for I had also been taught that the English are unable to utter a single sentence without inserting either an oath or a curse, so much so that the common people of France do not refer to them as English at all, but as 'Goddams'.

In making his statement the Earl was of course referring only to my face, as this was the only part of my person visible, and he was telling no lie. He was not the first person to call me beautiful, and besides, I had the evidence of my glass. I am a small person. When I was fourteen I measured just five feet from heel to crown, and I only ever gained an inch or two more even with maturity. Thus my features are also small, but of a truly becoming evenness, and yet relieved from plainness by my rounded chin, my small, slightly upturned nose, my high forehead, my smiling mouth – when I chose that it would smile – and most of all my green eyes, set wide and able (again when I chose) to glow. Perhaps they were glowing then, with pleasure.

He could also of course admire my hair, which was long and wavy, dark brown but with streaks of red in it, upon which I too wore a golden coronet (with more right, I think, than he.) For the rest, I was totally concealed by my cobalt blue gown which rose to my throat and brushed the floor as I walked. The gown was decorated with vermilion stars and was one of my favourites. But so far as the Earl was concerned, he was looking at an immature girl.

Yet was he here to choose a queen. 'My lady,' he said in French, with another bow, having greeted my mother.

'My lord,' I replied, and, my mother having seated herself, I gestured him to a chair, and sat myself.

'You do me great honour, my lady,' he said. 'Coming to Tours especially to meet me.'

'It was his grace's wish, my lord.'

'Ah.' It was, of course, a debatable point at that time, as to whether his king or my uncle was the true ruler of France, but he was here to mend fences, not break them. 'His grace King Henry sends you gifts . . .' he half-turned, and waved his hand, and his people, grouped behind him, displayed a variety of bric-à-brac, mirrors and silks and the like, items of which I already possessed sufficient. Clearly the English were not going to offer anything of real value until they had decided that I was going to belong to them.

'And I have none to offer in return,' I said, allowing him a smile.

'On the contrary, my lady, his grace seeks from you the greatest gift of all, your hand.'

'Should you approve of me, no doubt, my lord.'

I had stolen the initiative. He flushed, and seemed at a loss, but his embarrassment was relieved by the sound of a trumpet announcing that my uncle was about to indulge us with his presence.

Everyone rose and faced the doorway, the men bowing and we ladies sinking into a deep curtsey as Uncle Charles entered.

Uncle Charles, the seventh of that name to rule the Kingdom of France, has generally been regarded as one of life's great failures. Well, his mother was little better than a whore, and his father was mad; he was disinherited by his parents while still in his teens, and forced to see his country overrun by the armies of the man who had replaced him as heir to the French throne, Henry V of England; on a visit to Bordeaux he had had a building collapse around his ears, which left him with a lifelong suspicion regarding the solidity of his surroundings; he had been raised from the depths of despair by the exhortations of a peasant girl who saw visions and could inspire armies to victory – opinion is still divided as to whether she was a saint or a witch – and who stood beside him when he was crowned in the cathedral at Rheims, in total defiance of his father's treaties. But he had raised no hand to save Joan the Maid from being burned alive, and this had utterly ruined his reputation.

On the other hand, since Henry V's premature death (which had left a nine-month-old boy – Charles's own nephew and now my prospective husband – heir to the thrones of England and France, according to treaty), my uncle had slowly and carefully with wonderful perseverance worked to restore both the substance of his inheritance and the dignity of his name. And, married as he was to my mother's sister, he had always been unfailingly kind to me, even if I understood that the son of a mad father cannot always be expected to be sane himself.

As I have mentioned, Uncle Charles walked with a stoop, although he was only just past forty years of age, and cast anxious glances from side to side as he moved, as if fearing an assassin's knife, although he was always surrounded by heavily armed guards. More likely he was afraid of his son, my cousin Louis, a small, ill-featured rogue, just twenty-one years old, who walked immediately behind him. The Dauphin had already conspired against his father on more than one occasion, and their present reconciliation was not expected to last.

Compared with the English milords, Cousin Louis was very soberly dressed. But he was considerably better dressed than his father. Uncle Charlie's clothes were dowdy and crushed, suggesting that he had slept in them – which he did, often enough – and although he did not wear a beard, he had clearly not shaved today.

A stronger contrast between this king and that earl who had just changed my views of masculine good looks could not be imagined.

But again, in contrast to his slovenly appearance, Uncle Charles had an eye for beauty, and I am not speaking merely of myself or my aunt or indeed his mistress, a woman called Agnes Sorel, of whom he was inordinately fond. This splendid château outside the city of Tours, to which Mama and I had been summoned – Papa had been called upon to meet the

English ambassador some months earlier, but was indisposed on this occasion – had actually been built by another, but Charles had taken great pains to beautify it, and make it into a splendid home. It was his pleasure to spend much more time here than within the grimy and noisy confines of Paris, which, in any event, had only recently been regained for France.

Now he was all smiles as he embraced my mother, and then my sister Yolanda; then he embraced me as well, allowing his fingers to trickle up and down my spine. Brought up as I had been in the heady sophistication of the French court, I had no doubt that my good uncle would have replaced Mademoiselle Sorel in his bed with Mademoiselle Margaret of Anjou without a moment's hesitation, had he not known such an incestuous act would bring with it the condemnation of the Church and the end of his hopes for a profitable treaty with England.

'Well, my lord,' he inquired of Suffolk. 'What do you think of our little Anjou rose?'

'I think, your grace, that your description is at once apt and accurate.'

'Good, good.' The King seated himself, and smiled at the assembled company. 'Well, then, we must talk, eh?'

'After I have reported to the King, your grace.'

'Hm,' Charles commented, not so pleased at either the prospect of a delay or the sly reference to his disputed title. 'Hm.' He waved his hand and the conversation became general as the wine was passed.

Suffolk and I, being the principals, naturally gravitated together, and raised our glasses to each other.

'And just what will you relate to his grace, my lord?' I inquired.

'Why, that I have encountered the most wondrous creature . . .'

'Creature, my lord?'

This was the first time he had seen my eyes flash steel, and he was duly taken aback. 'It was intended as a compliment, my lady.'

'Then I shall take it as such,' I agreed magnanimously. 'Continue.'

'Whose cheeks are like apples, whose mouth is eminently kissable . . .'

I raised my eyebrows. 'You are speculating, my lord.'

'Whose demeanour is majestic and at the same time far older than her years,' the scurvy fellow continued. 'Of course it will be my everlasting sorrow that I cannot report personally upon those aspects of your beauty which are necessarily concealed . . .'

We gazed at each other.

'Can they have a bearing upon the outcome of this negotiation, my lord?' I asked. I was not the least put out by his forwardness. On the contrary I enjoyed it, coming from so handsome a man.

'I imagine they would seal the matter, my lady.'

My decision was taken. I wished to wed this king who claimed France, and whose ancestors had bedevilled this country I called mine for more than a hundred years. Could I accomplish my ambition, might I not change the course of history?

'Then do you rise early, my lord,' I said. 'They say the river is at its most beautiful at dawn. But approach it privily, I beg of you, or you will come to harm.'

I am well aware that many men learned in the medical profession assert that bathing is injurious to the health, and that an excess of it will lead to an early grave. I offer myself as an example that they are mistaken.

These professors are all from northern latitudes, where indeed indiscriminate wet can lead to coughs, colds and pains in the liver. But I had to this moment lived my life in a more temperate climate, and I had been encouraged to water ever since I could remember by my father's mother, Yolanda of Aragon, who had, alas, recently died. My mother also shared in this enjoyment, as did her sister-in-law, and thus once the winter winds had ceased to blow it was the

habit of the ladies of the French court to descend to the Loire
in the early morning, and there disport themselves. We even
contrived to bathe in the winter, by sharing a huge tub set in
the centre of Aunt Marie's boudoir, and I managed to
continue the habit in England, to the scandal of my
attendants. In England even royalty, it appeared, bathed but
four times a year. The common people did not bathe at all.

I digress. Our greatest pleasure was to be found in the
river. I would not have anyone suppose that these royal
ladies and their attendants were unduly lascivious. Well,
actually, they were. Not my sister Yolanda and I, of course.
Although we knew a great deal about midnight meetings and
discreet fumblings on empty galleries, we were regarded as
too young to take part in these delightful divertissements –
there was our virginity to consider. But we watched and
listened and learned, and especially envied the fair Agnes,
who was wont to walk the palace with her breasts un-
covered, revelling in her own beauty. Even had Mama
permitted us to follow her example, Yolanda and I were not
yet equipped to do so with any great prospect of attracting
male attention. But in the water we enjoyed ourselves as
much as any of the others, sure of our privacy, for our habits
were well known and guards were suitably disposed to keep
ogling yokels at a distance. Thus how my lord of Suffolk
was going to manage was his business.

Yet was I excited to discover if he *would* manage. I knew
that he could never come close enough to gain more than an
impression. But would he dare try? That would tell me more
about the Earl, and perhaps about Englishmen as a whole,
than anything he was likely to learn about me from a hasty
glimpse of exposed flesh.

Thus the following morning we bathed, filling the air with
our happy shrieks as we splashed water over each other,
while I kept an eye out for any trespassers . . . and had all but
given him up when I spied a boat, apparently out of control,
for it had no oars, drifting rapidly downstream towards us.

There was a great deal of hallooing from the far bank, and

from the bluffs above us as well. But the guards did not approach, for if the oarsman had indeed caught a crab and lost his oars, he was clearly an innocent trespasser whom it would scarcely be charitable to shoot with a crossbow – especially as everyone could discern that the hapless fellow was the English ambassador.

I was overcome with admiration. I knew the Earl had fought with distinction under Great Harry, but here he was revealing a knowledge of strategy and tactics which almost amounted to genius. Naturally at the sight of the boat, certain to pass close to us, while the Earl gesticulated and shouted for help in a most convincing fashion, my companions uttered great shrieks of pretended terror, and sank beneath the water until only their eyes were visible. But my maidenly alarm was obviously greater than anyone's, as I lost my head completely and instead of remaining concealed ran from the river, scrambling up the bank in a gigantic goosepimple to reach the safety of my clothes, an operation which took several minutes. I was exhausted, and so no doubt was the Earl, for he ceased shouting for aid and collapsed into the bottom of the boat, in which position he drifted round the bend and out of sight.

'Naughty Meg,' Uncle Charlie remarked. 'Do you take me for a fool?'

As a matter of fact, I did. But of course I could not tell him so.

It was his habit after dinner to sit me on his knee for half an hour, while one hand drew patterns on my back and the other on my front. He was, after all, the king as well as my uncle, and no one was going to call him out. Mama and Aunt Marie indeed giggled girlishly whenever he made at me, and remarked loudly how much his grace adored his sweet Meg. It may have been, of course, that he just had a weakness for the name Meg, as he often displayed a similar affection for his daughter-in-law the Dauphine, a Scots princess named Margaret, who was married – unhappily, it was rumoured – to Cousin Louis.

Only Mademoiselle Sorel looked at me as if I were a
snake. Not that she had anything to worry about. I found
Uncle Charlie's touch quite repulsive, and could not understand how she could submit to it, nightly and naked. But he
was the fount of all our well-being, and it was necessary for
me to smile and kiss his cheek and hug him, doing my
complexion no good at all upon his scratchy chin.

'Even I have never thought of such a gambit,' he
whispered in my ear. 'Tell me truly, Meg: did you not invite
the rascal?'

'Heavens, your grace,' I protested. 'I near fainted when I
saw him.'

One of the first arts a princess needs learn, of course, is
that of dissembling.

'But what of the Earl, your grace?' I asked. 'Did he drift
clear out to sea?'

A matter of some hundred miles.

'No, no, he was rescued by his people. They say he was
powerfully affected by his misadventure.'

'I should think so too,' I remarked.

My plan worked to perfection. The following day, 22 May,
Suffolk presented himself at the abbey of Beaumont-les-
Tours, where we were staying – not even Mama would
expose Yolanda and myself to the loose morals of the French
court on a permanent basis.

It was early in the morning, and we were all *en déshabillé*.
But as we were informed that the Earl had information of
great importance to give us, we trooped into the reception
hall, suitably chaperoned by several of the sisters.

The Earl was alone, his attendants having been refused
admittance. Now he made his usual leg, while his eyes
devoured me, clad as I was in only a thin robe over my
shift.

'Your grace,' he said, addressing my mother formally as
the Queen of Naples. 'I have the honour of proposing to you
a marriage between your daughter Margaret and my most

sovereign lord, Henry, the sixth of that name, King of England and France.'

Mama goggled at him, as she was wont to do when surprised.

I was quicker to respond, even if I also could not believe my ears. 'It was our impression, my lord, that you were returning to England to report to his grace.'

'That will not be necessary. I came to France with plenipotentiary powers, to act as I saw fit.'

The wretch! He had not sought to reveal that fact before.

'Well,' Mama said. 'I know not what to say. I must speak with my husband, and the King.'

'His grace King Charles' – Suffolk could not bring himself actually to utter the words 'the King of France' – 'and his grace the King of Naples have already signified their agreement to such a match, your grace.'

'Well,' Mama said again.

'Then it is settled,' I said.

Two days later the betrothal was solemnified in the church of St Martin in Tours. The Papal Legate, Peter de Monte, who had been summoned to Tours some days earlier just in case his offices were required, officiated, and Suffolk stood proxy for his king. Thus I laid my hand in his, and he closed his fingers on mine, and looked deeply into my eyes, and swore to love and honour me until death did us part, while I did the same to him. I was aware of a most powerful emotion. Well, I was only just fourteen – my birthday is 23 March – and here I was plighting my troth to the most handsome man of my experience. At that moment I had no doubt that much as I was overwhelmed by the presence of the ambassador, a mere glimpse of the King would drive Suffolk forever from my mind.

The betrothal was announced to the world by a happy peal of bells, following which we took ourselves to the abbey of St Julian's, where Uncle Charlie, who had attended the church, had laid on a most splendid feast for us. Now for the first time I was given the full treatment of a queen. I sat at the head of the table, between Charlie and Suffolk, with even Mama below me, and four countesses waited on me, carving my meat, holding my wine goblet, wiping my fingers between each mouthful with napkins soaked in rose-water. I had attained greatness.

That night there was a ball, at which I danced until four of the morning, my partner for most of the time being the Earl. And should he not have been, as for the time he was my affianced husband?

For the next two days there was a fair outside Tours, and a tournament-at-arms in which the French knights sought to break their spears upon the English, as they had been prevented from doing at Agincourt. I sat in the central box with Uncle Charlie, my mother, and the Queen of France, and dear Papa, who was restored to health. Many a bold fellow was unseated during this tremendous clash of arms, but my lord of Suffolk defeated all comers, and assumed the status almost of a demi-god in my eyes.

But manly jousts were not all that Uncle Charlie had arranged for us. There was a variety of strange sights to shock the multitude and have us ladies pretending to faint with consternation. These ranged from giant men who carried trees in their hands – and caused quite a flutter as the ladies, behind their fans, discussed the probability that a man more than seven feet tall would be proportionately *large* all over – to jousts between men-at-arms mounted on camels. These last were hilarious affairs, as although it turned out that a camel can run quite as fast as a horse over a short distance, he is much less amenable, as well as being much more difficult to sit upon. Thus the gallant knights often found themselves on the ground fighting for dear life, but against their mounts who were apparently anxious to bite them rather than against their opponents.

Never had I been so happy.

At this point I should make it plain that I was no stranger to the marriage stakes. Princesses are always in demand.

The first to come knocking at my door had been the Count of St Pol, when I was but four years old, seeking my hand for his son. This was a complicated business, as my father, inheriting through my mother a claim to the county of Lorraine two years previously – when I was scarce a year old – had promptly marched off to establish his position, been defeated, and taken prisoner. He was still a prisoner when the matter of St Pol was raised, and he was released on parole to attend to the matter. It fell through, and he was returned to captivity.

Two years later, Papa's position had appeared to be improved, the death of Queen Joanna II of Naples leaving him with a claim on that crown, as well as the lordship of Minorca and Majorca; he already had a legal claim to the kingdom of Jerusalem. Papa, of course, still languished in prison, but Mama boldly set forth to pursue the glorious Neapolitan goal; I was sent to stay with my paternal grandmother in Anjou.

For a while it seemed as if Mama's, and therefore Papa's, prospects were bright, and I became an object of some importance. Duke Philip of Burgundy, no less, proposed a marriage between myself and his eldest son, Charles, Count of Charolais. Needless to say I did not know the youth, and at the age of five undoubtedly would not have liked him in any event. I cannot help but wonder what a pair we might have been, as he accumulated the title of 'the Bold' and became a famous warrior, who, even if he was often ranged against me, never forgot that we had nearly been man and wife. He has recently met an untimely end on the pikes of the Swiss peasantry, but such a fate is infinitely preferable to that which overtook my actual husband.

Duke Philip's terms for the match, however, proved unacceptable to Papa – even though the contract would have secured his release – and again the proposition fell through.

Duke Philip was to raise the matter of my marriage again, in 1442, when he suggested the Count of Nevers as a possible husband. But by then the Lorraine contretemps had been settled and Papa been released from captivity, even as all his hopes had fallen to the ground, so once again I remained unbetrothed.

The fact was that while I was undoubtedly a princess, as my father was a king, he and I lacked substance, and most prospective fathers-in-law are interested in securing more than a pretty face for their sons, even if it is accompanied by a nubile and willing body. Papa was known as King René the Good; his full titles were, in order of precedence, King of Jerusalem, King of Naples, Duke of Anjou and Duke of Bar, Count of Guise, Count of Lorraine, Count of Provence and Marquis of Pont-à-Mousson. I was actually born in Pont-à-Mousson, this and Guise being the only two of the above in his possession at that time.

As for the rest: the Kingdom of Jerusalem was inherited through some distant ancestor; since the collapse of the Crusades it had existed only on certain ancient maps. Papa had never been there and very clearly never would, as the only force on earth which seemed likely to disturb the Saracens in their possession of the Holy Land was that possessed by the Ottoman Turks, at this time busy with their conquest of the Balkans.

Papa's claim to Naples was equally sound legally, and equally unlikely to be realised in fact. The Neapolitan Anjous, as they were known, although close relatives of ours, were of a more extreme variety. One of them, Joanna I of Naples, was reputed to have murdered her first husband before marrying three more. I have often been compared to this remarkable lady, in terms of beauty, for she was the most beautiful woman of her time. This is complimentary enough; and as for murder, I have myself found out that queens all too often find this desperate course of action necessary if they are to remain queens.

The second Joanna, whose death had given birth to Papa's hopes, has never to my knowledge been accused of murder. She has, however, the reputation of having bedded every man in her kingdom. This is clearly a slander, as being physically impossible but, though my own experiences have taught me that queens may well need to spread their favours to maintain themselves, Joanna II was clearly a libidinous whore.

It will therefore be gathered that these Neapolitans were a savage lot, and Papa was quite unable to make any headway against them with his various claims, while Mama's efforts in the field had equally failed. Then there was Lorraine, to which Papa's rights had been acknowledged by the Emperor, but he had still not been able to take possession. This left Anjou and Provence. Anjou (in which I spent most of my childhood, either at Angers or Saumur) was in rather close proximity to the English possessions in France, and had had to submit to the passage of marauding armies on more than one occasion. This had done the finances of the duchy no good at all. Bar was the same, and Guise and Pont-à-Mousson were very small. Only sunlit Provence provided dear Papa with any substantial income.

But Papa, alas, was not your hard-bitten, ambitious soldier, determined to achieve his inherited position regardless of who might fall by the wayside. Had he been so, he would hardly have been called 'the Good'. He possessed another nickname, that of 'Last of the Troubadours', and in fact he would far rather have composed a pleasant roundel than break a lance. He supported art in all its forms, far beyond his means, and thus it was that throughout my life we seemed always to be on the point of bankruptcy, relying entirely upon the good offices of Uncle Charlie ... and *his* finances were usually in pretty poor shape!

Thus my future prospects for a husband had risen and fallen in proportion to the current estimate of Papa's chances of success in realising any one of his inheritances, with less and less optimism in the marriage market ... until the arrival of the ambassador from the King of England.

Now, herein obviously lies a conundrum: if the Princess

Margaret of Anjou, daughter of an impoverished king, was not good enough to be a wife for the Count of St Pol, the Heir of Burgundy, or the Count of Nevers, how did she suddenly become the chosen bride of the greatest prince in Christendom?

As I have indicated above, at the time my only consideration was that the match was desired by both my father and, more important my uncle, for reasons of state. That it might also be desired by the English for reasons of state did not then occur to me.

The fact was, as I was to become aware soon enough, matters were not going well for the English. The early death of Great Harry had left them in disarray, which for some thirteen years had been skilfully concealed by the prowess of Henry V's eldest brother, John, Duke of Bedford, a man scarcely inferior in either stature or military genius to his more famous sibling. Bedford's reputation has been sullied for his burning of Joan the Maid, but there is no reason to doubt that he genuinely considered her to be a witch.

Joan's brief appearance and the consequent resurgence of French nationalism was what had really created a crisis for the English. My dear proxy fiancé, Suffolk, had actually been the man who had had to raise the siege of Orleans before her impetuous banners, but again, this had been obscured by the genius of the great Bedford. Bedford's death in 1435, however, left the mighty English war machine floundering.

The young king was then fourteen, or the same age as myself when our marriage was decided. No doubt boys as young as he have donned armour and ridden off to war at the head of their troops – he had sufficient lineage in this direction. However, he did not. The kingdom was placed in the hands of a Great Council, out of which there emerged, as rivals for control of the king's person, Humphrey, Duke of Gloucester, brother to Henry V and John of Bedford and therefore the uncle of my husband-to-be, and Cardinal Henry Beaufort, great-uncle to the young king. I came to

know both of these gentlemen well later on. Suffice to say
for the moment that they represented radically different
points of view. The 'good' Duke Humphrey, as he was called
by the common people – why has always escaped me –
wished to prolong the war with France: the Cardinal wished
to end it in a peace honourable to both sides.

Many had been the machinations of these two men to attain
their ends following Bedford's death. The Cardinal's plan had
been simplicity itself: marry the young king to a French
princess and have an end to the fighting which was costing
both sides so dear. For this purpose an embassy had been sent,
most secretly, to Uncle Charlie as far back as 1439, but the
Cardinal had been faced with a difficulty: there was no French
princess available. However, Uncle Charlie may have been
half-mad, and he may have been as devoid of true sense as I
always suspected, but he certainly possessed a good deal of
low cunning. He *did* have a princess handy, who was as French
in upbringing and outlook as anyone, and who, if not his
daughter, was at least his niece . . . and beautiful as well.

And now his plans had come to fruition. Or so I at least
thought.

Any foolish supposition I might have had that I would now
be whisked off to England there to surrender my virginity to
a great and handsome king and lover – an end I devoutly
wished to accomplish – was immediately dispelled. Uncle
Charlie was in the middle of a war. Well, when was he not?
This particular fracas was with the Duchy of Metz, and had
merely been suspended for the duration of the winter. He
had actually come to Tours to settle my affairs as a prelude
to resuming the campaign, now that winter was behind us.
To the siege of Metz he also summoned Papa, and as Uncle
Charlie paid our bed and board, Papa duly went. My
departure for England must be postponed until campaigning
was over, a matter of several months.

But this was also apparently satisfactory to Suffolk who,
having made so bold a decision without reference to anyone

in England, must now return and inform the English king, and his magnates, what he had done. Indeed he had to do more than that, for royal marriages are never a matter of pledges and vows alone. They are always connected to affairs of state, and Uncle Charlie, in agreeing to my betrothal, had made certain proposals to the Earl, proposals which the Earl had accepted. I did not then know what these were, or I would have felt less certain of the future.

Suffolk himself seemed entirely confident. As my proxy husband he sought me out before his departure to bid me farewell. 'I shall return, before the end of the year,' he assured me, 'with a suitable escort for your grace, to accompany you to England.'

'Will not my husband come himself, my lord?' I asked.

'I doubt it. He can hardly enter France except at the head of an army, and this we all wish to avoid. Have no fear, your grace, he shall await you in England with all the eagerness of a youthful heart.'

I clutched his hand. 'Tell me of him, my lord. Is he tall?'

'He is tall, your grace.'

'As tall as you, my lord?'

'Well, not quite, your grace.'

'Is he broad?'

'As broad as a man should be, your grace.'

'Is he as broad as you, my lord?'

'Well, no, your grace. But he is half my age.'

'Is his hair the colour of gold?'

'It has much red in it.'

'Like yours?'

'Why, yes, your grace.'

'And he wears a beard?'

'Not at this time, your grace.'

I was disappointed. I found Suffolk's beard most attractive. 'Tell me of his prowess,' I begged. 'Is he a mighty man with lance and sword?'

'Ah . . .' He looked embarrassed. 'His armour is the finest in Christendom.'

I was in no mood for analysing answers. 'And does he ride like a king?'

'His grace rides very well, your grace.'

'Does he take part in many tourneys?'

'Ah ...' He looked even more embarrassed. 'His grace is very learned,' he said.

'Does he hunt often? Here in France we hunt every day that it is possible.'

'Ah ... his grace is also very pious.'

I digested this, and then asked the vital question. 'Will I love him, my lord, as much—' I bit my lip, suddenly blushing as I realised what I had nearly said.

Suffolk had realised it too. But he was not the man to lose the chance of gaining an ascendancy, however slight. 'As much, your grace, as ...?'

'There are many men I could love, my lord,' I said. 'Were it in my stars.'

He cast a hasty glance left and right to make certain that we were alone, and then kissed my fingers. 'Sweet Meg, there is but one woman I would love, or could love, be it in my stars or no.'

He raised his head to stare at me. He was three times my age and he was married and a father. But what would you? I was fourteen, and I was in love. Girls of fourteen fall in love with great enthusiasm, and fall out again with equal vigour, often in a matter of weeks or even days. But while they love, their whole being is consumed with desire for the object of their adoration. Fortunately in most cases that object is on the far side of a high wall, seen only occasionally in the distance, but still reason enough for heavy sighs and even swoons.

I was not so fortunate. The object of my adoration was in my presence, and we were alone, and he was holding my hand and drawing me slowly but inexorably closer to him. 'Oh, Meg,' he said. 'Meg, Meg, Meg. I adored you from the moment I first beheld your face. And to see you the other day in the river, your gleaming body, your ...'

There was only one way to stop him committing an irretrievable disaster, and that was to stop his mouth. This I now did, with my own.

Perhaps he actually drew me against him while he was speaking. I do not know for certain. I do know that for several seconds our tongues were twined round each other, and his hands were searching my gown – there was no way through save from my ankles, and they were some distance away, fortunately – and inducing in me all manner of most delightful sensations.

Then he released me and stepped away, his face ashen as he realised what he had done. 'Your grace . . .' He fell to his knees.

It was some seconds before I could speak. My instincts were to throw myself again into his arms, but now prudence came to my rescue. Suffolk continued to kneel with bowed head, no doubt expecting me to summon my attendants and have him removed to prison and thence execution. I rested my hand on his shoulder, and his head came up, most sharply. 'It were best we forgot these last five minutes, my lord,' I said.

'Yes,' he muttered, his eyes once again devouring me. 'Yes.'

'And it must never be spoken of to a soul on this earth.'

'No, your grace. I swear it.'

'Then kiss my hand, and go, and return when the King is ready to receive me.'

He grasped my hand. 'Meg—'

'Go,' I said again. 'You must go, my lord.'

For a moment his fingers tightened on mine, then he released me, and bowed. 'I shall count the seconds until we meet again, your grace.'

I would have liked to accompany him on to the porch, and wave him out of sight, but that would have been to compound disaster with disaster. What I needed most was several minutes alone, to allow my heartbeat and thus my colour to return to normal.

I was not to be allowed that time. Before I could even catch my breath Mama was with me. 'What did he say?' she demanded.

'Adieu, Mama.'

Mama peered at me. 'Nothing more?'

'What more could he say, Mama?'

She continued to gaze at me, her mouth twisting into a variety of shapes, as it was wont to do when she was undecided. But she and I had never been close. While she had so gallantly used all her energy in attempting to forward her husband's cause, I had been left largely in the care of my grandmother. I had remained closeted with that dear old Spanish lady until her death, which had occurred only eighteen months before my story opens. She had then been quite old, but remained gay and yet thoughtful to the end.

Many is the tale she told me of wild Aragon, with its mountains and tumbling seashore, its forests and its handsome people. Of fights against the Moors – not that she had ever seen any; by the time Grandmama had been born the Reconquista was all but complete, the Moors being confined, as they remain, to the small kingdom of Granada in the south-eastern portion of the Iberian Peninsula. But she made it sound as if she had been personally present at these conflicts, which had been continuing for several hundred years.

I loved my grandmother, and was overwhelmed with grief when she died. But I was twelve years old, already a woman, and already understanding that I must play a woman's part. When Mama had returned to me, to solace my sadness and resume her proper station, I was a stranger to her. We did our best, but where I was grave and interested in the affairs of the world, Mama was frivolous and considered only her next flirtation. How many of them *were* merely flirtations, given the morals of the French court, I prefer not to consider. The fact was that there was no intimacy between us; and I suspect she was somewhat afraid of me, certainly of my sudden bursts of temper.

Thus now, while she wished to warn me against the impetuosity of my own desires, she could not find the words. Instead she said, 'The Earl is no doubt a worthy man, fit to serve so great a master. I trust you realise your good fortune, Meg.'

'Indeed I do, Mama,' I assured her.

In the privacy of my own chamber I could reflect upon what had happened. I had never been kissed before, or at least not in such a fashion. Not even Uncle Charlie, forever slobbering about me, had dared touch my tongue with his. It seemed as if Suffolk and I might almost have ended my virginity. Well, we would certainly have done so, in every way, had I not forced us to part.

I was, of course, fully aware of what passed between a man and a woman in bed; Grandmama had seen to that. And – like most young girls, I fancy – I was in a great haste to get at the business, while understanding that in the first instance, at least it must necessarily be done with a husband or one's reputation would be irretrievably ruined.

Equally was I aware that adultery with a queen was treason, which involved unpleasant deaths for all concerned. There was such a scandal in our own French royal family. Only a hundred years before I was born, King Louis X married a Hungarian lady, named Clemence, who was discovered *in flagrante delicto* with one of her pages. The unfortunate fellow was torn apart by four horses, while Clemence, being pregnant at the time, was allowed to give birth and then strangled in a dungeon. No one ever inquired too closely into the fatherhood of the child, who, as it turned out, lived less than a year, although for part of that time he was officially King of France.

Equally was I aware that a betrothal carried the same responsibilities as a marriage. In the eyes of the world I was Queen of England, and no man could change that, or ever has, although heaven knows a good many have tried.

All of these considerations gave me considerable pause

for thought. Yet I was in love. As soon cease to breathe as refuse to recognise that fact. And my lover was going to return, to claim me, in the name of another, before the year was out. Can it be wondered that I endured a few hot flushes as I brooded on pros and cons?

There was of course only one possible solution to my problem, but how to implement it was the question. Again I had to thank my dear grandmama for my upbringing. When she had noted that as a small child I possessed an unhealthy weakness for honey, she had cured my passion by the simple expedient of forcing me to eat honey for every meal for a week. At the end of that time I was so heartily sick of the sticky mess it was several years before I could bring myself to touch it again. Obviously I could not employ the exact same remedy in Suffolk's case. Even had it not involved a calamitous end to my life, he simply was not there. But he was there in my thoughts. And so I settled down to dream of him, every day and all day, throughout that long, dreary summer. When I went abroad, I pretended he was at my side. When I ate, I pretended it was he attending me. When I knelt in church – may the Holy Mother forgive me – I pretended he was kneeling beside me.

And when I was in my bed at night . . . this was the most difficult of all. Grandmama had told me what to expect from a man, but she had not been able fully to illustrate her thesis; and although I had come upon the odd page in what had best be termed *déshabillé* as he relieved himself, the object I would have admired and if possible examined was always hastily tucked away with terrified apologies.

Still I possessed a fertile imagination; and what with one thing and another congratulated myself, by the time the armies went into winter quarters again, that the Earl was exorcised.

It must not be supposed that thinking about the Earl of Suffolk was all I had to do that summer. It was a very busy time.

There was my trousseau to be prepared, masses of houppelands and surcotes – the cotehardie was going out of fashion – the former with a considerable *décolletage*, which was all the rage at the French court. These gowns were made of velvet, brocade, or silk, according to the season for which they were intended, and the materials were all a blaze of colour. There were fur trimmings for my neck and cuffs and hems, reticulated head-dresses and steeple hennins, the last quite the most difficult that it is possible to wear, and a constant menace when attempting to pass through doorways or in a high wind. There were gold net cauls to be worn beneath these extravagances, and in addition, an abundance of jewellery was required, but much of this came in the form of presents, gold neck- and hip-chains, necklaces, brooches, pectoral crosses and reliquaries, and of course rings of all shapes, sizes and values.

There were hundreds of other presents, but my favourite, not least because it was at once unexpected and unusual, was a lion cub, sent to me by the Duke of Burgundy, no less. Perhaps he was attempting to be witty, but, as my character was as yet unknown to anyone – even myself – it is more likely he merely sought to be different. I adored the playful little imp, and called him Albion, that being one of the names by which the country I was now to call my own had once been known.

For relaxation I pursued my two favourite hobbies, hunting whenever possible, and when it was not, curling up with a good book, the various tales of Boccaccio, of course. I must have read and re-read those treasured words a hundred times.

I also endured to keep up with the news of what was happening, which was not a lot at the moment, but one never knew when a peculiarly spicy piece of gossip might come the way of our little court.

For example, only four years earlier, one of the very noblest men in France by repute, named Gilles de Rais, had been burned at the stake as a wizard. His crime, it appears, was to have lured young children of both sexes into his castle, had his way with them, and then murdered them. According to the story as repeated to our appalled but titillated ears, he would continue to have his way with them even as they died, which is surely carrying the pursuit of pleasure a shade too far.

But imagine my feelings when I read of these hapless creatures, boys and girls of perhaps my own age, entering that gloomy castle, there to be raped and debauched again and again until they were put out of their misery in a variety of horribly painful manners. I could not help but wonder at the fate I was shortly going to have to face, leaving my own dear France to live in a country with a desperate climate, full of fierce people whose sole pastime, it was represented to me, was killing Frenchmen and raping their wives and daughters.

What would they do to me? In retrospect, I can say, it was a question to which I should have paid more attention. But when I considered it, I would think of noble Suffolk, and be relieved.

Thus the summer waxed and then waned, and I became impatient for the onset of the autumnal rains. But once again my girlish dreams and plans were set at nought by events beyond my control. That year the autumnal rains did not come, and so campaigning continued far beyond the normal season. This was an irritant to me; it was a disaster for the Duke of Metz, who had barely sustained himself throughout the summer and had looked forward to the withdrawal of the royal army in order to restock his larders and his ammunition, and generally prepare for another year's siege.

Uncle Charlie, therefore (or more likely, his military advisers, for he was no soldier himself) realising the weakness of the city, determined to take advantage of the continuing fine weather and remain in the field, in anticipation of concluding the matter once and for all.

In itself this would not have concerned me greatly, but

when in December the Earl of Suffolk again crossed the Channel and advanced to the limits of the English possessions in France, instead of turning south to visit me at Saumur, or summoning me to Tours to meet him, he continued across northern France to Nancy, where Uncle Charlie had set up his headquarters and his court. I then expected a summons to that city, but none came, and I was left to kick my heels in Saumur. It appeared that my part of the business being completed, it was not a matter of hard bargaining between the two sides as to my dowry and whatever else of benefit to either party might be obtained from my marriage.

It was a most frustrating time, as word reached us in Saumur of the magnificence of the Earl's retinue, the handsome knights and beautiful ladies who rode at his shoulder, the splendid balls and feasts and jousts which they were enjoying. Less satisfying was the news that on this occasion, as he had actually come to fetch me, Suffolk was accompanied by his wife! I felt an instant dislike for the fortunate woman.

Christmas was a very lonely business at Saumur.

And then in February, the summons at last came. Negotiations had been completed, and Mama and I were to join Papa in Nancy.

By now winter had set in in earnest, and it was a difficult journey. But I was buoyed up with anticipation and happiness. Everything was coming to fruition at last.

And so indeed it proved. We reached Nancy towards the end of the month, to be greeted by the news that Metz had just surrendered. Never had there been such celebrations, and these were but a prelude to what was to come, for my marriage was to take place.

This was solemnised in the cathedral of Nancy a week later, by Louis de Herancourt, Bishop of Toul, and was witnessed by a huge and famous company. Even my eldest brother John had arrived, as well as my other siblings. John was known as the Duke of Calabria, although of course he had never been to southern Italy; it was merely *de rigueur* for the eldest son and heir to the throne of Naples to be known by that title, rather as the English heir is called the Prince of Wales – that Papa did not actually possess the throne of Naples was irrelevant.

I had always thought John the most splendid of men, and had regarded him as having achieved a station far beyond anything to which I might aspire. How, in a short year, had things changed! I was now the most important member of our family, and I had met the finest man I had known in my brief sojourn on earth.

The Marquis of Suffolk – for he had been promoted as a reward for what he had accomplished – and I had had no time together before the ceremony; we had merely glimpsed each other from a distance. In the cathedral, however, he stood with my hand in his as he acted as proxy for the husband I had not yet seen. I suspect we both trembled as we touched each other, as he slipped the ring on my finger, and as, the service concluded, he bent his head to plant a husbandly kiss upon my cheek. But perhaps he had striven to exorcise me as I him, and for the moment at least we kept aloof from each other.

But it was difficult to sustain, for now there began an entire week of jousts and feasts and balls. It was necessary for the Queen of England to tie her scarf to the lance of her 'husband' before each list, and equally it was necessary for the Queen of England to accompany him into the start of each dance. Thus every day we were driven closer together. I smiled at him as he presented his lance, twined my fingers together in apprehension as he charged on his war horse, and trembled against him as we made a turn on the floor.

It was, be it remembered, the beginning of March, and perhaps the coldest time of the year. Thus jousting was no careless matter, and even the Marquis was unhorsed several times as his mount slipped on the soggy turf; he still emerged victor ludorum.

Equally, while there were fires blazing in every grate of the castle in which we lodged, castles are by definition draughty places, and one alternately roasted and shivered according to one's distance from the flames. I even forewent the pleasure of bathing for the time being. But the pleasure of being again in the Marquis's arms was heavenly. That week was one of the most memorable of my life, and without crisis. He did not attempt to call upon me, privily, and I was content to wait. Soon enough I would begin my journey to England and my husband, with my French family left behind, and the Marquis of Suffolk at my side.

2

As I have mentioned, Suffolk was on this visit accompanied by his wife. I gathered she was to take over the management of myself and my household from Mama, in view of my tender years, and in fact stand *in loco parentis* to me until such time as I should actually come into the care of my husband.

I had felt an instant dislike for this lady on first learning of her existence, an emotion motivated by simple jealousy that she should possess what I so ardently desired. The discovery that she would also possess virtually plenipotentiary powers of me during the coming month increased my dislike to sheer loathing.

We had of course been introduced on first reaching Nancy, but she remained a shadow until after the proxy wedding, when, as it was now time for my departure for England, she moved into my apartment to oversee the packing up of my belongings. Then my confused feelings for Suffolk became more confused yet.

Alice de la Pole was a tall, handsome woman, of quiet demeanour, and possessed of a ready smile. She was also no ordinary housewife, elevated to noble status by the deeds of her husband's family. Far from it. Her maiden name had been Chaucer, and her grandfather had been a well-known story-teller at the court of King Edward III. The poet had actually been a customs officer, which is no recommendation to be sure, but his son Thomas, Alice's father, had been well thought of. From the position of butler to King Richard II he had gained the favour of King Henry IV and his son, and been granted several manors and positions of responsibility which had made him into a wealthy man. More important, through his mother he was a cousin of the Beauforts, admittedly at a time when they were merely John of Gaunt's bastards, but this in fact made Alice a distant cousin of the King's.

My dislike evaporated the moment I came to know this lady, and we became friends and remained so through some very difficult periods, until, like so many people, she grew weary of the struggle and made her peace with the monster, Edward of York. But in 1445 that lay many years in the future.

Our friendship was the more remarkable because my first crisis as Queen of England occurred before I even left Nancy to begin my journey to my new land. The day before I was due to depart, Mama came into our apartment in a fine rage and threw a piece of parchment on the table before me.

'That Suffolk!' she declared. 'He has the effrontery to say that your establishment is too great. That it must be cut by two-thirds. Two-thirds!'

I had been so busy enjoying myself over the previous week I had given little thought to my establishment. I had, of course, throughout the summer known that lists were being prepared, and suitable persons interviewed, but never having actually had an establishment of my own before, I had been content to leave the entire business to Mama. Now I picked up the parchment, and will confess that I was surprised at the size of the list.

Mama felt that I needed: six ladies-in-waiting; four lords-in-waiting; four ladies of the bedchamber; six chambermaids; twelve seamstresses; six laundrywomen; four female servers and four male servers; four main chefs; two pastry-chefs; six bakers; six scullery maids; six scullery lads; four falconiers; and six dog-keepers.

These were in addition to my chamberlain, Louis d'Heristal; my confessor, Father Joseph, and four attendant priests; and two keepers of the royal lion – my pet Albion. 'Well, Mama,' I ventured, 'I am sure the English can supply us with scullery maids and lads, and laundresses. And even dog-keepers.'

'What nonsense!' Mama declared. 'I'll not have it.'

But she had to have it. Suffolk was adamant, and it was with a greatly reduced party that I eventually left Nancy.

Not that this was immediately obvious, for Papa and my brother John determined to accompany me as far as was practical – Uncle Charles naturally had no intention of approaching too closely to English soil, just in case the Goddams decided to settle the question of who was really King of France by inviting him to remain there for the rest of his life. But he and his court escorted me through the gates of Nancy, and there he said farewell, hugging me tightly while tears streamed down his cheeks. 'Oh, Meg, Meg,' he muttered in my ear. 'Have I not always been good to you?'

'Always, dearest Uncle,' I agreed.

'Then remember me, always, as your benefactor, and as one who has loved you dearly.'

I understood of course that for all his crocodile tears he was now thinking less of our personal relationship than of the benefits which would obtain were the Queen of England and the King of France to remain close friends, if not intimates. 'I shall remember, Uncle,' I promised, reminding myself that as queen my duty to my new country must always come before any debts owed elsewhere.

Thus we bade adieu, each supposing that we should never see the other again. Which is what indeed happened. Had I never seen Cousin Louis the Dauphin again, either, my life had been more fortunate.

*

Even without their King, many of the knights and ladies of the French court elected to continue with me for a while, for I was in the official charge of the Duke of Orleans, the King's brother, and so a very goodly entourage took the road from Nancy to Chalons, through the winter slush. Mama did not accompany me; she returned to Angers, with Yolanda. Like Uncle Charles, I am sure they too felt that they had seen the last of me.

Papa came as far as Bar-le-Duc, where there was another tearful parting, then the remainder of my party proceeded to Chalons, where the marriage treaty was to be engrossed and I was signed for and delivered, as it were.

Princesses are often treated like negotiable chattels, which, alas, is what they are, even when they are become queens.

But we were a merry party on the road to Chalons, only giving way to grief, on the part of my escort, when we reached that city and the signing of the treaty was completed. When I retired that night there was a perfect host of men and women waiting to bid me farewell, many with tears in their eyes. Amongst them was even Pierre de Brezé. This man was my uncle's chief minister, and as such was the most powerful man in the land. He commanded Uncle Charlie's armies as well as his court; it was he who had reinforced his position by introducing Mademoiselle Sorel to the King's bed.

He was also handsome and well-built, and not old – only in his mid-thirties – but he had always at least pretended to the role of senior statesman where I was concerned. Now he knelt before me and, having kissed my hand, retained it for a moment longer than decorum allowed.

'Sweet queen,' he said, 'this land of France will never be the same again, now you leave us.'

'Tush, good sir,' I replied. 'You will soon have forgotten all about me.'

'I? Never, your grace. I, Pierre de Brezé, swear to keep your image before me for the rest of my life. If indeed you would but grant me a keepsake to aid my constancy ...'

I endeavoured to regard him severely, but found it difficult: I was too astonished. Of course I understood that he was in the same position to Uncle Charlie as was my lord of Suffolk to King Henry VI, and that therefore probably whatever he professed was an act of policy rather than true emotion ... On the other hand, he *was* a handsome fellow, if cast in an entirely different mould to the Earl – being small, dark and swarthy, as well as younger – and I knew him to be a man both of wealth and at least passing power.

Besides, what woman can resist what was nothing less than an avowal of love, even if of doubtful veracity, especially when she considers that it can never be requited? So I gave him a silk scarf, which he pressed to his cheek before stowing it in his belt. Oh, to be able to foresee the future!

From Chalons we went to Paris, the first time I had beheld this queen of cities, although truth to tell I was somewhat disappointed. It was of course still the dead of winter; and if the snow had for the time melted, it now commenced to rain most dismally and persistently. 'The very skies weep for your departure from France, your grace,' said M. d'Heristal.

I discounted his sentiments; my early romanticism was already giving way to an understanding of the realities of life. Thus I saw Paris less as the most famous city in France than as a squalid accumulation of huts north of the river, and while there were some splendid buildings on the island itself, these were also so close-huddled it was almost difficult to breathe.

'Superbly chosen for defence,' Suffolk commented, ever the soldier as he eyed the fast-running current of the Seine to either side, and indeed history relates that the first Parisians accumulated on the Isle de la Cité to escape the marauding hordes from across the Rhine.

However, no criticism could be levelled at the cathedral of Notre Dame, which was quite the most splendid building I had ever beheld, or ever would. In this hallowed place, on 16 March 1445, I was received with all the honours due to a queen: a fanfare of bugles, the cheers of the populace, bowing princes and priests, even a fusillade of artillery from a safe distance outside the walls. Doves were released to flutter into the sky and a solemn service of thanksgiving for my safety was held.

I finished the day quite exhausted.

Hitherto, such had been the continuous goings-on in my immediate vicinity, I had had no private words with the Earl. I am not sure I dared wish them. Quite apart from the constant presence of his wife, and my own pleasure in her company, it was also necessary to let him know, as he was now my subject rather than I the object of his choice, that I was displeased over the matter of my establishment.

Thus, although I remained powerfully affected by his physical presence, I had allowed him nothing more than a disdainful smile from time to time; and if, in his role as my proxy husband, he was necessarily at my side whenever I appeared in public, and my hand was required to rest in his, I yet concealed any evidence of whatever emotions I may have felt.

On this night in Paris, when I had retired early (as I have said, quite exhausted by the strenuous events of the day), Madame Bailly, my principal lady, came to me and said that the Earl of Suffolk requested a private word. 'Shall I send him off, your grace?' the good lady asked.

I considered. But Dame Alice had already retired, I had not yet undressed, and at least part of my pique had been caused by the fact that *he* had shown no very great desire to be alone with *me* since his return to France. 'No,' I said. 'Show him in. And do you withdraw, good Bailly, out of earshot, but yet remain close enough for me to call you if I wish to do so.'

She obeyed, and a moment later the Earl was bowing before me, and casting a somewhat anxious glance at

Albion, who lay, as was his wont, against my chair, uttering little guttural gurgles in the back of his throat, again as was his wont whenever anyone entered my chamber other than my ladies. 'I thought you had forgotten I existed, save as a queen, my lord,' I remarked. 'Pray be seated. There.' I pointed at a chair some feet away, as he would have sunk to the floor at my feet.

He sat down, the while staring at me most intently. 'You know that I love you,' he said.

I could feel the heat gathering in my cheeks, but yet answered as calmly as I could. 'I would hope that every man in my kingdom will love me, my lord.'

He chose to ignore my attempts to turn the conversation into humdrum lines. 'That I have not approached you before is because you have been always surrounded by your family and a horde of French louts.'

I raised my eyebrows. Louts, indeed! 'Not to mention your wife, my lord.'

'Does this disturb you?'

'Not in the least. I find her delightful.'

He considered this for some seconds, then returned to his main theme. 'But now we are all but free of the French. Tomorrow, your grace, we shall be on English soil.'

'I am counting the minutes, my lord.'

'And there you will become the care of the Governor of Normandy, the Duke of York.'

'But not my husband?'

'No, your grace, King Henry will not leave England itself. The Duke is a cousin of the King.'

'I know this, my lord.'

'He is also a bitter enemy of myself,' Suffolk added.

'Indeed, my lord?'

'Therefore . . .' He slipped from the chair on to one knee, staring at me all over again. 'Meg, sweet Meg, I trust what I have accomplished is in accordance with your wishes?'

'You know that is so, my lord.'

'Then I would beg you to remember that, always, and no

matter what pressures may be brought to bear upon you.'

'Pressures, my lord?'

'You do not understand this England to which you are going.' It was then that he told me of the rivalry of Gloucester and Beaufort, which was tearing England apart, and told me that he belonged to the party of Cardinal Beaufort, and peace.

'Well, then, have you not scored a signal triumph, my lord?' I asked. 'As the marriage is accomplished? Surely all England knows of it. Pressures, you say? I am Queen of England. No man would dare attempt to set me aside.'

'No man, indeed, your grace,' he said, 'but there are ways of harming even a queen, through her servants.'

I frowned at him. 'You had best speak plain, my lord.'

'Your grace, dare I say it, is not considered by many people in England to be a suitable consort to our king.'

'Am I thought to be deformed?'

'You are known as the most beautiful of women, your grace.'

I smiled at him. When he spoke like that I could listen to him for hours. 'Do I then lack sufficient royal blood?'

'I would estimate your lineage is longer than that of the King's, your grace.'

'Then what is their objection? Simply that I am French? Has not almost every English king for the last two hundred years married a French princess?' I laughed. 'And before that, the Plantagenets were French themselves.'

He took a deep breath. 'What men speak of is that your grace comes to our land without substance.'

My smile changed into another frown. 'I suspect this too is well known, my lord. It is a poor point to be held against me.'

'Indeed, your grace. It was agreed, long ago, that no dowry would be required.'

'Then what is the difficulty?'

He rose to his feet, and I debated calling for Bailly, but he had not yet told me what was truly troubling him. In any event, as Albion resumed his growling, he did not advance towards me, but merely took a turn or two up and down the room. Clearly he had a great deal on his mind. 'Your grace, I came to France as minister plenipotentiary for the King of England. My brief contained two points. One was to secure the King a bride, the other was to end the war with France. I had not assumed a difficulty in either direction.'

I waited, now resting my chin on my hand; this was my first encounter with international diplomacy.

'However, it was my misfortune to lay eyes upon you, and to see you *en déshabillé* ...'

'My lord,' I interrupted, 'that subject is closed.' Misfortune indeed!

'I must speak of it this last time, your grace. When I beheld you, even before the river, I knew that no one but you could be Queen of England. You know I fell in love with you. Hear me out, I beg of you,' he said as I would again have interrupted him. 'I had supposed my feelings, if known to you, were concealed from all others. In this I was mistaken.'

'My lord!' I was frightened.

'Fear not. Nothing will come of it, to harm you at least. I had also supposed that your uncle was a simpleton.'

He paused, as if expecting another rebuke, but as far as I was concerned, Uncle Charles *was* a simpleton.

'Unfortunately,' the Earl went on, 'this is not the case. He is a very shrewd man indeed, not to say cunning. He it was observed my regard for you, and determined to turn it to his own advantage. He allowed me to return to England with my glowing recommendation of the match. It was when I visited him at Nancy that he revealed his true demeanour. The marriage would be permitted to go ahead, he told me, but only on his conditions. There will be no peace between England and France, but only a truce for two years. At the end of that time the truce will be translated into a lasting treaty of peace, to secure which England must surrender the county of Maine, together with those parts of the county of

Anjou as are occupied by our troops, to France – to be
returned, as I understand it, to your father in order that he
may maintain himself as a king.'

'And why should this not be so?' I demanded. 'Maine is
part of my father's patrimony; Anjou *is* his patrimony. Your
English occupation of it is illegal.'

He hung his head. 'Alas, your grace, the people of
England do not countenance the return of one yard of
English-held land to France. And they will say that King
Charles will never actually allow your father to regain his
land, but will take it for his own.' He raised his head. 'But
what was I to do? The alternative was to lose you. King
Charles was adamant.'

He was flattering me again. But I could only consider the
enormity of what he had done. 'My lord, you mean that in
English eyes you have given away English soil? There is a
backwards dowry, if you like. Who in England knows of
this?'

'No one as yet, your grace.'

'Then what will be your fate when it is discovered?'

'I am immune, your grace. At least on that score. I
obtained from Parliament, before I undertook this mission,
an indemnity giving me a free hand to negotiate this
marriage.'

'But you did not tell your Parliament what you had in
mind.'

'I did not then have the surrender of the county in mind,
your grace, as I did not know what was in your uncle's
mind.'

'And you fear they may now renege on their indemnity?'

He came to me and fell to his knees; he was clearly so
distressed I had not the firmness of mind to reject him.
Albion also rose, and stretched, looking very hostile, but I
patted him on the head and he slunk away into a corner,
although he continued to watch the Earl most carefully.
'They cannot touch me for surrendering Maine and returning
Anjou, your grace. Yet they will never forgive me for it.

They will bide their time, and seek to strike me down for some future mistake, as they will deem it. Without your support, I am a dead man.'

'My support, my lord?' A girl a few days short of her fifteenth birthday can surely be forgiven for feeling distinctly uneasy at having such a responsibility thrust upon her.

'You are Queen of England. If you are determined, there is none can say you nay.'

'Save my husband, my lord. Had you not best apply to him?'

'King Henry is a worthy man, your grace. Most worthy. But . . . I doubt he will support me as ably as yourself.'

I did not truly understand his meaning, and supposed he was but paying me a further compliment.

As I did not immediately reply, he seized my fingers. 'My life is in these hands, your grace. I beg of you to remember this, always, and to remember too that everything I have done has been done for love of you.'

'Sweet Suffolk,' I said, and was in his arms, myself slipping from my chair to kneel against him while our lips sought each other's, and his hands roamed over my back and shoulders, and even slipped down below my waist to give me a squeeze beyond decency. There is, perhaps, something distasteful in the spectacle of a married man of mature years discovering so violent an infatuation for a girl thirty years his junior. Reflecting now that I am of mature years myself, perhaps I *do* find the episode distasteful.

But then I was far from mature, and at that moment I was beyond reason or caution. Heaven alone knows what might have happened, for no Parliament on earth can indemnify a subject for deflowering his queen, had not Albion come to my rescue, rising on his haunches and giving vent to a very becoming roar – seeing that he was only a cub – which shook the rafters and had Bailly and several other women running into my apartment.

By then I had disengaged myself and resumed my seat,

the Earl was on his feet, and I was back in command of myself.

'What is this interruption?' I demanded. 'I did not call.'

'The beast, your grace ...' Bailly protested.

'Is undoubtedly hungry. Take him out and feed him.'

This was done, the ladies casting suspicious glances at the Earl as they left the room.

'But do you remain, good Bailly,' I said. 'I am ready to retire. I understand what you have said to me, my lord,' I told the Earl. 'And you may rest assured I shall always remember your words. And now, good night.'

He hesitated, glanced at Bailly and then at me, bowed, and left. No doubt he did a great deal of tossing and turning that night in his bed. I know I did.

Not on account of any concern for the future. The Earl dared not disclose anything that had passed between us, for fear of the scaffold. Besides, he loved me, and I think he did so to the instant of his death.

In any event, I had more immediately serious matters to consider. For next morning was the most important day of my life, to that moment. The Dukes of Orleans and Calabria escorted me to the English frontier at Poissy, and there bade me farewell.

'You go to greatness, sister,' John said. 'May your fortunes ever prosper.'

'And yours, dear brother,' I replied.

Never were two wishes more confounded.

I entered the town with my entourage, now entirely under the command of the Earl of Suffolk, but not for long. Drawn up to receive me was a large body of armed men, knights as well as some of those archers who had caused so much havoc to French chivalry over the years.

There were also maidens strewing flowers before my palfrey and screaming prettily at the sight of Albion who walked beside me on a stout leash under the control of his keeper, and a fanfare of trumpets, not to mention a priest to bless me, a choir to sing my praises, and, sitting his horse alone save for a very small boy, at some distance from the throng, the Duke of York.

It was all very impressive, and none more so than the Duke, who quite equalled the Earl of Suffolk in manly looks, enhanced by the invisible aura of possessing royal blood, and clean-shaven after the French fashion. I am not so fickle as to have you suppose I would in any circumstances have allowed him the same degree of affection as I had given Suffolk, but in fact it was very obvious to me from the moment I approached close enough to look into his eyes, and he had greeted me with an elaborate flourish, that here was no friend. The reason was that there were many who considered that the Duke of York had a better claim to the English throne than my own dear husband.

This needs to be explained. The great King Edward III, who had died some seventy years before my story begins, had several sons. Two died in infancy. Of those who survived to adulthood, the most famous is the eldest, Edward the Black Prince, who caused even more havoc in France than did his father. He however died before he could reign, and England was left in the hands of his son, a reckless boy, Richard II (who was by way of being my uncle by marriage, as he had obtained as his second wife Uncle Charles's sister Isabella).

Richard's rule eventually became so obnoxious that he was deposed by his cousin Henry of Lancaster, who then took the throne as Henry IV of England. Now this Henry, *my* own dear Henry's grandfather, was the son of Great Edward's third surviving son, John of Gaunt, Duke of Lancaster. Undoubtedly he usurped the English throne from his cousin Richard, but Richard had no sons, and had proved himself unfit to rule. Once he had been safely disposed of – deposed kings have a low life expectancy, as I can avow from my own experiences – there was scarce a voice in the kingdom raised against the assumption by the house of

Lancaster of the royal prerogatives. Even his other cousins
kept quiet, and they included the Princess Philippa, daughter
of Edward III's *second* surviving son, Lionel, Duke of
Clarence; as the English do not admit the Salic Law
forbidding women to inherit the throne, she legally had a
prior claim.

However, no doubt if Philippa *had* offered an opinion, it
would have been discounted. She was a woman; and
although she was not legally debarred, the English were not
interested in queens regnant in such troubled times. Philippa
therefore married a noble named Mortimer and was conveniently forgotten.

Any lien she might have had on the throne was equally
forgotten for two generations. During these years England
prospered, and when Henry IV died from some foul
pestilence picked up when he was crusading in his youth, it
prospered even more under his son Great Harry V. But Great
Harry had now been dead some twenty-three years and, as
I have related above, since his death, and that of his brother
Bedford more recently, England's prosperity had withered
along with her successes in the French war. Men began to
whisper that no good could come of an usurped throne,
forgetful as men are of the amount of good that had already
emanated from that tainted source.

Now Philippa's granddaughter, Anne Mortimer, had
married a distant cousin: Richard, Earl of Cambridge, who
was actually the younger son of Edmund, Duke of York,
Edward III's *fifth* son. This Richard never caused more than
a passing inconvenience to my dear husband's forebears, but
his son, also Richard, became Duke of York; as the son of
Anne Mortimer, he was in the direct line of descent from
Lionel of Clarence, John of Gaunt's elder brother. This was
the man who now greeted me with cool disdain, if equally
with all the homage due to a queen.

With him was a small boy, only three years old; a most
fine, sturdy lad, who for all his tender years actually wore a
cuirass and sported a small sword at his side. 'My eldest son,

your grace,' the Duke said. 'Edward, Earl of March.'

Had I the power of seeing the future, I would straightaway have kicked Albion and reminded him that the best breakfast a lion can have is a three-year-old youth. Lacking this power, I actually patted this dreadful monster on the head, and said, 'What a handsome child.'

'He takes after his mother, your grace,' the Duke said gallantly.

A strange situation. For had the Duke in his turn been able to see the future, as I was entirely in his power for the next few weeks, he would no doubt have arranged for me to meet with an untimely accident in order to leave his King a widower before the marriage had even been consummated. But there we were, destined by fate to be the bitterest and most vengeful enemies who ever walked this earth, supping together, and drinking our wine, and appearing to be the best of friends.

Actually, one cannot blame the Duke for not considering his new queen as being of much account on this occasion of our first meeting. I had had an exhausting fortnight since arriving in Nancy, and even before that I had found the business of travelling the breadth of France in winter a trying affair. No doubt I had stayed up too late over a long period of time, danced too often, and certainly I had over-indulged in food and wine. I was also labouring under some emotional uncertainty, courtesy of my lord of Suffolk. All of these contributed to taking the roses from my cheeks, the sparkle from my eyes, and to leaving even my beauty a suggestion rather than a glowing fact.

That night I began to sniffle, to the concern of Madame Bailly and Dame Alice, and to the annoyance of those English ladies who had come to France to attend me and were now constantly clustering around me. 'Your grace has caught cold from this beastly French weather,' remarked the Countess of Salisbury.

This suggestion did not endear her to me, and indeed she

was a woman given to dominance. She was, I discovered, a relative by marriage of the Duke of York. For that worthy had further enhanced his position by espousing no less a person than Cicely Neville, sister of the Earl of Salisbury, the Countess's husband. This man was one of the wealthiest landowners in the kingdom, and his brother, the Earl of Westmorland, hardly less so. As to the Earl of Salisbury's wretched son, whom some called the Kingmaker but who was to be the ruin of all my hopes, of him I will speak later.

Suffice to say that my lady of Salisbury was not of a mind to have all the carefully laid plans for my various receptions disrupted by a common cold. So, despite the objections of the Countess of Suffolk, – who, alas, could not match the Countess of Salisbury for imperious arrogance, the Salisburys being much the wealthier family – we departed next day for Mantes, where we boarded several barges for the journey down river to Rouen. Both countesses were in my barge, together with the Earl and the Duke and his son, but not, to my chagrin, Albion. 'I will not travel in the same boat as such a monster,' the Countess of Salisbury declared.

Now, I was the Queen, and there was no one could say me nay if I had chosen to make an issue of it. But I did not, entirely because I was feeling like death not even warmed up. By the time we reached Rouen, on 22 March (the day before my fifteenth birthday), I was lying in my couch on the barge shivering from head to foot, while my nose was streaming.

By now even my haughty attendants were concerned. They conferred in whispers, and when we drew abreast of our landing place, which was crowded with people, hailed one of the other barges to come alongside, when another muttered discussion took place. At this point the Countess of Salisbury came and sat beside me. 'Your grace is not well,' she remarked.

I assumed this was an English form of wit.

'We have discussed the matter and your symptoms, your grace, and have sent ashore for a physician. But for the time being it is our opinion that you should not land.'

'I am to make a state entry into Rouen,' I muttered.

'I know. This is very unfortunate. A great deal of money has been spent preparing for your entry, and people have come to town from miles around to celebrate their queen. They will be most heartily displeased if the festivities are cancelled. The Duke has therefore requested me to take your part, as it were ...' bold as she was, she had to hesitate at this juncture to observe my response, and indeed I all but sat up. 'Just for the day, your grace,' she hurried on.

I groaned, and fell back on my cushions. 'I have a cold, my lady,' I said. 'Will I not be better tomorrow?'

'Alas, your grace, we fear this is more than a cold.'

My eyes had drooped shut, but now they opened very sharply. 'Then what is it?'

'Your grace ...' she looked about to burst into tears, although I could tell she was actually acting a part, and very well, too. 'We fear it may be the pox.'

I fell back in a swoon. Well, as near as I ever did swoon, which is never in my life save on one dreadful occasion which will be related in its proper place. Yet my eyes closed, and my brain began to spin. I understood of course that she was not referring to the great pox, which is a sexual misfortune hardly to be found in a virgin. However, we mortals are subject to a variety of other unpleasant illnesses, caused it is said by noxious vapours which abound in the air we breathe. The most terrible by far is the mysterious Black Death, which a hundred years earlier had reduced the population of Europe by a third, and even nowadays recurs from time to time, bringing doom and disaster wherever it touches.

But second only to this horrendous fate is to suffer the smallpox. This disease is very nearly as universally fatal as the Black Death; a manifestation of the infection is the outbreak of obscene pustules all over the body and especially on the face. Even if the sufferer survives, he or she is all too often left with dreadful pits and scars on the skin. Was this then to be my fate? Just fifteen years old, hailed on all sides for my beauty, and soon to meet for the first time a husband who knew of me only by report? Can it be wondered that even my spirit gave way and I collapsed in tears.

And indeed, although I had not yet noticed them these dreadful water-filled little blisters were already appearing on my back, which was what had alarmed my ladies.

An hour later the physician was rowed out to my barge, on which the curtains had been drawn as no one wished any of the spectators on the bank to know the catastrophe that had overtaken their queen. Meanwhile the Countess of Salisbury had donned one of my gowns – with some difficulty and straining of the seams, as she was a woman grown and I still an immature girl – and was rowed ashore to pretend to be me making my triumphal entry into the capital of Normandy. I listened to the distant cheers and the cannonading with a heavy heart. No doubt I was done with such glories, forever.

The physician, whose name was Robert of Rouen, was a small man with a pinched face. He surveyed me for some moments before touching me, while humming most untunefully. Then he put two fingers on my throat, and hummed some more, before requesting Bailly to open the bodice of my gown. This she did with trembling fingers, thus exposing me to the apothecary's gaze; even at fifteen my breasts were well formed, if far from having attained their full size.

I have heard it said that young girls, in their sexual precocity, often fall in love with their first doctors, simply because these gentlemen go where no man has been permitted before. I can only say that most of these damsels must have been weak in the head or far more fortunate than I in their doctor. Even had my heart and mind not still been filled with my last embrace from Suffolk, I felt nothing but distaste for this weasely fellow who kept grunting to himself as he actually put his ear between my tender mounds. Why, I have no idea – save that he was a lascivious brute. It could not have been to ascertain that my heart was still beating – my heavy breathing should have assured him of that. I had just observed, for the first time, that there were pustules on my chest.

Having finished assaulting my femininity, he must now assault my very vitality, tilting my head back to peer up my nostrils, and even placing a disgusting finger inside one of the orifices, which set me to coughing all over again.

On the other hand, he now proceeded to give me the best news I had ever had in my brief life, although I did not immediately appreciate it. Retying the bows on my gown himself, he said, 'I do not think your grace has the smallpox.' I scarce dared allowed myself to believe what he was saying. 'There is another variety of the disease,' he explained. 'Which is commonly called the chicken-pox. It is not so virulent.'

'How can you tell which is which?' I inquired.

'It is not always easy, your grace. But there are certain indications. Both are characterised by the appearance of these pustules, but whereas in the case of the chicken-pox these are confined to the face and body, in the smallpox they invade the nostrils. There is no evidence of any such invasion within your nostrils, your grace.'

So that was what he had been doing. Almost I forgave him. 'You mean I will not die?'

'I think it is unlikely. Your grace is young and strong.'

'And I will not be marked?'

'Oh, I am afraid that cannot be guaranteed.' He saw my expression change from relief to dismay. 'But if your grace can refrain from scratching or bursting the pustules, there is every possibility that they will disappear and leave your beauty untarnished.'

I was not entirely mollified. 'And how long will this illness take to run its course?'

'Why, within two weeks your grace will be as healthy as ever before in her life. But for that time, you must needs have absolute rest.'

He left hurriedly, as I threw a shoe at him.

Of course I was relieved not to have the smallpox, but this chicken variety did not seem to be a great improvement, save in the matter of fatality – and a bride of fifteen, whose entire dowry is contained in her beauty, is inclined to prefer death to a ruined complexion. Adding to my distress was this announcement that I could not move for another fortnight when my husband, as I romantically supposed, was panting in England for my safe arrival in his arms.

The delay was hardly less irritating to the Duke and his cronies, who made their displeasure understood in no uncertain terms. But there it was. Doctors must be obeyed. And so I chafed, and they chafed. The day after the apothecary's visit, I was absolutely immersed in the horrid little water blisters, which seemed to cover every inch of my body. Naturally, as I was lying down, those on my back and bottom burst, and they all, burst or not, itched most terribly. But although I often cried out with the discomfort, I steeled myself not to touch one of them, thus revealing to myself that strength of character which was going to stand me in good stead so often in the future.

That I was not a woman to be trifled with should have been apparent to the Countess as well as the Duke, but they were too stupid to draw the proper conclusions; had they done so, the entire history of their nation might have been different. In any event, I refused to permit the Duke, or any man, and most especially Suffolk, to attend me while I was in so unhappy a state. This stricture did not of course include Robert the apothecary, who visited me every day – but I did not truly regard him as a man.

He congratulated me on my courage, and was again proved right when, after some ten of the most uncomfortable days of my life, the pustules began to disappear. How anxiously did I peer into my glass, and with what relief did I see that beautiful face peer back, with scarce a mark visible. I did not escape entirely unscathed. There were some shallow pits on my back and buttocks, as I have indicated, and there was one on my face, but it was situated immediately above my left eyebrow, and was therefore not easily to be discerned. In fact, I have often thought it added to rather than detracted from my looks.

Better yet, I was told that it was now most unlikely that I would *ever* contract the more fatal form of the disease.

On 7 April I was pronounced fit to travel, and thus bade Robert farewell, commanding Dame Alice to bestow on him some gold coins. I doubt she did this, for reasons which will soon become apparent, but at least I left him my gratitude.

I had of course been the recipient of many good wishes for my speedy return to health, as well as of prayers uttered in the cathedral in Rouen on the two Sundays of my illness, and, so I was told, in every church in England. This was very gratifying, but most pleasing of all to me was a letter from my own dear husband. It was the first time I had beheld his hand, and indeed the first time that he had addressed me directly.

His writing was rather a scrawl and difficult to decipher, but I gathered that he too was counting the days until we could be united. Although this was the closest he came to expressing any sentiments of love, I reflected that it would have been gross hypocrisy for anyone to avow love for someone he had never seen. The important thing was that he was *prepared* to love. As was I.

Thus I was in the best of spirits when I was finally able to proceed with my journey, as the fleet of barges carried me and my retinue down the broad flood of the Seine, despite the risk of encountering a *mascaret*, or bore, below Rouen. This is nothing less than a great wave caused by the incoming sea meeting the outflowing river, and when the tide is in flood it can be very dangerous, for it travels extremely fast, and can tear boats from their moorings or even wreck wooden piers and docks.

However, we reached Honfleur without encountering this

watery disaster, and there for the first time in my life I looked upon the broad waters of the English Channel. And did not like what I saw. The breeze was strong from the south-west, the skies were grey and it drizzled, and the seas were even greyer, save where they were torn apart by the wind into seething patches of white.

'When will we be able to cross?' I inquired.

'We leave tonight, your grace,' the Duke informed me.

'In this storm? Is that wise?'

'Tush, your grace, this is not a storm. It is but a cupful of wind, and from the right direction, too. We shall simply bowl along, and be in Portsmouth before you know it.'

From the moment of our first meeting I had found myself taking a dislike to this man. Now there was no use in hiding it from myself: I loathed him. But in this instance I could only hope he was right.

In fact he was, according to his reasoning. The English, because they are an island people, spend a good deal of time on the water – mainly in pursuit of their principal amusement: invading France – and are thus well acquainted with the idiosyncracies of wind and tide. Certainly the entire party seemed to have not the slightest doubt that we should put to sea, and thus the remainder of the day was spent in loading my retinue and myself on board the little fleet awaiting us.

The ship in which I and my ladies were to travel was the *John of Cherbourg*. It was what is known as a cog; that is, it had high sides, a raised deck fore and aft, two masts, and was very wide-beamed. Under the aftercastle there was a spacious cabin, and into this I was inserted, together with Bailly and the two countesses and various other females. On this occasion I exerted my authority, and insisted upon Albion accompanying us; he was chained on deck, to the alarm of the sailors.

Both Suffolk and York also boarded the stout cog, so that the captain was heard to remark, 'By Our Lady, my lords, should we strike a rock or encounter pirates, there is the

Queen and the premier lords of all England gone at a stroke.'

This earned him a buffet from Suffolk, but did absolutely nothing to reassure me. However, we had a hearty meal, on deck, as there was no room left in the cabin; the lords would have to sleep in the open, supposing they could. The wind remained to my mind extremely strong, but the Englishmen treated it with disdain and I was forced to match them.

I stayed on deck, clutching my hat over my ears, to watch the mooring lines being thrown ashore. One sail had already been set, and under this we drifted away from the dockside, whereupon the captain shouted, men scurried to and fro, Albion roared – one of the seamen had inadvertently trodden on his tail – the other sails were hoisted up the mast and, as the seamen say, we began to dance merrily over the waves.

This description is only half-true. Dance over the waves we most certainly did, the moment we were outside the harbour. But there was no merriment in it, at least for me. The rain had ceased and it was a splendid night, with a full moon illustrating the heaving waters. It would have been better had it been pitch dark. The movement of the sea almost immediately communicated itself to my stomach, my dinner departed, and then I was vomiting things I did not even know my gut to contain.

My ladies put me to bed, but it was the least comfortable of couches, being merely a thin mattress over bare boards. They fussed and offered me various things to eat and drink, which only made me vomit more. I wished for death, and actually prayed for either that rock or those pirates of whom the captain had jokingly spoken. But neither appeared, and in the course of time I fell asleep from sheer exhaustion.

When I awoke it was daylight, and the motion had calmed considerably. The Countess of Salisbury sat beside me. 'Are we arrived, my lady?' I asked. I was ever the optimist.

'No, no, your grace. But we are in the Solent, and will be at Portsmouth in time for supper. Would you not like to see your new kingdom?'

Her words inspired me, and I allowed myself to be washed and dressed, and thus appeared on deck to find the ship proceeding placidly up a broad stretch of almost totally enclosed water. To our right was a high-backed island, which was performing the excellent duty of protecting us from the wind and sea; to our left the land was low-lying and appeared marshy; but this was indeed England.

In my ignorance, I assumed that my journey was now over. As before, I was wildly over-optimistic. This Solent, that stretch of water enclosed by the Isle of Wight, is much larger than one might suppose. Allowing for the various sandbanks with which it is littered, and which prevent a ship from travelling in a straight line, it is well over twenty miles in length. Portsmouth, the harbour for which we were bound, was at the eastern end. To escape the worst of the weather, we had made our entry at the western end, past a formation of peculiarly-shaped rocks known as the Needles.

Now, we had just crossed the Channel, where it is some sixty miles wide, in the course of a single night. To cover a twenty-mile journey should therefore have taken us less than half of that time. Not a bit of it. My knowledge of the vagaries of sea travel was increasing all the time, and with every minute I liked it less and less. Our problem was mainly to do with these beastly tides. In the Channel they run east and west, and were thus athwart – to use the nautical term – our passage, which was to the north. Thus if we were set down a few miles in one direction for six hours, once the tide had turned we were set back up approximately the same distance. In the Solent the tides continued in this east and west flow, but unfortunately our course was to the east, and thus while we were bowled along for several hours, when the tide turned we were set back again almost to where we had started.

Where then was the wind, which should have provided the necessary impetus to enable us to overcome the tides? Alas, it seems that at sea there is either a great deal of wind, with the resulting danger to masts and lives – and stomachs – or there is not enough of it, with a resulting period of total frustration. There *was* a breeze, and it continued from the south-west, thus blowing us towards our destination; but it had dropped away from the gale of the night, and in addition we were now under the lee of the Isle of Wight. On entering the Solent, with an east-running tide of some four knots (it would have been impossible to use the narrow Needles Passage against the tide) and making about two knots ourselves, we covered some sixteen miles in the three hours left available to us. We could make out the steeples of the churches in our destination. But once the tide turned and ran the other way, again at some four knots, we actually lost twelve of those miles, though appearing all the time to sail steadily through the briny. This left us very little ahead of where we had started and, as it was now getting dark, our captain decided to anchor on the north side of the island in the shelter of a bay quaintly called Yarmouth. This was to make sure we did not run aground by attempting a night passage. 'Besides,' he informed us, 'if we can catch a fair tide first thing tomorrow, we will have it for six hours, and arrive safely at our destination.'

I refused to believe him, although my companions seemed very happy with the situation. But I was the one proved right on this occasion. After a remarkably comfortable night – for the motion of a ship at anchor in a snug bay is very soporific – we duly set off at dawn, again with a light fair wind and now also with six hours of fair tide. Alas, both the wind and the tide were less than on the previous day; instead of making Portsmouth as our captain had so confidently predicted, we reached within a mile of the harbour, when the wind dropped altogether, the tide turned, and there we were, forced to anchor for another night.

By this time the *John of Cherbourg*, overcrowded as it was, had become a noisome place. The situation was not helped by Albion, who not only emptied his bowels several times a day, thus requiring one of the sailors to be allotted constantly to stand behind him with shovel and pail, but also took offence whenever this worthy with his implements approached too close. I swear we were near a mutiny when we finally entered the harbour.

Here I had expected to be received by my husband, but he was not there. Instead, we had to disembark, and proceed by land back to the west, to the town of Southampton, where, I was told, the King awaited me, and past which we had apparently sailed on our way to Portsmouth, for the town lies up one of the inlets leading away from the Solent, but is difficult of approach from the sea because of mudbanks, and, needless to say, tides.

Thither therefore I took my weary way. It could have been a most pleasant journey for the countryside was attractive, and the people, for all Suffolk's warnings, appeared pleased to see me and cheered me most enthusiastically at every village through which we passed. Unfortunately it rained incessantly, and in addition to the wet from above we were forced to ford several fast-running streams and so got wet from beneath. However, on 14 April I reached Southampton. Without even being given an opportunity to change my clothes I was hurried to the local abbey, and there presented to my husband.

How often had I considered this moment, looked forward to it, dreamed of it! I had even relieved my conscience regarding my various sets-to with Suffolk by reminding myself that these had undoubtedly been caused entirely by my eagerness to be with my real husband, which had thus encouraged me to look upon my proxy husband too generously. Now had the moment arrived.

My first impression was very favourable. The King was at this time twenty-three years of age. He was tall, and if a trifle thin, this could be put down to his youth. He was clean-shaven and had a long face and perhaps a melancholy expression, but he was certainly not unhandsome. And as I approached him and sank into a deep curtsey at his feet, he smiled, which greatly enhanced his looks.

I had immediately observed, however, that of all the men in the room – and that included the travel-soiled Duke and Earl who stood at my shoulders – Henry VI looked least like a king. Far from being the best-dressed man present, he was the worst. He wore a black doublet and hose, the plainest of collars, and not a trace of jewellery was to be seen. His shoes looked like a labourer's boots, and had hardly been polished more often – a far cry from the pointed elegance on the feet of the men around him.

Now I had experienced such an attitude in Uncle Charles – although I would never have dreamed of marrying him – but what was even more disturbing was that there was no fire in Henry's eye, no stature to his stance, no visible evidence that here stood the son of Great Harry, ruler of the most formidable fighting race on earth. In fact, in this also he reminded me of my Uncle Charles, who was of course his uncle as well. Perhaps I had not properly considered this before. Now it concerned me greatly.

But at least no one present could doubt that I was a queen, and their queen as well. Despite the weather, I had taken care to dress at my best for the final stage of my journey. Though my shoes and the hem of my houppeland were stained with mud, the gown was none the less cloth of gold. I wore all the jewellery I possessed, and my hennin, a trifle dampened by the weather, brushed the lintel of the doorway under which I had just passed. I wore my hair loose, as befitted a young virgin, and it lay on my shoulders like a shawl.

Now the King gave me his hand, and I kissed his fingers, and was then gestured to my feet. 'Enchanting, madam,' he remarked. 'You are enchanting. Suffolk, I swear you are an honest man.' This caused laughter in the lords to either side, and perhaps some embarrassment to the Earl himself as he no doubt considered how dishonest had been his behaviour towards his sovereign's wife.

Still holding my hand, the King now turned to face the nobles and ladies behind him. 'Madam,' he said. 'I would have you meet my uncles. Cardinal Beaufort . . .'

The Cardinal – a large, stout, florid man (as are so many prelates) in his sixties – kissed my free hand and beamed at me most pleasantly.

'Humphrey, Duke of Gloucester . . .'

The Duke, the youngest and last remaining brother of Great Harry, was in his fifties. Like his step-uncle he was perhaps overweight, but his colour was too deep and his mouth too tight, indicating the choleric temper which was greatly feared. Unlike the Cardinal, he did not beam at his new niece, but rather subjected me to a piercing stare, as if trying to discern my bad rather than my good points. But I met him with a smile.

I had of course studied the current state of English politics during the months I had waited to reach the kingdom, and (as I have related) I was assisted in appreciating the situation by Suffolk. I thus understood not only that these two near-relatives were deadly rivals who loathed each other, but also why.

The causes of their mutual enmity went far deeper than the question of whose point of view should control the King, and therefore England's foreign policy. John of Gaunt, father of Henry IV, grandfather of Henry V, John of Bedford, and Humphrey of Gloucester, and thus great-grandfather of my dear husband, had not been prepared to rest on his legitimate laurels as a father, nor, apparently, had he found sufficient solace in the arms of his two legitimate wives. In the course of time his roving eye had encountered one Catherine Swynford – a great beauty, it is said. Well, presumably she had to be, to atone for a name like that. This woman my great-grandfather-in-law took to his bed on a more or less permanent basis in his declining years, and despite his age proved to be continuingly fertile. Catherine gave birth first of all to a son named John, and then one named Henry; there were other children, but these are all that matter to my story. Having done this, and feeling death approaching, he declared this secondary progeny legitimate, and gave them the name of Beaufort, from the castle in which they lived. John Beaufort was created Earl of Somerset by his half-brother, King Henry IV, and then Duke, and Henry Beaufort, on going into the church, pursued a number of grandiloquent schemes, which took him even to a contest for the Papacy. The forces against him there were too strong, but by adroit diplomacy he had secured his red hat, and now, as we have seen, was closest of all the ministers to his half-great-nephew.

This had become all the more important recently, because – supposing we set aside the scurrilous claims of that villain York – with the death of Bedford and the King as yet remaining childless, Humphrey was now the King's heir. And his *sole* heir, for when Gaunt had legitimised the Swynford's brood, he had expressly included the proviso that none of them could ever inherit the throne.

One would have supposed this would have settled the matter for all time. But Gaunt was dead. So was his son Henry IV, and his grandson Henry V. And Cardinal Beaufort survived. In the course of the years he had carefully amassed a fortune and was now reputed to be the wealthiest man in the land; it was said that he had, on more than one occasion, saved the King from bankruptcy by a timely and generous donation. The exact importance of this I did not yet realise, but it was well known to all that the Cardinal was the King's favourite relative, and that it was being whispered in the taverns that Henry might well be considering revoking his great-grand-father's edict, and with a stroke of his pen remove any disability on the part of the Beauforts to inheriting the crown.

Clearly this could never apply to the Cardinal. But the introductions were continuing.

'Edmund, Earl of Somerset.'

This was Bishop Beaufort's nephew, and therefore cousin to the King. I had heard a great deal about him, and his father, John, first Duke of Somerset, and his elder brother, the second Duke, who had recently died. As eldest surviving son of the first-born, Edmund was actually the senior member of the house of Beaufort. His father had been a great soldier and Edmund had aspired to emulate him, with a sad lack of success which had cost the English dear in France until he had been replaced by the Duke of York as Governor of Normandy.

But this was the man who, should the Beaufort line lose its disability to inherit, would be next in line to the throne after Humphrey of Gloucester! At the moment I met him, however, he was principally engaged in attempting to achieve the rank of royal duke that had been granted to his father and elder brother, but not as yet to himself. That he remained a potential rival for the throne, however, could not be doubted.

It may well be asked why Duke Humphrey had not taken steps to alleviate the situation. He was the principal heir, and his rights would have been fully transmitted to his son, were he to have one. Well, he had certainly tried, but without any success. Indeed, his choice of wives is amazing as he seems to have sought beauty rather than either substance or, more important, fecundity. This I know has been said of the choice of myself as queen, but I am the daughter of a King – and I am, or was, a mother. This cannot be claimed for Humphrey's bedmates. He first grasped the hand of a countess, Jacqueline of Hainault – the widow of Uncle Charlie's brother, my Uncle John – with the motive of obtaining the lady's estates and undoubted wealth as well as her favours. This upset her liege lord, my old admirer the Duke of Burgundy, and a long and bitter struggle ensued; it ended in the marriage being annulled and Burgundy terminating its alliance with England. Presumably while this was going on there was little time for begetting.

Tiring of this unsatisfactory situation, Humphrey abandoned his Dutch lady-love and married in her place his mistress, a commoner named Eleanor Cobham. I understand that she too was a great beauty – I never met either of the ladies to judge for myself – but she came to a sorry end. She is reputed to have sought the death of my own dear Henry, with the aid of some accomplices, by making a wax image which they exposed to the flames, to watch it melt away. They anticipated a similar fate would overtake the living man, in which case Duke Humphrey would have succeeded, and Dame Eleanor become queen.

What a picture this conjures up!

However, the Duchess's plans were betrayed, and a male member of the coven, who remarkably bore the name Bolingbroke – the title by which my Henry's grandfather was known – confessed, no doubt after being racked. He and the female accomplice, known as the Witch of Eye, both suffered the fullest rigours of the law, the witch being burned alive, the wizard being executed for treason in the English fashion: hanged, cut down while still alive, castrated, disembowelled, beheaded, and his body divided into four quarters. A third accomplice, Southwell, an ecclesiastic, died in prison.

Dame Eleanor, as the wife of a royal duke, was saved from any such ghastly fate. But she was forced to walk the streets of London as a penitent, barefoot and clad only in her shift and bearing a lighted candle, following which she was sentenced to perpetual imprisonment, being moved from castle to castle throughout the rest of her unhappy life.

These events had taken place only three years prior to my marriage, and had done nothing to improve Humphrey's always fierce temper. He had been forced to stand by and watch his beloved so maligned and mistreated, without being able to lift a finger to help her for fear of being himself implicated.

This very brief outline of the principal courtiers with whom I was destined to be surrounded gives a sombre picture of the situation in the English court at this time. But I was not the least concerned with the private ambitions or sorrows of those about me. My eyes were only for the King, my lord and husband. In him had I arrived at the summit of my ambitions, and with him I had no doubt I would rise higher yet, as together we scaled the paths of fame and glory, of love and parenthood.

Well, I suppose I am at least a famous person.

3

I may have foolishly supposed that my lengthy journey, which had really begun the previous year in Tours, from being Princess Margaret of Anjou to becoming Queen Margaret of England, had ended when I was at last face to face with my husband. But there was still a long way to go.

First of all, there was the matter of my wedding. It was not to take place until 23 April; that is, nine days after I had met the King. During that time I saw his grace once in passing; and once most deliberately, as I shall recount.

Impatient as I was to be the wife of the greatest king in Christendom – as was tirelessly repeated to me by everyone with whom I came into contact – I was not altogether sorry for the delay. In the first place, I wished for time to recover fully from the rigours of the sea voyage which had followed my illness with the chicken-pox. In the second, I conceived that it would give the royal seamstresses ample time to prepare for me an even more magnificent gown than that I had worn in Nancy, or at Notre Dame. And in the third place, I sorely wished to take stock of my situation, and to form a considered opinion of the man and the society to which I was now bound for the rest of my life.

My first wish was fully gratified. My week and a half's rest in Southampton restored me to the best health I had ever enjoyed.

My second was met with a sharp rebuff. 'Your grace will surely wear the same gown as for your proxy marriage,' declared the Duchess of Salisbury. She had now been reinforced by various other relatives, prominent amongst them the Duchess of York, who was known even to her friends as Proud Cis, and was a still more domineering character than her sister-in-law.

She was, as I have mentioned, a member of the Neville family, her two brothers both being prominent earls: one of Westmorland, the other of Salisbury. Of these Richard Neville, Earl of Salisbury, was the more powerful. I had met him briefly upon my arrival at Southampton, but as he was the husband of my first *bête noire*, I disliked him even before I set eyes upon him, and saw no reason to change my views then. However, the fact was that these brothers, owing to the steady accumulation of estates by their forebears over the years, were the wealthiest men in the kingdom, excepting only the Cardinal (and, surprisingly, Salisbury's own son, of whom I will speak later). But they were staunch adherents of their brother-in-law, the Duke of York.

Proud Cis it was who put the *coup-de-grâce* to my attempts at protest over my wedding gown. 'There is no money, your grace,' she said. 'It has all been spent on fetching you here. Your first gown will have to suffice.'

This was, to say the least, a startling revelation. I had been brought up in what may best be described as genteel poverty. My father was a king without a kingdom, and with the major part of his actual possessions overrun by the English. I had always been told that Uncle Charles was hardly better off, as while he *did* possess a kingdom, it too was largely overrun by these beastly Goddams over whom it was now my lot to rule. But I also knew that whenever Uncle Charles found my father to be near destitution, the royal French purse had been amply opened for our rescue, just as I knew it had been Uncle Charles, financially straitened or not, who had paid for the magnificent entertainments which had attended my proxy marriage.

If there was one thing of which everyone at Uncle Charles's court had been certain, however, it was that the King of England was rich as Croesus, and that I was going in a straight line from poverty to wealth beyond my wildest dreams. Well, I may say, my dreams were not so very wild; but I had certainly supposed that I should never again have to worry about what I spent, or how, or when. And here was I being told there was not sufficient money in the royal coffers to provide me with a new wedding gown?

I do not think I can be blamed for concluding that it was a plot on the part of these ladies (who as I have said were all of the persuasion later to be known as Yorkist, as opposed to the house of Lancaster) to make me appear dowdy and unable to dress to my new station. But when I appealed to dear Alice, she confirmed the dreadful truth. What with the continuing strife between the Cardinal and Duke Humphrey, the government of England had sunk into supinity, adequate taxes had not been collected. In a word, my future husband was strapped.

I took a brief refuge in tears – of anger rather than self pity like some milkmaid – and then determined on the only path open to me, but one which, I had no doubt at all, would carry me over all obstacles. 'I wish to speak with the King,' I said.

'The King?' They exchanged glances.

'My husband,' I reminded them.

'Only by proxy as yet, your grace,' the Countess of Salisbury pointed out.

'My lady, take heed that you do not regret those words,' I snapped, now thoroughly out of sorts, because it seemed to me that she and the others were having a private joke at my expense. 'I will see his grace. Now!'

'Your grace .. ' Proud Cis made an elaborate bow. 'That is impossible at this moment. His grace is at his devotions.'

I looked out of the window; the sun was well on its way to the meridian. 'Very well,' I conceded. 'I will see him before dinner. Better yet, I will dine with him.'

'Your grace, the King always dines alone. And his devotions occupy his time until the meal is ready.'

That will have to change for a start, I determined to myself; dinner at Uncle Charles's court had always been an occasion for great festivity. 'Then I will see him after dinner.'

'After dinner, your grace, the King will return to his devotions.'

'Madam,' I said, 'I find your attempts at humour unbecoming.'

She looked at me in surprise. 'I but state the truth, your grace. His grace spends much time at his devotions. More time than ever, this past week.' She glanced at her companions, who could not repress a titter. 'It is to prepare himself for the ordeal of marriage.'

I glared at her, at them all, then gathered my skirts and left the room. Outside, I encountered the Mother Superior, who was conversing with my own Bailly. 'Take me to the King,' I demanded.

Consternation! Dear Alice wrung her hands in dismay. Proud Cis and her friends ran behind me, saying this would never do, while the nuns ran to and fro, not knowing *what* to do, and Bailly quietly ordered me a palfrey. On this I mounted, wearing my indoor clothes, with not even a houppeland to keep out the rain. My hat, fortunately, was a plumed felt instead of a hennin, and quite easily manageable.

Actually, it was not raining at the time, which was a considerable change from the ordinary state of affairs I had observed in this benighted country. My grooms hastily followed me – my French lords had been dismissed at Rouen, and I was entirely bereft of male companionship save for these stout English lads, all of whom had clearly fallen in love with me at first sight – and I made my way to the Abbey.

Here my arrival caused as much consternation as my departure from the convent. Guards presented their halberds, squires hurried off to advise their various masters of my arrival, dogs barked, monks scratched their tonsures ... and I swept past them, demanding of each man as I encountered him the whereabouts of the King.

It turned out that Henry had just arisen from his devotions, and was washing his hands preparatory to sitting down to his dinner. Well, it was some time since I had washed my hands, either. 'Fetch me a basin and napkin,' I commanded the trembling monks. 'And show me to the King's dining chamber.'

This turned out to be the monks' own communal hall, a high-ceilinged and not unattractive place, had it contained any furniture other than benches and boards laid across trestles for tables. As I was surveying this scene and dipping my fingers into the tin basin brought by the anxious brothers, the Earls of Suffolk and Somerset entered, neither particularly well-dressed, and both looking very hot and bothered.

But they remained two very handsome men. 'Your grace!' They bowed together. 'There is something amiss?'

'I hope not, my lords,' I replied. 'I but wish to speak with my husband. And it seems the entire kingdom is conspiring to keep us apart.'

They clearly did not know what reply to make, but were saved from further embarrassment by the arrival of Henry himself, attended by the Cardinal and various other lords. 'Madam!' my husband exclaimed in astonishment. 'Forsooth and forsooth!'

I was to discover that this rather absurd oath was the only imprecation he ever allowed himself.

I sank to my knees before him, and he held my hands to raise me up. 'There is something amiss,' he said.

'I but wished to speak with my husband, sire,'

'But you do not as yet have a husband, madam.'

If I did not, then it was very careless of him to call me madam, as he did persistently, instead of mademoiselle!

'Legally you are so, sire,' I reminded him.

'But not in the eyes of the Church, madam. There is a

force greater than any laws that man may make. It is unseemly for you to visit me in this fashion, until the Church has given our union its blessing. Was it an urgent matter?'

By now I was well on the way to losing my temper. One would have supposed that any man with red blood in his veins would have welcomed a visit from a beautiful woman, especially as within a few days she was going to grace his bed. But I managed a smile, and kept my voice as sweetly seductive as ever. 'I but sought your advice on the gown I should wear for our wedding.'

'Why, madam, that is woman's work. There are more pressing matters.' Then his tone softened. You would please me, Meg, were you to be wed in sackcloth. Perhaps indeed that would be most fitting for us both, as we are sinners before the Lord.'

I would not give way. 'You flatter me, sire. But think of the effect on the populace. The Queen of England surely needs to look like the Queen of England?'

He frowned at me for a moment, and my heart sagged. Then he smiled. 'Of course you are right, sweet Meg. It shall be attended to. Now you must leave me. My lord!'

Both the earls started forward, but it was Suffolk who reached me first, and escorted me through the door.

'That will show those proud ladies,' I remarked.

'You are very forward,' he advised.

'I please his grace. That is all that matters.'

'You will always please him, sweet Meg.' He gave my arm a squeeze. 'You have but to remember that for his grace matters temporal take a poor second to matters spiritual.'

He escorted me back to the convent, but as we were accompanied by all my grooms and by most of my ladies, who had now caught up with me – these of course including his own wife – there was no time for him to offer me any solace. And it seemed I had to accept the governance of Proud Cis, for at least a few more days; her forceful personality utterly dominated that of dear Alice. But to her obvious chagrin, Cis received her orders and had to comply.

Next day a seamstress named Margaret Chamberlayne arrived: the best in the kingdom, I was told. She got to work without ado, while I gave Albion a good hug, to feel the heart of a lion beat against mine.

When the great day arrived and I was escorted to Tichfield Abbey, where Bishop Ayscough of Salisbury was to conduct the service, I was resplendently clad in a cerulean blue skirt with a chrome yellow bodice, both trimmed with ermine; my cloak was also of cerulean blue, again trimmed with ermine. My headdress was yellow, worn with golden cauls, and it and my collar were decorated with all the jewels my ladies could muster.

There was a great gathering of lords and ladies, all shivering in the drizzle, but all bowing and indeed gasping at my beauty as I passed them. For my part, I was delighted to observe that Henry was, for the first time in my company, dressed as a king, in red tunic and blue breeches, with the leopards of England and the fleur-de-lis of France emblazoned in gold upon his chest. He looked every inch a king ... and a man, too.

Standing with him were three men; or, rather, a man and two boys somewhat younger than myself, whom I now met for the first time. To my surprise, they turned out to be the king's stepfather and half-brothers! Perhaps this is putting it rather better than the truth. For here I was face to face with some more peculiar facts about this family into which I had married. King Richard II, of inglorious memory, had, it may be recalled, taken as his second wife the Princess Isabella, sister of my Uncle Charles. Isabella had been only twelve years old at the time, and from all accounts Richard was both inept as a husband – he could never produce an heir – and morbidly in love with his dead first wife, Anne of Bohemia. This had not prevented Aunt Isabella from falling in love with him. And remaining in love with him, even after he had been deposed and murdered, as the English are so fond of doing to their kings.

She did eventually return to France, married Charles d'Orleans, Count of Angouleme, who had some claims to be a poet, and died at the age of only twenty. Even in this short span of life, however, she had been suggested as a wife for Henry IV's son, then Prince of Wales, who was to become king as Henry V. Isabella turned him down without hesitation, as the son of the usurper who had done away with her own dear Richard.

Nothing loath, Henry then tried to secure Isabella's sister, but she too would have none of it. It was not until the utter defeat of the French at Agincourt in 1415, and the consequent surrender of the French monarchy with the infamous proviso that Henry should succeed Mad Charlie VI and King of France, that Henry's marital ambitions reached fulfilment: Charles had a daughter named Catherine, and this aunt of mine was not in a position to say no when her hand was requested by the conqueror of her nation. Aunt Catherine therefore became mother of my own dear Henry.

However, as all the world knows, only six years after the marriage, and when at last Great Harry had been able to spare the time from his constant campaigning to get his wife with child, he dropped dead, leaving the babe no more than nine months old. This was a serious position for a Queen Mother who was also a foreigner. Not unnaturally she considered herself to be the person best equipped to see her son through at least the dangerous first few years of his life. This did not suit the late King's brothers, Bedford and Gloucester. Their business, as they saw it, was to continue the war and bring to fruition Great Harry's claim to the French throne, which they did by having my future husband crowned in that same cathedral of Notre Dame at which I had been honoured as queen, and which at that time happened to be in English hands. This was obviously but a gesture; French kings, to be kings, need to be crowned in the cathedral at Rheims. But the English could not get there, so they put up with the next best thing.

The important point was, that while they were pronouncing

the infant Henry King of England and France, Uncle Charles was ignoring the treaty signed by his father and having himself crowned King of France – at Rheims. There was thus no way in which the English royal uncles could consider vesting the regency, and thus ultimately the conduct of the war and the claim, in the hands of a woman who was Uncle Charles's sister.

Aunt Catherine had therefore been politely set aside, given a reasonable home and income, and requested not to meddle. She was a high-spirited and, I am afraid, somewhat unbalanced girl of twenty-one. What would you expect? Unable to play a part upon that larger stage which had seemed to be her destiny, she turned her attentions to the smaller stage that was her new home, and out of her various attendants chose a certain Welsh squire, by name Owen Tudor, to be her favourite.

Soon he was warming her bed. Owen himself always claimed that he had been legally married to Catherine, but this is obviously untrue. Even if they had undergone a marriage ceremony in a church, it would still have been illegal; for no ex-queen may marry without the consent of her son and, where they exist, his regents. Catherine made no such application to the royal brothers; her son was still too young to care. Certainly when Bedford and Gloucester discovered the truth of the matter – as had to happen when my good aunt's belly began to swell – there was a great to-do. Owen found himself in the Tower of London and was fortunate not to have reached the block.

But the matter blew over, and in the course of the following few years Catherine bore her lover no fewer than three sons, not to mention a brace of daughters. Then, some eight years before my marriage, she died at the early age of thirty-six, no doubt worn out by amatory discourse and its consequences. Regrettably, I never met her. But here was the man himself, Owen Tudor, rescued from obscurity by his stepson, granted an annuity, and welcomed at court. The boys, his surviving sons, were Edmund and Jasper. Edmund was my own age, fifteen, Jasper a year younger. They were somewhat small fellows, like myself indeed, but lively and not unhandsome, although their hair was a bright carrot colour and their faces a mass of unbecoming freckles. I liked them at sight, and our friendship was to endure.

However, the smiling Tudors, the glowering Duke Humphrey, the cynical Cis, even the handsome, anxious Suffolk and the equally handsome but more urbane Somerset, were all as nothing this day as I placed my small white hand in the larger one of my husband. With due ceremony we were joined together for better or for worse. How many brides, I wonder, have obtained so entirely one-sided a bargain.

For the moment, however, I was utterly happy, my emotions crowned when I beheld my wedding ring. In it was set an immense glowing red ruby. It was I later discovered a gift from Cardinal Beaufort to the King, and had been made up into a ring for me. I had never owned anything quite so valuable, and felt that I glowed to match the stone.

Here was at last that fulfilment for which I had waited so long. I was not even disturbed by the lack of proper celebrations of this momentous event; these, I was assured, would follow my coronation, which was to take place in Westminster Abbey at the end of May. Until then, I was honeymooning.

In this regard, I had observed – during my admittedly brief sojourn upon this earth – that kings are entirely as other men. I had of course only met two. My dear papa was forced by circumstances beyond his control to spend much of his life away from the bed of his beloved wife. But whenever he did come home the pair of them disappeared into their bed-chamber behind locked doors, to emerge some hours later, tousled and happy. Uncle Charles could not keep his hands off any female, madame or mademoiselle, who happened to attract him. In other words, kings in my experience at that time were as lecherous as any other men, and had more opportunities for amatory success. Who would be so bold as to refuse a king?

Now, I had been brought up by my mama, and even more by my Aunt Marie and my grandmama Yolanda of Aragon, to believe that lechery should not be confined to the male sex – when the circumstances properly called for it, of course. From before I attained puberty, I had been encouraged to look forward to my marriage, and to my wedding night more than any other. That my husband should be a king, that he should be tall and handsome and clearly in the best of physical health, merely gilded the lily so far as I was concerned when it came to amatory matters. Having therefore been disrobed by my ladies with much chaff and ribaldry, wrapped in a voluminous undressing robe, wearing velvet slippers, my hair loose and tumbling down my back until it brushed my buttocks, I fairly ran along the corridor to the King's bedchamber while the ladies chased behind.

We were, it should be remembered, in an abbey. Yet the room struck me as being both small and poorly furnished, more suited to a monk – to whom it probably belonged in our absence – than to a king and queen. But even this did not dash my spirits. Nor did the fact that it was positively crowded with men. Proud Cis naturally demanded passage, but it was still necessary to brush against this lusting humanity, and I received more surreptitious squeezes in those few minutes than in my entire previous life. Again I was not to be deflected from my purpose, considering that to have pinched a queen's bottom must surely be an enduring memory for the lucky fellow. Thus I arrived before my husband, who like me was wrapped in a heavy robe. He wore, to my surprise, a nightcap, the tassle of which drooped past his ear and made him look uncommonly like a court fool (a commodity in which, it occurred to me, this court was singularly lacking).

I put the thought aside, to concentrate on the matter in hand. 'Sire,' I said, and sank to one knee.

'Wife,' he replied, and raised me up again. As he seemed hesitant, I kissed him on the cheek, this being the first time any part of our bodies save our hands had come into contact.

The lords and ladies cheered, and the King looked embarrassed. Now, as was customary, we were presented with a bowl of plum buns immersed in spiced ale, which brought the colour to our cheeks and seemed to make the King even more embarrassed. He set aside the bowl and clapped his hands. 'Good lords and ladies,' he said. 'I fear you must leave us.' An odd way of putting the matter, to be sure. But leave us they did, with many admonishments as to our happiness and pleasure.

At last the door closed, and we were alone. 'They are good people,' Henry remarked. ''Tis a pity so many of them hate me.'

'Hate you, sire?' I asked in some alarm.

'Perhaps it is the lot of kings to be hated,' he said, without any obvious resentment.

'But who, sire?'

He shrugged. 'My lords, for not leading them into battle in France.'

'Not my lord of Suffolk, surely?'

'No, no. He is a good man. The same can be said for Somerset, as he is my cousin. But York . . .'

'Who is also your cousin, sire.'

'Aye,' he said sombrely. 'Aye.' And then looked at me. 'But this is no conversation for our wedding night. Come, kneel with me.'

'Willingly, sire.' For a moment I was unsure whether or not this was some English form of love-play with which I was unacquainted. But my husband wished only to pray. Well, I had no objection to that. But when several minutes had passed and he continued to mutter to himself, while I had asked the Good Lord merely for a successful consummation, my knees began to hurt. I remained for some minutes longer, however, and then could stand it no more, and staggered to my feet. My movement did not seem to disturb the King, so I climbed on to the bed. As I did so I divested myself of my robe, for there was a roaring fire in the grate, and the room was distinctly warm. In any event, clothes would surely be an irrelevance in bed.

The King now raised his head and regarded me with consternation. As I was to discover, mine was the first naked female figure he had ever beheld, and even if we must make allowances for a certain immaturity in a fifteen-year-old girl, I may say without fear of contradiction that he was starting at the very top. But he did not seem pleased. 'Meg!' he admonished. 'You are obscene. Where is your nightgown?'

'I have none,' I said.

'Then get beneath the covers, and hide your shame.'

Somewhat abashed, I obeyed, and from their shelter watched him remove his robe. Its disappearance made little difference, as beneath it *he* was clad in a thick nightshirt. No doubt, I told myself, this was the English habit. But even my optimism suffered a blow when, on getting beneath the covers beside me, he lay on his back and gazed at the tent above our heads, not giving me a glance. This too I endured for several minutes, until I grew impatient, and rose on my elbow. 'You are displeased with me, sire.'

At last his head turned. 'Displeased? No, no, Meg. You are young. And French.'

Utter condemnation. But I refused to lose my temper. 'I wish only to please you, my lord.'

'I am sure you shall, sweet Meg. We will speak of it tomorrow.' Saying this he sat up, but it was not to fold me in his arms. Instead he reached out of the bed and snuffed the candle, and then lay down with his back to me!

Once more, several minutes of silence. But I was not going to be faint-hearted at this juncture. Resisting the temptation to poke him in the ribs, I sat up myself. 'Sire,' I said. 'We are not man and wife.'

That startled him. He rolled over and sat up in turn, with such violence I nearly fell out of bed. 'Forsooth and forsooth! Has our union not been consecrated by the Bishop, in this very chapel?'

'Indeed, sire. But no marriage is made, before God or man, until it is consummated. This is a universal law, accepted by church and state alike.'

He did not reply for several seconds, then he gave a heavy sigh. 'You are right, of course. I had not expected legalities in one so young.'

'Legalities?' I cried, quite forgetting my manners. 'I am your wife.'

'French,' he muttered. 'French,' as if he had just discovered himself in bed with a witch. He lay down again. 'Sweet Meg. I know nothing of this business.'

It was some seconds before I could speak. I could not imagine a grown man of twenty-three, who was not also a monk, who remained a virgin. As for a king . . . But again I refused to lose my self-possession. Perhaps I would be the gainer in this, for if he had never known another woman, he might never wish to. Again, the two kings of my experience had both indulged themselves in mistresses, and I had always before me the sorry spectacle of Mademoiselle Sorel virtually excluding Aunt Marie from the royal bed. 'Then, sire,' I said as winningly as possible, 'we will have to teach each other.'

How may the blind lead the blind? I am sure my instincts were in the right place, but his were not. I had to do all of it myself, and to say truth I was not very successful on this first occasion. We both slept heavily, exhausted, and next morning, as soon as the ladies had brought us each a restoring posset, he left in a great hurry to pray.

Proud Cis was scornful as she inspected the sheets. 'You are not yet a queen, your grace,' she remarked.

But perseverance has always been one of my principal characteristics, as this detestable woman was to find out to her cost in later years, and before we set off for London I was indeed Queen of England in fact as well as name. The event itself terrified Henry, as I could not stop myself crying out when finally he possessed sufficient manhood to stab me, and he thought he had done me a mortal injury.

The fact is that, separated from his mother while still an

infant, and brought up entirely by men, who sought only to combine scholarship with military prowess, no one had shown the least interest in teaching the poor man the facts of life. By the time he was in his teens and might have been expected, from the urgings of his own body, to wonder what lay beneath the skirts of the ladies of his court, he had already begun that turn towards the Church which now had him gripped in a vice.

Potent word. For he regarded sex as a vice which, as the Church instructed, should only be indulged in for the purpose of procreation. This meant that the deed could never be undertaken in any spirit of levity or, God forbid, lechery. In vain did I try to convince him that a certain amount of foreplay was necessary to prepare us both for the ultimate: he still found it necessary to pray for forgiveness after every bout.

And yet, remarkably, during our honeymoon he fell in love with me. I assure you that this is not the idle fancy of a frustrated woman. Every day he gave more evidence of his affection. Though always a reluctant lover, he began to spend more time in my company and less at his devotions. And when he discovered that the flower I had adopted as my own was the common daisy, he promptly adopted it as his own, too, and had it inscribed on most of his garments and such bric-à-brac as his salt cellars and cutlery.

I have sworn to be absolutely honest in these notes – no one will ever read them – and thus I must confess that with every day I spent in Henry's company I became more aware that Fate had dealt me a scurvy hand. I had assumed I was marrying great wealth: the incident of my gown notwithstanding, another fact of which I became increasingly aware was that the King, required to keep the most splendid state in the country, was a good deal less wealthy than people like the Nevilles or the Beauforts.

I had assumed I was marrying the son of Great Harry: well, so I was, but any son less like his father – at least as far as Great Harry's reputation went – could hardly be imagined. I had not stopped to consider that I was also marrying the son of Aunt Catherine, and therefore the grandson of Mad Charlie. Just how catastrophic this might turn out to be I had not even dreamed of.

I had assumed I was marrying a great warrior: at the time of our marriage Henry had never been within a hundred miles of a battle, nor had he ever broken a lance in the lists.

I had assumed, as I was marrying a man and a king, that I was marrying a great lover: of this I have already spoken.

Worst of all, I had assumed that it was my destiny to mother a brood of kings, who would once again make the name of England reverberate throughout the world. Well, I was not so naive as to suppose this would happen on my honeymoon, but the fact was that so perfunctory were Henry's entries that I even then doubted he would ever be able to impregnate me. However, I had also assumed that I was to become Queen of England, and this no man, or woman, could prevent.

I do not think I shall ever forget my entry into London. It took place on 28 May, and whatever the frustrations I had endured during the previous couple of months, this was the greatest day of my life, to that moment.

Not that the town was in any way attractive. It was less than half the size of Paris, and apart from the huge fortress, known as the Tower, which dominated it, was a mean and ugly place. But it was the heart of the kingdom.

I will confess to feeling distinctly nervous. I had been warned on all sides that the inhabitants of London were the most unruly, ungovernable, unreasonable and riotous mob in the whole world. They were virtually a law unto themselves; even the King must needs ask permission to enter their walls, and even a king was not guaranteed immunity from flying brickbats should he displease them. I had also been warned that they were vehemently anti-French. Thus I really did not know whether I was about to live the last day of my life, and wondered what it felt like to be torn limb from limb.

I need not have worried. It was of course as splendid an occasion as could be managed, and for once our efforts to please were assisted by the elements: there was not a cloud in the sky, and the sun shone magnificently. Equally, before our arrival, the conduits had run wine instead of water for the previous twenty-four hours. This is a business that needs precise calculation. A sober Londoner is unpredictable but on the whole good-humoured; a drunken Londoner is good-humoured but liable to become a wild beast if angered; and a twice-drunken Londoner is liable to be fast asleep. On this occasion, the amount of wine disbursed seems to have been just sufficient to keep the populace in an excellent humour, and yet awake.

Then your Londoner adores processions, and this was a procession to end all processions. First came a band of trumpeters and drummers, who with their fanfares and measured beat warned the citizens that the rest of us were following. They took up their position beside the Guildhall to maintain this racket throughout the proceedings. Then there was a bevy of beautiful virgins – at least so it was claimed – although their garments were so diaphanous as they cavorted while strewing rose petals to left and right that it is difficult to believe that they maintained that status for very long, supposing they did not die of distemper, for although the sun shone it was not warm. Next came a body of men-at-arms, in full armour, lances at the rest and visors raised, walking their horses proudly through the throng, and even smiling, as commanded to do, at the urchins who ran beneath their hooves.

These were followed by a detachment of the fearsome Welsh archers, popular lads, as the citizens correctly esteemed them as the destroyers of the French. Then there was a bevy of lords and ladies, dressed in their best, smiling and waving to the unwashed mob. Among them, I was happy to see, were the Duchess of York and the Countess of Salisbury, at last occupying their proper places, with *hoi polloi*.

Then came Albion, now half-grown, walking on a leash held by his keeper. His appearance caused a tremendous stir.

We were next. Our canopy was held aloft by the Dukes of Gloucester, Buckingham (a descendant of Edward III's youngest son) and York, the Earls of Suffolk and Somerset, Salisbury and Westmorland, and immediately in front of us walked Cardinal Beaufort.

Henry, in full armour, with the crown on top of his helmet, rode a great war-horse which caused me some concern as it occasionally pranced. I rode a white palfrey.

As I was cloaked, for as I have said there was a chill easterly breeze, I wore my first wedding gown; and as I was outdoors, a tall hennin in gold and silver, with masses of white gauze attached to crown and brim floating behind me. My hair was loose and joined in the general flutter, while as I raised my hand to the populace, again and again, my ruby caught the sunlight most splendidly.

The onlookers cheered themselves hoarse. It was the first and, unfortunately, last time that the people of London were so enthusiastic about their queen. Or their queen about them.

The procession finished with a magnificent banquet at the Guildhall, which did not end until late in the afternoon. Then, thoroughly sated, we left the city again, and proceeded by barge upriver a short distance to the village of Westminster. Here, on the very banks of the Thames, was situated the royal palace.

I was agreeably surprised at the sight of my new home, for I beheld a vast house, towered in many places to be sure but lacking the grim defensive measures which had attended every house in which I had hitherto resided. Even Uncle Charlie had spent his life perambulating from fortress to fortress, these being the only places in which he had felt remotely safe not only from the marauding English, but from the machinations of Cousin Louis. But there appeared no

such apprehensions in England. There is the benefit of living
on an island, where a foreign invasion is a difficult and
loudly proclaimed event, allowing ample time for defensive
measures or flight to be undertaken. The nearest enemies
able to distress England without crossing water were the
Scots, several hundred miles away to the north.

The interior of the Palace of Westminster was not so
attractive as the exterior. It was very like all the castles in
which I had spent my childhood, a place of over-large rooms
and draughty corridors, tramping guards and an almost total
lack of privacy. It was also situated exactly opposite to, and
at a distance of not more than a few yards from, Westminster
Abbey, the large church erected by King Edward the
Confessor some four hundred years previously. My husband
thought this a splendid convenience. He considered Edward
the Confessor the greatest monarch ever to sit upon the
English throne, however insulting this conception might
have been to his famous father and even more famous great-
great-grandfather, the mighty Edward III: the Confessor, so
far as is known, never once drew his sword in defence of his
realm, or in pursuit of another's.

The proximity of the church meant that a large part of
every day was overladen with the chime of bells or the
chanting of choristers. No one has ever accused me of being
irreligious, but there is a limit. I far preferred to walk on the
river terrace and look out at the rushing waters and the many
craft which plied upon them, for the Thames was the
principal thoroughfare from the city to the sea, and indeed
well into the interior of the country.

Our closeness to the abbey did have one fleeting advantage; when two days later I was crowned Queen, I had
merely to walk a few steps. Being crowned is of course to
be regarded as the apogee of any monarch's life. Until this
magical moment he, or she, may have the right to rule by
inheritance, legality, or even – dare I say it – usurpation. In
the case of a consort, she may, as in my case, already have
been married to the King, and therefore be recognised by all

as their queen. And yet until, before the assembled populace, she is anointed and proclaimed, in the name of God the Father, God the Son, and God the Holy Ghost, she is still a cipher against history. Should death overtake her before the magic moment, she will remain always a mere entry in the records.

In the case of a foreigner like myself it was even more important that my endowment with the regal honours should be seen, and accepted, by all. Here I am thinking less of the common people than of the lords and their ladies; only a handful of them, as I was well aware, had the slightest inkling of what was contained in my wedding contract. All these factors combined to make me exceedingly nervous as the moment approached. But in addition the simple business of being anointed and crowned is a startling experience, especially for a young girl who, though already a bride, remained suitably chaste and modest.

I was therefore all of a tremble when Henry offered me his arm and, wearing my second wedding gown – as being the easier to unfasten at the appropriate moment, thanks to the skill of Mistress Chamberlayne – we left the palace, with our usual escort of princes of the blood and their ladies. Once again an immense crowd has assembled, and once again my beauty was the cynosure of all eyes, with good reason on this occasion.

I was escorted up the steps of the abbey, and there greeted by Archbishop Stafford of Canterbury, the premier prelate in the land. This man was no relation of the King's cousin Humphrey Stafford, Duke of Buckingham, who was standing at my shoulder. But he should have been the second most important man in the land after the King, had he been more assertive in his manner. He preferred the scholastic life, however – which made him a great favourite of my husband's – and left the show to the Bishop of Winchester, Cardinal Beaufort.

On this occasion his duties must have been pleasurable enough. I was seated on the throne, and after various prayers

had been said, disrobed. That is, my ladies removed my
mantle and then unfastened my gown, to expose me naked
from the waist up to the eager gazes of the masses before the
steps.

This was a trying moment, for while the unwashed throng
were at a considerable distance and would surely be unable
to perceive more than a blur of white skin largely shrouded
in tawny brown hair, the peers of the realm and their ladies
were a good deal closer than that. They clustered to either
side and one or two actually stood at my shoulder, all
anxious for a closer inspection of this girl who was now their
queen.

I could only square my shoulders and fill my lungs and
wish I had more to offer, while reflecting that Proud Cis and
her fellows must be regretting their own fading beauty when
confronted with so much that was fresh and blooming. But
I am afraid I spoiled the whole effect by shivering uncon-
trollably when the oil was actually poured on to my
shoulders – the idiot priests had quite forgotten to warm it!

Still, the crown was set upon my head, my shoulders and
dugs – an unattractive English word for a woman's breasts
which I shall not use again – covered with my cloak, and I
stood to be presented to the cheering populace.

When I returned to the palace, the lords and their ladies
were waiting to be presented to me. Duke Humphrey of
Gloucester and Duke Richard of York I had of course
already met, as I had met Earl Edmund of Somerset. These
were all princes of the blood, as was Humphrey Stafford,
Duke of Buckingham. I have already mentioned him as
having an important role at my wedding. He was forty-three
years old, a stout, handsome man, every inch a Plantagenet
with his golden hair and strong face. I liked him immediately, and even liked his wife, despite the fact that she had
been Anne Neville before her marriage. In other words, she
was the sister of Proud Cis, and the royal cousins, Richard
of York and Humphrey of Buckingham, were brothers-
in-law.

With them on this auspicious occasion were their sons. Young Edward, Earl of March, I had already met in France. Still only three years old, he was as pretty and precocious as ever. Humphrey Stafford junior was much older, already in his teens, and an altogether more pleasant personality, if only because he was just old enough to have fallen madly in love with his queen, as was obvious to everyone. Henry Beaufort, Cousin Edmund's eldest son, had obviously suffered the same exquisite fate, although he was not yet even in his teens.

Behind the royal dukes there were the great lords, and of these the two brothers, the Earls of Salisbury and Westmorland, were the dominating figures. The elder of the pair, Richard Neville, Earl of Salisbury, was reputedly one of the wealthiest men in the Kingdom, and as the brother of Cis and Anne, until my appearance on the scene with the suggestion of a royal heir to follow, closely connected with potential successors to Henry.

He also possessed several sons, most of whom were in their teens. It was on this occasion that for the first time I came face to face with Salisbury's heir, also named Richard, then a boy of seventeen. As such, he was of an age to catch the eye of a fifteen-year-old girl who had also just become his queen. And indeed there was much to catch the eye. I beheld a tall, fair youth, who stood very straight, and already possessed a commanding presence. His clothes were very fine, his cap of the best velvet, and when he bowed to kiss my hand he almost managed to convey that *he* was doing *me* a favour.

I had not noticed him sufficiently before, although I had of course been briefed by both Suffolk and Alice as to who was what. This boy was in any event destined to play an important role in the government of the country. But his cunning parents had ensured an even greater future for their son by securing his marriage to Anne Beauchamp, only a short while before our meeting. Anne Beauchamp's father Richard, Earl of Warwick, had been a favourite of Henry V, and had indeed been in charge of my own Henry's boyhood education. He had also been the wealthiest earl in England. He had died six years previously, and Anne was his only survivor. Thus Richard Neville the Younger, by marrying her, would become at twenty-one both Earl of Warwick and in turn the wealthiest noble in England. Even had I not already formed a dislike for both his mother and his aunt, not to mention his father and his uncle, I have given enough cause for me to dislike *him*. Now, when he straightened, I for the first time looked him in the eye, and I felt a chill cross my shoulders. Perchance they were still suffering from their exposure and inundation beneath the sacramental oil, and yet I feel that on that sunlit afternoon I glimpsed the soul of a boy who would in time seek to rule the world.

To think that I sat in the presence of my two greatest enemies – the future King Edward IV and the future Warwick the Kingmaker – in all my power and glory, while one was a child and the other a stripling, and did not immediately seek their heads!

The next three days were given over to dancing and festivities, jousts and masques. It was all very jolly and gratifying, and everyone, even the Yorks and the Nevilles, were unfailingly kind and courteous. It was also very tiring, and Henry and I did no more than collapse into our bed exhausted in the small hours. Thus the unfortunate reality of our marriage was not yet apparent to me, and though Henry grumbled at the waste of time and money, and every day rose early no matter how little sleep he had had to cross the court to the abbey, where the confounded bells would be tolling, this was actually a relief. He did not insist I accompany him; left to myself I could take off the nightgown he had insisted I wear ever since our first night together and spread myself across our bed, stretching each arm and each leg as far as it would go, and think to myself, I am Queen of England! I am the Premier Queen in all Europe! Which meant the entire world!

*

Part of the business of the celebrations was to enable the great lords to give me presents, which they did, according to their means and their ideas of what would please me. I received a great deal of plate and jewellery, which was to stand me in good stead later on, together with various knick-knacks. But my favourite present of all was relatively worthless, at least when considered in the light of obtaining ready funds. This was a quite magnificently illustrated book of French romances presented to me by Talbot, Earl of Shrewsbury, England's premier soldier at that moment. The tales themselves of course could hardly be compared with those produced by my dear Boccaccio, but I would spend hours looking at the pictures.

Even more to my liking, I was required to sit down with the Cardinal and the other officers of the exchequer to determine my financial position. I took no part in the wrangling, not all of it dignified, preferring to leave such mundane matters in the very capable hands of the Cardinal, whose loyalty was assured. Out of it all I emerged with an annual income of four thousand, six hundred and sixty-six pounds sterling, thirteen shillings and fourpence. This pound sterling was the currency in which the English dealt, and arose from their financial relations with the Hanseatic League, the principal carriers of goods in northern Europe, who transferred funds from one place to the next in terms of 'easterlings', or pennyweights, which came to be known as a guarantee of sound coin and immediate payment. The English, themselves busy traders, had adopted this method of transacting business, in the process dropping the first syllable. As to sound coin and immediate payment, that was a different matter, but to a young girl who had never had two sous to rub together in the course of her previous life, my jointure seemed an enormous sum, especially when to it was added two thousand pounds' worth of land!

I think that first week of my wedded life was the happiest I had ever known. Or was to know. I was to be rapturously happy for brief periods in the future, but those were to be stolen moments, all too often overlaid with guilt.

But for the moment nothing suggested any possible change in my estate, save for the better. This last possibility lay entirely in the hands of my dear husband, and young and enthusiastic as I was, I had no doubt that it was merely a matter of time.

In the first instance, there was naturally much to be done to restore the court and the government to its normal state following the cessation of the celebrating of my coronation. The great lords, their ladies and their retinues took their departures from Westminster, each in turn calling at the palace to bid me farewell until we met again, with every indication of loyalty. 'Your grace is like a red, red rose,' vouchsafed the Duke of York. 'May you bloom forever.'

'I pray for your happiness,' agreed Proud Cis. 'Will you not bestow a kiss upon our son?'

The boy Edward was held up for my embrace, which I gave heartily, as I was all in favour of children at that time. She also had a clutch of baby daughters for me to dandle, and this too I did.

'Perpetual summer has come to England, your grace,' said the Earl of Salisbury.

'You have but to crook your little finger, and all the land will come running,' declared his son Richard. 'I at their head.'

What hypocrisy!

But then they were gone, and Westminster was a quiet place.

'How I have dreamed of this, Harry,' I said, nestling against him.

'Aye, they are a scurvy lot,' he agreed, obviously knowing them a great deal better than I.

'What shall we do today?' I asked, bouncing on the bed. 'I know! Let us ride to the hunt.' I had not hunted since leaving France.

'The hunt?'

'Do you not hunt?' I asked, feeling suddenly indigested. 'All kings hunt. As do their wives.'

'Oh, Meg, Meg, you are but a girl, and therefore can be forgiven anything.' He gave me a tender but entirely chaste hug. 'Hunting is a waste of time and energy, and a sore distress to the unhappy deer. I am to my devotions. I have sadly neglected them these past few weeks.' This from a man who during the weeks I had known him had spent at least six hours a day on his knees!

I saw him go, romped with Albion, but spent most of my time somewhat petulantly, I fear, to the concern of my ladies and especially of Alice Suffolk. But consider: I was young, I was anxious to live, I was filled with energy, and I was Queen of England. I needed to *do*. And I was required to spend my days listening to idle gossip about people I did not really know and who, at that time, interested me not a bit, while I concerned myself with my needlework. When I determined to make a thorough inspection of the palace, not excluding the kitchens, there was a great to-do and a rushing to and fro, but this was hardly to be compared with the excitement that occurred when I announced I wished to go for a ride. Squadrons of guards had to be turned out, bugles blew, grooms scurried, and ladies appeared to faint. I realised that were I to insist upon what I really wanted to do, go hunting, I might be the cause of several cases of heart failure, and decided to let it rest for the moment.

Nor was this the only cross I had to bear. Only a month after I became Henry's wife it was represented to me that it was not seemly for an English queen to have a French chamberlain. It was even suggested that it was not seemly to have a Frenchwoman as my principal lady of the bed-chamber. Bailly I flatly refused to part with, but I felt it necessary to acquiesce in the returning to France of M. d'Heristal. I was still in the mood where I wished to be as English as anyone else. Poor d'Heristal was broken-hearted, but in truth he had been as confounded by English manners as I myself, and as my chamberlain had turned out to be the fifth wheel of a coach.

He was replaced by an English knight, Sir John Wenlock, a man of middle years and sober mien – as a very young lad he had fought at Agincourt and held some lands in Normandy as a gift from Henry V – who seemed to find it necessary to act the father from time to time. I resented this, and from time to time threw things at him. However, as time went by, I came to value him at his true worth, and to understand that, having undertaken to serve me, he would do so unto death. No woman can ask more of any man, and we became friends, although our relationship underwent considerable vicissitudes in the course of the next twenty-five years.

Now as is well known, the ideal situation for a young bride, especially if she also happens to be a queen, is pregnancy. I could name any number of good princesses who have literally mothered themselves into an early grave in their eagerness to provide an heir to the throne, and I was fully prepared to take my chances in this direction. Unfortunately, man (or in this case, woman) proposes, and God disposes.

Now, I am as aware as anyone that nobody truly understands the mysteries of procreation. Many learned men have put forward innumerable theories, most of which are obvious rubbish. There is even a school of thought which insists that pregnancy has something to do with the fluid which flows from the male member when he is at the height of his passion. Even were it not patently absurd that the life force should be contained in a sticky liquid, the theory is defeated by sheer logic, for a woman is seldom altogether dry at these times, and who ever heard of a man becoming pregnant?

Equally there are those who declare that the mere act of marriage, the consecration and joining together of two bodies, and no doubt more importantly two souls, by God, is sufficient for the furtherance of the human race, this being the sole reason for which the institution of marriage was created, anyway. Would that this were so. But this theory does not explain the many married couples who remain childless – except to those who would say that they have sinned, whereas these unhappy people are normally the most blameless of characters. Even less does it explain the numerous bastards that abound in this world!

No, no. The most obvious cause of pregnancy is the entry of the male member into the woman, although no one can explain exactly why this should be so. My own theory, and I have yet to have it disputed, is that the woman is continually in a state of latent pregnancy, as it were; and that when properly stimulated by the male member she performs her duty. This alone would explain my own experiences, and my own inability to become pregnant by the King.

Henry loved me dearly. I am as certain of this as I am of the sun in the sky. But it was the love of a boy for a toy, or for a favourite horse or dog. He loved to hold me in his arms, to stroke my hair . . . but never my breasts or bottom, for fear of having to endure lewd thoughts. For this reason, equally, he never looked upon me naked after our first night. Sadly, it is again my experience that a man finds it very difficult to arrive at a proper state to penetrate a woman *unless* he is in the middle of some very lewd thoughts, preferably about her, of course. But about anyone, or anything, is better than nothing. This determination of Henry's meant that he was seldom in a proper state to do me justice.

Then, when he *was* in a proper state, as the entire business was carried out in the most perfunctory manner – again so as not to risk the insertion of any lewdity into our connection – there was absolutely no chance of his arousing my womanhood sufficiently to involve pregnancy.

It was a frustrating business. And a disturbing one, for above all others, the principal duty of a queen is to provide an heir. But I remained optimistic. I was young. Henry was young. All things were still possible. Which is not to say I would not have taken almost any route out of my boredom.

But there were none; at least, none obvious to a fifteen-year-old girl who had been brought up in the ideals of honour and faithfulness and the sanctity of the marriage vow – which was probably just as well.

I had, at the worst, supposed that I would from time to time enjoy the company of Suffolk, especially as Alice remained in close attendance on me. However, the most important event which followed the ending of the coronation celebrations was the summoning of a Parliament. This is a most peculiar English institution, quite unknown in France, in which the King appears before an assembly drawn from all over the land. It includes his great nobles, but it is mainly of the common people, and he actually begs them for money in the form of various taxes.

We have our *parlements* in France, to be sure, but these are individual to towns and districts and do not represent the country at large. The King of France has the power to summon the Estates General, an assembly of lords, commons and clergy gleaned from the entire country, should he feel it necessary – Uncle Charlie never summoned one at all, to my knowledge – but when any of these bodies has been gathered, it is invariably for it to hear what the King wants, not for him to discover what his subjects are prepared to give. But in financial matters, as in so many others, the English follow their own peculiar customs. It will have been gathered that there was no one more in need of money than my own dear Henry, but the idea that he should have to go cap in hand to the people he ruled and ask for it seemed to me the height of self-abnegation.

Now, I will be the first to admit that I know little of the business of financing a kingdom. I have never yet met a king who had sufficient money. Yet kingdoms are financed, by decree of the king, or by his will in other matters, whether it be borrowing or conquest. England is the only one I have ever heard of where it is a matter of argument and bargaining between king and subjects. This bargaining takes many forms. But mainly these common people take it upon themselves to say – to the King, mind you – we will give you the money you require, in return for certain concessions by you. A moment's thought will indicate where such a proceeding, carried to logical absurdity, would lead. Worse, these Commons, as they were proud to call themselves, deemed it their right to interfere in every aspect of the government, save perhaps the actual command of the army in war. But as Henry had no intention of ever commanding an army, this point did not arise.

Thus it was that, having made several arduous journeys to France, at the request of these very nobles and the Commons, having done a great deal of arguing and bargaining of his own, and finally returned with the prize he had been instructed to obtain – to wit, myself, and a truce between England and France as well – dearest Suffolk must now stand up in this beastly Parliament and defend his actions to these Commons!

The principal cause of criticism of his actions was that I had brought with me no dowry. That Suffolk had actually given away territory the English chose to consider their own in order to procure me remained a deadly secret. He defended himself with spirit, demanding what greater dowry could anyone desire than a truce which would stop, if only for a limited period, the shedding of English blood and the spending of English coin? This did not go down well with the war party, which was headed by Gloucester. But at this time they were in a minority, the Commons being reluctant to vote more money than was necessary for the continuance of government, and a merchant named William Burley, who was the elected head of these Commons, and went by the title of Speaker – as he gave utterance to the result of their private deliberations – called for a vote of thanks to the good Marquis for the great deeds he had accomplished on behalf of the country. This motion was carried with such acclamation that even Gloucester was forced to support it.

Suffolk seized the opportunity to strengthen his position,

aware as he was that there was a vast thundercloud just over the horizon, even if it was as yet invisible to any English eye, and requested a repetition of the indemnity he had been granted before ever going to France, absolving him from any blame or punishment for anything he might have done or agreed in the course of his embassy. This too was voted with acclamation.

I was anxious to do some demanding of my own, and seized my cue when Henry announced how satisfied he was with the outcome of the debate. 'I do not think the Marquis has been at all adequately rewarded for what he has done,' I remarked.

'Well, there is little else I can offer him, my poppet. He is already far wealthier than I, even had I any money to spare.'

'Money is an irrelevancy to a man like Suffolk,' I said. 'He craves recognition of what he is, the principal man of your realm, my love.'

Henry stroked his chin. He was not of the nature ever to argue, except where the point was purely academical, but I could see he did not agree with me, no doubt thinking of his uncles.

'What would please him most, and would equally please me most, my sweet,' I said, 'would be to have the Earl of Suffolk elevated to a dukedom.'

Henry was startled. 'A dukedom? My own dear love, Suffolk has no royal blood. It could only be allowed were he to perform some quite exceptional service to the Crown.'

I raised my eyebrows. 'Would you not say that Suffolk's services have been quite exceptional, dearest heart? But for his efforts, I would not be here now.'

Henry could really refuse me nothing, and so it was agreed. Pole was to become Duke of Suffolk. He was delighted when we told him. Alice was quite overwhelmed.

But before it could be officially announced, news reached us from Paris: an embassy was on its way, to discuss the handing over of Maine and the city of Le Mans, as agreed by Suffolk.

4

To say that we were surprised at this would be a considerable understatement, and I at least was furious. I had always known Uncle Charlie to be a devious, lecherous rogue, while Cousin Louis, if not lecherous, was even more two-faced than his father. But I had not believed they would be so uncaring of my popularity in England as so soon to project the marriage bargain into the forefront of national politics.

However there was nothing for it but to brace ourselves for the coming storm, and in fact, as I later discovered, there was some excuse for Uncle Charlie's action. He was not himself this summer. It may well be asked, when was he himself, or indeed, what was himself? But he was prone to extravagant behaviour, and extravagance can most readily be displayed in grief. Margaret of Scotland, Cousin Louis's bride and Uncle Charlie's favourite toy (after Mademoiselle Sorel and myself) was dead, at a most unseemly early age: she was not greatly older than I.

Apparently she had been hunting, and on returning to her apartment felt so over-heated she stripped herself naked and stood before an open window. Before anyone could draw breath, she had contracted a cold which became a congestion on the lungs, which left her unable ever to draw breath again. Uncle Charlie was apparently devastated, far more so than Margaret's cold fish of a husband, Cousin Louis. My heart bled for him ... but I was still intensely displeased that he should have so inconvenienced Henry and myself – not to mention poor Suffolk.

The embassy, which arrived on 14 July, was headed by the Archbishop of Rheims and the Count of Vendome. Both of these gentlemen were of course well known to me. And they were courtesy itself, beginning their proceedings by inviting Henry to visit France and meet Uncle Charlie, who was also of course *his* uncle, to discuss the whole question of Anglo– French relations. This seemed to me to be a splendid plan, as I would no doubt accompany my husband and thus be able to return to the haunts of my childhood in all the panoply of a reigning queen.

I also believe that such a meeting might have brought a great deal of good in its train, and helped us to avoid some of the horrible calamities which were soon to overwhelm us.

But the English lords were against it, and the idea fell through, although the French continued to revive it from time to time over the next few years.

There was no begging the question of the surrender of Maine and Le Mans, however. Henry was forced to summon his lords and inform them of the full terms of the marriage contract. It may well be imagined what a to-do there now followed, and in the midst of the tumult the blame was entirely laid at the door of Suffolk and myself. Neither of us could possibly be impeached, of course. Not only was I quite innocent of any knowledge of the negotiations until after they had been completed, but I was the Queen. While Suffolk, as we have seen, had taken care to have his indemnity reaffirmed only the previous month. But tempers ran high.

Obviously word of what had happened soon spread beyond the Council Chamber, and I was distressed to be cursed at as I rode through the streets. Some urchins even went so far as to attempt to pelt me with mud balls. None struck me, thanks to the vigilance of my guards, but it was a very unpleasant experience and it marked the end of my popularity with the English people, at least those of London and its vicinity. I may add it ended theirs with me. Henry, as might be expected, seemed confused as to what all the fuss was about. 'I do assure you, my poppet,' he told me, 'that you are far more valuable to me than some impoverished French duchy, especially as it legally belongs to your father in any event.'

I could not be sure I had been paid a compliment. More importantly, he quite refused to take any action against the scoundrels who had at least verbally assaulted me. 'Why,' he said, 'if I were to arrest everyone who had ever shouted a curse at me on the street, the kingdom would be depopulated.'

And no bad thing either, in my opinion. However, as he would do nothing, I therefore had to swallow my chagrin. But worse was to follow. The English are great believers in conspiracies. To them anything which is not immediately explicable has got to be the result of some secret machination shared by two evil minds. If Suffolk had given away 'English soil' in order to obtain my hand, it had to have been for a more sinister reason than to please his king, or even to bring a temporary end to the war. Soon the story was going the rounds that the man who had acted as my proxy bridegroom in France had also acted as my proxy husband, and the reason – as had of course been reported by the ladies – that there had been no obvious evidence of a consummation following my first night with Henry was that the marriage had long before *been* consummated.

'The wretches,' Alice declared, eager to defend her husband. 'It grieves me, your grace, to think how low the mind of man can sink.'

'The fools,' commented Henry. 'To suppose that a fifteen-year-old girl could possibly be attracted to a man three times her age.'

Suffolk and I merely looked at each other, knowing full well how close the lampoon was to having been the truth!

*

In fact, most of the nobility took the King's point of view, and the furore died down as the English flatly refused to hand over the duchy until the agreed time, two years hence. I will confess to a continuing uneasiness whenever I encountered any of the lords, or worse, their ladies, as I had no idea what was being whispered behind my back.

As it obviously would have been unwise in the circumstances to see too much of Suffolk, I began to spend a good deal of my leisure with the Beauforts. Not only were they close relatives, and their loyalty to the King and myself unquestioned, but they were also a boisterous, happy brood who made me forget much of my troubles. Even the Cardinal was eager to throw off the grave demeanour of the churchman and tell jokes and stories – of which he had an inexhaustible fund – while his purse was always at the ready to help Henry out of any small pecuniary difficulties, and Heaven knows there were enough of these. But I was disturbed to note, as I got to know him better, that Uncle Henry was not a well man. Well, he was of course quite an old man, being sixty-eight years of age, and he had lived a full and adventurous life. At fifteen, sixty-eight seems an unimaginable age. It still does, and I am now past fifty myself. But I was not so insensible as to realise that here was one of the very great props of Henry's throne, and therefore my own, and to pray that he might be replaced, when his time came to shuffle off this mortal coil, by someone of equal mettle.

Suffolk of course was Henry's chief minister, and, given Henry's disinclination to partake in business when there was anything better to do – meaning in his case a prayer to be uttered or a church or monastery to be inspected – he was virtually ruling the country. But Suffolk, even if my own very favourite man, was not of royal blood, and much as my heartbeat quickened whenever I saw him, even at my tender age I could recognise that his main concern was William de la Pole. Perhaps I even then sensed that there were troubled times ahead, without being able to put my fears into coherent thoughts. I could not help but wonder, however, how steadfast a support Pole would turn out to be should events conspire against us.

It was therefore more natural to think in terms of a Beaufort, but there were difficulties. Cousin Edmund was a fine, upstanding man, with a good deal of his Plantagenet forebears visible in his physical characteristics. He was also in the very prime of life, aged thirty-nine in this year of my marriage. Unfortunately, he was given to melancholy and fits of what in a woman would have been called the vapours, but this term could hardly be applied to a famous, if not terribly successful, soldier. He was also uncommonly superstitious. Well, perhaps we all are, but Edmund was very susceptible to prophecies. At some stage in his youth he had been told by a fortune-teller to 'beware the castle'. This created a tricky situation for anyone who believed in such rubbish, for where else was a peer of the realm to live save in a castle? The result was a great deal of inconvenience for those with whom the Earl came into contact. Even his own home was constantly being searched for intruders or even stray pieces of masonry which might not be in good repair, while when he visited, his host was distracted for days in advance by an army of esquires seeking to make sure there was no possibility of harm befalling their lord and master.

In addition to all this, when I first met Cousin Edmund, he was distracted because his brother John had died only the previous year. Edmund was still endeavouring to achieve his elevation from Marquis of Dorset to Duke of Somerset and thus to be recognised as one of the premier princes of the blood. He had actually inherited the Earldom of Somerset, but the question of whether he should be made duke remained in discussion.

He and his wife were, however, always unfailingly kind to me, and I adored their large family of children, especially their three sons. Henry, young Edmund and John were mere boys, younger than myself, but full of high spirits and rambunctious humour.

Cousin Edmund was being delayed in his claim to the senior family title because his brother had actually fathered a child before his untimely death. She was a female, and therefore could not inherit the title. On the other hand, her husband could, when she married. As she was but two years old, this happy event was necessarily some years in the future, but yet it attracted all the nobility with ambitions for their sons. In addition to the title, Margaret Beaufort was heiress to all Duke John's vast wealth, much of it inherited from her great-grandfather, John of Gaunt. The girl was a somewhat lugubrious babe, yet bound to be a lady of parts in the course of time. Edmund and his wife and I spent many pleasant conversations discussing this or that suitable husband for her – one who would *not* wish to claim the title – often while she sat upon my knee. Thus do we sometimes hold the future in our hands, without knowing it.

My own role in these family gatherings was a varied one. In the first place, I was the Queen, and must necessarily be treated with extreme reserve, and treat others with a corresponding decorum. In the second place, I was a married woman, and therefore to be considered as of mature mind and body, privy to all the secrets of lubricity. But in the third place, I was a fifteen-year-old girl who had hitherto lived a life of extreme freedom as well as activity, and in a court where the word 'freedom' was interpreted in the widest sense.

It was an enormous pleasure to hunt with the Beauforts, even if I knew that on my return to Westminster with my clothes soiled with mud, or even blood if I happened to get too close to the stag as his throat was cut, I would receive a stern lecture from my dear husband.

Equally was it an enormous pleasure to play at blind man's buff with the Beaufort children, laughing as I fell over in a heap with one of the boys, seeking a surreptitious squeeze of his codpiece even as he attempted to get his hand beneath my skirt, while Edmund and his good lady looked on benevolently.

No less was it a delight to discuss adult matters with Edmund, who revealed reassuring perspicacity.

But equally was I undoubtedly too often careless in my demeanour, and I well remember the day when I was thrown. Well, I say thrown: the beastly animal merely stopped without warning and I slid from the saddle before I could stop myself. Unfortunately the reason for the sudden cessation in his onward career was a muddy stream, into which my own momentum as I reached the ground, on my feet, very rapidly carried me.

I reacted without thinking, regained the dry land, gathered my skirts, and raised them to my thighs as I sat down in order to remove my soaked boots and stockings. It was at this moment that I heard the sound of hooves, and looked up to find the rest of the party hurrying back to the assistance of their Queen, and being brought to a standstill by the sight of, if I say so myself, the best-formed pair of gleaming white legs in Europe.

Others no doubt remembered that day as well.

When not with the Beauforts, or at my needlework, or reading, or playing with Albion, I fell into the habit of writing letters.

This began as inadvertently as everything else. In my anger at the appearance of the Archbishop and Monsieur Vendome to the probable disruption of my wedded tranquillity, I had sat down and penned a very stern note to Uncle Charlie. After all, if he was King, I was now Queen. I did not, at that time, know of his bereavement. Having sealed the letter and sent it off, I began to wonder if I had not been a little too bold, and awaited his reply with some trepidation. When it came I was greatly relieved. Uncle Charlie was his usual slightly scatter-brained self, accepted my reproaches most humbly, but explained he had acted as he did to assist me by forcing my new subjects to continue the truce for a while longer – it would surely, he pointed out, be untenable for me to be queen of a country at war with my own dear France.

It was difficult to argue with this, especially as one of the results of the embassy was indeed a prolongation of the truce for a further two years. Additionally, it was now he told me of my Scottish namesake's sad demise, and I felt compelled to send him my deepest condolences.

Thus begun, our correspondence continued. I do not recall everything we wrote about, but it was mostly mundane matters, although I may from time to time have imparted certain pieces of information about English affairs. It was certainly not done with any evil intent. But no doubt the very fact of the correspondence was noted by my enemies; and these, although I did not suspect it, were legion.

I did not at that time suspect anything of the currents whirling about me. I pursued my life with my customary vigour. If the younger Beauforts were the outlet for my animal spirits, I was happy to discuss affairs of state with Suffolk and Cousin Edmund, when the occasion arose. The occasion to discuss these matters with my husband *never* arose.

I also, not unnaturally I consider, endeavoured to make my home as comfortable as I could, and it follows that this means I endeavoured to make it as French as I could. It may be recalled that Suffolk had cut my household to the bone for reasons of economy, but Bailly and I did the best we could, although it was a difficult business.

Consider merely the matter of food and drink. Your Englishman, and in this case my husband was as English as any one of his subjects, likes his meat and his bread. Well, there is nothing I prefer than to sink my teeth into a tasty steak. But your Englishman likes his meat well done; I like to taste blood.

Equally, the Englishman's idea of bread is a huge tasteless white slab, made palatable only by the meat and gravy piled on its top. Not for him are tasty morsels which can be eaten by themselves. The exquisite pastries served up by my chefs gave Henry such acute indigestion as to cause rumours that

I was trying to poison the King!

In France, we endeavoured to add some interest to our diet by eating various vegetable matter. The fact is that meat, unless highly spiced – and spices were now becoming more and more expensive as the Turks closed the Mediterranean Sea to the free movement of goods from the East to Europe – is too often somewhat ripe by the time it comes to be eaten. Vegetables, and I am not here speaking of the various roots which are consumed by the common people, but of the green variety, can always be fresh, and even tasty. My endeavours to persuade the King to eat such things, however, proved unsuccessful.

'My dearest girl,' he would say, 'I am not a rabbit.'

Would that he had been. Our troubles would have disappeared.

The same comments can be made about drink. I do not think there is a more pleasant liquid than a goblet of good rich French wine. The English, unfortunate in their quite ghastly climate, cannot grow grapes. Instead they brew a liquor from barley, which they call ale. It is bitter and flatulent. One of my most abiding memories of the English court at table is of the trumpeting which went the rounds of the hall, men, women and children, as this explosive mixture combusted within their bellies.

I had hardly less trouble when I endeavoured to introduce dancing to our court. Now of course the English ladies enjoyed dancing as much as anyone; it was the King who found it frivolous and heartily disapproved of it, just as he disapproved of much of the music which I enjoyed listening to.

The greatest stir, however, was caused by my personal habits. I can say without the slightest fear of contradiction that the English are the filthiest people on earth. Bathing to them is an anathema. Well, one has to consider their climate, and it is possible that those who live even further north, such as the Scandinavians, may have similar deplorable ideas of cleanliness. But the consternation with which I greeted the news that even my husband entered water but four times a year, equally spaced between quarters, may be imagined.

Almost my first act on reaching Southampton had been to demand a tub from the good sisters where I was lodged, and then to soak myself while Alice wrung her hands in dismay, sure I was ruining my complexion, and Proud Cis and her fellows curled their lips in contempt.

Henry was equally taken aback by my insistence upon bathing. 'You do yourself no good,' he told me. And when we reached London, he asked rather anxiously, 'You will not bathe in the river, I hope, my sweet.'

I considered the matter and decided against it. The Loire, where I had enjoyed it, had been well removed from the sea, private, and filled with little bays in which there was no current. The Thames at Westminster ran at full speed, whistling past the palace like a runaway horse. There was a complete absence of any slack water save at the turn of the tide, which was seldom at a convenient moment. And most important, it was not only overlooked from every direction, but it was the principal thoroughfare of the kingdom, and carried on its broad bosom every manner of boat and ship, day and night.

So I was reduced again to using my tub, to the evident disgust of my menials. But I was not to be gainsaid.

I kept my equanimity throughout it all; there was always Albion to romp with when I felt utterly frustrated. But I was yet to experience an English winter.

In France the winters can be very cold, the more so the further one is removed from the sea. But it is a brisk, dry cold, lying beneath brilliantly blue skies. It tingles the blood, and the ice and snow provide many pleasures, from tobogan-ning to skating.

I have been told that only little more than a century in the past the English climate matched the French. But then, at the beginning of the fourteenth century, there came a succession of unheard-of tempests from which it seems the island has never recovered.

Thus in England winter is mostly a time of rain. Well, it may be said, so are summer, spring and autumn. At these other seasons of the year, however, there are occasional glimpses of the sun, and even one or two hot days. But in winter the whole land is covered beneath an impenetrable grey cloud, and the atmosphere becomes danker by the day. Nothing dries, dampness pervades, and with it comes a succession of coughs and colds so that it is impossible to hold a conversation without interruption of either sneeze or sniffle.

If there was any blessing in this most unpleasant time of year it was that even Henry wished to snuggle against me for warmth in our bed. Alas, it was only for warmth.

When we *did* have a frost, and I wished to go out and slide upon the ice-covered pond which lay within the abbey grounds, the Archbishop no less than the King was horrified at such frivolity, and I was sternly forbidden.

Nor do the English celebrate Christmas to any great extent. Henry did not celebrate it at all, except to spend some forty-eight hours on his knees. I joined him from time to time, but when I remembered the great jollifications and the flowing wine which would be enjoyed at Uncle Charlie's court I all but wept.

Actually, it was just as well that the royal household did not attempt to celebrate Christmas, for when I approached the Cardinal regarding my present to my husband, and suggested a golden crucifix, he pulled a very long face. 'There is no money, your grace.'

'I am not asking for funds from the exchequer, your eminence. I will pay for the crucifix out of my own moneys.'

'You have none, your grace.'

'Your eminence,' I said, as reasonably as I could, 'I was granted a jointure of more than four thousand pounds a year. Thus far, to my knowledge, I have spent none of this money. I wish to do so now.'

'I am afraid your jointure for this year has not yet been paid, your grace.'

'Am I allowed to inquire why not, your eminence?'

'There is no money available, your grace.'

'Oh, really, your eminence!' I protested. 'That is all I have heard since coming to this benighted country. Yet there must *be* money. Government is carried on.'

'By borrowing, your grace.'

'So? All kings borrow.' Dear Papa had lived on borrowed money all his life, and was still doing so.

'Indeed, your grace. But there comes a time when those with money are reluctant to extend further credit.'

'How may anyone refuse a king credit? Is not the whole kingdom his security?'

'That is a security which is difficult to realise, your grace.'

I felt like stamping my foot in frustration. But this man was my friend. 'Will you explain to me, your eminence, why all the lords are wealthy men, and the King, who is the greatest lord of all, is not?'

'Certainly the King should be the wealthiest man in the kingdom, your grace,' he agreed. 'But ... the lords grow rich by accumulating land, either by marriage or by wardship or by inheritance. Recently they have grown richer yet, by enclosures.'

'Enclosures, your eminence?'

'This country suffered grievously from the Black Death, your grace.'

'As did France, your eminence.'

'Indeed. But here in England there was no means of replacing the sudden fall in population by immigration. It has, perforce, been left to natural circumstances, which is an uncertain business.'

Well, I could have told him that!

'Thus much land, farmed for generations, was left fallow,' he continued. 'The lords either seized this land, or bought it for a song, enclosed it, and used it for farming sheep. As they do now. English wool has always been much in demand on the Continent. It remains in demand, but now there is so much more available. Thus the lords grow richer yet.'

'And the King cannot share in this wealth? He cannot enclose lands of his own? Better yet, can he not charge duties upon the export of this wool, to make sure some of the money gets into the royal exchequer?'

The Cardinal looked at me in surprise that I should have learned so much about high finance. Then he smiled. 'Why, your grace, the King can, and does, do these things. But perhaps his grace does not enforce the gathering of taxes as rigorously as he might. As his father and grandfather did. And then, of such money as is accumulated, much needs to go on the debts incurred by his grace's father in the French wars, and which are still being increased by the necessity of maintaining an army across the Channel. Much more needs to go on the ordinary business of government. And finally, of what is left . . .' he sighed. 'I am a man of the Church, your grace, and must be grateful for all the gifts that come our way, but I fear that his grace is often far too generous. This school he has founded at Windsor for indigent youths, the college he would endow at Cambridge – they all cost a great deal of money.'

'So that there is none left for me,' I said, at last giving way to anger. 'And I must let the festive season pass without being able to give my husband a present.'

'God forbid, your grace,' he protested.

'Do you have a remedy, your eminence?'

'Perhaps if I were to make you a gift of such a crucifix as you describe, your grace, then you could do with it as you chose. You could even give it to his grace as a present.'

'Your eminence . . .' I was overwhelmed. 'But you would be offended, were I to give your present to another. Even to the King.'

He gave a brief bow. 'I should be honoured, your grace.'

I became more than ever concerned that this noble man might not be with us forever.

Thus my first winter in England passed peacefully enough.

There were rumblings of discontent, amongst Lords and Commons, but I gathered this was a national pastime. It rained and rained and rained. And I did not become pregnant.

And then, just when I at last felt I was about to go mad with boredom and frustration, the clouds cleared away – well, partly – and I found myself enjoying the pleasures of an English spring.

I had arrived in England at the end of the previous spring, and undoubtedly it is the best time of the year in this windswept isle. Partly this feeling of euphoria is caused by sheer relief at having survived the winter, but there can be no gainsaying the fact that all of this rain made a profound impression upon the soil and everything that could be planted and grow. Suddenly I found myself surrounded by colour and scent whenever I went abroad. Particularly was I entranced by a bank of roses in the palace garden. These were thickly massed huge blooms, all of the richest blood colour. Remembering the compliment paid to me by the Duke of York after my coronation, I picked one and wore it in my hair, and was congratulated by Suffolk on the way it matched my colouring. Even Henry noticed it, and I came to a decision.

My emblem, the daisy, had caused some mirth among the English lords, as in this country the daisy is regarded as a common weed. I now resolved to take the red rose as my emblem instead and caused it to be sewn into all my garments, painted on to all my crockery, and stamped on my silver. It caused a stir. But none could deny that flower and patron were now matched for beauty.

That summer I enjoyed a great treat: Henry determined to make a grand tour of the country. To be sure, his object was not to see the people or allow the people to see him; it was to inspect various monasteries, for these he regarded as the true substance of his realm.

No one else agreed with him, of course, I least of all. But

his decision was applauded by his ministers for two reasons. Firstly, it would remove him from Westminster and let them get on with the business of ruling the country. And secondly, his upkeep would become the charge of wherever he chose to spend the night, be it abbey, monastery, castle or town – and the royal exchequer would be saved a heavy burden.

For my part, although the thought of traipsing round a succession of dreary monasteries filled me with total boredom, the thought of seeing something of my country and my people was exhilarating.

Our journey was in fact a very pleasant one, although not so extensive as I would have liked, as we never were more than a hundred miles from London. Henry preferred to travel very slowly, and to spend several days at each stop. This certainly enabled me to have a close look at those parts of the country we visited, and enabled the country folk to have a close look at me, they having been to this time existing on rumour. I was very pleased with my reception, especially after the growing hostility of the Londoners. In the country I was greeted with huzzas; local squires wrote poems in praise of my beauty, and red roses sprouted everywhere.

The King was also greeted with acclamation and much respect. This sadly did not last. As the exchequer had discovered for themselves, the business of feeding a king, when attended as he must be by his many servants, not to mention his queen and her many servants, is an expensive one. Whole flocks of sheep can be converted into mutton in a single weekend, whole barrels of ale drained to the wood, simply that the monarch need not go hungry, and Henry, whatever his lack of interest in the business of being alive, was very interested indeed in the concomitant of *staying* alive: eating and drinking.

Still, I reflected that the good people could hardly lay this particular travail at *my* door, even as I noted, every time we left a town or abbey, the expressions of relief as we departed. Our progress continued in a semi-circle around London, for Henry wished to visit the school he had recently founded outside the village of Windsor, some miles west of the capital, and called Eton. Windsor was the seat of a fine large castle built by one of his ancestors, and was where he had spent his childhood; he was, in fact, known as Henry of Windsor. Thus more than any other part of England he considered it to be his home.

Here we were received by the masters, and the boys, commoners all, and all from indigent backgrounds. These were being taught to read and write. Now I am very well aware that there are many commoners who have progressed well as merchants – dear Suffolk's ancestors had begun to accumulate wealth in that way – and who have proved very useful to the government, if only that their wealth might be taxed. Equally some of our best prelates have come from humble backgrounds, and it is of course necessary for even a parish priest to be able to read, or he could not interpret the Bible for the unwashed. But I am bound to say that the concept of teaching the true commons to read and write filled me with misgivings. A youth who can read becomes all too often a man who reads too much, and begins to wonder at what he has read, just as a youth who can write all too often becomes a man who writes conspiratorial letters. But Henry had different ideas. 'When every man in my kingdom can read, my poppet, and every woman too . . .' giving me an affectionate squeeze, 'then will England truly prosper.'

I reflected that by then it would hardly be his kingdom any more, even if he managed to accomplish this impossible feat during his own lifetime.

From Windsor we continued our perambulation until we reached Cambridge, situated in the east of the country, a flat low-lying area where a university had sprung up – composed of scholars who had fled England's original university, at Oxford, over some dispute or other – and not unnaturally, around it a town to supply the needs of the students.

Here Henry had founded a college, called, reasonably enough, King's College, and thus here again we had to undergo a meeting with penniless youths and their tutors, and be preached at and sung to. If I had been concerned at the concept of teaching indigent boys to read and write, I was far more concerned at the sight of this unruly and turbulent mob, who presumably had once been indigent boys themselves, and who were endeavouring to become our lawyers of the future. Of course we have a university in France as well, at the Sorbonne in Paris. I have never been there, but from all accounts the students at the Sorbonne are hardly more salubrious than those of Cambridge.

From Cambridge, towards the end of the summer we arrived at a place called Lynn. This is situated even more in the east of the country, where the land is very low. Indeed, at high water it is difficult to determine exactly where the sea ends and the land begins. Fond as I am of fresh water, the salt variety is the element that I like the least, and I could not help but recall that an earlier king of England, by name John, had been caught by the tide when attempting to traverse this part of the country, aptly called the Wash, and had been fortunate to escape drowning, while he had managed to lose all of his fortune to the surging waters.

But Henry assured me that the Wash was actually considerably further north than Lynn, which lay on the edge of a great swamp called the Broads, and that while flooding was not unusual in this part of his realm, it was seldom attended by any vast loss of life or property.

With this I had to be content, just as I had to pretend to enjoy this damp piece of England while we lodged at the Austin Friary and the King pursued his amusements of talking with the good friars, inspecting the buildings, and praying. But from this idyllic existence we were rudely aroused by a messenger from Cardinal Beaufort, begging the King to return to Westminster with all haste, as a crisis had arisen.

So home we went.

Perhaps we should never have been away until this particular crisis had been laid to rest. For far from having arisen, it was the same problem that had taxed us since that damnable embassy. Uncle Humphrey had spent the summer brooding on the iniquity of it all. I had hitherto been unaware of it, but Humphrey had had his own marriage plans for Henry, these being in accordance with his desire to continue the war with France. Thus he had proposed a Burgundian princess, a daughter of Duke Philip, at that time as bitter an enemy of France as any Englishman.

This plan had failed against the greater influence of Cardinal Beaufort and the peace party with the King, but it is interesting to consider the quirks of fate. It may be recalled that a marriage between myself and Philip's son Charles had been mooted when I was a little girl. Had both of these early plans come to fruition, I would have been Henry's sister-in-law rather than his wife, and from the safety of Bruges would have watched the calamities of his reign with equanimity. In Charles the Bold I would have found a husband worthy of my mettle. Instead of which, *he* wound up married to one of Proud Cis's brood.

However, it was necessary to deal with the present rather than bewail that which might have been. Uncle Humphrey had come to the conclusion that he had been robbed of both influence and prestige by the King's French marriage. That he loathed me I had never doubted for an instant, but he could do nothing to harm me as long as I possessed the love of the King.

Cardinal Beaufort remained Uncle Humphrey's true antagonist, but he had tried to bring down the Cardinal before, and most signally failed. He therefore now concentrated his efforts upon one whom he felt might prove an easier victim: Suffolk.

He was of course prevented from impeaching the Marquis – the idea of making him duke had been quietly shelved while his popularity was at a low ebb – by the act of indemnity passed by Parliament in 1445, and repeated this very year. Nonetheless Uncle Humphrey sought by every possible means to undermine Suffolk's authority, raking up every discreditable incident in his past – and what man does not have one or two discreditable incidents in his past? – and in particular concentrating upon two aspects of dear Pole's career.

One of these was fact: Suffolk *had* abandoned the siege of Orleans following the onslaught of the French armies reinvigorated by the presence of the Maid. But that was seventeen years before. He had been honourably acquitted of any blame in the matter by the Duke of Bedford himself, and it was fairly generally accepted by all that he could not possibly have hoped to triumph against the machinations of a witch. Uncle Humphrey now claimed that it had all been treachery, that Joan of Arc had done nothing more than negotiate with the English commander, visiting him in secret in the dead of night and using the charms of a seventeen-year-old girl to seduce the Earl, as he then was, away from his duty to King and country.

From this charge it was simple for Humphrey to proceed to his second, for the suggestion that Suffolk could be seduced by a seventeen-year-old girl led naturally to the supposition that, having tasted blood, as it were, he would himself be more than capable of seducing a fourteen-year-old future queen.

Now I have stated above that Humphrey could not harm me, as long as I possessed the love of the King. But here he was accusing me of high treason, for adultery by a queen is nothing less than this. Anyone reading these words may well say, ho hum, he tried this once before. The fact is, *he* had not, however much he might secretly have encouraged the Commons to put it about. Now he was saying it himself. I was outraged. 'He is uttering treason in accusing me of treason,' I told Henry. 'He must be arrested and brought to trial. He must either prove his accusations against me or submit to judgement.'

'My dear poppet,' Henry said in his usual placatory tones, 'how can anyone possibly prove such an accusation?'

'Then how can anyone dare make it?' I shouted.

'But you know, and I know, the whole world knows, that you are innocent of any wrongdoing.'

'The whole world does not know it, Henry,' I insisted. 'And they will soon believe the opposite if this foul uncle of yours is not checked.'

'He is your uncle as well,' Henry said defensively, looking distinctly apprehensive. A man who lacked the wit ever to lose his temper himself, he was clearly alarmed by my anger, never having experienced it before. Indeed, catching a glimpse of myself in the glass, with my cheeks pink and my eyes gleaming and my bosom heaving, I declare I was a sight to give any man pause, although not necessarily to terrify him.

Henry was looking for succour towards the Cardinal, who had remained with us.

'Your grace,' the worthy prelate now said, attempting to be as soothing as the King, 'it is Suffolk the Duke is after.'

'You mean,' Henry said eagerly, 'if we—'

'Do not even think it,' I snapped, astounded at such a suggestion of baseness. 'Suffolk is your grace's strong right arm. You will not find another. And I do not agree with your eminence. It is the King Duke Humphrey is after. Have you forgotten what happened to Richard II? He was accused—'

'By my grandfather,' Henry said mildly.

I ignored the interruption. 'He was accused of having surrounded himself with incompetent and traitorous ministers. But that was merely a means of striking at the throne itself. Yes, it was your grandfather, Henry. I am not blaming him, as Richard was incompetent.' Beaufort gave a warning cough. I was skating on very thin ice here, as there were sufficient people in the kingdom who would have said that Henry was even less competent of being a king. But as there were only the three of us present I was not going to be checked. 'The important point is, that if for any reason a cause is found to set you aside, your grace, then Humphrey would become King.'

I paused for breath, and the two men stared at me. Both knew I spoke the truth, but it was a truth no man had hitherto dared put into words. 'If only I had an heir,' Henry muttered.

'Yes, your grace,' I said, allowing all the steel I could muster to enter my voice. 'If only.'

'This is a very serious matter, your grace,' Beaufort said. 'I am bound to agree with the Queen that it must be settled. We must force the Duke to make his accusations in the open, before Parliament, and either substantiate them or withdraw them and submit to your judgement.'

Henry of course dithered, as a result of which Uncle Humphrey was permitted to go his own way, so that his attacks upon Suffolk, and by implication upon me, grew ever more virulent. As the autumn went by, others began to become agitated by the Duke's calumnies: whether they were for me or against me, they began to feel that as there can be no smoke without fire, there had to be a case to be answered. Thus at last Henry felt constrained to act, and on 14 December writs were issued summoning Parliament to meet the following February.

Henry, ever the innocent, would have called the Parliament to Westminster, but I inveighed most strongly against this, and by now I had got the Cardinal entirely upon my side. I do not suppose for an instant that this was either because he truly loved me, truly respected me as his queen, or truly believed in my innocence. He was concerned mainly for his family, and as it now seemed obvious that Uncle Humphrey was attempting to create a situation where at the very least he would have Henry declared incompetent and himself Lord Protector, as had happened in the reign of the late, unlamented King Edward II, the Cardinal had to consider where that situation, if it were to take place, would leave him, and indeed all of the Beauforts: one step away from the scaffold. He therefore supported my pleas. 'By the citizens of London, your grace,' he said, 'Duke Humphrey is called Good Duke Humphrey. Even were he to confess to treasonable designs, I doubt they would permit you to arrest him, this close to the city.'

Henry had to see the sense of this, and the Parliament was actually summoned to meet at Bury St Edmunds, which could be considered a safe distance from the turbulent mob.

Thus, after a very sombre Christmas, we adjourned to Bury in early February. Some people thought it unusual for the Queen to accompany the King to a parliamentary gathering, but I had no intention of allowing Henry out of my sight, for fear he might let the whole affair slip away into a nothing.

It was the coldest month of the year, and we rode north of the Thames into a snowstorm which was drifting to either side of the road. Bury itself was shuttered against the blizzard, but the shutters very soon opened to permit the townspeople to peer out at the masses of armed men suddenly thronging their streets, for by the recommendation of the Cardinal and myself we were accompanied by a very strong escort of royal guards, while the Cardinal had also written to all the lords he could positively trust – principally the royal cousins, Buckingham and Somerset – telling them also to come, accompanied by all their livery. The Duke of York, fortunately, was at his post in France, but Suffolk was of course also present, with a goodly number of men.

Salisbury and his brother, sons and nephews also attended, but as they were not in our confidence they were accompanied by no more than their normal retinues, and were quite outnumbered.

This concerned them, but as Uncle Humphrey had not yet appeared, they had no idea of what was going on. Salisbury called upon the King, and after looking askance to find me sitting at Henry's side, inquired into the reason for the large numbers of men quartered in and around the town.

'Why, my good Earl,' Henry replied, 'did you not read the writ? We are gathered here to obtain funds for my proposed expedition to France to meet with King Charles.'

'I was referring to the soldiery, your grace.'

'Why, my lord, in these troubled times, it is necessary to be well guarded. Would you not agree?'

With that, the Earl had to withdraw. Next day, 18 February, a week after our own arrival, word was received that Uncle Humphrey was approaching, accompanied by near a hundred men-at-arms. 'There you have it, your grace,' Suffolk declared. 'He means treason.'

'What are we to do?' Poor Henry looked quite terrified.

'Our plans are laid, your grace,' I assured him.

As indeed they had been, in conclave between the Cardinal, Suffolk, Somerset and myself. To attempt a confrontation with the Duke upon the open road would have been unwise, and might have led to a fracas. Instead we despatched a herald to meet him and, with every expression of courtesy and welcome from his nephew and niece, to inform him that quarters had been prepared for him in the North Spital of St Saviour's.

Uncle Humphrey was not an unintelligent man; indeed he was a very learned one, although intelligence and learning do not always go hand in hand. But his arrogance rendered his intelligence as nothing. That the King and Queen were apparently pleased to see him, despite all of the slanders he had been spreading about the Queen, seemed to him only his due, and without demur he allowed himself and his people to be led to his lodging, which was most comfortable. He did not apparently find it suspicious that the way he was conducted was round the town rather than through it. He therefore had no glimpse of the large numbers of royal retainers who were present, nor did he apparently consider it sinister that the position of his apartment required that the main body of *his* armament was quartered some distance away.

That night Suffolk, accompanied by Somerset, Buckingham and some other reliable lords, visited the Duke, disarmed him, and informed him that he was under arrest for treason. 'He was considerably taken aback,' Suffolk told us when he reported later that night. 'Indeed, he was quite speechless.'

Henry was relieved at this. The rest of the plan had also gone very well, and some thirty members of the Duke's entourage had been arrested, charged with treason, and rapidly despatched to various prisons around the country which were waiting for them.

Then it was just a matter of bringing Uncle Humphrey before Parliament to answer for his slanders. But this was not immediately possible, we were informed, as he had sunk into a coma. This was astonishing, but we were prepared to be patient.

Unfortunately, only four days later, Uncle Humphrey was found dead in his bed by his attendants.

5

We were utterly taken aback by this event. It was well known that Uncle Humphrey had for some time not been in good health, and equally that he was a man of furious temper. Obviously his outrage at being placed under arrest by the nephew he had terrified throughout his life had led to a seizure which had overwhelmed him. But that he should just die! It was almost as if the hand of Heaven had intervened on our behalf.

Or had it really been the hand of Hell? It was Uncle Henry Beaufort who first made us realise the unpleasant possibilities which could follow the tragedy. 'He has died,' the Cardinal said, 'while in your custody, your grace. People will talk.'

Possibly the understatement of the year.

'What will they say?' Henry asked, apparently genuinely bewildered.

Uncle Henry looked at me in despair, then pulled himself together. 'There will be those, who bear your grace no good, who will say the Duke was murdered.'

Henry went quite pale. 'Murdered? Uncle Humphrey? But that is preposterous. How would anyone dare say ...' He looked at our faces. 'That I had a hand in his death?'

'Well, no, your grace,' the Cardinal said. 'I do not think there is a soul in this kingdom would suggest that murder would ever enter your grace's mind, but . . .'

'They will think I ordered it,' Suffolk said in a low voice.

'Did you?' Henry asked.

Suffolk looked at me in consternation. 'Of course he did not, your grace,' I snapped. 'Your uncle died of natural causes. The Lords must be convinced of this. It is the truth.'

'What is to be done?' Henry asked, plaintively.

Perhaps all our hearts sank as we for the first time truly realised what a broken reed was our sovereign lord, in this, the first real crisis of his reign. 'The Duke's body must be exposed immediately,' the Cardinal decided. 'And not only the Lords, but the leaders of the Commons, too, must be brought to see it, that they may know the truth for themselves.'

This was done, but I am afraid to little avail. People remembered the tales told them by their grandparents of how King Edward II's body had been exposed, to reveal not a mark; but how his twisted features were indicative of the agony in which he had died, for red-hot irons had been thrust up his fundament to burn out his bowels while he yet lived. The Duke's features were no less twisted in anger, if not in pain, and all around us we heard the mutterings of 'Good Duke Humphrey' and expressions of outrage at his sad demise.

The Cardinal's immediate judgement was proved correct. There was not a single suggestion that Henry had, or could have had, any hand in his uncle's death. But it was freely gossiped that those about the King who had most to fear from any accusations the Duke might make had taken the necessary steps to secure their guilty secrets. It seemed that Fate, in ridding me of one treasonable accuser, had raised an entire nation of them in his place. Now for the first time I learned that they spoke of me as another French she-wolf. This was because an ancestress of mine named Isabella had been the French wife of that same ill-fated Edward II, and with her paramour, Mortimer, had caused her husband to be murdered. In a sense this was a compliment to me, because from the loins of that earlier she-wolf, inserted there by who knows whom – for it was well known that Edward II far preferred to dally with male genitals in preference to female, and the infant had been conceived before the Queen had discovered her passion for Mortimer – emerged the most fearsome warrior of his age, King Edward III.

Perhaps it was these very associations which put certain thoughts into my mind, which would eventually bear fruit.

At the time, however, I was aware only of distress. Consider! I was not yet seventeen years old, and I was being accused of adultery, treason and black-hearted murder. God knows Humphrey of Gloucester and I had felt a mutual antipathy, but I had never even considered his death. Although I had intended in turn to accuse him of treason, my aim had simply been to deprive him of any say in the government of the kingdom, certainly not of his life.

I was quite distraught. But not so distraught that I ceased to think or be aware of our problems altogether. Immediately these problems concerned our total lack of adequate financing, both for the requirements of government and of our domestic comfort. Duke Humphrey had been a wealthy man. And he had no children! I tackled the Cardinal the very next morning. 'Was not the Duke a very rich man?' I inquired.

'Very, your grace.'

'Then who will inherit?'

'That will have to be decided in due course, your grace.'

'In due course,' I remarked. 'That is always unsatisfactory.'

Of course he understood my drift. 'His wealth in coin is not so very great, your grace. His collection of books is vast, but of value only to another collector. His lands, as Duke of Gloucester, are really inalienable, as they will belong to the next Duke of Gloucester, whoever he may be. They might only be claimed by the Crown if the Duke were to be proved guilty of treason and attainted, and to be frank, your grace, I would strongly advise against proceeding down that path at this moment, in view of the mood of the country.'

'The mood of the country,' I muttered. But I had done my research very thoroughly. 'Of course the King and I must bend to your judgement, your eminence. However, is it not true that a considerable part of Uncle Humphrey's wealth is in the form of a jointure, obtained from his first wife?'

'That is true, your grace,' he said, frowning.

'No one can pretend *that* is part of the Duchy of Gloucester.'

'No, your grace. A jointure is usually held only during the lifetime of either of the joint holders of the property in question.'

'And both are now dead,' I pointed out, triumphantly. 'That property will now adhere to the Crown. As our personal fief. As *my* personal fief.'

'Your grace—' He wished to protest, but I would not let him.

'Your eminence, I would remind you that two years ago I was granted a jointure in money and land which I have never received, simply because his grace has never had any money or land to give me. I will have this land in its place.'

He shook his head, slowly. 'There will be talk, your grace.'

I stamped my foot. 'Talk! All I am told is that there will be talk. Well, they talk of me anyway, do they not? Slanders, lies, libels . . . let us at least give them something true to talk about.'

He argued no further and I had my way, becoming at last a woman of property. But he was right in estimating that there would be a great deal of criticism, and I was very glad to turn my back on Bury St Edmunds just as soon as possible. Which was soon enough in any event, for the death of his uncle quite dissipated Henry's interest in any proposed journey to the Continent to meet Uncle Charlie, and Parliament was prorogued without further discussion . . . and without voting any funds, which was a pity.

Henry felt that it was necessary for him to make a public display of his grief over the death of his uncle, and so we jointly travelled to Canterbury where we prayed and fasted and the King scourged himself. In short, we did all the right things, without eliciting much sympathy from the Commons, who continued to utter their foul insinuations. This occupied us throughout March – Uncle Humphrey had died on 28 February – and we had barely regained Westminster and, as far as I was concerned, some well-earned rest from the snow and rain and biting winds which had chilled me to the bone during our perambulations, when we were afflicted with a new calamity: on 11 April Uncle Henry died.

Now obviously it is in the nature of things that men, and women, are born, reach maturity, grow old, and die. Some people felt that Uncle Humphrey had gone a trifle early, but he had been fifty-six, and once a man passes fifty his time is clearly uncertain. Uncle Henry was seventy, and thus was at the very limit of his allotted span. Both men, therefore, could have been expected to die some time fairly soon. It was the occurrence of their deaths, within six weeks of each other, which was so unexpected. They had spent their entire lives in fighting each other, if only with words; now it seemed that Uncle Humphrey's death had deprived the Cardinal of his main reason for living.

From Henry's point of view, it was as if the roof of the house in which he dwelt had been blown away. Obviously he could not but reflect on his good fortune in that it had been Uncle Humphrey who had died first, and not Uncle Henry, but the fact was that almost since he could remember his life had been controlled and bedevilled by these two men. His Uncle John of Bedford, senior and superior to them both, had spent almost his entire life in France, only returning to England when it had been absolutely necessary to settle one of the more extreme differences between Gloucester and Beaufort, and in any event, he had now been dead himself eleven years.

So there was my poor dear Henry, at one fell swoop

deprived of the two men on whom he had been happy to lean, even if he had feared the one. He was so upset that when it was revealed that Uncle Henry had left him two thousand pounds – in gold coin! – in his will, he declined to accept it and gave it to the Church instead. I was appalled. While Uncle Henry had been alive it had never been possible to feel destitute, because at a pinch – as he had proved to us both time and again – he would step in with a timely loan. Now that source of funds was cut off, and my careless husband was giving away the last remnants of it!

We mourned Uncle Henry far more sincerely than we mourned Uncle Humphrey. But mourning for either was soon subdued beneath the necessity of government, or rather, of deciding who was *to* govern. Of one thing I was certain: there were to be no more royal dukes lording it over me. There were not even any uncles left, so it would have had to be one of the royal cousins. Well, York and I cordially disliked each other, Buckingham was inexperienced, and Somerset ... neither Henry nor I at that stage were quite certain what to make of Somerset. He certainly was not the man his uncle had been.

That left Suffolk. Here was a man who had always been a staunch supporter of the ideas of the late Cardinal, and thus a staunch supporter of the Crown, and more important than either of those from my point of view, a staunch supporter of the Queen. There was of course the small hurdle to overcome that Suffolk was in many quarters considered responsible for Uncle Humphrey's death, but at my urging the King tackled this crisis head-on. A new Parliament was called, in Westminster, and there Suffolk defended himself with great spirit against all the charges made against him, reminding the Commons yet again that in the matter of Maine they had given him, in effect, *carte blanche* to make whatever deal he could with Uncle Charlie, and pointing to the great good effects of the truce he had concluded, and recently renewed, and which, he was certain, would lead to a lasting peace between England and France.

I must confess that he was not very well received, but Henry himself sat in judgement, with me at his side, at least metaphorically – I made it very plain that if he returned without Parliament's approval of Suffolk's deeds and position he would have to face a very angry wife – and announced that he fully approved of all his minister's actions and expected the Lords and Commons to do so as well.

Rather taken aback by this unexpected display of forcefulness from the Crown, and perhaps themselves feeling rather adrift in the absence of Duke Humphrey, who had for so long led the opposition to the King's party, Parliament duly did agree. Immediately we rushed through a series of appointments to secure Suffolk's power. Henry was still reluctant to give him the dukedom I felt he deserved and should have, for fear of upsetting the other dukes, who were all of royal blood, but I had my dear friend made Earl of Pembroke, then Chamberlain, then Constable of Dover and Lord Warden of the Cinque Ports. Finally, in August, he was made Admiral of England.

The Lords could only look on askance, as it was clear to everyone that Suffolk and his Queen were the *de facto* rulers of England. To go against us would have been to go against the King, and no one was yet prepared to do that. We thus felt emboldened to remove Richard of York from his command in France, and sent him as Lord Lieutenant to Ireland instead. There were some sound reasons for this manoeuvre, politics apart. Richard had a great reputation as a soldier, but in France we were at peace, whereas in Ireland the word was unknown. The only pleasure an Irishman enjoys more than getting drunk and fighting with his friends is getting drunk and fighting with anyone in authority. I felt it would be a true test of the Duke of York's mettle to pit him against these wild creatures. And there was always the possibility that he might be killed.

There was the usual muttering, but Richard accepted the

post. I have always desired to be as fair to my enemies as to my friends, and I am bound to say that he was a strange man who undoubtedly knew that he had a better claim to the throne than his cousin Henry, who also knew he was by far the more fit to rule, and who disliked me and everything about me almost to the point of hatred, yet because Henry had been anointed King, felt unable to take the irrevocable and to him treasonable step of attempting a revolution. Until it was too late. In this he was utterly different from his eldest son. But of course, where Richard, Duke of York, was the son of Anne Mortimer and Richard, Earl of Cambridge, Edward of March, so-called the Fourth of England, was the son of Richard, Duke of York, and Proud Cis; his backbone had been stiffened by the Neville blood.

But these misfortunes lay in the future. For the time being Suffolk and I considered that we had achieved a triumph; York was replaced as viceroy in France by Somerset, on whose support we could always rely, and we felt that we had the kingdom disposed as it should be, whatever Henry's vagaries.

I felt more secure than at any moment since my coronation.

And was yet aware that I was not secure at all. As was Suffolk. We spent a great deal of time together that summer, in preparing our plans and persuading Henry to accept them, but always at the back of our minds was the realisation that our power – and indeed, in view of the general hatred with which we were regarded by the entire country since 'Good Duke Humphrey's' death, our very lives – hung by the merest thread.

Suffolk raised the question the first time we were alone together, at least as regards overhearing – my ladies were in a cluster at the far end of a large room. 'There is a matter I would discuss, your grace,' he said in a low voice.

I waited, suspecting what was coming. Nor was I wrong.

'I, the Lords, the Commons, nay, the whole world, your

grace, eagerly wait to congratulate you upon your preg-. nancy.'

I sighed. 'I am afraid you will have to wait a while longer, my lord.'

'Your grace, I hesitate to tread on indelicate ground ...'

'Speak your mind, my lord,' I told him. 'I shall not take offence.'

He hesitated for several seconds, then said, 'Your grace has been wife to the King now for more than two years. Can it be possible that there is some impediment to pregnancy, of which the world knows nothing?'

'My lord,' I said severely, 'you have been privileged to look upon my naked body. Do I look as if I suffer from an impediment?'

The poor dear fellow was scarlet to his ears. 'You remain the most beautiful woman I have ever beheld, your grace. But perhaps, the King ...'

'Is in every way a complete man, my lord. Except in so far as he regards matters of the flesh as unbecoming.'

He frowned, his colour slowly fading. 'You do not sleep together?'

'Oh, we do, most certainly. *Sleep* together.'

He pulled at his beard. 'I find that difficult to accept, your grace. I can only say that for a man to share a bed with you, naked, and not respond to the situation, well ...'

'We do not sleep naked, my lord,' I pointed out. 'His grace regards nudity as unseemly.'

'Forgive me, your grace,' he said. 'But ... do you *never* couple?'

'We do, from time to time, my lord.'

What a conversation. But at seventeen I was very innocent, and had no idea where I was being led.

'But with no result,' he mused.

'Perhaps because there is no passion, my lord.'

We gazed at each other. Perhaps he had no idea where he was being led, either.

But now we were close to understanding one another.

'Your grace . . .' he made as if to hold my hand, then thought better of it, as my ladies could certainly see us, even if they could not hear us. 'We are discussing a matter of life and death. Our lives and deaths. But perhaps even that of England itself.'

'There is yet time, my lord.'

'Is there, your grace? Can you be certain his grace might not be struck down, without warning, by some dread disease?'

'My lord!'

'I speak treason,' he admitted. 'Yet must I do so, your grace, out of the love I bear for you, and for my country.' Once again we exchanged looks. 'Do you understand, your grace,' he said, 'that should the King die, Duke Richard will be crowned?' I bit my lip. 'And do you further understand, your grace, that the day that happens, if it ever should, I will be sent to the block? If, indeed, I am not condemned to a worse fate.'

He paused to let that sink in, and watch my colour change. For as I well knew, the sentence of death for treason in England comprises hanging, drawing and quartering. Mere beheading is an act of mercy on the part of the King, and I could certainly understand that it was unlikely the Duke of York was going to feel much mercy towards the Earl of Suffolk, who had entirely replaced him as the principal man in the country.

Now, I had never seen a man hanged, drawn and quartered. It was a sight I looked forward to, in the course of time, having been informed that it is even more pulsating, at least for onlookers, than to watch a man being broken on the wheel, the most severe punishment in France. I *had* seen a man broken on the wheel, and frankly, found it difficult to imagine that any fate could be more humiliating, or painful. The unhappy culprit is first stripped to his skin, before the assembled populace, and then tied securely to a large cartwheel, on his back. The executioner then takes a metal rod, and with exquisite precision – he is well trained –

breaks each bone in turn, with a single tap of his dreadful instrument. He starts, of course, with the smallest bones, and gradually passes on to the larger. The victim screams and moans and faints, and is revived with buckets of water. The whole thing can take several hours.

The point is that, providing his heart is strong, no man dies of having all his bones broken, as the executioner is very careful to cause no loss of blood. Thus, still living when he has been reduced to a jelly, the unhappy fellow, still on his wheel, of course, is then raised on a high pole and abandoned, to be pecked at by the birds, while everyone goes home in a very exhilarated state of mind. One could well say, improve on *that*!

In England, the event is much more speedy, and the unhappy traitor is put out of his misery far more quickly, yet I understand that it is nonetheless a pretty sight. In the first place, having been exposed to the multitude, the culprit is hanged, that is, hoisted from the round by a rope looped round his neck. This unfortunate experience is continued until he is near to death, when he is cut down and stretched upon the platform. Now hanging induces a peculiar physical reaction in a man, one which, it could be said, would have been of benefit to my dear husband. It is while in this state, easy of access, one might say, that the malefactor is castrated by the eager executioner. Before he can recover from this misfortune, his belly is slit open so that his intestines spill out. As he is now about to die in any event, the executioner then removes his head, whereupon the body is quartered, the various parts of it being exposed in suitable positions, such as over the gates of towns, as a warning to others who might be tempted to raise their hand against their king.

It will therefore be understood that your English traitor gets off a good deal more lightly than your French. However, as I have said, much as I was looking forward to witnessing one of these executions, it was with a stranger in mind. The thought of even the lighter penalty being inflicted upon my dear handsome Suffolk made my heart thump uncomfortably.

Suffolk observed this, and now hastened to press home his point. 'I would not even like to wager on the safety of your grace,' he said. 'Consider, you would be in York's power, and who knows what evidence he would manufacture against you in order to keep you here rather than return you to France? The very best you could expect would be imprisonment for the rest of your life.'

At seventeen, that is a very long time. But even more horrific from my point of view was the idea of being at the mercy of Proud Cis! 'Do you have a solution, my lord?' I begged.

'There is only one solution, your grace. For the good of the realm, and the safety of yourself, you must have a son.'

For a third time we looked at each other. This time it was I who felt the heat in my cheeks, for I may have been innocent, but I was by no means a fool.

'My lord,' I said, 'what you propose would make us as much guilty of treason as if we had plotted against the King.' Which was, in fact, just what we were doing.

'Save that no one could ever know of it, save ourselves, your grace.'

'Indeed? And what of the father?'

Thus easily could I discuss a quite impossible subject; I was amazed at myself. And then found myself swallowing, as the Earl continued to gaze at me. 'I repeat, your grace, that no one would ever know of it, save ourselves. And do not think me too old for the task. My wife is at this moment pregnant.'

Good Alice. The mention of her name should have restored me to my senses. Instead my heart was pounding fit to burst. For if, in marrying Henry, I had gained an acquaintance with sexual matters, it had been like opening a book, the first page of which suggests all manner of future delights, and then having the covers slammed and the book removed from one's grasp before it was possible to proceed. I could not doubt that this man, whom I truly loved more than any other man I had ever met, would know how to turn all the pages ... and would wish to do so.

'It will, of course, have to be carefully planned,' he said, taking my silence for acquiescence.

'Indeed, my lord,' I agreed. 'If we were to be taken, *in flagrante delicto* ...'

Once again our eyes met, as if my words had suddenly illustrated what lay ahead. What indeed we both so ardently desired, but yet so feared. 'It were best you visited me,' he said.

'No, my lord. I have never visited you before. It would rouse suspicion.'

'Well, then ... How may I gain access to your bed, your grace?'

By now I was so excited I could hardly speak, much less think. 'I will see what may be done,' I said. 'It must be entirely by the way.'

'Pray it is not too long, your grace.'

'It will not be too long, my lord,' I promised.

Once again his hand moved, as if it would touch mine. 'I love you, Meg,' he whispered. 'I adore you. I worship the ground on which you walk. And I shall do so until the day of my death, and then await your presence in Heaven.'

'You think too far ahead, my lord,' I told him. For it seemed to me that if we succeeded in our nefarious plot, he might well have to await my coming in Hell.

What a conspiracy! I was only recently seventeen, and I was about to yield my body to a man of the world. My imagination ran riot, but also, as imaginations will, took in the consequences of betrayal. And yet, I would not be deterred from laying my plans. I had been kept almost in a marital cloister for too long. My heart no less than my body cried out to be loved with passion and energy, and, I admit it freely, with an excess of that lust and lewdity which so terrified my husband. Thus far in my life I had experienced not one of those four very desirable emotions, but I had read of them often enough in the pages of Boccaccio.

Thus, plans. It may be supposed that to lie with a queen is the most difficult of all tasks. This is not so. To lie with any woman is a difficult task, if she is not willing. But to lie with any woman, if she is an eager would-be participant in the deed, is as simple as snapping one's fingers.

The only necessity is a confidante. This I had close to hand in my dear Bailly, who was utterly faithful to me. She was also French, which was a great help, as French ladies are less rigid in their thinking than their English counterparts.

Bailly understood the situation as well as anyone, although I suspect she regarded herself as dealing less with a queen determined to secure the succession than with a young wife, frustrated and bored, who was seeking some outside solace. Well, I will not entirely deny that she was right, but it was the succession that loomed largest in my mind.

With Bailly in command, all doors were opened, quite literally, as she also acted as the go-between to arrange the event. On a day when my Henry was at his devotions – we were now again approaching Christmas and in Advent Week – my lord of Suffolk was attending a ministerial meeting in the Palace of Westminster when it became necessary for him to visit the privy chamber. Sadly, the one on the ground floor appeared to be blocked with some noxious matter or other, and he found it necessary to climb to the first floor, with a good deal of swearing of oaths. This privy was close to the royal apartment, and indeed connected with it, for the convenience of the King and myself, by a private passage. Once Suffolk was in it it was a simple matter for Bailly to extract him from it, and lead him secretly to my bed-chamber.

Now, it also happened that on this day I had been overwhelmed by a sick headache, and had told my ladies that I would remain in bed, totally alone save for Bailly, and was not to be disturbed under any circumstances until I called for them. We were thus assured of complete privacy.

Innocent as I was, I was not so dumb as to suppose that

a single coupling would necessarily bring forth the required result. It seemed to me that our aim would only be attained by repeating our endeavours over a period of time. Perhaps it was this prospect that first planted the seeds of doubt in my mind.

Equally, however, had I been constrained, ever since we had made the arrangement, by the thought that Suffolk possessed no royal blood. It was easy to remember, of course, that dear Henry's grandmother, Mary de Bohun, had possessed only a smidgeon, and for that one had to go back several generations, but nonetheless, it was there. Suffolk had absolutely no such claims. He did not even have a noble lineage reaching back to William the Conqueror's band of adventurers, which most of the English nobility seemed to find essential to a support of their position – his great-great-grandfather had been a merchant, who had been ennobled for that most useful of services, lending money to the King. My son would therefore have only my royal blood in his veins. This caused me to alternate between great determination and equally great uncertainty. I told myself that my blood was basically the same as Henry's, indeed, it was somewhat better, as my part of the family had so far avoided contamination by the strain of madness which ran through the Valois, and which I had always feared might be transmitted to my own children were Henry to be the father. Thus, determination. Then I told myself that even mad royal blood has got to be better than no royal blood. Thus, uncertainty.

Overlying it all was lust, which was growing within me hour by hour as the minute approached, combined with a lively apprehension at the thought of delivering myself, body and, well ... more body, into the hands of a man I now recognised to be an experienced roué.

It will be seen that I was in a fine state of indecision. I took off my nightgown in order that he should possess all of my glory at a bound, as it were, and put it back on again so that he should not think me wanton. Equally did I pace the floor, unable to quell the surging energy in my loins, and then return to my bed, afraid of exhausting myself.

I was in the middle of one of these last manoeuvres when the door opened, and the Earl was upon me. Literally, for without further ado he strode across the room, put his arms round me, and hugged me close against him while he showered kisses upon my face and mouth. Clearly he was in the grip of an even more powerful emotion than I, and for a few seconds we wrestled most erotically, with the result that my nightgown and his breeches alike found themselves discarded, and we were in bed, or at least, I was sprawled across the bed while he leaned over me, burying his head in my breasts and repeating, in between kisses and sucks at my nipples, how much he loved me.

Well, there could be no argument with that, at least as regards my body. But suddenly my own ardour had entirely vanished. I can only repeat: I was seventeen, and here I was being confronted with the prospect of a most horrendous crime. Treason and adultery, at the very least! And with a base-born man, however attractive, and however lovable. Equally, perhaps, at that moment there arose before my eyes a vision of dear Henry, and of dear Alice – two of the most blameless people I had ever encountered, or would ever encounter – about to be betrayed. By the necessity of the state? Or the mad desires of an over-anxious young girl and an impatient middle-aged lecher?

I was also being confronted with the evidence of his lust, which, unprotected by any codpiece, was simply enormous, far larger in every way than dear Henry. I had been rather taken aback at the sight of it even before he had carried me to the bed. Now it was banging away at my groin and thighs as it sought an entry ... and all of a sudden I was not sure that I wished to receive it.

It would be difficult for me to isolate which of these emotions was uppermost. I only know that I wriggled free of his embrace, and gained the head of the bed, sitting there with the pillow hugged against my stomach as a kind of shield.

He was quite confused, as might be expected. 'Meg!' he panted. 'Did I hurt you?''

Well, in fact I was feeling a little bruised, never before having been assaulted in quite so vehement a fashion. But I naturally dissembled. 'No, no, my lord,' I assured him.

'Well, then ...' he commenced, crawling up the bed towards me, a fascinating but rather terrifying sight, as his ardour had not a whit abated.

Hastily I rolled off the other side, still hugging my pillow. 'I cannot.' That brought him up short. 'I ...' I raised my shoulders and let them fall again. 'I cannot,' I repeated. 'I am sorry, my lord.'

He sat on the bed, now in every way discomforted. 'I love you,' he muttered.

'As I love you, my lord,' I promised him. 'But ... I also love my husband, and indeed, I love your wife. As should you,' I added somewhat tartly.

'I do,' he protested. 'But not as I love you.'

'What we planned was wrong,' I declared. 'I cannot commit adultery.'

He looked utterly crushed, in every direction. 'What is to become of us?' he asked.

'Why, my lord, we shall continue as before, ruling the country to the best of our ability, and putting our trust in God!' As he was now appeared clearly incapable of giving me more than a caress, I ventured round the bed. 'I shall never betray you, my lord. On the contrary, you will remain always the most important man in my life. I would but beg of you to understand.'

'Yes,' he muttered. 'Yes,' and endeavoured to draw me against him. In my inexperience I had underestimated the recuperative powers of the male member, at one moment a withered reed, at the next, on the slightest encouragement, again a couched lance.

Hastily I removed myself to safety. 'You must go, my lord, or they will send to see what has become of you.'

*

Thus seventeen. 'Did I act the fool?' I asked Bailly.

'Indeed, your grace. By being naked in your bedroom with the Earl, you committed the crime in any event. You could as well have enjoyed it.'

But I did not send behind him for a return encounter. I knew it would not do. And indeed I felt a sense of personal pride, that I had been tried in the crucible of adulterous love, and that my innate virtue had triumphed. There is all the difference in the world between a girl of seventeen and a woman of twenty-four, and besides, by the time I reached the greater age, I had been tried in too many other crucibles to regard adultery as of the least importance.

For the time, however, I was happy within myself, and, withal, my mind turned to the Church and good works, to the great pleasure of my husband. It was at this time that I was approached by a gentleman named Andrew Ducket, who was the Rector of St Botolph's, in Cambridge, with the suggestion that, as Henry had founded and endowed a college at the university, I should do the same, and that beside King's College there should proudly rise Queen's College.

I thought this a splendid idea, the more so as I was well aware that I was none too popular in that part of the country – or indeed, at this time, in any part of the country – and the foundation of a college bearing my name might well alleviate the feelings against me. I therefore granted a charter for the foundation of the Queen's College of St Mary and St Bernard, and on 15 April 1448 my good Sir John Wenlock laid the first stone.

Alas, building takes time, if it is to be done well, and my college was overtaken by events, with the result that it was not opened for students until 1464, by which time my circumstances had undergone a considerable change, and I was unable personally to attend this gratifying event. Instead all the credit was taken by that foul girl Bella, who at this time was yet to enter my life with her insinuating treachery.

*

It was obvious that this year of 1448 was going to be a difficult one as, by the terms of our agreement with Uncle Charlie, Maine had at last to be surrendered, and this event was certain again to arouse the populace against Suffolk. Thus it was a period when the Marquis should surely have kept a low profile, except in performing his duties as chief minister of England. Instead, the dolt created a fresh crisis by quarrelling with the Beauforts, of all people. I do not know if his naked romp with me had gone to his head, and he felt that he and I now must stand together, regardless of what might happen, or fall together into that horrible pit he had described. But in any event, he now chose to attempt to dispossess the Bishop of London, Thomas Kemp, in favour of a client of his own, one Molyneux. Such a course would have been disreputable in any event, but Thomas Kemp was nephew of the Archbishop of York, John Kemp, who some years earlier had been made a cardinal by Pope Eugenius, and Cardinal Kemp was a well-loved and indeed powerful man, and as a great friend of our late Uncle Henry, he was also assured of the patronage of the Beauforts.

Now there can be no doubt that Cousin Edmund was at this time feeling somewhat disgruntled. His administration in France was being unfavourable compared with that of Cousin Richard of York, whom he had replaced – and who, unfortunately, was earning great praise for his handling of Irish matters – and he had still not attained that dukedom to which he felt he was entitled. On top of all this he, in common with most of the royal family, felt that he was being pushed to one side by the machinations of the upstart Suffolk. The result of all this was that he determined to champion the cause of Kemp, and there was the most colossal row, with even gauntlets being hurled to and fro.

As the matter had an ecclesiastical fount, as it were, Henry naturally got into the act. He opted to back his chief minister, which was gratifying to me, but with his usual ineptitude he attempted to take the matter up with Rome itself, which did no more than earn him a stinging rebuke from Pope Eugenius. In the end it was the poor little Queen who had to sort things out, which I did by persuading Suffolk to drop his absurd suit, by persuading those members of the nobility who happened to be in London to drop their opposition to Edmund's elevation, so that he duly became Duke of Somerset, and finally, by persuading Henry to grant Suffolk the title he so richly deserved, so that *he* became Duke of Suffolk, and dear Alice a duchess. Bishop Molyneux we appeased by giving him the Privy Seal.

In one way the fracas served a useful purpose in that it distracted the Commons, who enjoy nothing better than to see their betters at loggerheads, and while they were thus preoccupied, the English garrison quietly marched out of Maine, and Uncle Charlie took it over.

In the midst of all this disturbance of our domestic life, I suffered a personal tragedy: it became necessary to put Albion down.

He had, as lions will, spent the past two years growing, and was now a vast animal, who, unfortunately, regarded all humanity, save only for his keeper and myself, as his mortal enemies. Now by the very nature of things, a queen is surrounded by people; and in addition to his natural dislike for such beings, Albion had also developed a quite remarkable jealousy of my person. This was flattering, of course, but he went too far when one day he actually chased the King from my bed. That Henry was *in* my bed was, as may have been gathered, a sufficiently important event to be treasured, and certainly made the most of. Albion not only ruined the occasion and upset the King, but also all but killed a guard hurrying to see what the noise was about.

With reluctance I had to let him go, trying to raise my spirits by reflecting that with him perhaps went my girlhood, with all of the errors and misfortunes linked to that trying period of a woman's life.

*

However, my hopes that our affairs would now be able to proceed on an even keel, as it were, were dashed early in the New Year. This actually began very well, with Parliament assembling at Westminster in the very best of humours, and willingly conceding us very liberal grants, which enabled us to enjoy a greatly improved table. My opinion on kings who have to go cap in hand to their subjects for even their daily bread has all been made plain, but it was a great relief to have money to spend at last.

Alas, our joy was short-lived. Before we had properly taken stock the plague appeared in London, and we hastily removed ourselves to Winchester. This appeared as a mere irritation at the moment, but now disasters crowded upon us. It all began with a raving lunatic named Francois l'Arragonois, one of those absurd knights errant to whom all needs to be glory, and who belonged to the party which considered that the surrender of Maine to the French was a negation of all that English valour had achieved on the Continent during the preceding hundred years. This walking disaster now proceeded to lead his troops back into the province, and sacked the town of Fougères.

We were aghast, the more so when we learned that Francois had been instigated to his disastrous course of action by our own viceroy, Cousin Edmund, the new Duke of Somerset, who seemed to have climbed back on to his high horse, and who now brazenly visited the captured town to share in the spoils. Naturally Uncle Charlie reacted violently to this breaking of the truce, and once again war between our two countries flared into bloody conflict. I was quite distraught. So was Henry, who promptly took off for the Welsh Marches, ostensibly to inspect monasteries there. I had no doubt he was removing himself as far as possible from the turmoil both in London and across the Channel.

I returned to Westminster, trying to put the pieces back together. Suffolk of course kept assuring me that all would be well, and indeed all might have been well, had Cousin Edmund shown the least aptitude as a soldier. Instead he was beaten from pillar to post by the French, and at last, on 29 October, Rouen itself, the capital of Normandy, fell. I anticipate. This was a long, bitter summer for me, made worse by Henry's absence. Normally I would have welcomed this, as allowing me to get on with the pursuits I enjoyed and he did not. But Suffolk, naturally, regarded the absence of the King on the far side of the country as an invitation to resume his contention of the year before last, having formed the not altogether incorrect conclusion that I had then been constrained by the fear of discovery.

The fact was, however, that I was now nineteen, a fully matured woman with a fully matured mind. Gone were childish crushes on handsome lords. My concern was for the country, and in this regard I could not help but consider our chief minister as the man who had got us into this unholy mess. And meanwhile the storm clouds were gathering. I would not have anyone suppose that the idea of abandoning dear Suffolk crossed my mind for a moment, either then or at any later date, but I was forced to spend a good deal of time trying to decide how he could be saved – an aspect of the situation which did not appear to cross *his* arrogant mind for a moment – and was thus even less disposed than two years previously to contemplate adultery.

Henry returned from his perambulation in November, and it was immediately necessary to face the storm. Parliament had already been summoned to meet on 6 November at Westminster. This time it was not in a good humour, owing to the repeated defeats in France. But we had faced critical parliaments before, and triumphed, although admittedly on those occasions we had had Uncle Henry Beaufort at our shoulder. Yet there seemed no reason to suppose we should not succeed in quelling the doubts so freely expressed by the Commons of the way the country was being governed.

Sadly, we were again undone by the intemperateness of Suffolk himself, or at least his followers, who it was difficult not to believe acted always on his orders. Be that as it may, the Lords and Commons had hardly assembled when one

Ralph, Lord Cromwell, a man from the eastern counties who was one of Suffolk's chief accusers, was jostled by William Tallboys, a Lincolnshire squire who was in Suffolk's pay. Both men reached for their swords, but were separated by the onlookers before they could come to blows. However when it was realised that this Tallboys was a very accomplished swordsman, which could hardly be claimed of Cromwell, the cry immediately went up that the squire had been sent by the Duke to pick a quarrel with the lord and remove him from contention.

As may be imagined, there was another most tremendous fuss. The Chancellor of the Exchequer, Marmaduke Lumley, promptly resigned, and he was followed a week later by Bishop Molyneux, who surrendered the Privy Seal. The official reasons behind these actions was that these gentlemen felt they could no longer work with Suffolk. This after they had worked with him for the past year at least, and he had near cost himself dear by trying to advance the faithless Molyneux! Clearly they felt that the Duke's star was about to set, and wished to dissociate themselves from him as quickly as possible.

Matters had by now come to such a pass that Henry felt it necessary to send Suffolk to the Tower until his case could be heard. Suffolk was naturally somewhat upset by this, but the King assured him that it was for his own protection, while I equally assured him that no harm would ever befall him as long as I lived. With this he seemed satisfied, and I, at a later date, was left to reflect that not even queens should make rash promises, the consequences of which can lie heavily upon one's shoulders for the rest of one's life. Parliament was then prorogued until January, enabling us at least to enjoy Christmas in peace. But I fear there was little enjoyment to be had in the royal household. We were again short of funds, and we knew we were facing a severe crisis in the New Year.

We determined to escape exposure to the London mob, and

spent the festive season at Windsor. Not, as I have mentioned, that it could be described as at all festive. We were short of support as well as of funds. Somerset remained in France, even supposing he could truly be counted upon. Buckingham could certainly be trusted, but we continued to regard him as a lightweight in the looming crisis. York remained in Ireland, but was a sinister presence across the water, and there could be no doubt that his in-laws, the Nevilles, were solidly ranged against us, or at least against Suffolk.

Suffolk, having been released from the Tower, himself retired to his East Anglian estates with Alice. Perhaps he had some premonitions as to the future, and felt that this might be the last chance he would ever have for domestic bliss.

I suspect all England, of whatever rank or persuasion, was but waiting for the reassembly of Parliament.

Henry and I returned to Westminster on 10 January 1450. We had no sooner arrived than most disquieting news reached us from Portsmouth, where Bishop Molyneux, apparently on his way to take ship for France – was he, I could not help but wonder, attempting to flee the state? – was set upon by a mob of sailors. These nautical fellows were merely incensed at their arrears of pay, and recognised in the scurvy bishop a government minister, perhaps being unaware that he had resigned his offices. Be that as it may, this disreputable rascal, anxious only to save his own worthless skin, laid the entire blame for the country's ills on Suffolk, and made sundry other accusations as well – not omitting a reference to the unbecoming intimacy which many had observed between the Duke and the Queen.

This abominable behaviour in no way saved his life, as he was promptly torn in pieces by the mob; but the accusations of a man who might have been supposed to know death was approaching him very rapidly carried a great deal of weight. I then knew that we had to steer a very determined course; my only fear was that Henry might be as unreliable as ever. I even sent to France to beseech Somerset's aid, but he was totally engaged in resisting the French, and could supply none.

Parliament re-assembled on 22 January, and without any further ado brought an indictment against Suffolk.

This indictment was a serious business, as it included the accusation of high treason. Before we could act to prevent it, the Duke was again incarcerated in the Tower of London, and this time by the will of Parliament rather than the King. This so-called Tower is a vast and forbidding fortress which was built by William the Conqueror to dominate the city, and it certainly does that. In more recent years it has often been used as a prison, as it is virtually impossible to get out of, except by due process of law. Naturally I was alarmed, and besought my husband to use his prerogative as ruler of the kingdom to set our friend at liberty. This Henry felt unable to do, no matter how strongly I pressed him. 'We must pray,' he determined.

Well, I am as good a Christian as anyone, but even at nineteen I had observed that it is impossible to count on the intervention of the Deity without knowing all the facts – as, for example, who else might be praying on the opposite behalf. We are all agreed there is only one God and obviously He cannot be expected to support both sides of any question; and undoubtedly Suffolk and I had sinned, in mind if not entirely in deed. However, there was nothing for it but to let the trial take place, although I was still resolved that no harm should befall the Duke, and I again assured him of this.

Suffolk had been imprisoned on 28 January. On 7 February he was brought before the House and formally charged, firstly with having sold part of the realm to the French, and secondly, with having treasonably fortified his castle of Wallingford. This second indictment was the snake in the grass. The first was easily disposed of by referring to the act of indemnity the Duke had obtained before beginning the negotiations for my hand. But the second ... we were entirely taken aback, and at my insistence, Henry ordered an adjournment so that the charge could be properly considered.

This was granted, but it served us little purpose. To me, the solution was simple: the duke's oversight in fortifying his castle without royal permission could surely be rectified by such permission being granted now. In any ordinary case this would have sufficed. But Suffolk's enemies – and they far outnumbered his friends – were determined to bring him down. Their arguments had all the dreadful logic of zealous lawyers. Suffolk *had* committed treason; he could not now be acquitted of that crime, any more than he could be acquitted of murder after the event.

'What is to be done?' Henry moaned, holding his head in his hands.

'There is only one thing that can be done, sire,' I told my husband. 'Perhaps it is right and proper that not even the King may set aside the law of the land in retrospect. However, no one can deny that the King has the power of commutation.'

He raised his head. 'He will still have to suffer. To be seen to suffer.'

'Some punishment for his crime, to be sure,' I agreed. 'You will banish him from the kingdom.'

'Yes,' he said eagerly. 'Yes. I will banish him. That will please them.'

This constant preoccupation with pleasing his subjects I found intensely irritating; I could not help but wonder when, if ever, his subjects were going to start pleasing *him*. However, I as usual dissembled. 'For five years, your grace.'

'Eh?'

'You will banish the Duke for a period of five years, your grace. That is quite long enough to have the people forget about him, and to bring him back to us all in the vigour of his manhood.'

'They will not be so pleased about that,' Henry muttered.

'Five years,' I repeated, my tone leaving no room for argument.

*

I sent a message to the Tower bidding the Duke to be of good cheer, and then myself attended Parliament, sitting in a gallery reserved for female onlookers, to listen to the debate and to make sure that my presence would deter Henry from backsliding.

The Commons were in a violent mood as the Duke was brought before them. Accusations were hurled at him from every side, and an immediate call was made for him to be impeached, which was the first step in the direction of the executioner. Throughout it all Suffolk stood foursquare to his accusers, but I could tell that he was extremely agitated, and despite my promises, counted himself lost. I gazed at the King, willing him to act the true Plantagenet at least this once. It took Henry some time to obtain silence. Then, after a quick glance at my gallery, he said, speaking more resolutely than usual, 'My lord of Suffolk has served this crown, and this country, right well throughout his life.'

'With respect, your grace,' the Speaker said, having the temerity to interrupt his King, 'past services cannot mitigate a charge of treason.'

'Yet in view of those services I can, and will, mitigate the sentence,' Henry declared. 'My lord of Suffolk is hereby banished from my kingdom.' He paused, and there was a gasp of anger from the Commons. 'For a period of five years,' Henry added.

Now the gasp became shouts of outrage. Fists were shaken, and there was even the clash of steel. I turned to Wenlock, who was as ever at my side. 'Summon the royal guards, Sir John,' I said. 'Remove both the King and the Duke from the Chamber.'

I too left, for my own safety, and with my ladies hurried to the palace. Here I was soon joined by Henry, ashen and trembling from his ordeal. 'For a moment I thought I had stirred a revolution,' he gasped.

'You acted the king, your grace,' I told him. 'I have never been so proud to be your wife.'

'Were you, Meg? Were you?' He looked like a small child, and I waved my maids away and took him in my arms. There he lay for some time, trembling like a babe, while I dared not ask the question which was trembling on my lips.

But at last he recovered somewhat, and I poured him a glass of wine, took one for myself, and sat beside him. 'I did not stay to the end,' I remarked.

'They were insolent, insolent,' he grumbled, breaking out in a fresh rash of trembling.

'What would you expect of the common people?' I asked. 'But they cannot harm you. They can do nothing but obey your decree. I assume the Duke was safely removed?'

He nodded. 'He regained the Tower without difficulty.'

'The Tower?' I cried. 'Is he not banished?'

'Sweet Meg, these things take time. The streets were crowded. I deemed it best to return him to safety until the furore has died down.'

'The poor man will be terrified,' I said. 'I must go to him.'

'No,' the King snapped. 'You will do no such thing.' I raised my eyebrows. Henry had never spoken to me thus sharply since our marriage. 'There would be talk,' he said in a lower tone, thus indicating that perhaps some of the rumours about the Duke and myself had reached even his ears.

'Very well, your grace,' I said. 'Providing you will assure me that there is no question of his safety.'

'He is perfectly safe,' Henry said. 'As soon as the tumult dies down he will leave the city and retire to his estates in Essex. I have allowed him six weeks to put his affairs in order. Then he will depart for the Continent.'

'Where will he go, do you suppose?' I asked.

'I suspect he will make a pilgrimage to Rome, and seek asylum in the Papal States. It will be safest, and he may even find employment with the Papal armies.'

I imagined my hero riding in full panoply at the head of the Papal troops, earning fresh glory, before returning. Five years! I would be twenty-four! I have, in fact, often wondered what might have happened had Suffolk indeed returned at the end of five years, covered in glory, to take his place at our side. But those are dreams, and I have had to make do with lesser men.

For the moment, I was only concerned with the thought of those five long years when I would not see his face. Or any other part of him. I wrote him a letter of farewell, couched in the most discreet terms, as was necessary, but yet, I hope, leaving him in no doubt of my feelings for him.

I hope he received it.

This terrible year of 1450 was determined to pursue its ghastly course. Suffolk's departure from London was not to be the quiet affair Henry had imagined. The citizens were lying in wait for him, and it was fortunate that he was provided with an adequate escort, for he had to fight his way out of the walls. We learned of the tumult with dismay, and I gazed at the King, for these were his subjects ignoring his writ in their riotous behaviour. But Henry seemed merely relieved that the Duke had gained the relative safety of his estates.

For the next six weeks, Parliament being again prorogued, we enjoyed some peace and quiet, although I knew I would never rest easy until the Duke was out of the country. His departure was set for 1 May from Ipswich, and on this day I accompanied Henry to the abbey to pray for his safe delivery in France.

It was ten days later that the dread news reached us. Suffolk had indeed set sail on 1 May. He had two ships and a pinnace, and bore down the southern North Sea for the Straits of Dover and Calais, where I had written Cousin Edmund to receive him and see him safely on his way. He never got there. He was within sight of the port; but then he was also within sight of Dover, and before he could make French soil he was accosted by a squadron of the King's ships. I repeat, they were the King's ships, and flew the royal leopards from their masthead. The Duke was summoned on board the largest of these vessels, the *Nicholas of the Tower*. This summons he obeyed. Some say that he was forced to do so, others that he went willingly. This is certainly possible; he may have hoped that he was to hear of his recall, the sentence of banishment set aside.

On the other hand, there was no way he could refuse, being greatly outnumbered. Any hopes he may have had must have been dashed the moment he boarded the warship, for he was greeted with the words, 'Welcome, traitor.'

The Duke was kept on board the *Nicholas of the Tower* for two days. I shudder to think what he endured during those last forty-eight hours of his life. Even if he suffered no physical ill-treatment, he must have been aware that his fate was sealed. I wonder what he thought of, what he remembered, as death rushed at him? Certainly I must have loomed large in his considerations. Did he hate me at the end, for failing to save his life? It would have been unjust of him to do so, for I had risked all for his cause. But not even I had realised the depths of anarchy to which the country was descending.

On the third morning, he was forced to leave the *Nicholas of the Tower* and board a pinnace, and there, sentence having been passed upon him, he was beheaded with, it is said, a rusty sword. We were told it took six strokes to separate his head from his body.

It is, of course, possible to say that he suffered a lighter and more dignified fate than had he been impeached, condemned, and executed in England. Looking back on him over the years, and attempting to forget my youthful passion for him, I can see him now as an over-ambitious man who sought to seduce a naive young girl in order to achieve his goal – for had I borne his child he would have had the kingdom in the palm of his hand.

But he deserved better, at the end.

6

We had left London for the Midlands town of Leicester, where Parliament was to reassemble, because once again there was plague in London, when we heard the news of Suffolk's demise. We were both profoundly shocked, and I, at the least, was also profoundly angry. 'The entire crew of the *Nicholas of the Tower* are guilty of murder, your grace,' I told my husband. 'They must be arrested, tried, and hanged, every man jack of them.'

'I doubt that is practical at this time, sweet Meg,' Henry moaned.

'You mean to let them get away with their crime?' I could not believe my ears.

'There is naught I can do,' he said.

'And no doubt you meant to let poor Suffolk's body rot where it was found on the sand outside Deal,' I snapped, as contemptuously as I could.

'No, no,' he said. 'The Duke must be given a decent burial.'

This at the least was done; Suffolk's body was claimed, and he was interred in his family chapel at Wingfield. I wrote to Alice offering my sincere condolences, but I did not receive a reply. She removed herself and her children – the eldest, John de la Pole, was just eight years old – back to her father's home at Ewelme, and although later on that year she was indicted for treason by Suffolk's enemies, the charges were quietly dropped. As I have previously mentioned, I am sorry to relate that during my later tribulations Alice made her peace with my enemies, and the boy John (whom Henry, as soon as was practicable, restored to the Dukedom of Suffolk) actually fought for the Yorkists, the despicable lout. Alice and I were to meet again, many years later, in the most doleful of circumstances.

But all that was in the future as we attempted to cope with the present without our most able supporter. In the short term, there was only one man to whom we could turn to continue the King's business, and this was Cardinal Kemp. He had proved himself our friend, and he was certainly loyal to Henry, but he was seventy years old!

I had no doubt whatsoever that it was Cousin Edmund to whom we would eventually have to give the seals of office, whatever our doubts as to his honesty of purpose, but he was still totally engaged in attempting to hold Normandy against Uncle Charlie, and could not spare the time to come to England. In any event, long before he could act, we were visited with an even greater calamity than the murder of Suffolk. The men of Kent rose in revolt!

Obviously a queen can hardly be expected to feel a great deal of empathy for any of her husband's subjects who dare to rebel against his writ. But even were I an impartial observer I would be bound to say that there was no legal justification whatsoever for such an action as these villains now undertook. They claimed to be revolting against the misgovernment of the realm. But the man accused of misgoverning the realm had just been murdered. This claim was therefore false, and the true facts of the matter came out when their leader announced that his name was Mortimer. He said no more than that, at this time. However, the implications were clear, that he was a scion of *the* house of Mortimer, into which, as I have related, Philippa Plantagenet had married, and which therefore held a stronger legal claim to the crown of England than Henry.

Mortimer was of course also the house of Richard of York. Now, as all the world knows, this Kentish Mortimer was ultimately proved to be no Mortimer at all, but an Irish scoundrel named Jack Cade, already guilty of murder and wife-desertion and Heaven knows what other crimes. But when this fact became known, it aroused even graver suspicions in at least *my* breast. Cade was an Irishman: York was presently lieutenant-governor of Ireland. Cade had taken the name of Mortimer: Mortimer was a name York was himself entitled to use. There seemed to be no doubt at all that the entire business had been instigated by Cousin Richard, with a view to testing the water, as it were, regarding the true feelings of the people when it came to a contest between Mortimer, or more properly, York, and the house of Lancaster.

Which aroused an even graver suspicion. Cade's rebellion took place almost the moment the news of Suffolk's death got abroad. Had it not been timed, by a far greater intelligence than that possessed by our Irish scoundrel, to erupt the very moment the one man Cousin Richard might have been afraid to meet on the field of battle had been removed?

Be that as it may, the rebels, whoever their true leader, reckoned without the resources available to the King. Not that these were immediately apparent. There was a great to-do, a hurrying and a scurrying, a whispering and a wailing. People remembered that previous uprising of the men of Kent, only sixty-nine years before, when the rebels had seized control of London and looted it to their hearts' content, besides executing several of the then king's ministers who were obnoxious to them.

However, it was also remembered that the king in 1381, Richard II, had boldly sallied forth to meet the rebels, and engaged them in conversation while one of his aides struck down their leader, at that time a reprobate named Wat the

Tyler, and generally discomfited them. This seemed the obvious plan to pursue in our present circumstances.

Unfortunately, there were certain differences between then and now. Richard II had been but sixteen years old, with all the impetuosity of youth, and with every promise of developing into a warrior as famous as his father, known as the Black Prince, or his even greater grandfather, Edward III. No one suspected that this apparently fearless boy had within him the seeds of both incompetence and tyranny.

Henry, on the contrary, was in his twenty-eighth year, and though, like Richard, he had a famous warrior as a father, he had already demonstrated all too often his total inability to rule. Nor, with his well-known religious inclinations, was he likely to sanction such a bold stroke as that with which Sir William Walworth had despatched Wat the Tyler.

More to the point, Henry had long lost the impetuosity of youth – he had never actually possessed it – and he was far too afraid of being torn in pieces ever to confront a mob.

Yet something had to be done, and quickly. Cade soon commanded some twenty thousand men, and these were by no means all footpads and cutpurses. There were a goodly number of squires in their ranks, and an even larger number of disbanded soldiers, returned from the French war; observers spoke of their excellent discipline and their profusion of armaments, and they were encamped on a large piece of open ground not far south of London, fittingly known as the Black Heath.

On the first news of this potentially disastrous situation, the Parliament at Leicester was broken up, and we hurried back to Westminster. Naturally we received counsel from every side, most of it conflicting, but in the first instance we despatched emissaries to meet with the rebels and discover what they were after, while we hastily summoned support. Cade's demands were as might have been expected, in retrospect: principally he wished the Duke of York installed as our chief minister to reverse the trend of Suffolk's policies; he also wanted Cousin Edmund replaced as commander-in-chief in France in the hopes of ending the French advance through Normandy.

Our emissaries said that they would report on these demands to the King, and withdrew. But by then our military preparations were complete, and a royal force, commanded by Sir Humphrey Stafford, advanced to put an end to these unlawful proceedings. Alas for our hopes. Stafford – no relation of our Cousin Buckingham who bore exactly the same name – proved incompetent, allowed himself to be drawn into an ambush in an oak wood when the rebels appeared to be retreating, and had his entire force cut up. He himself was killed, whereupon Cade donned his armour and resumed his march on London, his ranks now greatly swelled as news of his victory at the Seven Oaks became widespread.

There was consternation at Westminster. Henry had actually accompanied his troops into the field, although he had remained securely in the rear when Stafford made his fatal advance. The King now came scurrying back to London by boat, and I was disgusted to observe how terrified he was. 'They seek my head,' he wailed. 'What's to be done? What's to be done?'

I was very tempted to suggest the only solution I considered the least practical; raise another army and put me at its head! But I doubted anyone would listen to me. Instead Archbishop Stafford – a cousin of our slain military commander – proposed that he and Cousin Buckingham should form another embassy to Cade to learn what he now wanted. Well, obviously the rascal would up the ante, following his victory. He professed his utter loyalty to the King – although he made no mention of *me* – but continued to insist that Cousin Richard be recalled from Ireland, and now also demanded the punishment of those lords he claimed had shared with Suffolk in the disgrace of returning Maine to the French.

Head of this list was Lord Saye and Sele, an admitted adherent of Suffolk's, and therefore of mine. But the

Archbishop recommended that this unhappy man be sent to the Tower as a gesture of our 'goodwill' – towards a pack of murdering peasants, mark you – and further, that notwithstanding Cade's professions of loyalty, it would be best for Henry and myself to withdraw from Westminster to the safety of Kenilworth, where there was a very strong castle, and there wait on events.

To my consternation Henry enthusiastically agreed with these pernicious proposals; his one ambition seemed to be to remove himself as far as possible from any confrontation with his subjects. How his father must have been rolling in his grave! But when I protested, the Archbishop bent a very severe gaze on me and said that his recommendation was mainly with my safety in mind, for he could not answer for my head should I fall into the hands of the mob.

The suggestion made me more angry than afraid. Heaven knows that there have been several queens in history who have perished violently, but I could not think of one who had been torn in pieces by a mob! Surely the entire chivalry of the land would rally to the support of a beautiful twenty-year-old girl in such a dire extremity. Indeed I was minded to put it to the test. But, weak as I then was, I allowed myself to be parcelled up and removed to the country. My mood was not improved by having to watch my lord and master visibly trembling throughout the entire journey, and I flatly refused to share his bed. 'A queen,' I told him, 'sleeps with kings, not fugitives.' I would have liked to add that she also sleeps with men who act like kings, but I thought better of it, and in fact I had not yet done so. I expected him to be angry, but he merely mumbled at me. I got the impression that he was actually relieved.

Meanwhile, Archbishop Stafford's plan turned out quite well, although at some cost, and with no credit to himself. On Henry's withdrawal Cade promptly marched on London, where he was admitted, those louts being in the first instance disposed to support him against the 'Frenchwoman'. In

London he summoned Lord Saye and Sele and his son-in-law – a man named Crowmer, the Sheriff of Kent who had prudently sought to flee before those to whom he had recently been administering justice – to be tried for treason, and when he could not find a judge to hear the case, had them beheaded without a trial at all. He also sought to get his hands on Alice, but she was already safely at Ewelme. Another of Suffolk's adherents, Ayscough, the unhappy Bishop of Salisbury who had presided at my marriage, was murdered by his tenants.

This was all very ominous, as the greatest of Suffolk's adherents, myself, was still at large. But now Archbishop Stafford's prognostications began to be realised. Cade's people became bored with sitting around waiting for something to happen. They commenced to drink, and then to pillage, with a certain amount of rape thrown in for good measure, and the citizens of London saw their houses and families in danger of destruction. This very rapidly restored them to the royal cause.

Archbishop Stafford had locked himself in the Tower and refused to budge, but gallant seventy-year-old Cardinal Kemp was there, and he rallied the Londoners into an army of sorts, supported by the noble William of Waynflete, who had succeeded Cardinal Beaufort as Bishop of Winchester, and was to prove a good friend over the years. There was a battle at the bridge, and although losses were about even the rebels retired to their original camp. Now the Cardinal played his trump card, and sent a messenger to them promising them a royal pardon if they would only disband and return to their homes. He knew of course that this was what they really wanted to do, as I was beyond their reach and they all had some plunder to realise. Thus they drifted away. Cade understood what was happening, and endeavoured to maintain himself, but with his numbers hourly diminishing was forced to flee for his life. Finally he was brought to book by a most gallant fellow named Alexander Iden, who had been appointed sheriff in place of the unfortunate Crowmer, and beheaded.

Henry now sallied forth from Kenilworth, breathing fire, and toured the south-east; every rebel he could lay hands on was summarily executed. I found this most distasteful, not merely because the Cardinal had promised them pardon, but because Henry had been afraid to face them when they had weapons in their hands.

This entire episode may be regarded as a watershed in my life. For five years I had pretended that my husband was a good and noble lord, handicapped only in his business, both as husband and king, by his extreme leaning towards religion, which effectively placed him beyond criticism. For those five years, therefore, I had stifled my own instincts, both as queen and woman, in order to be the sort of wife he obviously wanted. But now he had revealed himself to be a dishonest coward. And now too I had had revealed to me the awful uncertainty of life. For a good deal of my prevarication with Suffolk had been caused by the comforting thought that there was always tomorrow, when the Duke and I might discover an opportunity to enhance our love in security and mutual delight. Now the Duke was dead.

There is no question that in that summer of 1450 I ceased to be a girl, and became a woman. More important, I came to realise that I must either abandon my husband and my kingdom, and flee in shame and disgrace back to Anjou – where I would hardly be welcomed in such circumstances – or look to myself, and myself alone, as the only person who could save both myself, and England, for the house of Lancaster.

I am of course writing with hindsight. I know now that various decisions were taken in my mind, that summer. But they were decisions of so momentous a nature that it was some time before I summoned the courage to accept them. My metamorphosis, if begun, took some years to accomplish. In the very short term, both the King and I were belaboured by so much continuing adversity that it was all we could do to maintain ourselves, much less plan for the future.

We were not the only ones to be in mourning that year. In France, Agnes Sorel died. From all accounts, Uncle Charlie was desolated, even if there is some difference between a king and queen who have lost their chief minister and been faced with a serious uprising in the space of a few months, and a king who has lost his favourite whore. In any event Charlie, who had at last given way entirely to lechery, immediately replaced the Lady of Beauty with her cousin, named Antoinette de Maignelais – like Agnes, a protégée of Pierre de Brezé – who was reputed to be even more beautiful than the fair Agnes, and of even looser morals, for apart from surrendering her own body to my ravenous uncle, she also acted as procuress, supplying him with a whole troop of handsome prostitutes, whom he dressed as queens and bedded in profusion.

This was a man of forty-seven, mark you, who had never done a worthwhile thing in his life! I could not help but gnash my teeth when I compared my position – so young, so beautiful, so anxious for physical love, and so insecure – with his, the old reprobate, behaving like some Eastern potentate, and with apparently not a care in the world!

Henry and I were at least entitled to look for some respite after the crushing of Cade's rebellion. Instead we were immediately faced with a new crisis as Richard of York, unbidden, crossed from Ireland. He declared that he had come to save England from misgovernment – virtually the same words used by his lackey, Cade.

My immediate reaction to the news that he had landed in England was to issue a warrant for his arrest on the grounds that he had left his post without permission. Henry, having gained not an ounce of backbone from spreading vengeance through Kent, as usual dithered. Cousin Richard acted. I was not present when he appeared at Westminster, commanded the guards to step aside, and forced his way into the King's presence, wearing full armour and with a sword at his side.

Henry was terrified. Well, what would you expect? The long and the short of it was that he submitted to a lecture from his imperious cousin, and agreed that York should remain in England as a member of his Council.

I was horrified. York on the Council meant that York *was* the Council. And so it proved. Cousin Richard had barely taken his seat when he was elected chairman. He had barely been elected chairman when the Council presented a petition – ultimatum would have been a more accurate description – to the King, requesting him to name an official heir to the throne, and 'recommending' that the only correct choice was Richard Duke of York. 'This is an outrage!' I stormed at Henry.

'It is a legal matter,' he explained. 'Since Uncle Humphrey died, the matter of my heir has been in abeyance. But a king must have an heir.'

'And have I no rights in the matter? What about when I bear you a child?'

He gave his wan smile. 'Dear Meg, you know that is now unlikely. We are not blessed.' Not blessed, I thought. Were you only to mount me like a man ... 'But, should such a happy event take place,' he went on, 'why, Cousin Richard would be set aside.'

As if such a man would ever deign to step aside, having been placed in such proximity to the crown he dreamed of wearing!

The hand of York now lay heavy on those who were considered of the King's party. One of his first acts was to recall Cousin Edmund from France. Now, I have to be honest and admit that Edmund had made a complete mess of our French affairs. While we had been fighting for Suffolk's life before Parliament he had been contriving to be defeated time and again by Uncle Charlie's troops. The crowning blow had come at Formigny in April, which had resulted in the total expulsion of the English from Normandy. In addition to his other excesses, Uncle Charlie was now calling himself Charles the Victorious, although of course it was Pierre de Brezé and Dunois who had actually commanded his army.

Edmund had had to retire to Calais, the country around which was all that was left of our once extensive domains on the Continent, after something more than a hundred years of endeavour. Thus perhaps it was a military necessity that so unsuccessful a commander should be recalled. But York was out for blood. No sooner was the Duke of Somerset on English soil than he was arrested, on a charge of having treasonably surrendered various towns to the French, and conveyed to the Tower. 'What are you going to do?' I asked Henry.

'Well, there is no doubt that Somerset will have to answer for his administration,' Henry said.

'You mean to allow him to appear before Parliament? And then be tried, impeached, and sentenced to death. Like Suffolk. Then no doubt you will send him into exile, like Suffolk, so that he can be waylaid and murdered.'

Henry refused to look at me, as was his wont when I was in a rage. 'There will be due process of law,' he muttered.

'Law!' I cried. 'There will be due process of York's will, you mean. Henry, Edmund is your cousin. The same blood flows in both your veins. You cannot permit this.'

'I cannot stand in the way of the law.'

'You cannot stand in the way of York, you mean,' I cried, and stormed from his presence.

But what was to be done? The King was ambling aimlessly on his way, relying on the one simple fact that he *was* the King, and therefore was, he supposed, untouchable. Whereas I could see York's design as clearly as if he had outlined it to me himself. He was the legal heir, both by blood and now by definition of the council. But the house of Lancaster remained a popular one, and would as long as the memories of Bedford and Gloucester and Cardinal Beaufort, and above all Henry V, remained. York shrank from plunging the country into civil war – like me, he was only just maturing towards that inevitable consequence of his ambition and my determination to defend the right. Besides, there were still too many powerful men able and willing to fight for the King. But if they were whittled down, one by one ... Suffolk was gone. Cousin Edmund, head of the house of Beaufort, was surely only the second name on a very long list. After him would no doubt come Buckingham, and then, the royal cousins eliminated, York could move more openly against our lesser supporters.

Was I then helpless to avert this looming catastrophe? Clearly, to rely on the King was but to hasten the event. I needed to act. But how? In this dire extremity, I discovered all that latent courage and determination of character I had always possessed. Suffolk had been sent to the Tower, supported by my promises. Thanks to the pusillanimity of the King and my own misunderstanding of the lengths to which our enemies would go, those promises had turned out to be worthless. I could never forget that.

Now Somerset had been sent to the Tower. I had promised him nothing. I was not absolutely sure I liked the man. But he was my only hope. If he went, then so did I. I did not doubt this for a moment. Thus I had nothing to lose by demonstrating this to the world, and letting events move forward from that starting point. However, I knew that I needed to act both with caution, and at a time when whatever I accomplished could have its greatest effect. I therefore practised patience, dissembled, busied myself with the business of a queen who is uninterested in affairs of state, arranged and oversaw the marriages of several royal wards, received young ladies at court, and added to my income by securing from the King a patent allowing me to export any tin and wool gleaned from my property free of duties ... and waited, until York, with that easy over-confidence which was his greatest weakness, left the capital to visit his estates in the north.

Immediately I summoned Wenlock, and told him what I wished. He was aghast, the more so when I further told him that the King knew nothing of it – and must know nothing of it until the deed was done. Thus the next day I left Westminster, with an escort of ladies and only a few gentlemen. I wished boldly to ride into the city, challenging the mob to waylay their Queen. This Wenlock refused to countenance, and so we boarded a barge at Westminster Steps.

Yet news of my progress obviously spread very rapidly. Apprentices and housewives abandoned their duties to cluster on the embankment and stare at me. I smiled at them all, and even from time to time waved at them. My ladies were very nervous, but I insisted they wave too. And before the Londoners understood what I was about, I was at the water gate of the Tower, which is somewhat ominously known as Traitor's Gate. But I cared not a fig for that.

Here there was another to-do, as the Lieutenant was taken entirely aback. But when I insisted upon entry, he could do nothing less than obey. I was the Queen.

This was the first time I had been inside this large, and to say truth, grim establishment. I found myself within very cold stone walls of immense thickness, surrounding some lawns and inner courts which did little to alleviate the general gloom.

The Lieutenant was even more alarmed when I announced that I had come to visit the Duke of Somerset. 'He is imprisoned by order of the Privy Council, your grace,' he stammered. 'And can only be released by such an order.'

'Did I say I have come to release him?' I demanded. 'I have come to visit a man who is at once my cousin and a trusted friend. I wish to discuss affairs in France, of which he surely knows as much as anyone. He is also my subject. As are you.'

That finished the protestations, and I was escorted into another one of the several towers which give this castle its name, up an interminable flight of stone steps, and into a remarkably spacious if somewhat sparsely furnished apartment.

Edmund stood in the centre of the room. He was well dressed, and had clearly suffered no ill-treatment. Like everyone else, today, however, he was utterly taken aback at the sight of me, and promptly fell to one knee. I turned to the Lieutenant, who, with his lackeys, and my ladies, had followed me into the cell. 'You may close the door behind you,' I said.

He looked as if he would have protested, but I had adopted my most imperious gaze, and he backed from the room. My ladies equally hesitated, and I waved my hand to send them scurrying behind the guards. The door clanged shut. Edmund had remained kneeling. 'Do you not find the stone cold and hard, cousin?' I inquired.

Hastily he stood up. 'Do you know what you do, your grace?' he asked. 'It will be all over London in fifteen minutes that you are closeted, behind a closed door, with a man accused of treason.'

'I mean it to be known,' I told him. 'I have not made any secret of coming here.' I approached him. 'Edmund,' I said, 'you know full well there is a conspiracy against the King.'

'I believe so, your grace. But no one else will accept it.'

'I know it to be so. We need all the true and trusted men we can discover.' I stood immediately before him. 'Edmund, would you die for the King?'

He gazed at me, his handsome face rigid for several moments, while I can only surmise what manner of thoughts chased themselves through his brain. Actually, I can well surmise, in view of his answer. 'I would die for *you*, sweet Meg,' he said.

I am prepared to swear that when I undertook this famous pilgrimage it was merely to force the issue, as it were, while recruiting a strong right arm. For our cause. Now it dawned on me that *our* cause was actually *my* cause, in the eyes of any man with courage enough to draw his sword on our behalf. There was no man in the kingdom, least of all the royal cousins, who had ever come into contact with the King and considered *him* worth dying for. I extended my hand.

'Then live for me, dearest Edmund, and carry my banner to victory.'

He seized my hand and kissed it, and before I properly knew what he was about, had kissed my sleeve and my shoulder, drawing me ever closer, until I was in his arms. Of course, I understood that, like Suffolk, Edmund had long worshipped me from afar. Now I was disposed to assist him. He was younger than Suffolk, and appeared stronger, and he had royal blood – indeed his blood was as good as the King's – and our cause was even more desperate than when Suffolk had made his infamous proposal. Besides, I now knew the awful consequences of postponing what was inevitable. Thus I surrendered my lips to Edmund's, reminding myself that it was for the good of the state.

Equally, like Suffolk, he was aghast at what he was doing, as his hands performed a perfunctory but animated journey around my back, my buttocks and my breasts, before falling away, to accompany him once again to his knees. 'Your grace!' he muttered. 'I am guilty.'

'Of loving me?' I asked. 'It is not a crime I propose to charge you with, cousin.' He raised his head. 'I wish you to be my strong right arm,' I told him.

'I am yours, your grace. But—'

'I can promise you no rewards other than being the principal man in my kingdom.'

He licked his lips. 'But—'

'You will carry out my wishes, and none other. Do you swear this?'

'I swear this. But, your grace—'

'You are impatient, Edmund.'

He was on his feet again, and I felt it expedient to step against him, allowing him to hold me close and kiss me again. Despite my brief amatory tussle with Suffolk, I swear I was more aroused than ever before in my life. But I kept my head. 'Impatient,' I repeated, and freed myself.

'But your grace,' he said, 'I cannot help you until I am free from this place. And I doubt that will ever happen. This is a castle, is it not? And I have long known that I would perish in a castle. It has been prophesied.'

This was what apparently he had been trying to convey for the last five minutes; I had misunderstood his ardour, but I fear he was always a cold fish, ruled by his head rather than his heart. And a superstitious fish, to boot.

'You do not wish to believe in scurrilous prophesies, my lord,' I assured him. 'As for the matter of your release, you may confidently leave that to me.'

My visit caused a sensation, but this was what I wished to happen. Henry looked at me as if I were a stranger – which I was to him, from that moment, less a wife than a guardian and mentor – and my ladies regaled anyone who would listen with the tale of my courage and determination. And theirs, of course.

I once again stepped forward as my husband's champion. York was still out of town. I thus attended the Council myself. They were astonished at my entry, leaping to their feet in alarm, as if I had come with a file of archers at my back.

I smiled at them. 'My lords,' I said, 'pray be seated. That I have the temerity to interrupt your deliberations is because there are grave matters to be brought to your attention.'

They looked at each other, and then the Cardinal, as I had guessed he might, invited me to be seated.

'Your eminence, your grace ...' this to Archbishop Stafford, 'my lords, as you may know, I have taken it upon myself to interrogate the Duke of Somerset as to the affairs which are in question. Your eminence, your grace, my lords, the Duke is a royal cousin, and I am convinced there is no more loyal man in the entire kingdom. He would die for the King. Can you say that of every man in the country?'

They exchanged glances.

'Your eminence,' I continued, 'your grace, my lords, England has a *King*. That perhaps on occasion he prefers to delegate his authority is entirely because he considers it of equal importance to care for the Holy Church as to care for his kingdom.' I gazed at the two prelates, who were bound to nod their agreement with Henry's principles. 'Yet is he the King. And now he would *rule*. Is there any man here would dare attempt to prevent him from exercising his legal prerogatives?'

That shook them. The one man who was attempting to do so was absent. 'His grace has but to make his wishes known, your grace,' Stafford muttered.

'His grace is indisposed,' I said. This was not actually a lie: Henry was in a state of total consternation. 'He has requested me to make his wishes known to you.'

They waited with some apprehension.

'Firstly, his grace requires that all charges against the Duke of Somerset be dropped, and that an order be issued immediately for his release from the Tower.'

They hesitated. 'The Duke of York ...' someone ventured.

'Your eminence,' I said, 'your grace, my lords, pray tell me, who is the King of England? Henry of Windsor, or Richard of York?' That concluded that particular argument. 'His grace also wishes it known,' I continued, 'that it is his desire that all the nation, but especially London Town, understands that he is the ruler of this land, and commands you to accompany him to a service of thanksgiving at Westminster Abbey, on Sunday next.'

Henry was first aghast at my temerity, then piqued at my having so usurped his authority, and then delighted at the prospect of a thanksgiving service. At my insistence he allowed himself to be dressed in full armour, with the leopards of England and the fleur-de-lis of France quartered on his chest. The news of the proposed service was sent abroad, and Richard came hurrying back to town, accompanied by his Neville cousins and a host of retainers. But he was too late. All London was on the streets, cheering for the King and his noble lords; York and the Nevilles could do

nothing more than join the procession, and display their
loyalty to the throne.

Next day the Duke of Somerset was made chairman of the
Council.

York endeavoured to recover his position, of course. As
soon as the Council was convened he demanded the
dismissal of Edmund from his offices, on the grounds of
incompetence, if no longer of treason. But Henry, stiffened
by my resolve, and also by the evidence that he had but to
assert himself to make even his nobles bow before him,
refused. Cousin Richard could do nothing more than withdraw, and consider what might best be done next.

Thus we gained a signal triumph. However, all things in
this life need to be paid for. The Council had barely
adjourned its meetings for Christmas when I received a visit
from Edmund, who requested a private audience. As I had
had a private audience, at my own insistence, in the Tower
only a few weeks before, no one was disposed to carp now.

I knew of course what had to follow. It may well be asked,
who was required to pay whom for what? Had I sat back and
done nothing, Edmund would undoubtedly have been
impeached and executed. My fate would then have been to
watch my husband treated as a nonentity by York, to be
treated as such myself, and upon my husband's death, either
to have been confined in some draughty castle for the rest of
my life or to have been shipped back to France, that ultimate
female disaster, a returned wife – it matters naught that one
is returned as a widow.

Well, then, it may well be asked, did either of us gain
anything more than that for close on thirty years of
unremitting conflict? Edmund certainly not. The seeds of
destruction were already germinating within him, simply
because he lacked the talent to carry through his ambitions.
But for me, I would say yes. I have *lived*, whatever the end
result. Besides, it has never been my nature simply to bend
my back and let fate belabour it. And had I remained at
home, Edmund would have been dead much sooner than

actually happened. Yet he chose to consider that I had made some kind of promise to him, by allowing him my lips.

Well, perhaps I had. It was only a few months since Suffolk's death, and but three years since I had been unable to follow the inclination of both my loins and my heart, because of the strictures of my head. But now my three parts had united. As I have said, I knew that I could never love my husband; from that realisation it was a brief step to understanding that I had *never loved* him. This of course does not excuse adultery, in any woman, much less a queen. But I was carried along in a mood of impetuous grandeur: I alone had saved us from Richard of York, and I needed, and needed to sustain, the love of the man who was prepared to be my champion.

Equally was I carried along on a wave of exhilaration, that for the first time in my life I had grasped the reins of my own destiny, with utter triumph. I was not in the mood to drop them now. I also reflected that this man might give me the son I so desperately needed and wanted; after all, he had several of his own.

But most of all, as I am being honest, was I carried along in a gush of sexual desire. I may have mentioned that Edmund was a most handsome man, and some years younger than Suffolk into the bargain. He grew more handsome by the moment, as he now knelt before me, congratulated me on the success of my coup, and swore his eternal love and loyalty. I raised him up, and was in his arms. Within seconds we were naked, and entwined.

What am I to say? Obviously we had both committed a grave sin, but it was not one which could be confessed. As for explaining, I have already done that, even knowing as I do that there can be no adequate explanation.

But the accomplishment of the deed was sheer heaven. Edmund had lived many years in France, and had studied all the sensual arts as practised in that most erotic of countries. They were arts of which I had been told, of course, that I might greet my husband with enthusiasm rather than dismay. Unfortunately, as I have related, my dismay arose from the fact that not one of these arts had ever been practised upon me by my husband.

Now that lack in my upbringing and experience was put right. I was at once delighted, disturbed, debauched and thoroughly damned, I have no doubt, as Edmund's lips and tongue sought out my every secret crevasse. What a way to treat a queen, I wondered. But then, his manhood followed his lips, and I was at once transfixed and transported. That metamorphosis which had begun with Suffolk's murder was completed, and I was for the first time entirely my own woman.

Yet would I willingly have belonged. But that was not to be. Sadly, one of the most curious aspects of manhood – in all its euphemisms – is the remarkable fashion in which, once spent, it reverts on the instant from the love which will conquer all obstacles to the humdrum concerns of daily life.

I lay in my bed, aglow from head to foot and front to back, and discovered I was alone.

'I must be off,' Edmund said, pulling on his garments.

'So soon?' I rose on my elbow, surely a bewitching sight.

'Someone may suspect.'

'No one can approach us as long as my dear Bailly stands guard.'

He paused in donning his jerkin to frown at me. 'Is she trustworthy?'

'Absolutely.'

His frown deepened. 'She has not done this duty before?'

I sat up, tossing my hair from my face. 'I am your queen!'

Of course that wasn't an answer, but I was not prepared to lie, and he was not prepared to force the issue.

'When can we meet again?' I asked.

'Ah . . . when I return to London, in January.'

'In January?' I shouted. Granted that it wanted but two weeks to Christmas, that still seemed an eternity distant.

'I have been away from my family for too long,' the

wretch explained. 'It would arouse suspicions were I not to spend the festive season in their company.'

Practising the arts of love on his wife, no doubt!

Had I been a whore, he would have paid me before leaving. Had we even been normal cousins, I might have touched him for a loan. But I was the Queen, and had already stooped far enough. Thus I let him go, and faced a most dismal Christmas. Our financial affairs were again in a mess, and it was necessary to borrow to pay for our Christmas dinner, while when Henry sent into the city to arrange additional funds for the celebration of Twelfth Night, he was refused.

I was astounded. How may a king be refused a loan? Very easily, it appears, in England. The King's credit had run out. We had no dinner at all on that most important day.

However, things improved for the rest of the year, and in fact, looking back, I would have to describe 1451 as possibly the most peaceful year of my adult life. In March I became twenty-one, an occasion of some importance, which was celebrated throughout the kingdom, and resulted in many handsome presents. I assumed ever more of the King's prerogatives, and doing this, with the assistance of Edmund and Cardinal Kemp, managed to stabilise our finances, so that we actually had money to spend.

Henry spent his time, as usual, at his devotions and inspecting monasteries. Our affairs in France went from bad to worse as the French overran Guienne. But the people seemed to accept this as inevitable.

Henry no longer visited me carnally, but Edmund and I managed to share a bed on several occasions. Each of these events was as delightful as the first, and as we grew more intimate I was encouraged to do some exploring of my own. He was a consummate lover, possibly the only task for which he actually possessed any talent at all. My own feelings remained ambivalent. In his company I was utterly stimulated. Out of it, I experienced increasing doubts. And

I grew increasingly disturbed at my failure to become pregnant.

My plans for this were all laid, of course. The very moment I missed a monthly period I intended to force myself upon Henry and refuse to take no for an answer. But nothing happened, and I could not help but wonder if the true disability was my own.

Yet as I have said, it was a happy, peaceful year, looked at from Westminster and forgetting what was happening in France. I saw to it that we did not go short this Christmas, or on Twelfth Night! Of course I was aware that the true cause of the absence of any strife around us was the refusal of Cousin Richard to attend any meetings of the Great Council as long as Somerset was in the chair; he spent the entire year at his castle in Sandal in the north, brooding. This somewhat surprised us, although he had indulged in such a period of deep consideration of his position before. But he had his position as heir to the throne to protect; he could not tell what machinations we might be up to behind his back, and he dared not risk his popularity with the mob.

In fact, we were up to no machinations in that direction at all, except the most vital one of all, that of getting me with child – and that was known only to Somerset, Bailly, and myself. Perhaps I should have acted more positively. But I was still only twenty-one, and I was very aware of both my guilt and my anomalous position. The King had no suspicion of my liaison with Edmund; it never occurred to him that there might be people who ever actually *wanted* to have sex. However, he was very aware of the part I was playing in the government of the realm, and I could tell that he was not entirely happy with it. He was a great stickler for legality, and even if he had been bullied into making York his heir, I knew that for me to commence an overt campaign to have that ruling altered might be to have my husband interfere, and perhaps even exclude me altogether from affairs of state. So I resolved to bide my time. I still possessed the confidence of youth that the Duke would overreach himself very soon, and present me with the opportunity I desired.

When Cousin Richard did overreach himself however, it was like a thunderclap. At the beginning of February 1452 we received news that the Duke of York was marching on London, at the head of an army!

7

As usual we were thrown into a tizzy by this sudden turn of events, and again as usual, it was necessary for me to bolster my lord and master. Even more as usual, Henry was inclined to let matters take their course, for Cousin Richard, with great cunning, was declaring that he was returning to London with no enmity against the King, but only to serve him, by procuring the dismissal of Somerset, who he claimed was ruining the kingdom. As for his army, this was simply for his own protection, as he feared assassination. 'There,' Henry said. 'He is at heart a loyal fellow.'

'Husband,' I said, 'if you will believe that you will believe anything.'

Henry's trouble was that providing it was what he wanted to hear, he *would* believe anything. However, in this case, with hindsight, I believe that Henry may have been right, *at that moment*. In view of what was to transpire, I feel that York had still not taken a decision regarding the ultimate step of declaring his superior claim to the throne. Equally there could be no doubt that dear Edmund *was* mismanaging England every bit as successfully as he had mismanaged France, and indeed the country was fast approaching a state of anarchy, with the law in the hands of the local magistrates, who dealt as they favoured or disfavoured, regardless of the rights of the case, or of any fear of a higher authority bringing them to book. Equally, however – from my point of view – none of these evils was in any way as great as that of having the Duke of York king in fact if not in name.

Fortunately, I managed to convince Henry of our mutual danger, and of course Edmund himself was ardently my supporter. The result was that we summoned an army of our own and gave every indication of being prepared to meet force with force. Naturally this was not my true plan, for our commander was Cousin Edmund, while Cousin Richard was leading his own people – there could be no argument as to who was the superior soldier: it would have been like pitting a farm boy against a knight in full panoply. As far as I was concerned, we were carrying out a gigantic bluff, much as I had done just over a year earlier when removing Edmund from the Tower. And again it worked, up to a point.

As the Duke, having crossed from Ireland, was approaching from the south-west, I had our people block and barricade all the roads into London, while Henry, again at my suggestion, took a leaf out of Cade's book and raised the royal standard on the Black Heath, a very suitable place on which to mobilise a large number of men, and strategically, an ideal position from whence to cover any attempted crossing of the Thames from the south and in the vicinity of the city. Here we waited, while York approached. Now, with that fatal hesitancy which his dreadful son entirely lacks, York – realising that if he persisted he would be held in arms against his lawful king – turned aside from a confrontation and pitched his camp at Deptford some miles distant.

Good Bishop Waynflete was with us, and we despatched him to inquire of the Duke's purpose. He returned with the usual utterances of loyalty, making the one point: that the Duke of Somerset must be placed under arrest forthwith. Were that done, Cousin Richard promised to attend the King on bended knee.

By now it was occurring to me that Richard's insistence upon the arrest of Edmund had more to it than a desire either

to remove a rival or to save the kingdom from misgovernment. Could it possibly be that he suspected our criminal
connection? I myself have always been good at keeping
secrets, especially where they are of such potency, and
Bailly I knew I could trust with my life. The only other
person in the conspiracy, because it was nothing less, was
Somerset himself. Obviously I had to trust him. But he was
a man, and men are wont to boast of their conquests. A man
who has conquered a queen may well regard himself as
having scaled the highest mountain in the world.

When I put this to Edmund he hotly denied it. But then,
he would. Either way, I began to feel that York was perhaps
too dangerous to be permitted to remain at large – in fact,
alive – even if he were to agree permanently to absent
himself from London ... if he was going to spend his time
dreaming up such pernicious and absurd rumours. Well,
obviously they would appear pernicious and absurd to
anyone who had ever regarded my beautiful, innocent face,
and the eagerness with which I accompanied my husband to
his devotions – from time to time.

I thus laid a plan. It should always be remembered that I
was, even then, fighting for my very life. Certainly I was
fighting for my position as Queen of England, which *was* my
life. When one is in such a position, one can admit to no
feelings of honour, no considerations of the judgement of
one's fellow men and women, or even of history. Only
survival matters.

'The important thing, your grace,' I explained to Henry,
'is to meet with the Duke of York face to face, and thrash out
your differences, and not at a time and a place of his
choosing, when perhaps you may not be suitably attended,
but one of yours. Such as now, indeed, when you are
surrounded by your military might.'

'Hm,' Henry commented. 'Hm.' This was as much as
could have been expected; after all, there was a decision to
be made.

'He will never come to us here,' Somerset grumbled.

'Of course he will, if we accede to his demands,' I said. 'Cousin Edmund, as of this moment you are under arrest.'

'Eh?' the poor fellow cried.

'Guards!' I called, and they hurried forward.

'Your grace—' Edmund was quite purple in the face.

'Trust me, my lord,' I whispered. 'Now, your grace, why do you not send to York's camp to inform the Duke that his demands have been met, and that you expect him to attend you as soon as possible, to swear eternal allegiance?'

Henry was quite confused, so I sent the message myself. 'There will be a great to-do,' my husband complained. And about time too.

Cousin Richard arrived that very afternoon, attended by his squires but with none of the Nevilles in tow, and stalked into the royal tent wearing full armour, glared around the room as if he were the victor, gave me no more than a cursory glance, and then discovered Cousin Edmund standing immediately behind the King's chair. Thereupon he let out a bellow which must have startled any adjacent cows into assuming their rape was imminent. 'Goddam and bigod, I will not have that man in my presence!' he shouted. As if he were King!

This was indeed too much even for Henry. 'Forsooth and forsooth,' he remarked indicating to us all that he was enraged. 'I will decide who may or may not be in my presence, my lord Duke.'

Richard looked quite put out at this unexpected resistance, and it was some moments before he could speak. 'Your grace assured me that the Duke of Somerset was under arrest.'

'Why, that he is.'

'And yet he stands at your shoulder, your grace?'

'Where a man stands has nothing to do with whether or not he is under arrest,' Henry riposted. He loved debates of this nature, which had no point and certainly no possible outcome.

'You have tricked and deceived me, your grace,' York said, having regained control of himself. 'I will take my leave and consult with my associates.'

Henry looked at me for his next move. But I was now prepared to take over the situation personally. 'I do not think the King wishes you to leave, my lord Duke,' I said, in my most dulcet tones.

York glared at me – I was the only woman present – then at the King. 'What do you mean, your grace?' he inquired, loading his voice with all the menace he could.

'His grace means, dear cousin,' I informed him, 'that as you are here, it were best you remain, until the various matters at issue have been resolved, and you have renewed your oath of allegiance. You need have no fear for your safety. If you will look outside the door of this tent, you will observe that we are entirely surrounded by armed guards, and that your escort is being most hospitably entertained.'

If looks could kill I would have dropped dead on the spot. But then, if I had had my way, Cousin Richard would have preceded me. How would history have been changed!

However, it was not to be. Richard and his adherents might openly flout the King's writ, drag his chief minister before a mock court, and cut off his head ... but the King would not thus out of hand execute a royal duke. In this regard, he was supported by Edmund. I had tossed, and lost.

But only the ultimate. York was forced to take a fresh oath of allegiance before he was permitted to return to his people. I have often wondered what he told them. Meanwhile, my actions had, as on that earlier occasion when I had freed Somerset, reminded Henry, however briefly, that he was the king, that he was a Plantagenet, and that men and women were supposed to tremble before his frown. I know that two principal causes have been produced for the catastrophe which overtook my husband the following year: the unexpected pregnancy of his wife, and the collapse of the English cause in France. I would suggest a third, and greater: this brief spell of acting the king, affecting a mind that was totally unfitted for such a task.

Be that as it may, the country suddenly woke up to the realisation that it did, actually, possess a king. Over Easter, Henry issued no fewer than a hundred and forty-four pardons. 'I am determined to end this factional disturbance,' he told me.

He then gave orders for our French affairs to be taken in hand. Calais, and those cities which still remained to us, were to have their fortifications overhauled and put into the best possible state of repair. Best of all, he persuaded my old admirer John Talbot, Earl of Shrewsbury – he who had given me one of my favourite books as a wedding present – to take the command.

Talbot was undoubtedly the finest soldier of his age, and had been so since the death of Bedford. However, he had been consistently set to one side by the ambitions of Suffolk, York and Somerset. He was now in his sixties, which is a great age to lead armies in the field from the back of a horse while wearing plate armour, and had spent the past couple of years as York's replacement in Ireland. Now he emerged from this semi-retirement to espouse our cause. We felt that all would be well.

These serious matters attended to, Henry set off on one of his grand tours of the country, intending to end the state of anarchy which prevailed. He began in Norfolk, then travelled down to the West Country, swung round Exeter and Bath up into the Welsh marches, then visited Hereford and Ludlow before returning to Kenilworth for a brief break.

But in October he was away again, to Stamford and Peterborough, before winding up at his beloved Cambridge.

I do not know what, if anything, he accomplished on this chevausée; I did not accompany him, although I did meet him at Kenilworth at the end of the summer. For me it was a very pleasant time, with my husband far away, Edmund close at hand, and our affairs at last, it seemed, in order.

Even from France the news was unfailingly good, as Talbot reconquered most of Guienne.

Apart from dear Edmund, and my continuing disappointment regarding the matter of an heir to the throne, the summer was mostly taken up with matrimonial affairs, two of which were to have an enormous bearing on the future. In the first place, before Henry ever set off on his travels, Edmund brought his niece Margaret Beaufort to court. Margaret was now nine years old. I would not describe her as a pretty child, in terms of looks, but as she was the heiress of our late cousin, John Beaufort, and thus to most of the estates of John of Gaunt, she was extremely pretty in every other possible way – looked at from the point of view of a prospective husband. I might have managed to have Edmund succeed to the title of Duke of Somerset, but I could not of course interfere with Cousin John's actual wealth, which was enormous, and which had passed intact to his only surviving child.

Now, since John's death, which had occurred in 1444, or eight years previously, when Margaret had been a babe in arms, she had been her uncle's ward. This meant that he had had the use of her income, although he could not touch her capital. This in turn had meant that Edmund had been, for the past eight years, a very wealthy man, if only in terms of cash flow. He now sought, in his newly restored power, to seal the matter once and for all. His purpose in producing Margaret was to obtain the King's permission to marry her to his own eldest son, also named Henry. Thus Henry Somerset would succeed immediately to his uncle's estates and wealth, and, in the course of time, to his father's title, and all the mighty Beaufort resources would be united in a single body.

The idea seemed eminently sensible to me, and I said so. Alas, in arousing my Henry to act the king, I had also aroused a stick to be laboured on my back. Henry had suddenly discovered all manner of ideas of his own.

Although no one would have supposed it, he had not been insensible to the various recurring financial crises within the royal household. And it may well be imagined that if from time to time the King and Queen went hungry, those who relied on the crumbs from the royal table went a good deal hungrier. This had taxed my husband particularly in regard to his half-brothers, whom he was sworn to support throughout their lives. It therefore occurred to him that a useful step in the direction of relieving all of our problems would be to marry Cousin Margaret to Edmund Tudor, who was now a well-formed but entirely penniless man of twenty-two, the same age as myself. Not only would this make Tudor into a very wealthy man, but as his loyalty to the throne was unquestioned, he would be a source of ready cash in the future in the class of the late Cardinal himself.

Well, what kings determine, lesser mortals need to accept. Edmund Beaufort was left to rue his decision to present the young lady at court before his Tudor namesake had already been wed, while Edmund Tudor at once stepped into the higher ranks of the nobility. To give him a title commensurate with his wealth, as the dukedom of Somerset was unavailable, Henry created him Earl of Richmond, while his younger brother Jasper was made Earl of Pembroke. My own feelings about this matter were naturally ambivalent. I desired nothing but the best for Somerset, but at the same time to have a half-brother-in-law who is as rich as Croesus is a very comforting feeling. Naturally neither I nor anyone else at that time had the slightest inkling of the remarkable effect this marriage would have upon the future, even if, as I write, the matter has not yet been resolved.

The second marriage in which I was interested that summer also had royal connotations, and was also to have the most profound effects on all of our lives, although these effects have already been brought to a conclusion, it would appear.

John, Duke of Bedford, my husband's late and great uncle, had been a lusty fellow, equally at home in a bed as on a battlefield. When his first wife had died, he had taken as his second the most beautiful woman in Europe. It must be understood that I am writing of a period when I had just been born, and was therefore not yet to be considered. The lady's name was Jacquetta of Luxembourg, and she was the daughter of Peter of Luxembourg, Count of St Pol. As I may have remarked before, what a remarkable wench is this thing called Fate! It will be remembered that this same Count of St Pol, in my infancy, had sought my hand for his son, and backed off because Papa's prospects had appeared to be in decline. Thus I could very easily have been Jacquetta's very youthful sister-in-law – she was some twenty years older than I.

The Duchess of Bedford had no doubt been very happy in her marriage, although as so often happens when one weds a statesman and soldier, the Duke had had very little time to warm her bed, and certainly could never find the time to impregnate her, thus being even less successful in this regard than his famous brother. But like his brother, as he died six years after the marriage, Jacquetta was left, as had been my Aunt Catherine, a young widow ... without even the solace of a son.

She followed the same path. Well, what young woman of spirit would not? But being the most beautiful woman in Europe, she had sought out not a mere clerk of her bedchamber, as Catherine had done, but the most handsome *man* in England, so it was said, a certain Sir Richard Woodville. And being slightly more aware of what she was about than Aunt Catherine, she had actually married the fellow.

This did not save her from a right royal roasting, or Sir Richard from a spell in the Tower, but as with Aunt Catherine and her Tudor paramour, she and he were forgiven, and allowed to retire into the country and spend the rest of their lives in obscurity. However, there are some people meant by fate to be obscure, and others who are unable to escape the glare of public hatred and adulation –

they are but two sides of the same coin – no matter how hard they try. Jacquetta and Richard certainly did not seek to return to fame and fortune. They busied themselves with loving each other, so successfully that in the course of time they begot no fewer than seven sons and six daughters – an amazing display of fecundity on the part of the Duchess which appeared to leave her entirely unmarked.

In this summer of 1452, Richard and Jacquetta's eldest child, a daughter, was fifteen years old, and therefore to be married. Now, when the handsomest man in the country marries the erstwhile most beautiful woman in Europe – even if she was by this time reduced to second place – the odds are that they will produce handsome children. This was certainly true of the Woodvilles. And of them all, this eldest girl was the pick. Her name was Elizabeth (or Isabelle as we would say in France) and I will confess that, having accepted an invitation to the nuptials, I had quite a pang when I first beheld the bride.

Surpassing beauty in a woman older than oneself may be accepted with equanimity, on the basis that she will be the first to wither. However, surpassing beauty in a woman seven years *younger* than oneself is no laughing matter.

Of course I very rapidly reflected that there was no cause for concern. Bella Woodville was tall for a woman, perhaps a shade too tall, where I am of a height which makes all men wish to cuddle me protectively. Bella had long, straight yellow hair, extremely attractive, and like silk to touch, but essentially passive in its nature; my wavy, tawny mane was the sort that always attracted a second glance, even in repose. Bella's features, although flawlessly shaped, were for that reason a trifle severe. No one could fault the straightness of her nose, but it was a shade long. No one could carp at the rosebud of a mouth, but it was a shade small. No one could criticise the shape of her chin, but it was somewhat pointed. The whole presented a more serious picture than my own up-turned delight, my wide mouth, my rounded chin. Bella's eyes were blue and cool. Mine were green and seething with emotion. When we became intimates, I discovered that she possessed a very good figure, but certainly at the age of fifteen she remained a slender girl, while at twenty-two I had already reached my voluptuous maturity.

The biggest difference between us, however, was in our characters. I was all eager passion. I am still, no matter what the vicissitudes of my life. Bella was withdrawn, almost quiescent. However, she was not weak. Indeed her single-mindedness, of which I was unaware at this time but which was concerned entirely with achieving wealth and power for herself and her family, was to carry her to the very heights, equal with myself, but also to scatter a few corpses on the way – not least from amongst her own siblings.

These remarkable changes of fortune lay in the future. For the moment I was only aware that here was a rather gorgeous, but also rather gormless, girl, distantly connected to the royal family, in the course of being married to a country gentleman named John Grey. He was the son of Lord Ferrers of Groby, and a man with absolutely no prospects of ever rising above his present station. Whereas I was the Queen, bestowing my gracious presence upon her nuptial feast. I was actually far more interested in her mother, of whom I had heard a great deal, and whom I was now meeting for the first time. Aunt Jacquetta – she was my aunt-in-law by her first marriage – seemed pleased at my attention, as they were all somewhat overcome at my decision to attend their little party. Thus I felt at my most generous, and in the course of conversation threw out the suggestion that once Bella had settled into married life, a place might be found for her at court, amongst my ladies. They were delighted, and accepted. What more could a young girl wish, or hope for, than a place at court under the auspices of the Queen herself? A great deal, apparently, if your name was Elizabeth Woodville. But of Bella's ambitions I then had no inkling.

*

I sometimes think that 1452 was my last happy year. Of course it is difficult to know when a year actually begins and ends. Is it truly as represented by the calendar? In this year I was happy, and my happiness overflowed into the following, briefly.

I will confess that I did not even shed more than the necessary tears when Archbishop Stafford died. If I have not mentioned his name very often in these notes, it is simply because there was not much to mention about him. He had anointed me at my coronation – with cold oil; he had signally failed to cope with Cade's rebellion; and in every other aspect he had proved to be of little value as either man or prelate. Now he was gone, and we were able to elevate the faithful Kemp in his place. This was a great source of comfort to me at least.

At Christmas we had money and merriment. The only fly in our ointment was the machinations of York, who was now busily spreading scurrilous rumours among the people of London. These scoundrels had never liked me, and they eagerly caught on to every calumny that could be spread about me; and there were a great number. Somerset was outraged, partly because of course the principal rumour was true and involved himself. But there was nothing he could do about it other than summon Parliament to meet at Reading, well away from the mob, where we could better control events. To Reading, therefore, we trooped at the beginning of March.

At that moment I was happier than ever before in my life: for the first time in my life I had missed a menstrual period!

The fateful coupling had undoubtedly taken place during the last week of January, when Henry was ill with some distemper or other and I was officially sleeping alone – and Somerset was residing in the palace following a meeting of the Council because the roads were too bad for him to return to his own home. We spent two or three glorious nights together, the longest we have ever achieved, but as we *had* spent nights together before without accomplishing anything (other than our mutual exhaustion) I saw no reason to assume anything would happen on this occasion. As I have mentioned, I was almost supposing that I did not have it in me to be a mother, which, when I regarded delivery machines like Jacquetta Woodville, made me want to spit.

But, there it was. I had menstruated immediately before Somerset had been forced to spend the night. Thus I was due again the third week in February. And nothing happened.

We were already on our way to Reading before the penny dropped. Or rather, before Bailly mentioned the matter to me. I wanted to shriek with joy, although of course, as Bailly was quick to point out, one swallow does not make a summer. On the other hand, just in case, it was necessary immediately to implement my contingency plan, which was to be followed, by, at worst, a premature delivery.

Henry had by now recovered from his cold, and on our arrival at Reading I immediately snuggled into his bed, telling him how much I had missed his warm comfort during his illness. He was pleased at this, but less so when I became carried away. I did actually succeed in my intentions, but it was a long, hard struggle. I am bound to say that, had anyone been there to witness it, the thought that such a perfunctory proceeding could possibly produce a pregnancy would have been laughed out of court. When one considers that throughout history it has been the lot of us weak and helpless women to be raped and pillaged by every itinerant soldier who has passed our way, I am sure it will not be argued that I was the most unfortunate of my sex, in that I possessed a husband who could not even mount his wife with any sense of satisfaction – to either of them.

However, on this occasion I was content, although now it was necessary to wait another couple of months before I could declare my condition. As if to celebrate my secret good news, Parliament – sufficiently packed by Somerset – was also in a high good humour, voted us lots of money, and was duly prorogued until November. York and the Nevilles did not even attend, and Edmund was in complete control.

It was thus in the fullest confidence that towards the end of May I approached the King and informed him that I was pregnant.

His reaction was disturbing. He merely stared at me for several minutes, so much so that I began to think he had not heard me. 'I am to bear your child, your grace,' I said, as winningly as I could. When one has to tell a lie of such proportions, it is best to leave no stone unturned.

He stretched out his hand to touch my cheek, and gave a sad smile. 'Oh, Meg,' he said. 'Dear, dear Meg. How much do you hope. You cannot be pregnant. We are not blest, you and I.'

Nor could I convince him that it was so. As a result no bells were rung, and the people were largely left in ignorance of my happy condition. I say largely, because of course a queen's pregnancy cannot be kept entirely secret, especially when there were so many people whose lives and prospects would be so dramatically altered should I bear a son. Somerset was like a dog with two tails, and it was all I could do to convince him that it was necessary his pleasure should be for the King and the house of Lancaster rather than for the babe and its mother. I very much fear his untoward behaviour did not go unnoticed.

I can only surmise the effect my news had on the York household when it reached Sandal Castle. Cousin Richard naturally chose to ignore it, as there had been no official announcement. Proud Cis was more concerned. Undoubtedly she was counting the months until she should be queen, and the thought that she might be pipped at the post was too much for her to bear. She hastened to pay a visit to town, for a reason totally unconnected with myself, or so she claimed. But of course, being in the vicinity of Westminster – whither we had returned – felt courtesy demanded she call on the Queen.

We were now well into June, and although, as I was only supposed to be some four months gone, I was wearing a voluminous skirt, her practised eye – she had recently given birth herself to a son named Richard, who was to become that despicable fellow Gloucester – understood at a glance that this was no rumour.

'Your grace is blessed,' she remarked, and departed.

It was a triumph I should have savoured, but suddenly I found myself surrounded by catastrophe.

It had really begun, although I had not been fully aware of it, with Archbishop Stafford's death. Henry had already experienced the death of an Archbishop of Canterbury, Stafford's predecessor Chicheley, back in 1443. I had not known the King then, of course, but from all accounts he had been sorely troubled, and had had to be reassured by Cardinal Beaufort that Chicheley's demise was in no way a reflection upon him. Kemp now did his best with this new situation, but in ten years Henry had become even more given to melancholia.

This single blow he might have overcome. But now, early in this month, news was received of the capture of Constantinople by the Turks. This event had long been supposed likely, and indeed the hapless Byzantine emperors, as they persisted in calling themselves even when their 'empire' had shrunk to the size of an English county, had sent numberless embassies to the west imploring our aid against the heathen foe. Unfortunately, to any proper Christian, the Byzantines with their peculiar notions of religion were every bit as heathen as the worshippers of Mahomet, and little help had been forthcoming.

Yet campaigning in those faraway and overheated lands was in the Plantagenet blood. Richard the Lionheart had spent a fortune careering the length and breadth of Palestine; Edward I had been on a crusade when he learned he had become King of England; and more recently important than either, Henry Bolingbroke, following his exile from England, had taken himself to Constantinople to fight the Turk, from whence he had returned full of martial vigour, and experience – and disease – to claim the crown. Indeed, there were not lacking those to say that had Henry V taken his military genius and his Welsh archers to the Balkans instead of Agincourt, he would have done Christianity a service far preferable to the prolongation of a dynastic squabble.

These things lay heavy on a mind so given to religious reflection as my Henry's. He was no soldier himself, but had he possessed the resources I have no doubt he would have funded an army for the relief of the Byzantines. He had lacked the money, and now it was too late. He brooded, and could not help but connect this general Christian disaster with our own recent bereavement. He brooded even more when, like Proud Cis, he could no longer deny the evidence of his own eyes. I was most certainly pregnant, presumably by his unenthusiastic thrusts. Thus he was to be a father. I have never been sure which of these two aspects of the situation affected him more. But they both certainly affected him.

Now, in the middle of July, came a crowning blow. Our affairs in France had appeared to be on the way to recovery, thanks to the efforts of Talbot. But on 17 July, at Castellon, Talbot met with a shattering defeat. He himself was killed, his army fled every which way, and English rule collapsed. By the end of the month, after more than a hundred years of virtually unremitting conflict, the English determination to conquer France had left them with possession of a single seaport: Calais.

People whispered the news in the street, afraid to utter the dread words aloud. Henry V and Bedford, Edward III and the Black Prince: those mighty warriors had spent their entire lives and considerable talents in pursuit of the single goal, and now it was ended.

The English do not like losing wars. Actually, few people do, but some are forced to become conditioned to it by circumstance. The English had become accustomed to winning.

These repeated blows – Stafford's death, Constantinople, my pregnancy, and now this crowning disaster in France –

undoubtedly had a serious effect upon Henry's fragile mind, especially, coming as they did, after a year in which he had exercised the royal power to its fullest extent for the first time in his reign. I know I am not alone in feeling that he did so very successfully. But Henry, always given to self-doubts, now began to consider whether his self-assertion might not have been an affront to God, and thus had induced these calamities. Whatever the truth of the matter, we had the greatest calamity of all on 10 August. On that day the King lost his senses.

I know in many cases what I have just stated is an euphemism for madness. But I mean it in its most literal sense.

Since my pregnancy, Henry and I had not slept together. He regarded it as against God's will to have sexual relations with a pregnant woman. I held no very strong views on that score, but I was entirely concerned with making sure my babe remained healthy and anxious only to be born. Thus I had a chamber to myself, and was awakened early on this morning by Wenlock, who was with difficulty restraining several gentlemen of the bedchamber from clustering about my bed. 'Your grace!' my faithful chamberlain stammered. 'Your grace! The King ...!'

I will confess my first thought was that Henry had expired, and my mind immediately ranged over all the possibilities and inconveniences that would follow, but I was also getting out of bed as rapidly as I could while Bailly hurriedly wrapped my swollen nakedness in an undressing robe. In this extreme state of *déshabillé* I hurried to the King's apartment, accompanied by his gentlemen as well as Wenlock and Bailly, and there, at first glance, assumed my worst fears proved correct. Henry lay upon his back, absolutely motionless, staring at the ceiling.

Then I realised that the King was actually breathing, though slowly and stertorously. I looked at the gentlemen. 'His grace will not move,' one of them said.

'His grace *cannot* move,' said another.

This seemed to me to be absurd. I stood beside my lord, and said, 'Will you not bid me good morning, your grace?' There was not a flicker of response. He is playing some game, I decided. 'Will you not attend your devotions today, your grace?' I inquired, a trifle sharply.

Still not a movement. 'He cannot move,' repeated the gentleman who had earlier made this point.

'His eyes are open,' I again snapped, well on the way to losing my temper. I bent over him. 'Henry. It is I, Margaret, your own sweet Meg. Will you not speak to me?'

Still no response. I became aware that while he might choose not to move, or be unable to do so, his bodily functions had not ceased during the night. He sadly needed attending to.

I straightened. 'See to your master,' I commanded. 'And Wenlock, summon the Council.'

The good lords came hurrying. But I had made sure Edmund arrived first. He accompanied me to Henry's chamber. The King had by now had his linen changed and the room was somewhat more salubrious than earlier. But he remained as I had left him, utterly immobile, staring at the ceiling.

'It is a seizure,' Edmund declared.

Which was no more than what the physicians had told me. 'He is certainly incapable of transacting business,' I agreed.

Edmund stroked his chin. 'Which means . . .'

'That someone needs to transact it for him.'

'A regency,' he muttered. 'The last time there was a regency was difficult. Duke Humphrey was regent in England, Duke John in France—'

'And the good Cardinal stood between them to keep the peace. But times have changed, Edmund. There are no royal uncles, today. There is no France to be ruled. There are only cousins. And a wife.' He gulped. 'It must be me, Edmund,' I said. 'Or it will be York. And I need not tell you what that would mean. For us both.'

He gulped again. 'They would not make Queen Catherine regent.'

'You are our chief minister, Edmund. You must see to it.' He gulped again and hurried off, while I was filled with every manner of foreboding – and with reason. It truly is an unjust world where we women are forced to rely on men, in so many cases weaker vessels than ourselves, to accomplish what we know to be necessary. Edmund, for all his good looks and dashing appearance, his Plantagenet heritage and his undoubted love for me, was about the weakest vessel going.

Naturally, at the news of the King's unhappy situation the Lords and the Commons flocked to Westminster, and before we knew it Parliament was assembled, despite being pro-rogued. Edmund explained the situation to them, and proposed that I should be made regent for the King, in the name of my as yet unborn child. This was what I had instructed him to do. I had *not* instructed him to follow his remarks with the admission that his proposal was unique, and only to be recommended by circumstances. The Lords bayed at him like wolves, while the Commons hummed with hostility.

I have never been absolutely sure in my mind whether the tide ran against me (as either a woman or a *French* woman), or against the certainty that should I be made regent, Somerset would have been continued in office. He undoubt-edly would have been, although had I been made Queen Regent I would certainly have taken a much more positive role in the government.

Perhaps this is what they feared most of all.

Whatever the reason, our bid failed, although we managed to achieve a compromise. Thanks to the efforts of our faithful Archbishop Kemp, it was decided to leave matters in abeyance for the next few months in the hope that Henry might recover. The Lords did not like this, Richard and his adherents least of all, but no one was prepared to oppose the Archbishop; nor could anyone pretend that the government would suffer because of Henry's incapacity. For my part, I was happy to see the decision left until I was again in full possession of myself – and perhaps an heir to the throne as well.

I must admit that I was agreeably surprised that Cousin Richard did not make more of a fuss at the time, or claim more than he did. He pleaded illness, and did not even come to Westminster. This was a great relief to us, but we should have known better; he was merely laying his plans.

Meanwhile, every effort was made to bring Henry back to life, as it were. I am bound to confess that I found the situation very alarming. I knew, of course, that Henry's maternal grandfather had been mad, and that there was, indeed, a strain of madness running through the entire Valois family. Happily, we of Anjou were a collateral branch.

The important point was, however, that from what I had been told of Charles VI, his madness had revealed itself as nothing more than the occasional odd behaviour, until one day, quite well on in his reign, a wild woman had seized the bridle of his horse and told him he was about to be assassinated. Presumably she too was mad. In any event, the effect on the King was dramatic; he seized his sword and started laying about himself with shrieks of rage. This was perfectly understandable. But then for the rest of his life, even after the witch's prognostication had proved false, he had been given to these maniacal outbursts when no one within reach – even his wife – was safe from bodily harm.

Not of course that the fair Isabeau was often within reach. She spent most of her time in remote castles teaching young squires the arts of love; and I am not speaking of writing poetry, either.

Again, while Uncle Charlie was also decidedly odd on occasions, he had never actually resorted to swiping people with a sword. In view of his lechery one is forced to conclude that he inherited more from his mother than his father. Of Cousin Louis I prefer not to speak at all, although

I shall have much to *tell* in due course.

But in no case had any of this apparently hereditary madness manifested itself in a total collapse of body and mind, although it is true that when affected, Charles VI did not (or more likely, refused to) recognise his queen. Presumably there are parts of the mind and body which function even when one is asleep, or one would die every night. These alone were keeping Henry alive. For the rest, he would not speak, and he did not appear to hear or see. He was incapable of the slightest movement, and had to be fed like a small baby for whom no breast is available. His bowel movements appeared uncontrolled. All in all, he was a pretty unpleasant prospect.

But his symptoms, I repeat, bore no relation to any I knew of in the family. However, he was the King; and every effort had to be made to restore him to his proper self. Some of these methods were distinctly nasty, as the surgeons varied in their hypotheses between attempting to shock him out of his stupor, by means of such things as pins being suddenly thrust into his buttocks or buckets of ice-cold water being thrown over him, or regarding him as what he appeared, a new-born babe, which necessitated that he be clucked at like a hen and called all manner of stomach-turning names. None of these so-called cures had the slightest effect.

I could do little either to help or hinder this process. Had I been in full possession of my health and strength I might well have tried the power of sexual persuasion, however distasteful this would have been. But at the time my only concern was my babe. That autumn was the longest I ever spent, but at last, on 13 October, I was brought to my bed. My ladies fussed about me, there was a great to-doing, but I took it all in my stride, as it were: this was the moment I had been waiting for all my life. And there I was at last, with a bouncing baby boy tugging at my tits.

The Lords were summoned immediately, as summoning the King would have been a waste of time. Now I wished York could have been present, just to see his face. But it was almost as gratifying to witness the adulation of those who *were* present. That the baby was a Plantagenet could not be doubted, from the pale blue of his eyes to the reddish gold of his hair. Of course this first hair all disappeared fairly shortly, but it was replaced by locks of a similar colour. That the Duke of Somerset had such hair was no cause for comment; so did his cousin, the King.

Now the King was first in my mind, but I would not let my son be shown to him until I could be present. This I was able to accomplish two days later when, accompanied by my ladies, Somerset, Buckingham and Archbishop Kemp, I attended the King's bedchamber.

The occasion was a sore disappointment. Henry remained immobile, even when I placed the babe in his arms. 'What is to be done?' I asked the Archbishop, tears in my eyes.

'We must pray, your grace.'

I have commented on the difficulties of relying on prayer. In fact, I dared not, in view of the manner in which I had achieved my triumph. I had to face the world as the proud mother of the next King of England, which I did, I think successfully. I determined to call my son Edward. There had been three Henrys on the trot, and the line seemed to have declined. I thought of Edward III and his son, Edward the Black Prince. There were names to conjure with.

Besides, York's eldest son was named Edward. My Edward would far outdo that lamentable youth, I was determined. Well, perhaps he would have, given time.

Meanwhile, we continued in the grip of a constitutional crisis. For Christmas, I had Henry removed to his favourite surroundings, those of Windsor Castle, still in the hopes of restoring his mind. But he showed no interest, not even in the uncomfortable journey. It was plain that the nettle had to be grasped, especially as ghastly lampoons were beginning to appear in the streets of London, suggesting that their future king was a bastard! I would have had the perpetrators sought out and boiled in oil, but Somerset, no doubt bowed down by his own guilt, hesitated. I thus persuaded him to issue writs for the summoning of Parliament, and formally to place before them my application to be regent for the kingdom in the name of my son, until the recovery of their King.

The Lords and Commons duly assembled. I may say that with Buckingham, who was now one of my most fervent supporters (having followed the fashion of all those men with whom I was thrown into intimate contact of falling in love with me) I more than once during this period presented Edward to his legal father, but without the least success. However, Edward was undoubtedly heir to the throne, and Archbishop Kemp assured me that he had every hope of success. Indeed, the Archbishop harangued the assembly and put my case most forcibly. Listening from the gallery I was delighted, and felt as confident as himself.

I also could not help but notice, however, that our old friend was old indeed, and appeared unwell. The next day he was dead. Obviously, as I have had occasion to remark before, old men do die; it is perhaps what they are best at doing. But the occasion was so inconvenient as to raise in my mind at least the consideration that he might have been assisted on his journey to his Maker.

Not that there was anything I could do about it. Once Kemp had breathed his last, matters hurried onwards, and away from me. The very next day a deputation of the Lords, headed by Cousin Richard, insisted on seeing the King. Their ostensible purpose was to obtain his decision in the matter of the new Archbishop, but obviously they were intent upon satisfying themselves as to his true condition. I was not allowed to be present but apparently they formed some fairly definitive conclusions, for the *next* day, Richard was appointed Protector of the Realm.

Before I had had the time to digest this calamity, Richard himself arrived, supported by his in-laws in great numbers. They were by no means rude. Why should they be, when all had fallen into their laps? Richard even attended me, privily, on bended knee. 'Your grace will surely understand,' he explained, 'that in the most troubled times, there is no woman in the world, not even one with your undoubted talents, could seek to rule this realm. Believe me, I would yield to you in all things, but as the acknowledged heir to the throne I feel obliged to discharge my responsibilities to our subjects.'

'Sweet cousin,' I told him, 'your words are like balm to my troubled spirit. However, I feel obliged to correct you in one small point. The heir to the throne lies here.' And I pointed to the crib beside my chair.

'Your grace,' the rascal said, 'I wish you and your child joy. However, let us be honest. The prince will not be fit to rule this realm for at least another sixteen years. Happily, at some time much sooner, he will be pronounced king, if the country will have it. At that time, I will step aside as heir. But he will still need a regency for those very many years, and I may claim without dissembling that there is no man in this land more capable of discharging that duty than I.'

Naturally I noted that he referred to the prince as *my* son, and had thrown in the remark 'if the country wills it' regarding Edward's succession. Yet his fine words faced me with a problem. Because what he was saying was the absolute truth. As to whether the most suitable *man* in the kingdom was a better choice than the most suitable *woman* was entirely another matter. In any event, again there was nothing I could do. Somerset had no party. York's party consisted of eighty-five per cent of the Lords and hardly less of the Commons. Buckingham might shake his head and gnaw his lip, but he was not about to oppose his cousin, Richard of York. While I, who would have opposed him with every bone in my body, was enduring the second most debilitating of feminine circumstances in that I was feeding my child.

Thus it seemed that I was left entirely at the mercy of my bitterest foe. Not to mention his wife!

*

Now I am sure I have left no one who may peruse these words – should anyone ever, which God forbid – in any doubt as to my feelings for Richard of York. And yet honesty commands me to say that not only was he the only *man* in England suited to rule, which he immediately and amply demonstrated, but that, having obtained supreme power, and being supported by the vast majority of both Lords and Commons, he was in a position of authority actually known to no man since Great Harry's death. And he did not abuse that power.

He possessed an undoubted right to the throne. When one considers his sons (and even more than Edward of March, that mean, snivelling boy Richard of Gloucester, who likes it put abroad that he is a poor deformed creature when everyone who knows him acknowledges that he is as fit as a horse and as strong as one too, and who has stooped at nothing to achieve his ends – and will probably go on doing so in the name of his lecherous brother) one cannot help but be astonished that dear Henry had another nineteen – albeit mostly unhappy – years to live, or that I am alive today to pen these lines.

But at this time Richard of Gloucester was still dandled on Proud Cis's knee, and York was scrupulous in preserving the niceties of his position. He visited the King to acquaint him with what measures his government was undertaking – a futile exercise as Henry continued to stare vacantly at the ceiling – and greeted me on bended knee. True, he immediately dismissed Somerset from all his positions and sent him to the Tower. But this was only to be expected. I at least made sure that there was this time to be no question of any charges of treason or possible executions, even if I had to acquiesce in dear Edmund being imprisoned. This was, York explained, for his own protection, and I could see his point.

It is equally true that York had his own nominee made Archbishop of Canterbury, but here again it was difficult to carp; the man in question was yet another royal cousin. His name was Thomas Bourchier, and he is – for he is still alive, and still Archbishop, although past eighty years of age! – the third son of William Bourchier, Earl of Ewe, by Lady Anne Plantagenet, daughter of Thomas of Woodstock, Edward III's youngest son, which made him a first cousin of Buckingham, and in varying degrees a cousin of all the rest of us. He was a learned and devout cleric, at this time just past fifty, already Bishop of Worcester. I had no doubt at all that there were many more deserving prelates in the land. Nor could I doubt that Cousin Richard had chosen him because he was sure of his support. But Richard was a most consummate politician. In choosing Bourchier, he was also sure of Buckingham's support; and as Buckingham, in turn, was one of *my* principal supporters, I could do nothing but acquiesce.

These important matters determined, Richard proceeded to rule with great vigour. Our exchequer was too bare to permit him to undertake any adventures in France, but I do not believe he would have risked them in any event, as it would have necessitated him leaving England and the King – and me. But the country was restored to order, and became a happy place. No one can accuse me of being ungenerous to my foe, although I was not blind to the true situation. Cousin Richard was not governing England well for the sake of Henry; he was governing it well for the sake of the next king, and he fondly supposed that was going to be himself. Obviously this possibility hovered above us day and night, for a man who cannot move, and appears dead in all but his ability to breathe, digest and defecate, can be expected to cease doing those things at any moment.

What would happen then no one about me wished to consider. York had denounced the lampoons regarding Prince Edward's birth, but there could be no doubt he believed them. Therefore, in his eyes, he remained the rightful heir. Should Henry die, would he declare himself king? Or would he accept the regency for Edward? In either event, it would be in his interest to see that my son never reached an age to assume the government. Long before then he would either have to die, or be proved a bastard. And in either of *those* possibilities my own life was irrevocably concerned.

It will be seen therefore that this was not a happy period for me. Somerset, who I knew would fight for me, was in the Tower. Buckingham, who I now also knew would fight for me, was at large. But neither of these royal dukes, or even the pair of them combined, could possibly be considered a match for Richard of York, supported as he was by the Nevilles. I had to discover a strength equal to theirs, and for the time being I had no idea where to turn. I thus took refuge in the passage of time, in the hopes that some youthful paragon might arise to be my champion – both Somerset and Buckingham had sons, and Henry Beaufort at the least was at once handsome and strong and gave considerable evidence of military talent . . . but he remained very young.

My apparent supinity in the face of this complete overturn of my fortunes was made the easier by several factors. One was of course York's forebearance; I was in no way restrained, I was always treated with the greatest respect, even by Proud Cis, and best of all, my finances took a decided turn for the better. As York was an adept at collecting taxes, for the first time since my marriage my jointure was paid in full for the year.

Then there was my position as a young mother, than which, I can assure you, there is no happier situation. Of course I understand that the early days in a child's life are fraught with dangers, that only one in three of these precious morsels of humanity ever attains the age of ten, much less adulthood, and that mothers are therefore often left anxious, brooding creatures. But at that moment I was blest. Edward was the healthiest, sunniest babe that could be imagined. This was even a cause for alarm, as such a characteristic was so blatantly more in keeping with Edmund's temperament than Henry's. But no one commented and I was delighted as I watched him grow, and envisioned the future when, clad in plate armour and with my banner flying above his head, he would lead his armies into battle.

There was, however – dare I say it? And why not, as I am saying everything else – a third cause for my contentment that summer.

It may be recalled that two years previously, on the occasion of the marriage of Elizabeth Woodville to John Grey, I had carelessly thrown out the suggestion that the gorgeous young woman might, in the course of time, become one of my ladies. She and her mother had been delighted at the idea; but nothing had immediately come of it, as within two months of her wedding Bella was pregnant. Well, what would you expect where so lovely a creature was concerned, and where she was actually fortunate enough to be married to a man rather than a monk?

She retired to the country, gave birth to a bonny boy, and within another two months was pregnant again. These exciting events occupied her for a full two years. However, in the spring of this year of 1454, when I was torn between care and fear for my child, and frustration at being refused the regency for my husband, Jacquetta appeared at Westminster with her daughter, and intimated that they would like to take up my offer.

I understood at once that although Jacquetta herself was still delivering children with almost monotonous regularity, she feared for the health of her daughter should Bella continue to be assaulted, the very moment her womb was clear, by the impetuous member of her lusting husband. I say I understood, even if I did *not* understand why any woman should actually fear this, having had so little of it myself. It should be remembered that what with my pregnancy, and the fact that it ended in the midst of a constitutional crisis, which had only been resolved by dear Edmund's incarceration, I had been totally exempt from anything which might be called true solace since my unsatisfactory set-to with Henry the previous March. This is a long time for any woman, particularly for one with red as well as blue blood in her veins.

Yet I was very disposed to take Bella into my company. She was young, and the rest of my ladies were growing older. She was intelligent as well as beautiful. She appeared to wish only to please me. And she had two little boys: one slightly older, the other slightly younger, than my own dear Edward. I envisaged them as permanent playmates, true paladins who would grow to splendid manhood together.

Bella was a delight. Within a few days of her arrival I had ousted poor old Bailly from her duty of sleeping with me – she snored most terribly – and replaced her with my young friend. I do not propose to enter into our relationship in any detail, save to observe that when two women love it is on an altogether more noble plane than anything that can be accomplished by men, without in any way suffering in sensuality. In this regard I use the word love in its profane sense. Bella did not love me spiritually; to her I was a stepping-stone to better things. I did not love Bella spiritually; to me she was a comfort at a time of trial and deprivation. I wanted, and she was not prepared to resist the embrace of a queen.

But we could each appreciate the other's beauty, even if, both being very young – I was only twenty-four and Bella seventeen – our desires were limited. More importantly, we were friends. Or so at least I thought. I can hardly be blamed if nowadays I regard friendship as a very uncertain quality.

By such means I passed that long and dismal summer, and saw the leaves falling. Together with my ladies I celebrated a very sober Christmas, and sent a message of good cheer to Edmund in his unnatural quarters. I prayed, but with very little hope of my prayers being answered – until they were, in a most miraculous fashion.

On 27 December, Wenlock entered my chamber. I was on my hands and knees on the floor, with Bella, playing with the little boys, but one look at his face told me I should not be annoyed at the interruption. 'Your grace,' he said. 'This day his grace has sent offerings to the cathedral here in

Westminster. As well as to Canterbury.'

I stared at him, for some moments unable to comprehend. Bella clapped her hands.

We packed immediately and made our way to Windsor. Trembling, I entered the King's bedchamber, Edward in my arms.

Henry was sitting up in bed, his attendants beside him as well as several priests. 'Why, Meg,' he said, 'how well you look.'

'Your grace.' I stood beside him, and held out the child. 'Our son, Prince Edward.'

'Forsooth and forsooth,' Henry commented.

'He looks just like his father, your grace,' Bella said. She had accompanied me, of course; we were inseparable. Just what she meant, I did not care to consider at that moment. Henry interpreted it in the best possible way.

'He has my eyes,' he said.

'Will you hold your son, your grace?' I asked.

'Oh, willingly, madam.' He cuddled the little boy. 'We are indeed blest.'

It was 30 December, and suddenly all was well with the world. It never was again.

8

As may be imagined, we took immediate steps to have the news of the King's recovery proclaimed to the land.

Our first move was to call upon Bishop Wayneflete and the Prior of St John's to visit Henry and determine his sanity. This they did, announcing that they could find nothing whatsoever the matter with him.

As a matter of fact, Henry's illness was quite the most remarkable thing of which I ever heard. He had absolutely no recollection of anything that had happened, or had been done to him, since the August of 1453, and this despite the fact that the marks of some of the attempted 'cures' were still visible on his body. Despite our efforts to keep him fed, he was weak from lack of nourishment, and for several weeks, he was quite unable to walk more than a few steps, from having lain in his bed for so long; but these understandable weaknesses and a variety of bedsores apart, there was no sign of any ill-health.

The priests being satisfied, the Lords were summoned, and whatever the chagrin most of them must have been feeling, they too were forced to admit that the King was in full possession of his faculties. Meanwhile, I had been very busy having Wenlock prepare all manner of documents for his grace to sign the very moment he could hold a pen. Indeed, it was necessary for me to hold his hand and guide the pen, for I regarded time as of the essence.

The four main decrees issued by the King were the ending of York's Protectorate, the removal of Bourchier from the chancellorship – not even I could remove him from the archbishopric – the release of Somerset from the Tower, and, most important of all, the elevation of Prince Edward to be Prince of Wales, which established not only his paternity, but also the fact that he was the next King of England. York was clearly unhappy with the situation. He could not argue the point, but he looked from the chair in which Henry was sitting propped up with cushions, to the chair in which I was sitting, Prince Edward on my knee, his eyes stern as steel; he had no doubts who had actually issued the command ending his power. But there it was, he had to go; and off he went, leaving Windsor to travel north to Yorkshire, where he had his castle of Sandal. With him went the Nevilles, no less unhappy with the change in their fortunes.

Back to Westminster came Somerset. He visited the King on bended knee, gave thanks for his recovery, and soon enough found an opportunity to be alone with me and fold me in his arms. 'Oh, Meg, Meg,' he whispered, kissing my neck and ear, while his hands did all manner of delightful things inside my undressing robe. 'I had all but despaired.'

'Never despair, Edmund,' I told him. 'But ... this situation may arise again.' He pulled his head back in consternation, his cheeks ashen. 'Where no one knows the cause of an illness, or can even establish the symptoms,' I pointed out, 'no one can possibly produce a cure. It is unlikely that Henry is going to gain any additional mental strength as the years go by.'

'Then what is to be done?'

'That must be our first concern. Certain it is that we must be prepared to act in our own interests, should his grace show the least sign of a relapse.'

What exactly we should do, when there could be no doubt that Parliament would again confer the Protectorate upon

York should Henry's illness recur, was difficult to determine. My sole concern, of course, was to maintain myself until Prince Edward could be of an age to take up the reins of government. But I knew that no matter how precocious my son might turn out to be – and I had every intention of educating him to be the most precocious prince ever born, both in arms and politics – it would be a dozen years and more before he would be able to rule.

It therefore seemed to me that my best prospect was to create a party which would outweigh York's, and this promised to be difficult as he already had the heavy brigades on his side. But all things are possible, and I actually began to consider the odds on my seducing Richard of York's nephew, young Warwick, from the support of his father and uncle – even being prepared to use the word seduce in its most literal sense if I could feel certain of success – when events were entirely taken out of my hands, and the country was launched upon that perilous and destructive course which I pray to God is not yet done, whatever my own present fortunes.

We had survived another English winter and were enjoying the balmy breezes of spring, with Henry in good spirits and rapidly regaining his strength, and Edmund as usual issuing decrees of which no one took the slightest notice, when we received word that the Duke of York, accompanied by his Neville brothers-in-law, the Earls of Salisbury and Westmorland, as well as the Earl of Warwick, had finished cogitating about his situation and had raised an army, with the avowed intention of marching on London.

This disagreeable news caused much less anxiety than in 1452, simply because we had coped with the situation in 1452. However, I was well aware that York was unlikely to fall into a similar snare this time. What is more, as our information indicated that this time he was planning to approach more from the north than the west, keeping him out of London was going to be a more difficult matter. I had no doubt at all that the Londoners would rise in his support should he be allowed to enter the city. Henry recognised the differences in the situation as well as I, but most unusually he was full of aggressive intent and also revealed some sound common sense. Having summoned the royal army, he placed Buckingham in command rather than Somerset. 'I need you at my side, Cousin Edmund,' he said. 'For are you not my chief minister?'

Edmund of course was flattered; he did not seem to understand that even Henry, whose interest in military matters was minimal, had realised he was not fit to command an army.

The various musters due to be supplied by the royal magnates duly assembled until we had beneath our banner some two thousand men, while reports arrived every day of York's progress towards us. He had not got beyond Ludlow, however, when Somerset called upon me, most anxiously. 'There has been a message from York,' he muttered. 'Directed to Bourchier, but intercepted by my people. He swears his allegiance to the King, and asks only that I be set aside, when he will disband his force.'

'That is exactly what he proclaimed in 1452.'

'Indeed. But this time he wishes proof of my arrest before he will parley with the King.'

'Has Henry seen this?' I asked.

'Not yet. The messenger was brought directly to me.'

I considered. But I felt it was time to settle this matter once and for all. The King was the King. If York raised his hand against him, all the country, all the world, would have to know that he was a traitor rebel. 'I think we should burn that letter, cousin,' I said. 'And give Richard sufficient rope with which to hang himself.'

Some people may suppose I made a mistake. I had no doubt at all of my purpose. But foolishly I underestimated not the enemy, but the absurd points of view of my dearest friends and indeed lovers. I entirely agreed with Buckingham, all martial ardour now he was commander-in-chief of the royal array, that we should move our forces north of

London to Watford, which sits astride the great Roman road
called Watling Street. Watling Street leads all the way to
Chester, and was the only practical route for an army of any
size to take if it would approach the capital from the north
with any haste. Here we could array ourselves in the best
possible position, and leave it to the rebels to make the first
move.

This decision was taken, and I hurried off to prepare
myself and to send Prince Edward to a place of safety.
Imagine my chagrin when Buckingham and Somerset came
behind me, and informed me that it was the King's wish that
I also should retreat to a position of safety until the business
was decided. 'That is nonsense,' I declared. 'My place is
with the King.'

'It is the King's express wish, your grace,' Somerset said,
and added in a lower tone, 'and my own most devout
request, dearest Meg. We will all be the more certain of
success if we know no harm can come to your own sweet
person.'

Weak vessel that I am, I agreed, having made both
Somerset and Buckingham swear that they would do nothing
rash, but also that they would allow York no advantage in
any conference. I then retired with Prince Edward and my
principal ladies to Greenwich to await the outcome of the
approaching crisis.

What I am to relate, therefore, comes at second hand. But
it is as my faithful Wenlock, sent as my representative, told
me. And a sadly mismanaged affair it was to turn out to be
in my absence.

All began well. The royal army reached Watford on the
afternoon of 21 May and there encamped, while scouts were
sent out to discover the whereabouts of the rebels. But York
had also employed scouts and spies; indeed, he sent a fresh
envoy to avow his loyalty and demand only that Somerset be
tried for his misdeeds – chief among which, of course, was
misconduct with the Queen. Henry, I am happy to say,

refused to countenance such a suggestion, and for once lost his temper, swearing that he would give up his crown rather than surrender Somerset – which would have been to acknowledge the said misconduct. Dear Henry, I am happy to say, never once suspected me of betraying his bed. Sadly, I cannot claim this was because of an excessive trust in me. As Henry found sexual matters quite distasteful, and forced upon reluctant manhood by the marriage vows, he was quite incapable of imagining any man, or woman for that matter, wishing to indulge in amatory discourse *outside* of marriage.

In any event, his outrage left Cousin Richard with no alternative other than to continue his rebellion, for to back down would have brought *him* to the block soon enough: I would have seen to that. So far so good. But Richard's envoys had naturally reconnoitred the King's arrangements while delivering their message, and upon learning that Henry was blocking his most direct route south in a strong position, Richard turned his host aside, intending to bypass his King and gain London before he could be stopped.

Word of this manoeuvre being brought to Buckingham, he made the, in my opinion, dubious decision to continue to attempt to block his enemy's path, and on the morning of 22 May left Watford to march the seven-odd miles to the town of St Albans, through which passed the only other practical road to the capital. I say the decision was dubious for two reasons: firstly, the two armies were too close for so sudden a manoeuvre; and secondly, unlike Watford, St Albans is virtually an open town, difficult to defend. It would have been far better to hover on York's flank, and force him to battle at a disadvantage.

However Buckingham was haunted by the very real fear that Cousin Richard would somehow escape him and reach the safety of London, and I must admit that, having decided on his strategy, Cousin Humphrey seems to have acted with a great deal of energy. His people, accompanied by the King, who still appeared eager to confront the rebels, left Watford soon after midnight, and by the most strenuous efforts gained St Albans by eight o'clock in the morning. There they immediately set to work to put up what fortifications they could, having learned that the rebel army was somewhat larger than the royal and that it would be necessary to stand on the defensive. But it was too late. The preparations were incomplete when the Yorkists hove in view, taking up a position on a ground known as the Key Field. From here they once again attempted a parley, but Buckingham refused to treat with them, and at ten o'clock Cousin Richard took the momentous step of commanding his forces to assault the royal position.

Cousin Humphrey, as I have said, had thus far acted with the greatest of energy. Having marched for several hours he had put his men to work, and they had blocked with a palisade both the roads into St Albans. There had been no time to do more, but from behind these palisades they awaited the Yorkist onslaught with equanimity. It was here that Humphrey's lack of real talent as a general revealed itself. Having blocked the two roads, he assumed the battle could be left to take care of itself; he made no effort to adopt any other defensive measures, or to consider the possibility of a counter-attack at an advantageous moment. Very probably this moment would never have occurred, as the royal troops were definitely outnumbered, but had the town been adequately defended there is no reason why they should not have repulsed the Yorkists time and again, despite the fact that Cousin Richard had with him several of those infernal bombards called cannon. It is my experience that rebel soldiers, when they do not immediately gain the day, are more likely to lose heart than those fighting for the right.

But the town was not adequately defended. Where the royal troops were situated, all went well. Unfortunately, between the two roads there was an open space – guarded it is true by a wall – but not by any soldiers. It was because of this fortuitous space that young Warwick gained an entirely spurious reputation as a general. His body of men was forced into it by the sheer weight of numbers to either side, busily attacking the two roads. It may even be that Warwick, who I can say from personal experience was not the bravest man in the world when it came to physical danger, was happy to lead his men against a non-existent foe, waving his broadsword and bellowing 'A-Warwick!' at the top of his lungs as was his wont.

Having thus absented themselves from all danger, his men found themselves in a vacuum, as it were, confronted only by this not very high wall. They could not go back without revealing their cowardice; to go to either side would be to join in the fracas; just to sit and wait for the outcome of the battle would have earned them no credit ... so they went forward and scrambled over the wall, taking their Earl with them – in no very dignified manner, I suppose, as heaving someone wearing plate armour over even a low wall is a clanking, wearying business.

Once over the wall, they passed through a few deserted back yards – the good citizens of St Albans had prudently either fled the town or locked themselves in their cellars – and then found themselves on St Peter's Street, the main thoroughfare through the town. They were now, of course, behind both bodies of defenders.

As may be supposed, this splendid if inadvertent coup gained the day. No soldier likes to find his enemy appearing behind him where he thought himself safe; it is a most disturbing sensation. The royal troops fled every way, and with them, I am sorry to say, went several of their commanders (including that useless Irishman James Butler, Earl of Ormonde and Wiltshire, who threw his armour into a ditch the better to aid his escape).

Not all the royalists ran away. Buckingham's son Humphrey, the fine, upstanding youth I had noticed making sheep's eyes at me after my coronation, died fighting, as did the son of the famous Hotspur, Henry Percy, Earl of Northumberland, and his nephew, Lord Clifford, the son of

Hotspur's daughter. Buckingham himself was taken prisoner when trying to rally his beaten forces.

And Edmund, dear, dear Edmund? He died as only such a muddled character could have contrived to do. Many years earlier, as I have recounted, he had been told by a fortune-teller to beware of castles. He had survived two terms of imprisonment in the Tower and might have been supposed to have discounted the prophecy; in any event, there was no castle in St Albans, or indeed in its neighbourhood, to concern him. But having fought most gallantly – he may not have had much military talent but always a good deal of courage – he and a devoted band were carrying out an embattled retreat when they paused for breath, and perhaps a hasty gulp of ale, for they were outside an inn. Unfortunately, at this moment Edmund looked up, and discovered that the inn was called the Castle. At this he apparently entirely lost his head, shouted, 'We are betrayed,' and instead of continuing his retreat, rushed into the midst of the enemy like the veriest German berserker, and was cut down.

When this news was brought to me I was stunned. I cannot honestly swear that I had loved Edmund, as perhaps I would have loved Suffolk, given time, as perhaps I did love . . . but love for another man at that time lay in the future. Yet Edmund was the first man to whom I had truly yielded my body – I had *offered* it to my husband, but he had declined to take advantage of the situation – and he was the father of my son. I wept most bitterly, and vowed revenge, even if I had absolutely no idea how such a desirable end was to be attained.

And what of King Henry VI, my most noble lord and master? Well, he had donned full armour on the morning of the battle, with the leopards and the fleur-de-lis on his breast for all to see, and he must have remained with Buckingham on St Peter's Street until Warwick's people broke into the town. At around this time he was wounded in the neck by an arrow. I do not feel enough has been made of this. I am not speaking of the wound, which was slight and caused no physical ill effects. But the fact is, as I have said, that he was so dressed that no one in either army could have doubted he was the King. I am not unaware that there are kings, and kings of England too, who have commanded others to wear their armour in battle, and themselves preferred the plainest of garbs, in order to preserve their hopefully valuable lives. My Henry was not the sort of man to stoop to such a cowardly ruse – some would say he lacked the wit. More importantly, he could not help but remember that his father had gone into battle wearing not only distinguishing armour, but his crown as well! So it would seem plain to me that someone in the Yorkist camp had determined the best solution to their problems would be the death of the King. I would vote for Warwick in this regard.

In any event, the idea was not taken to fruition. Having been struck, and uttered a few 'Forsooths' to reveal his feelings, Henry retired to a thatched cottage, and there rested while his adherents died in his name. He was found in this refuge by Cousin Richard, in all the splendour of his undoubted triumph. As the King was still very much alive, and as Somerset was by now established to be dead, the Duke of York dropped to his knee and apologised to his King for any inconvenience that might have been caused. No doubt the fracas *was* a trifle inconvenient for those whose bodies were being thrown into a communal grave outside the town.

So there we were, our hopes dashed upon the field of battle, and myself feeling in a state of bereavement. Indeed I cannot be blamed for fearing the worst. Even if he had not uttered the words himself, York's adherents had openly accused me of adultery – in effect treason – and now, by force of arms, he was every bit as supreme as had been Henry's grandfather following the defeat of Richard II's army. My mind insensibly roamed back through history to women like that Clemence of Hungary, strangled in her dungeon, a fate which also overtook my kinswoman and kindred spirit, Joanna of Naples. Perhaps I delved even further into antiquity, and remembered an early French queen who had been torn apart by four horses for her misdeeds. My blood ran cold. But I determined to defy them to the end.

However, today we live in a more refined age; and besides, for all their ferocity, the English never do seem to have waged war on women. Perhaps I should say on princesses or women of the nobility. The worst I really had to fear was being packed back off to France, although that would have been horrendous enough, and I am not speaking merely of the ordeal of another Channel crossing. Amazingly, none of these things came to pass. While I and my ladies waited at Greenwich for the axe to fall – perhaps literally – York calmly took possession of the realm ... as Protector. Truth to tell, in view of all his claims, he could hardly do otherwise and retain credibility in the eyes of the world. Twice he had taken up arms to rid England of the rule of Somerset while professing the most total loyalty to the King. And now Somerset was dead. Indeed, strictly speaking, his objective being achieved, York should now have retired into private life.

I doubt he would have done that in any event, but he was helped by circumstances. Only a few days after we had received news of the battle, I received a visit from Proud Cis. I assume that her husband had governed her in how to behave for she was most circumspect, while I, having been warned of her approach, received her with all the dignity I could muster, the tears washed from my face, my only token of mourning my black garters, which she could not see. Bella stood at my side, and thus I gave my enemy the privilege of coming face to face with the two most beautiful women in the kingdom.

She made an elaborate bow which all but dislodged her hennin, and had yards of tulle floating in every direction. 'Your grace,' she said, 'I bear ill tidings.' Not for the first time I decided that the English idea of wit did not coincide with my own. But it appeared that she did actually have tidings even more ill than those I had already received. 'His grace is unwell.'

'I had heard the wound was slight,' I said.

'I do not speak of the King's wound, your grace. That is all but healed. Alas, his mind has again collapsed, and he lies helpless. Your place is at his side.'

The crowning blow! I could do nothing but dissemble. 'Where?'

'He is at Hertford, your grace.'

This town is situated only a few miles from St Albans. Obviously I conceived it my first duty to regain control of the King's person, but in addition I was curious to visit the site of this famous conflict, so soon to be forgotten because of those that followed. 'Then I must leave at once. Will you arrange an escort?'

'It awaits your grace's pleasure.'

'And suitable transport for Prince Edward?'

I waited for her reply with bated breath; were she to deny the title ... But Proud Cis never batted an eyelid. 'That too, is arranged, your grace.'

Not for the first time I must pause to reflect on the strange behaviour of this man York. I was at his mercy. More, my son was at his mercy. Had he or I, or both, met with an accident, there would undoubtedly have been those who would have cried murder. But as I was not very popular with the English mob, and as my son was loudly called a bastard in every quarter, any furore would soon have died down and left King Henry without any of the support I was able to give him in the trying times ahead. Yet York continued to behave with impeccable honour. This has led some commentators to describe him as an absolute paragon, one of the noblest men in English history. Well, perchance he was, although any man who could father three such monsters as Edward of March, George of Clarence and Richard of Gloucester had to have a bit of the monster in himself.

However, I suspect it is more likely that he entirely

discounted a twenty-five-year-old woman as an adversary. As for her son, holding the previous statement to be true, he would have considered that as there could be no arguing with his rule until Henry's death (which, despite the relapse, was not immediately foreseeable) he had a good deal of time in which to have the heir set aside. My hypothesis is the more likely, because this is in fact the plan he now carried out.

For the time being, however, my efforts were entirely directed toward the King. This is not to say I did not pay sufficient attention to everything else that was going on about me. Actually, it was remarkable how rapidly, considering that there had actually been a battle between the forces of the King and those of his cousin, the entire country got back to normal. Even St Albans had been cleaned up and there was little evidence of the blood that had been shed, although the commander of my escort was eager to show me the important sights such as the Castle Inn – perchance I shed a tear as I envisaged the death of dear Edmund – and the house where the King had been found – a most mean dwelling with a thatched roof – as well as the famous wall over which Warwick had clanked to glory.

'There was the decisive moment, your grace,' the scurvy captain told me. 'Had the King possessed such a general as Warwick, it would have been a different story.' The fellow was of course a Yorkist. Yet, in common with just about everyone else, I believed him. Possibly the only person in the entire realm, or even Europe, who properly evaluated the Earl's true military capacity was his even more youthful cousin, Edward of March – but this was to have dire results.

Meanwhile, peace had descended upon the land so completely one might have been forgiven for supposing the conflict had been naught but a dream. The fact is that the common people had not even been aware that there was going to be a military confrontation, much less a battle, until the matter was settled, and once it *was* settled, everyone was relieved to see how little had changed. York was again Protector, as he had been in the past, and was again making the country obey the laws. Bourchier was again Chancellor, and aiding and abetting his cousin in every way. Henry was again incapable. So what was new? Only the demise of Somerset, and I have to confess that Edmund had been almost as unpopular with the Commons as was I.

People thus proceeded about their own affairs. Early in the summer, for instance, Edmund Tudor married Margaret Beaufort, thus seeming to end the Beaufort interference in national politics. But this was not so. Edmund Somerset had left three sons, and the eldest of these, named Henry after his uncle the great Cardinal, seized the first opportunity to pay a visit to Hertford, where the King remained, in a total stupor quite the equal of a year before.

Now, I had marked this youth well at the time of my coronation. He was, it may be recalled, somewhat younger than myself, and in my first few years as queen we had often romped together at his father's home. Now he was grown to manhood. I had of course seen a great deal of him during recent years but, my interest being entirely consumed by his father, I had perhaps not paid him sufficient attention.

Now I beheld a very fine-looking young man, perhaps even more handsome than his dead father. As to his qualities, I had at that time no ideas, but I was prepared to make allowances. I am speaking of his qualities of leadership and as a soldier – I could never afford to forget that in real terms he was my stepson and half-brother to the future King of England!

Henry Beaufort was naturally deeply grieved and angered by his father's untimely death, and confided to me that he dreamed only of revenge. I assured him that I did also, but that it was absolutely essential to do nothing rash. He knelt before me, placed his hands between mine, and swore to obey me in all things and at all times. I fear that not for the first, or the last, time in my life, I allowed myself to be swayed by a handsome face and honeyed words.

I was far more immediately suspicious of the friend who accompanied him. This was the youthful Clifford, another who had lost his father at St Albans. I never doubted Clifford's determination to avenge his father, and therefore his loyalty to me, but so vehement were his declarations that I could not help but doubt his ability to remain true to his oath of patient obedience to my wishes.

What those wishes might be I had at that time no idea. Survival remained the key, and it was the King's survival as well as my own. The last time he had been afflicted it had continued for well over a year, and a repeat of this period stretched interminably before me. To my great gratification, however, and the consternation of the Lords, Henry regained his faculties only a month after being taken ill. Once again I hastened before him with pen and paper, but York was slowly learning how to look after his interests. He had undoubtedly been informed by one of his spies in our establishment that the King was showing signs of recovery, and before I could get his fingers wrapped round his pen the Protector was in our midst.

'Sweet your grace,' the scoundrel said, kneeling before us. 'How you do tax your beauty with affairs of state. But there is no need for letters and decrees. Parliament is anxious to acclaim its King. I have come to escort King Henry thither. When he sits before them, he has but to make his wishes publicly known, and I swear they will be carried out.'

I felt like stamping my foot, but I kept calm. 'Tush, my lord Duke,' I protested, 'his grace has just left his bed after a month. Such a journey would be highly dangerous.'

Alas, not for the first time, my husband opened his mouth against my wishes and my interests. 'But I feel perfectly well, sweet Meg,' he protested in turn. 'I wish to return to Westminster, and I wish to address my Parliament.' Was there ever a woman so plagued?

'However,' York said, 'if your grace would prefer to remain here . . .'

I was in a quandary. I had no idea what might happen to Henry without me. On the other hand, I had no means of protecting him; and if York did indeed mean him ill, then I was certain he meant me a great deal more ill. I chose to remain in Hertford, Henry Beaufort having promised to ride like the wind to bring me tidings of what was happening long before any of York's people could get to me.

But once again York could afford to proceed with absolute legality. I had forgotten what an effect he could have upon Henry when they were alone together. News reached me that the King, addressing Parliament, had expressed his entire confidence in the rule of the Protector, with whose name he associated the Earl of Salisbury, and his now-famous son, the Earl of Warwick.

With this public pronouncement to his credit, York could even afford to be magnanimous, and he agreed to Henry's request that young John de la Pole, son and heir of my dear Suffolk, should be made Earl of Suffolk and inherit all his father's lands. Alice was delighted, and I believe it was at this time that the Poles began their drift away from the House of Lancaster to that of York.

He was not the only defector. To my consternation Wenlock now informed me that his private affairs necessitated his giving up the position of my chamberlain, and resigned. I had no doubt at all that here was another wretch changing the colour of his rose.

Here I should make a digression to explain the nomenclature of the war which, although none of us truly suspected it, had actually begun at St Albans, and which is now known as the War of the Roses. Many reasons have been put forward for this, some of them very fanciful, such as that a dispute arose one day between the Dukes of York and Somerset who were walking in the Westminster gardens. Somerset declared that he would be forever faithful to the Red Rose of Lancaster, meaning of course myself, whereupon York, thrusting his hand into some convenient bush, plucked a white rose, and said that in that case he would always be faithful to the White Rose of York.

This is romantic stuff, and I have no doubt at all that in some future age a scurrilous poet may well attempt to pass it off as fact. However, its absurdity is patent. My lords of York and Somerset were never given to strolling together in the garden like two lovesick maidens, and the only roses which were permitted to grow around the Palace of Westminster were my own blood-red variety. Nor was there such a thing as a white rose of York at that time.

The facts are these. Those who loyally supported the King and the house of Lancaster were equally loyal supporters of mine, and my emblem was the red rose. This is well known. The Yorkists had no emblem until, several years after the outbreak of hostilities, Edward of March fought and won a battle, immediately before which it appeared – from I suspect the reflections on a misty morning – that there were three suns in the sky. These suns were close together, and might well have appeared like a white rose in its fullest bloom. Edward as I say won this battle, and thereupon searched for a symbol to represent his victory. This he found in the white rose, which then seemed most appropriate, as it opposed my red. And this is how it came about.

When Henry returned to Hertford, where we had set up quite a little court, he had to face a very angry wife. I was appalled at his behaviour, and told him so in no uncertain terms.

'Praising that scum is bad enough,' I said, loading my voice with venom. 'But by agreeing to perpetuate the Protectorate you have virtually excluded my son from the succession.'

'Now you know that is not so, sweet Meg,' he protested. 'It is but a temporary measure, until I am fully restored to health. You have no idea what a trial it is to go to battle, what it is like to feel cold steel tearing your flesh . . .' He was in tears, and I was forced to comfort him, while indeed praying that I might have the privilege of undergoing such a trial at least once before I died. It is odd how some prayers are answered, and others, perhaps to more purpose, are ignored.

But at the time I was helpless, my position rendered again almost intolerable by the King having yet another relapse towards the end of the year. Truly I came close to despair, and was only kept from collapse by the courage of my dear Bailly, and my even more dear Bella. How I trusted her in those days, and how I was able to forget the ills of the world when in her arms. In the light of what I now know of the wretched girl, the truly surprising thing is that she stayed in *my* arms, when my power seemed lost for ever. But no one has ever accused Bella Grey of lack of judgement; she knew I was not finished yet.

All in all, 1455 was a year I would prefer to forget. As I have said, Henry contrived to lose his senses again before Christmas. Some accuse me of having driven him into decline by my constant exhortations to him to act the king. But what would you? He *was* the King, and I was the Queen, and we had a son who was heir to the throne. And all three of us were treated as utter nonentities. People did not even doff their caps to us in the street!

The future appeared very grey. I could get no succour, even in words, from the Continent, where everything was at sixes and sevens. Papa and my brother John were campaigning in Naples, as unsuccessfully as ever before, my sister Yolanda had married a scurrilous rogue named Frederic de Vaudement who hated me, while Uncle Charlie and Cousin Louis had finally broken, and Louis had taken refuge with his uncle Philip of Burgundy. This last might have appeared as an advantage to me, as Cousin Louis had never been my friend, but Uncle Charlie seemed distracted by the event – when he was not being distracted by his harem – and anyway it would have been catastrophic, in my circumstances, to have appealed to French arms to reinstate my husband as the true King of England.

From all this it will be gathered that I was already considering making a fresh appeal to force. I understand that this is unseemly in a woman, but before I am criticised my position should be understood. I was a queen, but my husband was no longer a king except in name. I was a mother, but my son was everywhere regarded as a bastard. (That this happened to be true was my secret alone and had nothing to do with my situation.) And I was a woman, young, beautiful and passionate, who had seen two lovers into the grave and was stuck with a husband who was either incapable of movement or regarded any connubial movement as obscene.

I think I deserve great credit for my forebearance and patient determination to extricate myself from this slough of despond into which I had been pushed. The true surprise is that I did not start eating the carpets or seducing one of my pages.

Instead, I made plans. And when, in February of the following year, Henry again returned to his senses, I was ready and at his side with pen and paper – this time having given strict orders that *no* one was to be admitted until I gave permission.

'There is much to be done, my sweet,' I told the King, wiping sweat from his fevered brow. 'The country is in a sorry state.' This was not entirely true. Under York's firm government the country was in a better state than it had been for some time. But I had no doubt I could rule it better yet.

'What time is it?' my hapless husband asked.

'Late,' I assured him. 'I have these decrees which urgently need your signature.'

'What day is it?' he ventured.

It actually was a Sunday, but I knew full well that for Henry to discover that would be to end all business for a good twelve hours. 'It is Friday, my sweet,' I told him. 'So it were best to get all this business out of the way today so that you can spend the weekend at your devotions.' I held out the pen, and put the first sheet of parchment before him.

'What month is it?' the King inquired.

'It is February, my sweet. And in answer to your next question, it is the Year of Our Lord 1456. Now if you will just sign these papers ...'

For the first time he looked at them. 'These are all in your handwriting, my poppet.'

'Well, of course, my love. They are important matters.'

Now he read them. 'We have done all this before,' he complained. 'To no avail.'

'Which is no reason why we should not avail now,' I pointed out.

Henry duly signed and the decrees were presented to Parliament, resulting in the usual fuss. I was disgusted to discover that even Buckingham wished to temporise, and with the murderers of his son! The upshot was that while the title of Protector was taken away from York, he remained a member of the Council, while Bourchier remained Chancellor. So what had I gained? I am afraid Henry and I had a storming row, with the result that for the first time in our lives he used harsh words to me. That is to say, he shouted, 'Forsooth and forsooth, woman, but you are a trouble-maker!'

Well! I had never been shouted at like that before. And I was only trying to safeguard the future of my son. I gathered up the Prince and left, going to a house I owned at Tutbury where I spent a month amusing myself with Bella and hunting, while we strove to educate the Prince.

I had assumed that Henry, once he recovered from his emotional distress, would send for me; but he did not. Actually, he was embarking upon one of his perambulations around the kingdom, regardless of the spreading gossip concerning a king and queen who preferred to live apart. In these circumstances, having waited several weeks for a summons which never came, I took the Prince and myself to Chester. For Edward was not only Prince of Wales; he had also been made Earl of Chester, which is approximate to

Wales, and I wished to present the Earl to his people. This was a most gratifying experience. These rough and ready borderers assembled in their thousands to acclaim both the Earl and his beautiful mother. I was all but mobbed by men anxious only to kiss the hem of my gown or to touch my boots. I was thrilled, and could not help but notice that every man carried either a bow or a sword, and quite a few both. Here were natural fighting men ... and they loved their Queen. It was a relationship which was to endure.

Henry's summons for me to be at his side arrived in August, and I travelled from Chester to Coventry, where I entered the King's bed. He affected to have entirely forgotten our quarrel and, knowing his uncertain mind, it is very possible that he had indeed done so. To Coventry there now came a variety of people, including those in whom I was most interested, and I persuaded Henry to summon a Parliament to meet there in October. This was done. I had spent a great deal of time during the intervening month discussing affairs with those lords I knew would support me, and although Buckingham continued to temporise – I could not help but feel that since St Albans and the death of his son he had developed a profound feeling of unease regarding York's abilities as a soldier when compared with his own (and of course he was always unduly influenced by Bourchier) – he was forced to go with the tide. Thus the October Parliament was a triumph. I again had Bourchier ousted, and replaced as Chancellor by Wayneflete, and I had York sent back to Ireland as Viceroy. Now I was in control, and I was determined that it was going to remain that way.

9

My first recourse had to be to create a party bigger and more powerful, in every sense, than that of York. This I set out to do, but at the very start I received a severe blow. Naturally I had supposed that the King's half-brothers would be the foundation stones of my strength. Nor was I wrong, in so far as they were able. But on 3 November, before I had even caught my breath as it were, Edmund Tudor died.

When someone of your own age dies, whether he or she is a relative or not, it gives pause for thought. But there it was. Edmund Tudor, Earl of Richmond, had caught some frightful distemper and was carried off before any of us really understood what was happening. This applied most of all to his wife. Poor little Margaret, only thirteen years old, was big with child. One is bound to say that thirteen is a trifle young to endure the horrors of pregnancy, although of course I would willingly have undergone this trial myself when only a year older. But thirteen is even younger to have in addition to undergo the miseries of widowhood.

Additionally, of course, she remained England's premier heiress, to snare whom would be the dream of any itinerant lord short of money. In the interests of her own well-being I packed her off to one of her castles, in Pembroke, hoping she could lie-in there in peace while I made arrangements. On 28 January she gave birth to a boy whom she named

Henry. It is amazing to think that of the entire House of Lancaster, that babe and I are the only survivors. And now that twenty-three years have passed, Henry Richmond is no longer a babe!

But I anticipate. As I have said, I had ideas of my own for Margaret Tudor, and later that year I married her to Buckingham's younger son, Henry Stafford.

Meanwhile, the court remained at Coventry. This was because the citizens of London had grown so virulent in their attacks upon me I was not prepared to return anywhere close to them, save to burn their scurvy town to the ground. And when I say the court, I mean myself and the Prince. As soon as the weather warmed up, Henry began another perambulation. He went from Stafford to Coleshill to Chester to Shrewsbury to Leicester to Kenilworth to Hereford before returning to Coventry in September.

I was glad to see him go. More and more it was obvious that he had absolutely no interest in the business of being King, and even less interest in the business of being a husband. Had it been possible to get rid of Bourchier altogether, and make Henry Archbishop of Canterbury in his place, I have no doubt he would have been one of the most famous men of his age. Well, I suppose he is. But for all the wrong reasons.

Meanwhile I ruled, with a great deal of satisfaction; and dare I say it, not a little success. When one rules, of course, one cannot hope to please everyone. But at least I put our finances in some order, as I insisted upon the careful collection of duties and arranged a whole succession of marriages amongst the younger nobility from each of which we gained some revenue. But I am afraid my popularity dwindled even more. The English, it seems, do not approve of women who show an untoward interest in money – Bella has recently discovered this for herself – and to add to my problems some idiotic French sea captain carried out a raid on Sandwich and burned the port. The mob naturally said I had instigated this misfortune. In fact, I was furious, and fired off an angry missive at Uncle Charlie, who equally naturally – and probably truthfully as he had absolutely no idea of what was going on *in* his kingdom, much less outside of it – disclaimed all knowledge of the event and described the perpetrators as pirates.

It was of course necessary to deal with Bourchier a good deal of the time, but in the main I left that to Wayneflete, who was, as ever, a tower of strength. My principal aide was Buckingham, who gradually began to exercise the same relationship to me as had Suffolk and Somerset. I am here speaking entirely politically. Stafford was not the sort of man I could ever have taken to my bed. Oh, he was handsome enough, and I would say he was an accomplished lover. But he had none of the *fire* I desire in a man. He carried out my wishes as Queen in so far as it was possible, but he was always harping on such things as keeping a middle way, pleasing the greatest number, and above all – and most irritatingly – maintaining good relations with his brother-in-law Richard of York.

Now I ask you, how may the mongoose lie down with the snake? But Buckingham persevered, and soon found an ally against which it was difficult to make progress: the King himself.

For in the January of 1458 Henry was enjoying – if the word is at all appropriate – one of his periods of lucidity, which were always accompanied by an over-estimation of his powers and his abilities. I have of course always held that a king's powers are limitless, providing only that he has the mental stature to ride roughshod over all opposition. I would have been perfectly happy had Henry developed such a personality, even if, in the course of it, he would have ridden roughshod over *me*! In fact, I would have welcomed a bit of roughshod riding, because the truth of the matter was that since the death of Somerset, now three years in the past, not a single male member had even approached my portcullis, much less breached it. Three years! When one is in one's twenties, this is a terribly long time to lie fallow. And when a *woman* is in her twenties, the threat of thirty, which in my case was now only just over two years away, looms like a thundercloud with its certainty of the ending for ever of youth.

However, for a brief moment, Henry was riding rough-shod in every direction except the one which lay to my bed. Thus in January he summoned a Great Council, to meet at Berkhamsted, a royal manor some miles north-west of London. 'We are going to put paid to all of these animosities, once and for all,' he declared.

Now I wish to make it perfectly plain that this whole charade, and what followed, was Henry's idea, not mine. In addition to his other physical and mental disabilities, my beloved husband had what can best be described as a very selective memory; that is, he only remembered what he wished to remember. Certainly he appeared to have entirely forgotten that he had once before summoned a Great Council, in 1447, to a place where he could command events, at which time Duke Humphrey of Gloucester had been arrested and shortly afterwards been found dead. Now Henry may have chosen to forget this but Cousin Richard was not likely to; and sure enough, although he obeyed the summons, he arrived accompanied by the Nevilles and by a force of armed men sufficiently large to be described as an army. What is more, he spurned the quarters prepared for him by the King and took his people on into London itself, where he was sure of a welcome and total safety. Needless to say, as Henry had a large armed force himself at Berkhamsted we seemed on the verge of a resumption of hostilities.

I am bound to say that as far as I was concerned, such a course would have been the ideal way to 'put paid to all of these animosities, once and for all'; I had no intention of abandoning our forces on any future battlefield to the doubtful strategy of Buckingham or worse, the King himself. I was full of memories of the Maid of Orleans, and intended to don armour myself when next it came to a physical confrontation. But Henry had shot his bolt for the year. I do not know, because he did not confide in me, whether he did have any plan for overawing the Yorkists by force of numbers, but when he discovered that they were not to be trapped he returned to his favourite pastime: that of doing absolutely nothing except pray.

Others were more active, in the cause of peace. There was a great to-ing and fro-ing between the two camps, conducted mainly by Buckingham and Archbishop Bourchier. I was helpless while this was going on. I understood that there was no way I could get at York while he was holed up in London, and was concerned mainly with ways of drawing him out. But before I had reached any decision, I was confounded to be approached by Henry and Buckingham, accompanied by the Archbishop, and told that the matter was settled: the parties were entirely reconciled and we were all to attend a service of thanksgiving on Lady Day, 25 March. I had no sooner digested this astounding piece of news than I was struck between the eyes by another. This famous service was not to take place at our own Westminster Abbey, or even in the safe seclusion of Berkhamsted church, but at the cathedral of London itself, St Paul's, in the very heart of the city. And of the mob.

It occurred to me immediately that we had been entirely outmanoeuvred, and were about to be at best arrested *en bloc*, at worst torn to pieces by the ravenous apprentices. But nothing I could say could shake the King's purpose. To him a service of thanksgiving was closely akin to the greatest happiness in life; and besides, words of honour had been given on all sides. Words of honour, indeed! I contemplated flight, but realised that if I did so, and Henry went ahead with this absurd plan, as Buckingham and young Somerset and young Clifford and indeed all the Lancastrian lords had been commanded to accompany him, I would be left absolutely bereft of support. There was nothing for it but to prepare to die with dignity. I dressed myself in my best, instructed Bella to stay always at my side so that we could at least expire in each other's arms, left the Prince of Wales – so soon, it seemed to me, to be an orphan – with Bailly, and accompanied the King into the city.

Presumably we are all familiar with the tale of Daniel in the lions' den. I assure you that the prophet could have felt not an ounce of the emotions I experienced as I walked my palfrey down those cobbled streets, between the ranks of the assembled multitude. They regarded us in silence. Well, I suppose it might have been worse – they could have been baying for our blood. But Henry was at his most regal, which perhaps did not amount to much. On the other hand I was at *my* most regal, all tall hennin and flowing houppeland, golden cauls and jewelled fingers, as I guided my palfrey forward, looking from left to right with as confident an expression as I could muster, and I flatter myself that I counted for a great deal.

We reached St Paul's without so much as a clod being hurled at us, and there found waiting the Yorkist throng, a perfect mass of armed men. I presumed our trials were but beginning. But when we dismounted and formed up to enter the cathedral, I received the biggest surprise of all. The whole thing had apparently been arranged by the King and the Archbishop, with the enthusiastic support of Buckingham and York ... and the wretches had told me nothing. So now, the King and Bourchier having mounted the steps to a fanfare of trumpets, York advanced and offered me his arm. I could do nothing less than place my hand on his, and together we in turn climbed the steps, for all the world like a pair of lovers, while behind us, I discovered by means of a hasty glance, was a perfect procession of pairs, every one composed of a Yorkist and a Lancastrian, arm in arm. Cousin Richard smiled at me. 'Now I truly feel, your grace, that our troubles are behind us,' he said.

The man was either a fool or a liar. I suspect he was both. This was the third time he could have turned things decisively to his own advantage. A single *agent provocateur* planted in the crowd to assault – in the guise of a Lancastrian supporter – a Yorkist, would have created a riot; and once the London mob gets out of control it is more often than not days before it is returned to order. They were Yorkists to a man, and we were in their midst. Any number of the darkest deeds could have been committed without anyone being able to point a finger at the Duke who could have emerged with his minions as the only survivors, forced by circumstances to take the crown from the dead king and the murdered queen.

But nothing happened. We celebrated our reconciliatory mass, kissed each other fondly, and went our separate ways. I gathered up the Prince and departed for Chester. I felt safer there, and besides, I was recruiting a little army of my own amongst the fierce borderers, who always greeted me with huzzas. Henry went on his travels in his usual way, and with his usual embarrassing lack of awareness of the requirements of royalty. For example, I learned to my chagrin that when he was at St Albans, in a fit of generosity he presented the monks at the abbey with a magnificent red cloak, which he took from his own back. The monks were most gratified, until they realised that they would have to return the gift – it was the only cloak the King possessed.

How may a country be ruled by a man like that?

My own endeavours to gain a decisive advantage over the opposition were continuing to be frustrated. In pursuance of my plans, I determined that my next step should be to obtain possession of Calais, which I had much in mind as a possible refuge in case Henry had any other mad dreams of exposing me to the London mob – I could not see us being so lucky as to survive two such encounters.

Now, Calais was under the governorship of young Warwick, who, trading upon the reputation he had gained as a soldier at St Albans, was trying to create a reputation as a sailor by patrolling the Channel; with a view, he claimed, to preventing the French from carrying out another raid on Sandwich. This naturally gained him great credit with the mob, even if it was an indirect shaft aimed at myself. My idea was that he should be removed from his post and replaced by young Henry Somerset. I was proceeding slowly but surely, winning over the various lords who were not Warwick's actual relations to my point of view, when the scoundrel spoiled everything by encountering a French fleet in the Channel and totally defeating it.

Now, it may well be that Warwick had vastly more talent as an admiral than as a general, or it may be that he was aided by a favourable combination of wind and tide which confounded the French – I have never been able to get to the bottom of it – but the fact was that he suddenly became a total hero to the mob, who apparently regarded him as the ultimate reincarnation of my deceased father-in-law.

So bang went all of my plans. I was told by Buckingham that to remove Warwick from his command of the Channel at this moment would have been to instigate an instant revolution.

I therefore had to practice patience and lay my plans anew. It may well be asked, at this stage, why I was in such a constant state of agitation. After all, I was to all intents and purposes in control of the government, and the world at large had believed the Great Reconciliation we had perpetrated the year before. But I was not to be fooled. The Yorkists, I knew, were just waiting for events to fall into their laps. This could happen in any one of a number of ways. In the first place, there was no saying when the King would have another relapse; it seemed certain that he would, and medical opinion held that as he grew older the chances of a *permanent* mental collapse would increase – they were thinking, no doubt, of his maternal grandfather's case.

In the second place, the very business of government brings unpopularity. The common people, and the common English people more than most, are always more inclined to break laws than to observe them, certainly when it comes to paying taxes and duties. Any government which rigorously enforces the law – and I was determined that in my government the law would be upheld, especially where it related to financial matters – must inevitably lose its popularity. When, as in my case, the government is not popular to begin with, its decline in favour is even more rapid. Additionally, not only are governments prone to a decline in popularity through humdrum affairs of state, but they are also liable to unforeseen disasters. In fact, in this regard, Warwick's achievement in temporarily ridding the Channel of French pirates was a disservice to his uncle's ambitions; a few more raids like the one on Sandwich, if permitted, would have had the mob clamouring for my head.

In the third place, and I suspect this was the nub of the matter, your Englishman feels that there is something unnatural about a nation of warriors being ruled by a woman. Well, I suppose this absurd notion is not unique to the English; one thinks of the Salic Law. But it is most hypocritical in the English, both because they do not admit the validity of the Salic Law, and because at the drop of a gauntlet they will extol the martial virtues of their Queen Boudicca, who some fourteen hundred years before my time had the great distinction of burning London Town and massacring, it is claimed, eighty thousand of its inhabitants. As London today contains only thirty thousand inhabitants one is forced to assume even the Venerable Bede used to draw a very long bow – but Boudicca remained a lady whose feat I longed to emulate, the more so every time I was forced to enter the gates of that confounded city.

There was a fourth reason for Yorkist confidence in the future, one closely related to the third. Not only was I a woman, but I was a Frenchwoman, or so they claimed, although there are equal parts of French, Italian and Spanish blood in my veins, as a glance at my family tree will illustrate. And I was also a young and extremely beautiful Frenchwoman, whose lubricious personal habits clearly consisted of leaping into bed with a different man every night. Would that it had been so! I am not denying that the charge might have been true had there been any suitably lubricious men around my bed. But since Somerset's death these had been singularly lacking, if we exclude the young bloods, none of whom, however handsome and filled with ardour – and undoubtedly all madly in love with me – I felt I could trust to the required extent.

Thus it will be seen that inactive enjoyment of my present position of power was highly dangerous for me. I had somehow to bring the Yorkists into open defiance while I enjoyed such a position.

As may be supposed, this was a busy and distracting time for me. Consider: I was endeavouring to govern a country which a foreign observer has described as ungovernable; I was trying to be the wife to a total nitwit, but who was the fount of my power; I was seeking ways to gain an advantage over enemies who sought my blood; I was attempting to maintain our financial position without driving the populace into rebellion; I was forced daily to repel the advances of a horde of young men every one of whom was certain he could make me the happiest woman in the world; I was convulsed with physical energy, and desire, which I had little means of dissipating ... and I was the mother of an adorable five-year-old boy who was more important to me than all the rest put together. Indeed, the rest put together were only there because I was determined that Prince Edward would one day inherit the crown.

But I fear I was inclined to spend too much time with my son and his principal playmates, Thomas and Richard Grey, as well as with their mother (who, after all, was at this time *my* principal playmate!). I was therefore not greatly pleased to have my various cogitations interrupted by the arrival in England of Cardinal Francesco Coppini, a Papal Legate, no less. It may be recalled that a dozen years or so before, Henry had had a difference of opinion with Pope Eugenius IV over who should be the next Bishop of London, Henry supporting Suffolk in his choice of the detestable Molyneux, while Eugenius had chosen Young Kemp. That had ended in the discomfiture of the King, and relations between Westminster and the Vatican had somewhat cooled. However, soon after this dispute, Eugenius had died.

He had actually been pope for fifteen years, which is a long time nowadays. In these troubled times, the Pontiff is always either very, very old when he is regarded by his fellow cardinals as suitable to reach the top of his profession, or if he is young, he is regarded with suspicion because of his youth and ambitions by a sufficient number of the cardinals to be awkward. In either case history indicates that the result tends to be the same: His Holiness is required to take his place at God's right hand in fairly short order, by one means or another – the favourite appears to be acute indigestion. Thus in the eleven years since Eugenius' death, two popes had come and gone, and we were now in the reign of a third. This man, who had just taken up the burden of representing God on earth, was named Enea Silvio de Piccolomini, or, as he liked to be known in the literary world – for amongst his other accomplishments he had actually published a novel, which I suppose is unique among popes – Aeneas Silvius.

Piccolomini had gained a considerable reputation as foreign minister for the Vatican during the preceding pontificates. Now he was enthroned as Pope Pius II. It is an aspect of new popes that they attempt to set the tone of their pontificate, and at the same time ensure for themselves a place in history, by *doing* something, preferably something their immediate predecessors have not done. There have been those popes so unfortunate as to inherit an ecumenical council set up by the previous incumbent, who have been able to do nothing more than continue it. Setting up such a council is, however, one way of doing something. Another is to inveigh against the public morals. This is usually unpopular, and leads to acute indigestion even quicker than usual. And once upon a time, there was a third: to preach a crusade. This has usually been against the infidel, although there have been popes who have preached crusades against various Christian sects, or even against the emperor, because they could think of nothing better to do. There was even one who preached a crusade against a king of England, that same poor fellow John I have mentioned previously, who came adrift in the Wash.

However, crusades have become progressively less popular as they have become less effective; that is to say, as the infidel has grown progressively stronger and thus been less profitable to crusade against. Neither of Eugenius' immediate successors had been able to stir up much interest in a crusade against the Turks who were battering down the walls of Constantinople.

We were therefore all somewhat surprised when Pius II announced that it was his great aim in life to send a crusade against these same Turks, who were now stronger than ever before, and were ruled by a formidable sultan who, officially named Mehmet, rejoiced in the nickname of Hunkar, or Drinker of Blood. Men with such soubriquets, especially when no one can have any doubt they are well earned, are depressing enemies. We in Christendom said to ourselves, ho hum, but this Piccolomini has a limited imagination for a novelist.

We were soon to learn, however, that Pius was very serious about his crusade, as was manifested by his decision to send legates to every country which he deemed able to take part in it. Thus to England there came Cardinal Coppini, the Papal Legate.

Now here, in fact, Piccolomini revealed a great deal of imagination based – as is the case with so many story-tellers – on no very obvious facts. There could be no one in Europe able to doubt that the government of England was in a state of penury. Equally there could be no one able to doubt that if any money to finance a foreign campaign was to be raised in this green and wet island, such a campaign would be mounted against the French in Normandy rather than the Turk in the Balkans. Piccolomini may have counted on the well-known religious affiliations of the King, but he should have known that Henry was not the man to lead a campaign against anyone.

On the other hand, it did occur to me, when I met the good Legate, that if he side-stepped the government and dealt directly with the lords, it might do everyone a power of good. The idea of the Duke of York, the Earl of Salisbury and the Earl of Warwick setting off in all their panoply to confront the Drinker of Blood and his janizaries appeared to me a splendid one; if there was one thing that seemed certain, it was that these banes to my existence would not return.

I therefore, in the King's name, convened a Great Council, and presented the Legate to the Lords. Henry was present, of course, and full of martial ardour. 'I do assure you, my lords,' he told the assembly, 'that but for pressing matters at home I would take the cross myself and lead you all to glory.' He was politely but sceptically applauded. Unfortunately, it turned out that every nobleman in England had a pressing matter at home to attend to, and Coppini's plea therefore fell on stony ground.

Even more unfortunately, however, the ground was not as stony as it had first appeared. I was ignorant of this fact, and that the Legate remained in England, travelling round the country and visiting each of the lords at his home, seemed to me to be but an example of Papal stubbornness. I was to discover my mistake a little later on.

At the time I felt it more important to pursue my own objectives, which were now close to fruition. For that summer I received another unexpected visitor. 'A fellow called Dou . . . dou . . . a Frenchman,' Bella explained. 'From France.' She was always very positive.

I imagined a messenger from Uncle Charlie, and received him. His name was actually Doucereau, and he was an odd

little fellow with twisted features who was obviously
destined by fate to wind up at the end of a rope. He had a
letter for me that I opened with trembling fingers, because I
did not recognise the handwriting. However, I did recognise
the silk scarf in which the letter was wrapped. It was the one
I had presented to Pierre de Brezé immediately before
leaving France, thirteen years before.

Thirteen years! And now ... 'Sweet Queen, most lovely
and gracious lady of her age,' Pierre had written. 'Forgive
my effrontery in communicating with you. But the fact that
you once allowed me a token of your esteem gives me
courage beyond my station. Your grace, I have watched your
progress from afar with admiration, but equally at times with
fear. I need say no more. By now you will know as much of
the prefidious English as do I. I but wished you to be certain,
at all times, that should you ever be in need you have but to
return me this scarf, which has never left my pocket for
thirteen years, and I will attend you with all my might, all
my purse, all my courage, and dare I say it, your grace, all
my love, without a moment's hesitation.'

This is the sort of letter that any woman with red blood in
her veins can receive any day of the week. I was quite
delighted. At the same time, being *au fait* with events in
France, I understood much that had not actually been written
down. The fact was that Pierre de Brezé was no longer Uncle
Charlie's number one. The King of France, as I have earlier
suggested, as he grew older had become the world's
principal lecher, whose sole interest in life had become
centred on that area of the female body between the neck and
the knees. Pierre had early discerned this tendency, and had
thus projected his protégée Agnes Sorel into the royal bed.
Nor had he been lacking in resource when Agnes had come
to an untimely end, for it may be remembered he had
immediately procured the services of her even more lovely
cousin, Antoinette de Magnelais. But Antoinette, however
attractive, had no longer been able by herself to please the
King's fancy. Thus he had created his harem, and on

Antoinette's demise Pierre had found himself no longer in favour.

He was not the sort of man to retire. He *had* in fact retired from court to his country estates in Normandy, but only to continue intriguing to regain power from that base. I knew, for instance, that he had been in correspondence with the Dauphin, who was still hiding in Burgundy, afraid of arrest should he ever return to France. I even surmised that his interest in me might be less as a woman than as the Queen of England, for fear of a resurgence of English power sufficient to resume the Hundred Years War was a recurrent nightmare in France, and it was much more likely to happen were Richard of York king than in an England ostensibly ruled by hapless Henry, and in reality under the control of his Francophile wife.

I repeat, all of these things I well understood. But yet the thought of such a man as Pierre de Brezé worshipping me from afar and offering me his strong right arm went to my head. I equally understood that he would of course by now be in his fifties. But what mattered that? In my teens I had been enamoured of a man thirty years my elder. Pierre was not that far my senior. And I knew him to be a *man*. But more important, a friend, in whom I could trust. And he was French!

I replied immediately, acquainting him with both my current satisfactory situation, my fears that it might not last, and my wish to pre-empt my enemies. Equally promptly did he come back to me and, being Pierre, suggested to me a course of action which was as simple as he assured me it would be successful.

In fact, his plan was one which I have mentioned I was surprised the Yorkists had not used against ourselves before now.

I had learned from my various agents that Warwick was returning to England from Calais for a visit, and that he would, as was required of him in his capacity as governor of that essential link between our possessions in England and

France – in fact it was our *only* remaining possession in France – be calling upon the King at Coventry. I made doubly sure that he would do so by having Henry write to command his presence, the reason given being that he wished to hear all about the Earl's great naval triumph at first hand, with the suggestion that a reward might be in order.

As I had suspected, Warwick could not resist such a bait, and so walked into my trap. He came with a large retinue of men, as I had expected. But the King had a larger retinue, not anticipating trouble, to be sure, but there in case of it. And in the crowd was my *agent provocateur*.

The fellow's name is irrelevant; he had been sent me by Brezé. A convicted criminal, he knew he was bound to die, and had accepted the commission in order to save his wife and children from Pierre's wrath. He wore a cloak that effectively concealed his clothes, but as the Earl was approaching the King's house, he threw the cloak away, to reveal himself wearing Warwick's livery with its unmistakable badge of the bear and ragged staff. Drawing his sword, he attacked the King's soldiers, shouting 'A-Warwick! A-Warwick! Now is the time! Strike! Strike!'

I was watching events from an upstairs window, and everything went entirely according to plan. The hapless criminal was cut down before he could do much harm, but the ripples caused by his action spread through the crowd; everywhere royal troops and supporters turned on the Earl's, and Warwick himself, realising that he was outnumbered – and once again revealing that fatal dislike of his for engaging in physical combat – hurriedly departed, calling his people to follow him. They did this with alacrity, and a full-scale riot was avoided. But I had gained my point. Warwick fled to Calais, leaving his cause in disarray. Henry was deeply affronted by what he had to regard as an attempted *coup d'état*, and promptly summoned Parliament. The good Commons were also deeply affronted, as they more than any others had believed in the Great Reconciliation, and demanded that Warwick appear before them to explain his conduct. But this of course he was not likely to do, and despite my efforts to stiffen the King's resolve, they could arrive at no decision as to what to do next.

However, while they were in this pro-Henry, and thus by necessity pro-Margaret, mood, I managed to secure agreement that the revenue from the Duchy of Cornwall, which was part of the Prince of Wales's apanage, should be paid directly to the Prince's household ... of which I, as his mother, had total control. For the first time in my life I felt absolutely solvent. I could now turn my attention to settling the Yorkist matter.

But in fact, they were the first to make a play. At the beginning of the summer, I had, as was by now my habit, taken the Prince on a visit to his Chester earldom. It was about the one place in the entire kingdom where I was certain to be welcomed, and on this occasion several thousand men turned out to acclaim me. I had of course been forewarned of the sort of welcome I could expect, and had used my first receipts from the Duchy of Cornwall to have made a large number of tiny silver swans, as a white swan had been adopted by my son – by me, really, on his behalf – as his badge. Now Edward, who was five years old and a fine sturdy lad, went among his men, myself at his elbow, and presented each man with one of these swans. Obviously the expense was considerable but I flattered myself that it was worth it, for when we were finished they cheered themselves hoarse, and their captains assembled around the Prince and me and swore they would die for us. Well, for me, at least. I then conceived the idea of marching my army to the south-east, into the vicinity of London. I could muster ten thousand men, a very great number, and if I knew I could not keep them together for an indefinite period, I felt that it could do no harm to let those insolent apprentices see for themselves that the Queen was no one to be trifled with. And if any of the Lords took heed as well, so much the better.

As it happened, it is probable that these military matters

reached the ears of the Yorkists. Salisbury was in any event
smarting under the business of his son, for Warwick was
quite unable to show his face in England in case he was
arrested, and was no doubt bombarding both his father and
his uncle with pleas for them to take his business in hand.
Whatever the truth of the matter, I was on my way home
from Cheshire in September and had reached Eccleshall in
Staffordshire, when I received news that not only was
Cousin Richard mustering and arming retainers in Yorkshire, but that the Earl of Warwick was preparing to depart
Calais and return to England, at last assured of the support
of his relatives.

Even more urgently, it was reported to me that Warwick's
father Salisbury was already in the field, with five thousand
men at his back, and was marching on Ludlow, where he
expected to be joined by his brother-in-law.

It seemed to me that the rascals had played into my hands,
because my force was assembled, and in a situation which
militarists call interior lines; that is to say, we were closer to
the men of Salisbury than were the men of York, and while
together their combined forces might have been a match for
us, separately we outnumbered each of them by almost two
to one. Thus here was an opportunity to deal them each what
might turn out a fatal blow, and still have time to take my
people south to cope with Warwick should he dare land.

Best of all, King Henry and Buckingham and Archbishop
Bourchier and their temporising were all far away. I was in
command, and could handle the situation as I thought fit. I
therefore ordered my general, James Touchet, the fifth Baron
Audley, to march at once against the Earl of Salisbury and
defeat him. I knew we had a considerable majority in men,
but at the same time I despatched a message to a nearby lord,
Stanley, calling upon him to muster his people and come to
my support. I have been criticised for this, as apparently
being unaware that Stanley was Salisbury's son-in-law.
Well, of course I knew this. And of course I did not really
need his help. But it struck me that it would be a good

opportunity to determine once and for all upon which side of
the fence Stanley stood. As it turned out, finding out where
Stanley stood was a very difficult task; the scoundrel replied
that he was marching to my assistance with every available
man ... and then never moved.

As I have said, at that time I was not greatly interested
either way, except to be certain he was my enemy. The
Prince and I rode with my army, until on the evening of
22 September 1459, we arrived on the banks of a stream at
a place called Blore Heath – it is situated some fifty miles
south-east of Chester – and on the far side descried the tents
and banners of Salisbury's army.

'We have them, your grace,' Audley declared.

'Will we fight them now?'

'No, no, your grace. We will wait for dawn.'

'But will they not endeavour to escape during the night?'
I inquired.

'No, no, your grace. The Earl of Salisbury would not do
such a cowardly thing,' the old warrior assured me.

I could only hope he was right, but I spent a restless night
and was up before dawn, which was still quite early. It was
a great pleasure to hear the martial stirring around me, the
clank of armour and the clash of arms as swords were made
ready and bowstrings strung. My misfortune was that I had
no armour of my own. I had had a suit made, suitable for a
queen, but it was in Coventry, as I had had no idea we were
at all close to conflict. In any event, I doubt it would have
done me much good, for Audley was a typical male. 'No one
can possibly expect your grace to wield a sword,' he
explained with great earnestness. 'And concern for your
safety would greatly hamper my knights. Nor,' he added as
I would have argued, 'are there any qualities of generalship
now to be required, your grace. They are there, we are here.
If they do not come to us, we shall go to them. It is as simple
as that. Look ...' he pointed. 'There is a finely situated
church tower in that village. From the top of such a vantage
point you will be able to oversee the entire battle. And there,

your grace, I swear to you that I shall bring the Earl of
Salisbury, a prisoner. Or if not, his head.'

I have often been accused of being the most bloodthirsty
woman who ever lived. This is a vile slander. However I do
not think I can be reasonably blamed for loathing a man
who, with his wife, had opposed me from the moment of our
first meeting, whose son had destroyed my husband's army,
and who was responsible for the death of my dear Edmund.
In any event, being in arms against his lawful King, he was
doomed to a traitor's death if taken alive. So I nodded, and
said, 'His head would be most acceptable, my lord.'

I was actually offering the Earl clemency.

I retired to the church tower, with an escort, and of course
the Prince. My ladies I had already despatched to a place of
greater safety. I would have retained Bella, had she been
with me, but I had given her permission to spend some time
with her husband during my visit to Cheshire. So on this
occasion I really was a queen among lions; alas that the lions
were all on the wrong side! I gained my vantage point, and
looked out at the September sun glinting from the armour of
my troops, and watched the Yorkists march down to the far
side of the stream; there they glowered at Audley's people,
while no doubt shouting threats and imprecations. Our men
stood their ground with perfect fortitude, willing the enemy
to attack, which would have been all in our favour as the
stream would have to be crossed, and the bank was much
steeper on our side than theirs. The Yorkists understood this
well enough, however, and after a period of fighting the
battle with words and the occasional arrow-shot, they retired
to their encampment and began taking down their tents,
apparently with every intention of departing.

This was exactly what I had feared they would do,
although why they had not carried out their intention during
the night was a mystery to me. But not for very long. It
seems that the scurvy wretches had never had the least
intention of withdrawing. Salisbury had estimated correctly

that rather than let him escape, Audley would wish to cross the stream himself. This is what he now did. My brave men of Cheshire scrambled down their steep embankment and into the water, waded across the stream, and then clambered back out again. But it was not possible to do this without a great deal of disorder. Men stumbled and fell, both in the water, causing huge splashes, and on the dry land beyond; swords and bows were dropped and trampled on in the mêlée; horses neighed and reared and more than one noble knight became unseated, a serious matter when one is wearing plate armour, and I watched with horror my army disintegrating into a mob.

This situation was also observed by Salisbury, whose men were not the least disordered by breaking up their encampment, as they had never actually started to do so. Now they suddenly appeared in ordered ranks; their archers loosed a flight of arrows which completed the discomfiture of my people, and almost before I knew what was happening the Lancastrians were fleeing in every direction. 'Your grace,' one of my escort cried, seizing my arm. 'We must get away.'

I freed myself and ran down the steps as fast as my skirts would permit. 'We must rally them.'

'Your grace ...' he ran behind me, and caught my arm again. 'Would you deliver yourself into the hands of the Yorkists?'

That gave me pause for thought.

'And what of the Prince?' the rascal asked, clearly much more afraid for his own life than mine. 'Is he not your first responsibility? Your grace, we have lost a battle. But there is much yet to be fought for.'

And so I allowed myself to be mounted and led away, Prince Edward at my side. But my heart was heavy. My first essay at commanding troops had been disastrous. However, I could reflect that I had not been in tactical command. And Audley had expiated his incompetence; he was among the dead.

*

The Battle of Blore Heath was undoubtedly a tactical defeat. But, strangely, it turned out to be a strategical triumph. Word of the rising of the Yorkists had by now naturally reached the King, and Buckingham had been marshalling the royal forces. Both he and Henry were astounded at my appearance, exhausted and travel-worn, to give them the news of our defeat, and hard on the heels of that came the additional bad news that York had joined his brother-in-law ... and that Warwick was also in England, and marching to unite his people with the rest. We were thus faced with a formidable force, and it might almost appear that our cause was lost.

However, Wayneflete was with us, and not for the first time he came to our rescue with his fertile brain. The news of the uprising had been circulated throughout the south, and with it word of how the hapless Queen and her escort had been set upon by the Yorkist wolves, all intent upon rape and murder. This cheerful little tale – and there were none to gainsay it, as Audley was dead and the rest of my men had fled back to their Cheshire homes – had a powerful effect. I will not claim I became any more popular with the mob, but possibly they felt that if anyone was going to rape and murder the Queen, it should be their prerogative. In any event, they began to feel that the Duke of York had gone too far, and in this belief they were spurred on by Wayneflete's agents.

The good bishop's advice to us, therefore, was to keep moving and avoid a conflict while suborning the Yorkist troops by promises of clemency if they abandoned their leaders who had so rudely attempted to profane the Queen. This worked like a charm, although we spent an anxious summer hurrying from here to there while York desperately attempted to bring us to a confrontation, either for another reconciliation or to settle the matter once and for all. But all this time Wayneflete's agents were at work, and the Yorkists suddenly found their numbers dwindling as their people went home.

Suddenly it was all over. A certain captain named Anthony Trollope, a veteran of the French wars and a man much admired by the large band who marched beneath his banner, and who had hitherto been a staunch supporter of the Yorkist cause, declared for the King and brought his men into our camp. With such a man, and such an accretion of strength, on our side, we were invincible. York fled to Ireland, Salisbury and Warwick to Calais, there to reconsider their positions. We were triumphant.

Obviously we had to capitalise on our success. At my insistence, Henry promptly called Parliament, the selection of which Wayneflete carefully oversaw to make sure it was composed of none but supporters of the Lancastrian point of view. This was gratifying, and seemed to guarantee us an easy ride.

In fact, Parliament, which assembled at Coventry on 20 November – in all England, London remained the one place where the Yorkist cause was still supported – was in fine loyalist fettle, and went farther than I could possibly have hoped. I had originally sought only the removal of Warwick from Calais and his replacement by my own nominee. Since Blore Heath I had also determined that some measure should be taken to weaken York's position and his ability to raise a private army whenever he chose, and the same thing applied to Salisbury. But Parliament promptly passed bills of attainder against all the Yorkist lords, including even Cousin Richard!

This meant that the Duke of York and all his followers were common outlaws, liable to be executed on arrest, and that their property became forfeit to the crown. I could not believe my ears, while Henry smiled with satisfaction. He had no intention of implementing the bills, of course; it was not in his nature. He was merely content to have proved his power.

I had *every* intention of implementing the bills. I did not actually seek anybody's head, at that stage – I still had a lot to learn – but the thought of being able to lay my hands on all the vast estates of the Nevilles, not to mention those of York himself, and of being able to treat Proud Cis and her sister-in-law as dirt beneath my feet, was a heady one. Unfortunately, Parliament, having reacted violently against the Yorkists, now reverted to its normal supinity and found itself unable to vote us any money with which to implement my plans: the Yorkist strongholds were of course defended by large bodies of men, and we would have needed an army to dispossess them.

But that seemed a detail soon to be corrected. For the moment, although I did not then realise it, I was at the apogee of my fortunes.

We spent a happy Christmas at Leicester, despite our usual shortage of ready funds. But my brain was already considering means of alleviating this situation, on a permanent basis.

More disturbing was the news that Signor Coppini had left England. In itself this would have been a relief, but he had not returned to Italy. Instead he had joined Salisbury and Warwick at Calais, whence, we learned, he had announced to all who would listen that he was fed up with the goings-on at King Henry's court. Well, I ask you! What he meant was he was fed up with me because I treated him with contempt. He also suggested that we might have been responsible for the fracas which had resulted in the attainder of the Yorkist lords. Here he was on sounder ground, to be sure, but as he had no proof we could afford to treat that allegation as well with contempt.

But the thought that the Papal Legate, who might well be able to influence his master, should have thrown in his lot with our opponents was a disturbing one.

However, for the moment all seemed well. Early in this most fateful year of 1460 Henry set off for London and the south, for his usual round of monasteries. I remained at Coventry, where I was among friends, although as soon as the weather improved I intended to return to Cheshire to see my faithful soldiers and aid them to overcome their depression following their defeat at Blore Heath. I would have gone at the beginning of June, but Henry wrote and asked me to remain for a while as he was himself returning to Coventry. I of course agreed to this. The King and I had drifted into a very even relationship. We were man and wife, and the fact that I *was* his wife, had proved an able and determined supporter of the royal prerogative, and was the mother of the heir to the throne – thanks to his amatory prowess, as he supposed – was all that he required of me. We no longer slept together for any purpose, but when we were under the same roof he would always pass an hour of the day with the Prince and myself. With Bella and Bailly, often joined by Wayneflete and Henry Somerset, we made a pleasant little party.

Henry never sought to probe into any aspect of my privacy; in that respect he was less even than a brother to me. Thus he knew nothing of my correspondence with Brezé, or of any other of the steps I had taken to secure his supremacy. He did of course know that I had been present at Blore Heath, and would sometimes chide me for taking on too much of the male role, but always in the most friendly and gentle manner. Had all other things been equal, I suspect we would have slipped gently into old age together, as I suppose do so many other married couples who have long overcome the requirements of their passion ... or perhaps, like us, never known mutual passion at all. As to whether I would have been able to accept such a passive role for the remainder of my life, I do not know. I think perhaps I would have forced myself to it, taking my pleasure from watching my son grow to manhood and in the course of time sharing in the glories of his coronation and reign. But it was not to be.

I cannot be blamed for seeking to make our hard-won supremacy permanent. Parliament, it seemed to me, had been less than honest in voting for the attainder of the Yorkist leaders, and then not supplying the funds enabling us to take possession of their lands and castles – it was obvious that the Commons, while anxious to prove their loyalty to the Crown, were not anxious to see the Crown grow so sufficiently, and independently, wealthy as to have no further need of them. And as, in this regard, no one could have the least fear that the King might use any excessive wealth for any other purpose than to endow a few more churches and schools, it was clearly me of whom they were suspicious.

I bore it all with equanimity, confident in the strength of my position. Henry and I spent a pleasant few weeks at Coventry, and then he was ready to be off again, just as I was off myself, my first stop being Eccleshall in Staffordshire, the town whence I had marched against Salisbury the previous year, and where I was certain of a warm welcome.

I had barely reached here, on 28 June, when news reached me that two days previously Warwick and Salisbury had landed in Kent. This was disturbing, as it may be recalled that it was the men of Kent who had started all the trouble in this region by their revolt in 1450. Just ten years before. Now they were at it again, but with a far more formidable leader – or pair of leaders – than Jack Cade.

I naturally sent messengers to the King, and to Buckingham, demanding to know what they intended to do about this fresh rebellion. But before I received a reply, worse news arrived. On 2 July, only six days after landing, Warwick and Salisbury were welcomed in London. From there, with a large army, they began their march to the north.

With London in the Yorkist pocket, we clearly had the most severe crisis of the reign on our hands.

10

Henry and Buckingham were actually aware of the forces gathering against them, and had summoned an army of their own, centred on the town of Northampton. Hither Prince Edward and I rode to join them, and I can tell you it made my heart swell with pride at the welcome we received, the wild huzzas of the common soldiers, the bared heads and bended knees of the knights. Red roses were everywhere, and I do believe that had the hapless Warwick come upon us at that moment he and all his host would have been torn limb from limb.

However, I still intended such a fate for the miscreant. I knew he was there, and I knew his worth: in my opinion he had none. I also knew that his father was still delayed before the Tower, and Richard of York, by far the superior soldier of the trio, had not yet drawn near. This time, I was resolved, there was going to be no shunting aside of the 'little woman'. I had allowed that mistake once too often.

My husband received me with his usual slightly apprehensive courtesy. Buckingham was downright pleased to see me, because of the effect my presence had on the men's morale. Neither made the slightest demur when I required the maps to be spread in front of me, and the enemy dispositions, so far as they were known, indicated. In fact, Warwick's whereabouts and dispositions were immediately confirmed by the arrival of the Bishop of Salisbury – the successor to the unfortunate Ayscough who had married Henry and me and been murdered by Cade's mob – with the inevitable request for a parley. This we rejected out of hand, and the Bishop rode off. But we had gathered that Warwick and his people were only a few miles away in the direction of London.

I now took control of the army. Before us there lay a brook called the Nene. It was not a severe obstacle, but I remembered very well how my last army had been disorganised by having to cross the stream at Blore Heath in full sight of the enemy, and I was determined that there should be no recurrence of that unhappy affair, especially as on this occasion it was we who possessed the dreadful bombards, for Buckingham had been labouring hard and well to make the royal army the best equipped in the land.

I thus commanded the host to ford the brook, and this was accomplished on the afternoon of 17 July, whereupon we pitched our tents and I confidently awaited the morrow. But I was restless – who is not, before a battle? – and as Henry was apparently determined to spend the entire evening on his knees praying for victory, I determined to betake myself amidst my faithful lions, and speak with them.

The men were settling to their evening meal when I arrived, on foot, accompanied by only dear Bella, Sir John Fortescue and the Prince. Instantly they broke into cheers, and gathered round me; one archer even offered me a chicken leg, which I daintily gnawed, while quaffing a mug of ale. Thus refreshed, I smiled at them. 'We have much to do tomorrow,' I told them.

They cheered some more; encouraged, I proceeded into a regular harangue. I assured them that in my veins there flowed the blood of fighting kings – not their kings, to be sure, but I did not go into detail – and that I was determined to share their peril as well as their victory. I reminded them that not only were they fighting for the son of Great Harry, but for the son of that son, and here Fortescue raised the

Prince on to his shoulders to let them see their future king. Their cheers all but split the heavens, and must have shaken the spirits of the Yorkists as they tramped through the night.

Then I made what I can now acknowledge to be a mistake. But at the time it seemed both necessary and attractive to spur them on to even greater efforts. My speech was based upon my reading of the lives of the great commanders of the past, and of these, the one whose spirit most attracted me was Julius Caesar. I would be less than frank were I not to admit that, as a woman, there were other aspects of the great Roman handed down to us through the ages which attracted me even more than his military prowess. (I would have been entirely within my rights to have felt that way even had I been a man, as Caesar was apparently very broad-minded when it came to sexual matters.)

Caesar never fought a battle without first haranguing his troops. Well, neither did Boudicca, although she was less successful in the long run. But they both, following appeals to patriotism and loyalty and glory such as I had just made, added a *pièce de résistance*: the promise of enormous wealth once the victory was gained.

This I felt constrained now to do to bring my faithful lions to the very pitch of desire for the coming fight. But I was in no position to promise them, from our limited funds, a liberal donative. Nor, I surmised, would there be much to be gained in promising them the looting of Warwick's camp; he had travelled far and fast, and would have carried little of value, while his treasure chest undoubtedly remained with his father in London.

London! When I considered how much distress those apprentices had caused me, how openly they had evidenced their support of the Yorkists, how they had pelted me with mud and accused me of adultery ... 'But gain the day tomorrow,' I told my eager men, 'and the road to London Town lies open before you. More, I will promise you this: we shall batter down the very walls of that traitor city, and then I will give you a free hand within. London, my friends, my people, my *lions*! There is a prize which will make every man jack of you as rich as Croesus.'

How they cheered, as I reflected that Boudicca had promised her Brigantes nothing less ... and delivered the goods! But those words were to come back to haunt me.

For the moment, however, I was well satisfied. I knew I held a winning hand, saving only some divine interference, and with Henry busily praying in his tent – he remained at it all night while I was trying to sleep only a few feet away – there did not appear to be any risk of that. However, as I have mentioned before, this business of divine support, or opposition, is not a certain one. I may have supposed I had an ace in the hole in possessing a king on his knees, for if I was conscious of my own sins I had no doubt at all that Warwick had as many on his plate, and thus we should have balanced each other out and left the field and the glory to Henry.

But who can tell what goes on above the clouds? How do we know which scoundrel has managed to elbow his way through the holy throng to arrive at God's right hand and mutter in His ear? Once one is dead, one never dies, we are told. Therefore it is even possible that Richard II was there, urging on the Deity to end the usurpation of the house of Lancaster; or Pope Eugenius, reminding the Almighty how Henry had once opposed him. Undoubtedly we possessed advocates no less able and enthusiastic; Cardinal Beaufort would certainly have spoken up on our behalf, I have no doubt. But Uncle Henry had always had a tendency to sleep in, and on this 18 July 1460 we were up and about early. Perhaps too early for him.

None of these apprehensions entered my mind when I awoke shortly before dawn. Henry had at last fallen asleep, so I let him get on with it while Bella strapped me into my cuirass. This and a metal hat – such as that worn by the common soldiers, which is really merely an upturned soup-bowl to protect the skull, with a brim to shade the eyes – was all I wore in the way of armour. I did not of course intend to take part in any mêlée – I was far too tiny for that – and I was disinclined to wear breeches or leg armour in case the enemy hailed me as a second Joan of Arc and called me witch, although as they had previously called me every other name possible I wonder why I bothered.

Once properly dressed, I arranged my people. The bombards I gathered in a group, and situated them on the road up which Warwick would have to come, and across which I established my main battle. This distribution of artillery was not considered sound by the military men – that is to say, it had not been tried before and above all others the military mind is the most conservative – but I would not be gainsaid. 'Warwick will almost certainly be with the centre,' I explained to Buckingham. 'Do we blast him and his people and then advance, and it matters naught what happens on our wings.'

He shook his head uncertainly, but again I would brook no argument. The guns emplaced, the Prince, Bella – her husband was commanding a company – and I went along the entire Lancastrian line, exchanging words with all I could and enjoying their huzzas, until a forest of banners appeared in the distance, and we realised the Yorkists had arrived. Instantly Buckingham was all masculine ardour. 'Do you now withdraw, your grace,' he begged me. 'This is man's work.'

'I will withdraw,' I agreed. 'But only as far as yonder hummock, from where I still intend to command this battle. Do you watch for my signals. One wave of the flag means fire the bombards. Two waves means the army will advance. Is that understood?'

'Indeed, your grace. Will three waves mean retreat?'

'There is going to be no retreat, my lord Duke,' I assured him. 'Where is the King?'

'He remains in his tent, your grace.'

That pleased us both and off I went with Prince Edward and Bella and Sir John Fortescue to my commanding hummock. The scene before me was calculated to stir the blood. The Lancastrian force was extended over perhaps a mile frontage, facing south along the high road and the pastures which extended to either side. The common soldiery had their pikes at the ready; they wore a variety of garments, but little armour except for the flat hat which I was myself sporting. Behind them our archers were busily stringing their bows; they wore leather jerkins and had their sleeves rolled up. Behind them again were our mounted men-at-arms, equipped with plate armour, lances at the rest, great swords on their thighs, endeavouring to keep their mighty warhorses under control. And immediately in front of our main battle were our massed bombards, the gunners, busy men who wore leather caps as well as jerkins, making sure their slow matches were well alight, mixing their powders and inserting their round stone cannon balls into the muzzles of their infernal machines.

Above them all floated the various pennons and banners of the lords and knights; I could make out those of Buckingham, of course, and Somerset, Percy and Egremont, Shrewsbury and Beaumont, Grey of Groby – at the sight of which Bella clapped her hands for joy – and Grey of Ruthin. But of course the greatest banner of all flew the leopards of England, even if it fluttered above the royal tent rather than over any portion of our army. How I dreamed of the day when I should watch my son leading his men into battle beneath that flag!

Approaching us in the distance were the Yorkists, like ourselves a mass of men and armour and flags. They revealed no very special order of march, and at a distance it was difficult to identify any of *their* banners and so determine which of their lords was in command where. It was of course still very early in the morning, and I reflected that no doubt the sun would soon be illuminating all for me; but at that moment, glancing over my shoulder, I realised that it was extremely unlikely that we were going to see the sun at all that day. The eastern sky was a mass of great black clouds which seemed to approach us and grow heavier with every moment. 'I shall fetch our cloaks, your grace,' Bella announced, and descended the rear of the hummock to where our servants waited.

The prospect of a summer shower did not concern me in the least. I was preoccupied with gauging the distances between the two hosts, for it was my intention to introduce doubt and disorder into Warwick's ranks at the earliest possible moment by the sending of some cannonballs into those ranks, a manoeuvre which would give my gunners, I anticipated, ample time to reload and repeat the treatment if the Yorkists continued to advance.

And now I reckoned the distance about right. 'Do you wave the flag, once, Sir John,' I told Fortescue.

This he did, but the signal was not immediately noticed by my generals, who were all watching the approaching enemy. I felt it necessary to wait for a few minutes before signalling again, in case Buckingham mistook my one wave for two and ordered a general advance before conditions were right.

This second wave was observed and acknowledged, and the order was given to the gunners to commence firing. They turned to their task … and the heavens opened. The clouds had by now arrived overhead, and the deluge which followed was quite the heaviest I have ever experienced. The water teemed down so hard that for a few minutes it was impossible for me to see even my own army, and in that time I was literally soaked to the skin. Deafened by the pounding on my helmet, I removed the offending steel and my hair was immediately plastered to my head and neck even as my gown was plastered to my body.

To say that I was annoyed at this untimely interruption in my affairs would be an understatement. I was furious, as I realised then that some beastly dead Yorkist advocate had undoubtedly got hold of the ear of the Almighty in place of my own defenders. For the rain did not merely have the inconvenience of soaking us; it put out our slow matches. When the squall passed on, as it did in no more than ten minutes, it revealed my gunners peering at their weapons of destruction in stricken consternation, while from the hitherto sizzling matches there escaped only thin wisps of smoke.

The rain had also of course soaked the bowstrings and left the archers, on both sides, bereft of offensive power, and it was very obviously going to be a case of cold steel. But yet I did not despair. If the very heavens were fighting against me, I was yet determined to conquer, and awaited with equanimity the continued advance of the Yorkist army. Nor were my people unduly disconcerted, so far as I could make out through the vast cloud of steam which was arising from our ranks.

At this juncture Bella reappeared with our cloaks, which were now entirely superfluous as, the squall past, the sun had actually come out and was bathing the scene in a most delightful light. Had it been possible to delay the clash for another hour, during which time our bowstrings would have dried and it might have been possible to relight our matches, I think there could have been no doubt of the outcome. But Warwick, if no military genius, was not entirely a fool, and knew that he would never have better odds than at this moment, and so urged his men onwards.

The meeting of two armoured hosts consists of a loud clang, punctuated by the cries of the combatants. I watched in a mixture of horror and admiration, exultation and envy as the swords slashed and the shields clanked, and men screamed as they lost their footing and were trampled underneath, and the banners were brought down and immediately re-erected. The little Prince was every bit as excited as I, as indeed was Bella, although she was concentrating upon attempting to keep track of her husband's banner. I had no need to worry about mine; *his* royal device continued to fly over the royal tent, where he had no doubt resumed his devotions. The forces were evenly matched, and mine gave as good as they got. I have every reason to believe that victory would still have been ours, had not, after about an hour of this hand-to-hand fighting, Grey of Ruthin, may his name be ever accursed, done a Trollope in reverse.

I hasten to repeat, this was Grey of Ruthin, not the gallant husband of my darling Bella. And what possessed the lout or persuaded him to play the traitor still defeats me. Trollope had been suborned, or so he claimed, by a consideration of the King's pardon to anyone who would abandon the Yorkist cause. There could be no such attractive prospect for one who abandoned the *King*'s cause, and on the field of battle, as well, a course which invariably carries with it universal condemnation.

But there it was. Grey of Ruthin commanded very nearly a quarter of the royal army. Worse, seeing his people throwing away their red roses and hearing them bellowing 'A-Warwick!' left the rest of my army wondering who would be the next to turn his coat. In it seemed no more than a trice the battle was ended, with our Lancastrians fleeing in every direction.

My little party on the hummock was struck dumb with the horror of it. Every head turned towards me, but I was struck dumber than anyone. I honestly could not believe my eyes. With our bombards, and myself in command I had not supposed for a moment that there was the slightest risk of us losing the fight. Even when my bombards had been put out of action, I still was certain of victory. But to be betrayed by a base rascal ... I do believe that much of the iron that later supported my character entered my soul at that terrible moment. However, I was still commander-in-chief, even if I no longer possessed an army to command. 'Fetch my horse!' I said. 'I must go down there to rally my men.'

'You would lose your life, your grace,' Fortescue protested. 'The day is lost. Your only hope is to escape yourself.'

I glared at him, and then looked back at the battle. It had become a rout, and I knew he was right. Besides, there was the Prince, who was every bit as bewildered as the rest of us by this sad dashing of our hopes. 'The King!' I exclaimed.

'I will see to the King, your grace,' Fortescue said. He

escorted me down the rear of the hummock and saw the Prince and myself to horse.

'Your grace,' Bella said, 'I would beseech your permission to seek my husband.'

I could not refuse her, but my heart was heavy with foreboding as I leaned from the saddle to squeeze her hand and kiss her lips. We had spent many a happy hour together before disaster had struck. 'Do you take care, my dearest girl,' I said.

'Until we meet again, your grace,' she said, her eyes filled with tears.

My party was a small one; six men-at-arms, two maids, the Prince and myself, together with half a dozen baggage horses on which I had packed the military treasure chest in several saddle-bags. I had no faith that Henry would not disburse that most essential aspect of maintaining an army to the first person who asked him for it, and thus considered it safest to keep it close by me. Later events proved I was correct, at least up to a point.

I knew we had to avoid Northampton, and I also knew that my only hope of real safety was Cheshire and Wales. Thus we first of all forded the Nene, and then rode to the north-west. On the next rise, however, I drew rein to look back. I was actually seeking a glimpse of Fortescue and the King, but I could not see them. Instead I saw one of the saddest sights it is possible to envisage. I watched my gallant lions attempting to save themselves, also by fording the Nene. But with the Yorkists at their heels they were being murdered left and right, and many of those who escaped the sword were drowned in the swift-flowing water. 'We must make haste, your grace,' said the captain of my guard, Tallboys.

I nodded, too sad even to speak, and we rode on. People stared at us, and shouted out for news of the battle, but none supposed they were addressing their queen in the bedraggled woman who passed before them; I had discarded helmet and breastplate, and shrouded myself in my cloak. We purchased some food, but I remained reluctant to enter a town, and so we camped for the night in a lonely copse, relying upon Fortescue's acumen to follow our trail. I hardly slept. My clothes had dried on my back and were stiff and uncomfortable, and there was no means of removing them or cleaning myself up. So Edward and I snuggled down together. 'Will we beat the Yorkists the next time, Mother?' he asked.

'Of course,' I assured him.

'I shall chop off all their heads, when I am king,' he announced.

'Of course,' I agreed. At that moment I was entirely in agreement with him. But even I did not understand how deeply had our situation affected that six-year-old's observation of the events surrounding him.

Perhaps shortly before dawn I did doze off, to be awakened by the thud of hooves. My guards were immediately on their feet, fearing the worst. But into our small encampment there rode not vicious Yorkists, but one of Fortescue's pages, a fourteen-year-old boy named John Combe, who threw himself from his horse at my feet. 'Your grace,' he sobbed, and he was weeping. 'Oh, your grace.'

I grasped his hands to raise him up. 'Tell me. The King?'

'Taken, your grace.'

I gasped. 'Sir John Fortescue?'

'Taken, your grace.'

'The Duke of Buckingham?'

'Slain on the field, your grace.'

I could not believe my ears. 'The Earl of Shrewsbury?'

'Killed in the rout, your grace.'

'Lord Percy?'

'Slain, your grace, as are Lord Egremont and Viscount Beaumont.'

My head reeled with the extent of the disaster. 'Did any of my lords escape?'

'John Grey of Groby escaped, your grace.'

'Oh, thank God for that.'

'And the Duke of Somerset.'

'Somerset?' Here at last was a spark of hope; Grey's survival had been a relief, for Bella's sake, but he was no general; he was not even, strictly speaking, a nobleman, merely the younger son of a knight who had not yet himself received the accolade. Henry Somerset, however young, would have to be my next army commander. 'Where is he?'

'I do not know, your grace. The Duke and Lord Clifford were seen riding to the west, with a small escort.'

'The west,' I said with some satisfaction. We would rendezvous in Wales, and raise a new army ... but first we must get there. As for the King – well, I could find little sympathy for a man who kneels in a tent while his men, and women, are preparing to die for him, and in many cases are actually doing so. I presumed that Henry would now be murdered, as is the English habit, and hoped that his fate would not be too painful or humiliating.

But I could not help but reflect that if my husband was dead, then my son was King!

It was of course not possible to keep the terrible news young Combe had brought from my attendants; they had all gathered round to hear what he had to say, and at the end of it they all looked exceedingly gloomy. At least, in my innocence, I assumed that the lowering glances they were exchanging were those of despair. I was yet a child in my understanding of the baseness of human nature. I thus endeavoured to cheer them up. 'Come along,' I said. 'Let us be on our way before some dreadful Yorkist happens upon us. Once we are in Wales, our fortunes will be restored.'

This time they exchanged somewhat sceptical glances, but packed up the camp and we got to horse, a sorely lonely little party. My first objective was Eccleshall in Staffordshire, where I was sure of a welcome, and where I had left stout Bailly and the rest of my ladies before riding off to war. Unfortunately, it was of course known to the Yorkists that I had escaped from Northampton, just as it was understood that I was the true driving force behind my husband's determination to rule. This was flattering to me, but also dangerous, because the Yorkists could not help but feel that if they could secure my person – or better yet, my death – their position would be greatly strengthened. They were also aware that I maintained a house at Eccleshall, and that it was likely I would visit there on my way to Wales, for they had deduced as well as anyone where my only hope of succour lay.

I of course was unaware of this, and merely wished to gain the comfort of a home of my own – where there would be a change of clothing as well as food and a hot bath – as rapidly as possible. Thus the following day, as we proceeded along the high road near Malpas, with the happy knowledge that Eccleshall was only a march away, we beheld a body of horsemen in front of us. They had been patrolling the road, that was obvious, and when they saw us, they gave a halloo and came towards us.

Ever the optimist, I first supposed they were Lancastrians sent out to look for us. It was young Combe who recognised them. 'That is the banner of Lord Stanley, your grace!'

I hesitated but a moment. Stanley, it may be remembered, was the son-in-law of Salisbury, and I had sent for his assistance before the battle at Blore Heath. He had failed me then, and I had no doubt he would fail me now, or rather, wish to hand me over to his father-in-law. And that was a fate not to be considered. 'Ride,' I shouted. 'To the south. Good Tallboys, do you protect the rear.'

This the captain did, instinctively, I presume, his men unslinging their bows and sending several arrows into the Yorkists, which certainly discomfited them. I later learned that our would-be captors were not commanded by Stanley himself, but by one of his servants, a man named John Cleger, and perhaps they lacked the resolution they would have shown had they been under the eyes of their lord. In any event, after a brief fracas, they withdrew, and we were allowed to make good our escape. We galloped our horses until they were thoroughly blown, Edward hanging on to my waist for dear life. Then we drew rein and awaited the arrival of Tallboys, who duly came up, but with only four of his men. 'That was gallantly done, Captain,' I told him, bestowing on him one of my most winning smiles, before which the worst of men have been known to tremble with ardent desire.

However, it seemed he was not in the mood to be pleased, even by a beautiful woman who was also his queen. 'Harry Brown is dead,' he said.

'I am right sorry to hear that,' I said.

'He was my friend, and now he is dead.'

'You may be sure he died in a good cause,' I told him, somewhat tartly.

He did not look relieved by that, and we resumed our journey in sombre silence, as usual to pitch our camp as far away from any human habitation as we could find. 'Be of good cheer,' I told them. 'Tomorrow we will be in Eccleshall.'

'And what will we find there, your grace?' asked one of the two women.

'Why, friends, and warmth, and shelter . . .'

'If the Yorkists have not got there first,' Tallboys commented.

'If the Yorkists are there, we will fight our way through them,' I told him as confidently as I could. 'And make for Wales and safety.'

'And some more of us will be killed,' he grumbled. 'To what purpose?'

'To what purpose?' I cried. 'Why, to preserve the life of your Queen. And your King,' I added, stroking Edward's head.

My people – I now use the word 'my' loosely – once more exchanged glances. Then Tallboys said, 'If the King has truly been taken and deposed, then you are no longer queen.'

It did not escape my notice that he had omitted to address me with proper respect.

'No man may depose the King, save the Pope,' I declared, more in hope than certainty. 'If you fear that his grace has been murdered, why, so do I. But in that case, your King stands before you, and it would become you to do homage to his grace.'

Another hesitation and exchange of glances. 'He is no king,' someone muttered.

I got to my feet to face them. 'Are you then traitors, like Grey of Ruthin?' I demanded, refusing to admit my fear that Edward and I might be enjoying our last moments on earth.

'Come now,' Tallboys said, 'admit that the boy is Somerset's bastard.' I was struck dumb with the effrontery of it, while Tallboys realised that he had gone too far to retreat. 'We had best have done with it,' he said.

'You'll not murder her,' said the second woman.

'It is the only way,' Tallboys insisted.

If I had had a sword I would have run him through there and then. 'I'll not be party to the murder of a woman and a boy,' the woman said. Not the King and his mother, mind you: a woman and a boy!

'What are the odds?' asked one of the men. 'Leave them here. Without horses, the Yorkists will find them soon enough.'

Tallboys glowered at me. 'There are things to be done to this woman which we would enjoy,' he said, while my stomach rolled in revulsion.

'I'll not have rape, neither,' the woman asserted. 'She was a queen.' She was clearly setting up to be a shrew, yet I would have forgiven her anything ... save her assumption that my regality lay in the past.

'Well, we'll have what we can,' Tallboys growled, and picked up my saddle-bags, which, as I have said, contained all my available funds.

'And what about these?' asked one of his men, coming up to me and grasping my hands. Before I could believe what he was about, he was pulling off my rings, including my beautiful ruby.

Not to be outdone, another of the scoundrels seized the bodice of my gown. I struck at him, but my arms were pulled behind my back, my collar was ripped open, and the golden crucifix I wore about my neck was torn away, the chain naturally snapping in the process. I panted with anger and outrage, and was thrown to the ground with a jolt that winded me. Edward did his best to protect me, and was also dealt a buffet which stretched him beside me, crying with outrage. 'I will have your heads,' the little Prince screamed, a resolve I had already made, if silently, but the villains ignored him as they poured the contents of the saddle-bags upon the ground.

'Share and share alike,' demanded the woman who had saved me from rape. 'Let me see that ring!'

'That's worth all the rest put together,' Tallboys told her.

They argued, quite forgetting our presence, it seemed. I rose to my knees and attempted to straighten my clothes, and heard someone whisper, 'Hist, your grace.'

It was the young boy, Combe, who had taken no part in the robbery, but had rather moved away from the scene of the crime; he was now some twenty feet distant, with the horses. I did not hesitate, recognising as I did that our lives, and certainly my chastity – such as it was, but to that moment I had only had carnal relations with two men in all my life – were not yet safe. I scrambled to my feet, grasped Edward by the hand and ran towards the gallant youth.

'She gets away!' someone shouted, but I was already up to the horses. Unfortunately, Tallboys had had his men strip the animals to give them a rest, and I was not up to riding bareback, certainly not with Edward in tow.

'Behind me!' Combe shouted. His was certainly a large animal, and the only one which was fully saddled and bridled. I lifted Edward on to the saddle behind him, then he gave me his arm and I scrambled up behind the Prince, pulling up my skirts to ride astride, something I had not done since my young girlhood. But there was no time to lose, even if I was unsure how three on one horse could hope to escape from a mounted pursuit.

As it turned out, however, there was no pursuit. My

faithful servants were more interested in my money and jewels than in my person, and could not trust any of themselves sufficiently to stand guard over the ill-gotten gains while the others chased behind me. In addition, I suspect that none of them, not even the foul Tallboys, really possessed the moral courage to murder a queen, and thus they were in fact heartily glad to see the back of me.

This did not change my feelings towards them. I wished only to see them hang; or better yet, hanged, drawn and quartered; or better than any of those, broken on the wheel, every one of them, not excluding the women. And I could tell that Edward felt the same, even if he was too young to have any idea of the torment it was possible to inflict upon another human being.

I do not think I can be blamed for my anger, my desire for revenge. These people had been my servants. I had never shown other than kindness towards them, and if I expected them to be prepared to risk their lives for my son and me, were not we prepared to risk our lives for the entire kingdom, which necessarily included them and their loved ones? I have always endeavoured, as I am sure I have amply demonstrated, to see both sides of a question. It might have been possible for me to accept that these people, who had lived intimately with me for several years, had finally despaired of their situation and wished to abandon me. I might have understood that, if I would have found it hard to forgive. But that they should call their King a bastard I could never forgive. Even if he was.

Again, I could perhaps have understood and accepted that it might have appeared the obvious course to murder the Prince and myself, on the principle that the dead tell no tales. Buried on that empty heath, our bodies might never have been discovered and we would simply have disappeared during our flight. The blame would certainly have been apportioned to a band of Yorkists. As for being threatened with rape, well, it would have to be a sorry woman who, in such a position, is *not* threatened with rape, as that would surely indicate that she was not worth raping. I assure you that I would have borne my fate with fortitude, as I did eventually have to on another occasion.

I anticipate. This too I could have understood. But to be robbed of everything I possessed down to my wedding ring ... and my wedding ring was almost my most precious possession. No, I do not think I need to apologise for the diabolical desire for vengeance that consumed my brain.

Meanwhile, however, our position was more than ever parlous. Three on a horse – a woman, a boy and a child – there was no hope of us escaping the next marauding band of Yorkists we might encounter. I remained a beautiful woman, but in no circumstances could I at that moment possibly be mistaken for a queen, and so the very next *man* we encountered would almost certainly reintroduce the subject of rape – and would probably be less easily distracted than Tallboys. In addition, there were the sheer physical problems of our situation, among the worst of which, from my point of view, was the discomfort of sitting astride the bony back of a horse, poorly protected by my summer gown. As soon as it became evident that Tallboys was not chasing us, I slipped from the horse and walked beside it; the poor overburdened creature was incapable of proceeding at more than a walk himself, in any event. There was also the question of food: we had none.

All of this was very disturbing to Master Combe, who felt responsible for us, a very grave weight indeed for a fourteen-year-old to carry. I did my best to reassure him that he had done all that could be expected of any man, but he continued to sigh most heavily. As I am being perfectly honest, I can confess that when we stopped for another night, various ways of taking his mind off his problems, as well as mine off my problems (and incidently of rewarding him for his valiant loyalty) crossed my mind. But did no more than cross. We were all exhausted, hungry, thirsty and very dirty, all aspects of discomfort which lessen desire, and in addition the poor lad was obviously and utterly in awe of me.

So we all spent a thoroughly uncomfortable night, lost in some pretty uncomfortable thoughts. But next day the sun shone, and we came to Eccleshall.

My household was naturally in a state of considerable disarray. A Yorkist party had been there the previous day and, not finding me, had ridden on. It thus turned out that Tallboys' treachery, and the delay consequent upon us having to walk the final part of our journey, had actually been a stroke of good fortune. However, there was no saying when they would return, so we did nothing more than have a hasty meal and a bath, and change our clothing before setting off again. It was at this juncture that I offered young Combe a permanent position as my page, an honour he eagerly accepted; I suspect both of us were looking to the future, for he was a comely lad.

Then it was an even longer and more arduous journey across the Welsh mountains to reach the seaside fortress of Harlech. This took over a week, and made our flight from Northampton seem like a picnic, save in one important respect. My guards and ladies on this occasion, marshalled by Bailly, were all totally loyal; and once we entered Wales, we were amidst friends. Often enough were we accosted by bold mountain men, armed and bearded, all of whom huzzaed when they realised my identity – I was again dressed and accoutred as a queen, even if a trifle short of jewellery – and then fell to their knees and swore that I had but to give the word and they would march on London Town themselves to rescue the King. This was very gratifying, but it left me in something of a quandary, as I had absolutely no idea whether my husband was alive or dead, reigning or deposed. Neither did they. This made me all the more anxious to reach Harlech, which I eventually did at the end of the month.

Here I found Henry Somerset and young Clifford, and several other lords besides, as well, of course, as our Earl of Pembroke, Jasper Tudor, who held the Welsh command, and

was as concerned as anyone to discover what had happened
to his half-brother. They all appeared overjoyed to see the
Prince and myself. Well, I was overjoyed to see them,
although I was too worn out to reveal it. Indeed, I took to my
bed with a distemper and remained there for a fortnight,
while the strength slowly flowed back into my veins.

This recuperative period was very necessary, because I was
scarcely back on my feet when news arrived – from London.
It was the very worst outcome of the Northampton disaster
I could possibly have imagined in my darkest nightmare!

Henry had indeed been captured, together with Fortescue.
It was the old story: the King had merely refused to leave his
tent, because he was the King! There was no word of what
had happened to poor Sir John. But Henry had been taken to
London by Warwick, who was naturally cock-a-hoop at
having gained another great victory; there were those
speaking of him as the finest soldier in Europe, if not the
world. There are conflicting reports of what happened at the
King's entrance into the capital. Those who brought the
news to Harlech claimed he was forced to wear a crown of
straw and was mocked by the populace before being lodged
in the Tower like a common malefactor. The Yorkists have
claimed that he was treated with every mark of respect, that
Warwick marched before him with drawn sword, and that he
was lodged most comfortably in the Bishop's Palace by St
Paul's.

Actually, whether he had been ill-treated or not meant
little to me; he was still a prisoner . . . and he was still King.
And he had made not the slightest suggestion that he should
be joined by his wife and son. Not of course that I would
have gone to London even had I been summoned; I am fond
of lions, but I am not so foolish as to walk unarmed into their
den.

I digested this news, and then made my decision. It
mattered naught what propaganda the Yorkists choose to put
abroad: the King *was* a prisoner. We did not know their

plans, but it seemed most likely that they were but awaiting
the appropriate moment to do away with him and proclaim
Cousin Richard in his stead. Thus it was my bounden duty
to continue the struggle, free him, and restore the fortunes of
the house of Lancaster ... and my son. And in fact, our
fortunes at this juncture appeared to take a certain turn for
the better. While I had been lying ill, brother Jasper had gone
off to North Wales on what was really little better than a raid
and a recruiting tour. But he had been blessed with good
fortune, and now sent me a message that the fortress of
Denbigh had fallen into his hands, and that the entire
countryside was up in arms and sporting red roses. My
decision was instant. Edward and I departed for Denbigh,
where we were indeed received with acclamation. Denbigh
is, of course, adjacent to Cheshire, and in an instant, it
seemed, I commanded an army of several thousand men
anxious only to do battle on my behalf. I felt that my
fortunes were entirely restored and summoned my captains
to join me that we might make our plans; then we were
assailed by fresh news from London.

Up to now, it will be realised, the entire Yorkist campaign
had been managed by Warwick and his father. It was
Warwick who had won the Battle of Northampton, and taken
Henry in triumph to London. It was Warwick and Salisbury
who had determined the conditions under which the King
should be kept: very pleasant conditions, it appeared, and I
was chagrined to learn that my husband – who would never
hunt with me – had actually been seen hunting, in the best
of humours, at places like Eltham and Greenwich. But it was
not Warwick and his father who controlled the future. They
were but agents for York. And Cousin Richard had now
crossed the Irish Sea and was in their midst.

What happened next was, as is usual with news received
from afar, confused. But uniformly disagreeable. It appears
that Richard had had a good long think about the situation,
and had determined that it was time to stop shilly-shallying.
I would estimate that in this we may discern the hand of

Proud Cis. Be that as it may, he once again did his trick of
bursting in upon poor Henry, wearing full armour and with
sword on thigh, and thereby terrifying my husband into a
state of nervous shock. This was, of course, not a terribly
difficult thing to do.

Having got Henry to promise him anything he wished,
York, similarly ready for battle, next descended upon
Parliament. This Parliament had been convened by Salisbury and Warwick, with the intention that it would agree to
anything York intended. Now I am sure anyone who may by
chance peruse these lines – perish the thought! – will by now
have obtained a fairly good estimate of my opinion of
parliaments. But on this occasion, happily, they proved my
contempt in error, and in a most singular manner. The Duke
of York, as I have said, wearing full armour, marched into
their Chamber and up to the vacant throne, stood beside it,
and demanded to hear from anyone who would deny his
right to sit upon it. Well, no one was prepared to do *that*, but
the number of Members who actually raised a cheer at the
prospect could have been counted on the fingers of two
hands; the remainder sat in stony and even sinister silence.

This was a serious setback to such a character as Cousin
Richard, whose mind was always consumed with doubt as to
whether or not he was doing the right thing. Our report was
that he turned pale and stammered, and then hastily withdrew from the Chamber. Outside, of course, he soon
recovered his courage, as no doubt Cis and her brother and
nephew got at him, and the affair was more easily managed
in the Council than on the floor of the House, so that while
I was gratified to learn that he had been rejected in his
attempted *coup d'état*, the ultimate result was not less
disastrous for our cause. It was determined that while Henry
would remain King for the term of his natural life, York
would be Protector throughout that life, and would succeed
upon Henry's death.

If ever a man was given licence to commit murder this
was it. But even worse, the determination of the Council was

that my son was not the King's, and could never succeed to the throne. Was ever a woman more insulted!

The news left us devastated. But I at least was determined to continue the fight and regain my son's inheritance. Unfortunately, it was obvious that immediate action was out of the question. There were several thousand bold fellows, Cheshiremen and Welshmen, who appeared anxious to follow me, but the most loyal of men require arms and pay. Our bombards had been lost at Northampton. My treasure chest had been stolen by my servants. My lords were all fugitives, far from their estates.

In these circumstances I sat down with my immediate entourage to discuss the situation, and we reached certain decisions. The main one was that I had to seek at least financial assistance from some other power, and the nearest power which might be expected to help me was that of the Scottish King. James II was the younger brother of poor Margaret Stuart, Cousin Louis's deceased wife. He was thus by way of being a relative, at least by marriage. He was not actually an enemy of England, but he was known to be covetous of certain fortresses in the north; and it was determined by my advisers that a deal could be struck.

This, like my promise of the sack of London to my followers before Northampton, was to turn out badly. In fact, I did not like the idea at all. The concept of the Queen of England going, begging bowl in hand, to another court, did not appeal to me. It appealed to me even less when I discovered that my transportation to Scotland would have to be by ship, as that was the only way my safety could be guaranteed. I looked at my lords askance when they told me this. How could they guarantee my safety on a *ship*? I had not set foot on anything larger than a barge – and then only on the Thames – since landing at Portsmouth as a girl of fifteen, fifteen years before, and I had resolved utterly that I would never put to sea again as long as I lived. But now it was proposed that I should again be cast upon the briny, and the louts did not hesitate to point out that the top end of the Irish Sea was a far more serious prospect than the English Channel, especially with the year as well advanced as it now was.

Yet I allowed myself to be persuaded, partly because Henry Somerset offered to accompany me, and protect me . . . and do a great deal more besides. The fact is that, as I may have mentioned, after seven years of total non-connection with any member of the male sex, I was virtually a virgin again, and yet exposed to a continual round of lusting male company. I had also surmounted – been driven over, would be a more accurate description of my experiences – a series of mental hurdles which I had long dreaded. Age was the most important of these. I was now thirty, and this is not a figure which a beautiful woman can enjoy with equanimity.

I had also definitely reached the end of my marriage. I did not expect ever to see Henry again, and in any event I knew that, supposing I did see him again, I was certainly not likely to entertain him in my bed. But I was still beautiful. And I was still a woman. And I did still have red blood flowing in my veins. I had resisted temptation for too long, but when I reached Harlech my resistance was low. It was at this time, while I lay ill in bed and with a raging torment in my mind, that Henry Somerset came to sit with me. Soon he was smoothing the hair from my fevered brow, and soon after that he was discovering other hair to smooth from a no less fevered part of my anatomy. Only Bailly knew what was going on, and Bailly had long been desirous of seeing me tucked up between the sheets with a handsome lord.

Now obviously, weak as I was, this was a situation which demanded some consideration. In defence of my earlier actions, I had mentally come to consider Edmund Somerset as my husband, more of my husband indeed than the King. But if that were so, Henry Somerset was my stepson. In any event I knew him to be my son's half-brother. I was not at all sure how the Church might react to such a liaison. But then I reflected that Henry was not really my stepson, because his father had not really been my husband. Regarding having sexual connections with my son's half-brother, I reflected on the career of a distant relative, the Count of Armagnac, who at the time I write has fathered three children by his sister and still prospers, as do his offspring. As for the Church, the less it knew of the matter the better, or I could find myself excommunicated. Of course it would have been a tangled mesh had I become pregnant by Henry; my son would have been at once Prince Edward's half-brother and his step-nephew, and probably quite a few other things besides. But I had no doubt he would also be another strong right arm with which I could assail Cousin Richard.

Thus I had accepted Henry's caresses, and indeed returned them. My delight grew as I discovered certain aspects of humanity which had not previously occurred to me. Of the three men with whom I had previously shared my bed – I am including Suffolk here, even if it was an in and out affair – two had been old enough to be my father, and the third had had both the equipment and the mentality of a monk. Here for the first time I found myself being tossed by a young man; Henry was actually younger than myself. It was a most delicious experience. I will not pretend he was an accomplished lover. Suffolk and Edmund had had some acquaintance with the true arts of love as practised in Europe; Henry had never had those advantages. His life had been lived in England, where romantic love is unknown and the setting of woman on any kind of pedestal to be worshipped has never even been thought of. Henry was of the 'View halloo! A-cunting we will go!' brigade and the sexual act in his presence was strongly reminiscent of a charge of infantry, pikes to the fore.

But perhaps, after my travails of the past few years, this was what I needed at that moment. And, being a mere youth, Henry had the happy knack of being able to resuscitate himself very rapidly between engagements. When I say that I remained in bed for a fortnight after my arrival at Harlech

I will confess that the last few days were in a state of
delightful, if somewhat bruised, lassitude. After that (until a
set of quite remarkable circumstances which I shall shortly
relate) I kept him always at my side, and a good deal closer
than that when the lights were turned down for the night. It
was certainly my liaison with Henry that caused me to
regard young Combe – ten years younger even than
Somerset – in a different light, even though, being a chaste
and modest woman, I rejected the idea of having two lovers
at the same time.

However, the important point is that Henry persuaded me to
undertake this journey to Scotland, looking for support. We
took ship, had an unpleasant voyage, and arrived in western
Scotland in mid-December, which I may say, is no time to
visit that freezing country.

I will deal with my sojourn in Scotland in a short while.
What I did not know was that, in my absence, my
Lancastrian lords had again taken the field. The leaders in
this enterprise were young Clifford and the Earl of Wiltshire.
There could not have been two more unstable noblemen in
the entire country. Clifford did nothing but swear vengeance
for his father's death, while Butler of Wiltshire, having run
away from the battle of St Albans five years before, had
spent his time since in a desperate quest to re-establish his
reputation.

Now, when I left Wales, I had been under the impression
that no campaigning would – or indeed could for lack of
funds – be undertaken at least until the following spring, by
which time I hoped to have returned with Scottish money
and perhaps even Scottish arms. And so it should have been,
but for Cousin Richard's fatal complacency. I suppose he
cannot be blamed for having supposed he had won the game.
Henry was his prisoner, he was Lord Protector for life, and
now news was brought to him that the only person on this
entire earth he truly feared, myself, had taken ship and left
the country, bound no man knew where. York therefore

determined that it was safe to leave London and spend Christmas at his favourite residence, Sandal Castle in south Yorkshire. Thither therefore he repaired, taking with him not only Proud Cis, but also his second son, Edmund, Earl of Rutland, as well as Salisbury and his duchess. In view of what was to happen, I am bound to say that it was a great pity York's eldest son, Edward, Earl of March, and Salisbury's eldest son, Warwick, did not elect to spend the festive season with their parents.

York may have been right in judging his ability to leave London in the care of others. But he was chancing his arm in traversing the wild northern country accompanied only by his personal guards and those of Salisbury. They reached Sandal safely enough, but by then the news of their presence had spread, and it had reached the ears of Clifford and Wiltshire, brooding at Chester. Instantly this pair conceived that they had the opportunity entirely to redress the state of affairs in our favour. Well, in fact, they were not far wrong. Hastily they raised from among my loyal supporters an army which has been put as high as eighteen thousand men, and marched the hundred-odd miles from Chester to Wakefield almost before York knew of it. When he did learn of it, he found himself in a dangerous position. However, he was a tried campaigner, and his castle of Sandal was a strong one. He resolved to stand a siege until relieved, and to this end sent messengers in every direction, but principally, we may surmise, to his eldest son Edward, who was now a lusty eighteen-year-old, and to Warwick, to come to his aid with all their available people.

We now must leave the realms of fact for those of fable. According to the Yorkists, what happened was this. The Duke and his brother-in-law, both experienced soldiers as I have said, are sitting behind their fortifications and daring Clifford and Worcester to do their worst (which, as they lacked cannon, was not very much against stone walls) when who should step forth from the ranks of the Lancastrians, and taunt the Duke of York with being unwilling to fight a mere woman, but ... Her Grace the Queen, Margaret of Anjou. Well, I would like to suppose I would have done that. But the fact is I was at that moment crawling ashore in Dumfries, soaking wet, shivering with cold, and racked with sea-sickness.

Now, to continue the Yorkist tale, the Duke, this experienced and most capable soldier who held the kingdom in his hand and could be certain that vast numbers of his supporters were marching to his rescue, and his brother-in-law (a man of hardly less stature) regarded his honour as at stake if he did not meet this woman in open combat, and so sallied from his castle against overwhelming odds and was defeated and killed, together with Salisbury. This last at least is fact. So it is fact that York was accompanied into the unequal fight by Rutland, who was taken attempting to flee, and personally decapitated by Clifford, shouting gleefully, 'Your father slew mine, and now I slay you.' That Rutland died begging for mercy is probable, knowing the youth.

Now we return to fiction. The battle won, Margaret of Anjou kicked and humiliated the dead bodies of her foes, caused their heads also to be cut off, and had them stuck on stakes above the gate of York city. Well, this happened. Their heads were there when I visited York a month later. But it was certainly not done at my command. I would probably, above all else, wish to be able to be in two places at once. The benefits in being able to perpetrate such a feat are almost unimaginable. Alas, contrary to what many have claimed, I am a woman and not a witch. It was simply impossible for me to have been in Scotland, where it can be proved I was, and at Wakefield, where it cannot, at one and the same time.

And yet, for the rest of my life – and probably for the rest of eternity – I was and shall be chased by this foul calumny, for all that the facts are indisputable. I even suspect that in the course of time some disreputable poet may make a great scene of it, to illustrate my villainy! The truth of the matter is, in my opinion, that York, finding himself besieged, and determining that I was *not* present – had I been he would have seen the royal standard – *then* decided to sally forth and chance his arm, for fear that I might be on my way.

In any event, this victory gained by Clifford and Worcester, which seemed at the time so complete, so utterly ruinous to the Yorkist cause, was in fact in the long run far more ruinous to ours. Richard of York, however personally hateful to me, was (as I have endeavoured to show) a gentleman and a man of honour, who, most importantly, lacked the stomach to *seize* a kingdom. Now he was dead, and I and my supporters were left to face his son, probably the most terrible avenging angel that has ever soared from the pit of hell to blight the slopes of mankind.

And of womankind, as well.

11

While these momentous events were taking place in Yorkshire, I was trying to obtain a welcome from the Scots.

These are very wild and savage people, who grow wilder and more savage as they are removed from any centres of civilisation, and these are in any event thin on the ground in this benighted country. They wear the oddest clothes, the men in some areas indulging in very short skirts, as if legs on either sex were ever intended to be revealed to the common gaze, the women wrapping themselves in brightly patterned shawls and cloaks. Their complexions are universally ruddy, although it is difficult to determine whether this is an hereditary matter; or caused by the howling and bitterly cold gale which blows constantly in these parts; or, most likely of all, by the drink they all indulge in – man, woman, and child – which is amber in colour, makes one's hair stand on end at the same time as it lights a fire in one's belly, and often leaves one entirely prostrate.

They are quite as aggressive in their habits as the Irish, to whom some experts think they are related. Unfortunately, while the Irish hate the English but are separated from us by a turbulent sea, the Scots hate the English and are separated from us by no more than a few hills. Thus they have since time immemorial been a bane to those of my people who would live in the north, while they have always assumed any

Englishman who strays across their frontier is worthy only of robbery and murder, and the same applies to any Englishwoman, although in the case of females there is usually a preliminary ceremony.

On top of all of these drawbacks they speak a quite incomprehensible language, which does not appear to be related to any other, and which spills over into their attempts to use a civilised tongue, with the result that even their efforts in English or French are largely unintelligible.

These were the savages into whose hands I now voluntarily delivered myself. No sooner had we stumbled ashore, I at least feeling like death and chilled to the marrow by my several days tossing on the Irish Sea, than we were seized and treated as shipwrecked mariners – and English shipwrecked mariners to boot.

However, we, or rather I, had a concealed strength: I was French. For the Scots, however ferocious, are yet greatly outnumbered by their southerly neighbours. Every so often an English king has bestirred himself, raised an army and marched across the border to carry out a bit of rape and pillage on his own account. These incursions the Scots, through lack of numbers and internecine rivalry amongst their own nobles, have only rarely been able adequately to resist. They still speak nostalgically of Bannockburn, when their immortal King Robert the Bruce defeated an enormous English army, but that army was commanded by the unedifying English King Edward II. More realistically they recall with shudders the invasions carried out by Edward II's father, Edward I, who is remembered as the Hammer of the Scots, or the defeats inflicted by Edward II's son, Edward III, or by the adherents of Henry Bolingbroke, my own grandfather-in-law.

They have therefore always required an ally to assist them or at least to distract their enemies. As the French have usually found themselves in the same position *vis-à-vis* the English, the two nations, or at least their royal houses, have insensibly inclined towards each other. As we have seen,

James II's sister was married to Charles VII's son, in the hopes of binding the two families even closer. Well, ambitions of this nature are always likely to be interrupted by death, but yet the link remained, and the fact that I was Queen of England and a fugitive was offset by the fact that I was a French princess and a fugitive. That is to say, I and my companions were not immediately murdered. And I was not even raped!

Yet we could hardly have landed in Scotland, in search of aid from the Scottish king, at a worse moment. Only a few months before, while I was hiding in Wales, James II had found it necessary to take action against one of his rebel nobles and had sallied forth against the fortress of Roxburgh, which he besieged with all the modern might available to a sovereign, including cannon. It did not rain on James II. Would that it had! His bombards were busily tearing great chunks of masonry from the walls of this castle when one of these chunks flew in the direction of the watching King and killed him on the spot. The poor lad was not yet thirty, being a few months younger than myself, and had been a most popular and successful monarch up to the last moment. The country from which I desperately needed assistance was therefore now in the hands of a small boy, or rather, of a Regent – and this was the King's widow, Mary of Guelders.

You can imagine this news gave me pause for thought, on several counts. Here were these savage lairds and their clansmen without hesitation placing the destiny of their country in the hands of a woman who was even more foreign to the Scots than I was to the English. What a contrast with the behaviour of my English lords. Or was this Mary of Guelders a quite exceptional woman? I knew of her, of course, but only vaguely; her lineage was nowhere as good as mine. Her mother, however, was the sister to Philip, the current Duke of Burgundy – who had proposed a match between me and his son, Charles, Count of Charolais (and later to the Count of Nevers). Once again I had to consider the quirks of history; had I married Charles, this Queen of

Scots would have been my first cousin by marriage.

I understood she was some years younger than myself, although the date of her birth was not generally known. However, she had hardly been older than fifteen when, with the encouragement of Uncle Charlie, she married James of Scotland in 1449.

Her married life had been in the strongest possible contrast to my own. She had married a vigorous, strong and warlike king; I had married a nonentity on whose head a crown had happened to be perched. She had been delivered of four strapping children by her husband; I had had to seek outside assistance. She had lost her husband in battle; mine had not had either the courage or the wit to sally forth and conquer or die sword in hand; and she was now Regent and supreme authority in her adopted country, where I was a fugitive from all authority in mine. The only point at which we met was that we were both young, both beautiful – or so I was told – and both warlike in our own natures. When James had had his unfortunate encounter with flying masonry, Mary, who accompanied her husband everywhere, had taken over the conduct of the siege and carried it to a successful conclusion.

This then was the character to whom I now had to apply for succour, whatever my personal feelings. And the necessity was growing by the day. For the Scots of Galloway, having decided that I *was* Queen of England, and therefore not to be raped and murdered, had determined that *as* Queen of England, I must be very rich and therefore to be robbed in every direction. When I explained to them that I was absolutely penniless, and that unless they fed me and my people they would have our deaths on their consciences, they became quite surly.

However, they also realised that I had to be of some value in some direction, and so sent off messengers to Mary, with the result that after a Christmas quite without celebration I received an invitation, or more properly a command, to repair with my people to Lincluden Abbey. There I would be given shelter, and there the Queen of Scots would be prepared to give me an audience.

My spirit rebelled against being treated with such disrespect, but I had no alternative hope of support. So to Lincluden I went, with my small entourage, which of course included both the Prince of Wales and Henry Somerset, as well as my faithful John Combe. And there I embarked upon one of the most remarkable episodes of my life.

On arriving at the abbey we found pleasantly spacious apartments awaiting us, and I was informed by the Prior that his household was one of the Queen of Scots' favourite residences. This was gratifying, and I was impressed by the surroundings, which were wooded and pleasant with a distant glimpse of the sea. I was also intrigued and a little concerned by the Prior's words: had I come to Scotland to encounter some female edition of Henry?

'Her grace is a religious person?' I ventured, anxiously.

He considered this. 'Her grace most certainly believes in God,' was his ultimate reply.

Thus I had to be patient, but on being advised that the Queen was approaching, and feeling much more hale and hearty than for a long time, as I had been sumptuously fed and given copious quantities of this amazing Scots liquor, whisky, to drink, I commanded my people, and most especially Edward and Henry, to don their best and had Bailly do her best, for me, although I possessed nothing that was not somewhat tarnished.

Then, in the quadrangle of the abbey, I awaited the arrival of the Queen of Scots. It was, be it remembered, early January and bitterly cold. I could not help but again feel I was being cruelly imposed upon. But I made the best of it, to be utterly surprised when Mary finally did arrive.

She entered the courtyard on horseback, accompanied by a guard of men-at-arms; her ladies followed some distance behind. I must say that she sat very well, controlled her mount perfectly, and slide from the saddle on to the step which had been placed for her with the utmost grace. I did my best not to goggle as I wondered if I had not inadvertently strayed into the presence of some Norse goddess.

Mary was very tall; she was not far short of six feet in her bare feet, and at the moment she was wearing boots. Her figure was a match for her height, without in the least being either fat or ill-proportioned. I know there are people who will always consider a forty-two-inch bust to be an ill proportion, but in fact it is a thing of beauty when allied to a flat belly, wide hips and long, powerful legs. Of course these other attributes of my hostess were not immediately apparent, as her habit, made of cloth of gold, was as extravagant as everything else about her, but I did understand that I was in the presence of a woman for whom the word voluptuous was totally inadequate.

And if the unveiling of these private delights was a matter for the future, there was nothing to interfere with the beauty of her face and hair. Mary had golden hair, which curled and snaked its way past her shoulders. She had big features – well, she had to, with such a body. But here again all was splendidly shaped, the high forehead indicative of intelligence, the wide-set eyes indicative of the clarity of her vision, the straight nose indicative of her imperious will, the wide mouth indicative of her generosity, and the square chin indicative of her determined character. From which it may be gathered that I found my hostess decidedly attractive.

Fortunately, her reaction was similar. 'Why, your grace,' she said, 'you are even more beautiful than by repute.'

As I could hardly have been looking worse in my bedraggled and sorely tried condition, I found this very complimentary. Perhaps my exhilaration dwindled a little as I introduced Queen Mary to my entourage and saw her bestowing quite as interested a gaze on Henry Somerset who was an even more handsome man than his father, but I was prepared to use every means at my disposal to gain this woman's help, even if it meant sacrificing Henry – hopefully on a temporary basis.

In fact it was to mean sacrificing a great deal more than that, as I very rapidly discovered. Following another sumptuous and very alcoholic repast – it appeared that the Queen of Scots had entirely fallen in with the habits of her adopted country – she announced that we queens were to have a tête-à-tête to discover where our mutual interests lay. I was all in favour of this and was prepared for some hard bargaining, but I am forced to admit that I had not the foggiest idea what I was in for.

The Queen escorted me to her own bedchamber and there dismissed all her attendants, so that we were alone. She then, there being a roaring fire in the grate, proceeded to remove every last vestige of her clothing while I watched in amazement, coupled with some envy at the revealing of so much feminine pulchritude, for she possessed an excess of everything, even pubic hair. Naked, she then proceeded to roll about on her bed in a most lascivious fashion until, discovering me watching her with some apprehension, she sat up in a cloud of golden threads, and said, somewhat defensively, 'It warms me up. Why do you not do the same, sweet Meg?'

I blame the whisky for what happened next. Naturally I do not wish to go into details, but with the liquor affecting my brain I could see nothing wrong in adopting her suggestion, and to roll about her bed naked in front of the fire was indeed warming, rapidly made the more so as Mary then resumed her rolling as well. The bed was not so large, and in a matter of moments I had been tumbled almost more thoroughly than ever by a man.

Soon becoming exhausted by these erotic antics, I fell into a deep sleep, from which I awoke perhaps an hour later with a gonging headache, a feeling of languorous well-being and, when I sat up and looked at myself and began to remember, a tremendous sensation of guilt. I then looked left and right for my hostess and found her sitting in a chair in front of the fire, still magnificently nude, and sipping from a goblet while she watched me. Perceiving that I was awake, she asked, 'Does your head hurt?'

'Abominably.'

'It usually does, after a midday nap,' she agreed. 'But then, it hurts more if one does not nap.' She filled the other goblet and brought it to me, a magnificent sight. 'This will make you feel better.' But what happens when this in turn wears off, I wondered. However, as I was in her hands – quite literally – I did not see an alternative; and, after drinking, the afternoon once again took on a rosy hue. She sat beside me to caress me. 'We must talk,' she said.

I didn't really know what we had to say at that moment, but I was again surprised. 'You need men and money,' she remarked.

'Why, yes, so I do,' I replied, caressing her in turn. Well, it was what she obviously wanted and there was a lot to go round.

'I may be able to help you,' she said, apparently ingenuously.

'I should be for ever grateful.'

'How grateful?' Mary inquired, giving a very tender portion of my anatomy a little pinch.

My eyes, which had been closed, promptly opened. It did occur to me that I was showing my gratitude at that moment, in the most generous possible manner, by giving her the freedom of my body. But I supposed that to say so might be unwise. 'Tell me what you wish.'

'I seek security.' Again, surprise. I would have stated unreservedly that the least insecure woman in the world had to be she holding me in her arms. 'For us both,' Mary continued.

I nuzzled her neck. It is remarkable how situations can grow on one. 'A treaty of eternal friendship between our peoples,' Mary murmured, doing some nuzzling in her turn, somewhat lower down my body. 'And love between their sovereigns. Which shall be signified by a marriage between the Prince of Wales and my daughter Mary.'

As Edward was just turned seven and the Princess Mary was four years younger, this seemed entirely satisfactory. 'Of course.'

'The fortresses of Berwick, Alnwick and Bamburgh.' The proposal came from the region of my navel, and perhaps on both counts left me speechless, and possibly caused some tension in my muscles – my knees came up and encountered her head. Mary looked up, her gaze reproachful; she disliked being interrupted in her pursuit of pleasure, or business.

'My lords would never agree,' I said.

'My dearest Meg, if I assist you to regain your power, I would expect you to use it absolutely.' The proposition sounded attractive. 'Besides,' she went on, resuming her explorations, 'as we would be eternal allies, what would it matter?'

Carrying on negotiations in these circumstances was very difficult; concentration was the problem. Dearest Mary had apparently a good deal of experience in what she was doing, whereas I was realising that my girlish cuddles with Bella had been almost totally innocent. Thus I agreed to give up the fortresses, once I was fully restored to power.

'Capital,' Mary said. 'I just know that you and I are going to be the very dearest of lovers, sweet Meg, for the rest of our lives. There is just one thing more.' She was busily exhausting me all over again, and I lay back on the cushions with my eyes closed, no longer really interested in affairs of state. 'Your young Somerset,' Mary said coyly, lying down beside me, 'is a most handsome fellow.'

That opened my eyes again. But really, the woman was insatiable . . . and omnivorous. She seemed to recognise that some explanation might be necessary. 'Well,' she said, 'I mean, he is not as handsome as you are beautiful. On the other hand, dearest Meg, I am a poor lonely widow. We must be honest with each other; there is something you cannot do for me.' Never have I felt so inadequate. 'Nor I for you,' she added magnanimously. 'Besides, if we share a lover, will we not be drawn even closer together?'

During the next week I found myself living, it seemed, one long orgy. I have no doubt everyone knew what was going on, but the clergy and the Queen of Scots' attendants seemed to accept our unnatural behaviour as entirely natural, while Henry of Somerset discovered himself in a seventh heaven, with two of possibly the three most beautiful and voluptuous and *willing* women in Europe eager to share their all. Mary, who seemed able to retain her head for business regardless of what was happening around her duly presented me with a treaty exactly as she had outlined it during our first set-to, betrothing Prince Edward to Princess Mary, binding England and Scotland to a perpetual alliance, and handing over to the Scots the border fortresses of Berwick, Alnwick and Bamburgh, the treaty to come into force the moment I was again ruling my kingdom. I signed without a moment's hesitation: ruling my kingdom was what I sought, and everything else was but an aside.

It was a happy, inconsequential time, which I sorely needed after all the trials and tribulations I had undergone during the preceding half-dozen years, and I fear I might never have left Lincluden Abbey had not affairs of state suddenly pressed me as hard as any of Mary's endeavours. Word arrived from Jasper Tudor of the remarkable victory at Wakefield.

We were stunned, and then overjoyed. Mary was not quite so pleased, as the news meant that I was no longer absolutely dependent upon her for help. But I was still entirely lacking in funds, and although I was eager to join my victorious army and complete the destruction of the Yorkist cause, I knew my men would have to be paid. Mary thus provided me with money – not enough, but then there is never enough money for great affairs – and she also insisted upon sending with me, as a bodyguard, a regiment of her own Highlanders – just about the most uncouth men I have ever encountered. But despite their skirts and red and bony knees, despite the fact that they wore no armour and were armed with but a small sword which they called a claymore, a yet smaller round shield, and an even smaller dagger, known as a skean-dhu – do not ask me why, despite their being seldom sober, never obeying an order, and always fighting among themselves, they were no men to cross. In fact, I could not help but wonder if the Queen of Scots had given them to me to rid herself of them!

We parted tearfully, having spent a last long hour tumbling each other about her bed, and then I set off – as I hoped, to glory and a restoration of the house of Lancaster.

My journey south to York, where my army was encamped and awaiting me, took about a week, and was fraught with difficulty. The roads and the weather were bad, and the Highlanders, once they were across the border, could only with great difficulty be restrained from reverting to type and thus to rape and pillage. There were several unfortunate incidents, and my reputation suffered. However, I was given a great welcome at York, and escorted by Clifford and Wiltshire and Jasper to see the rotting heads of York and Salisbury, which had been mounted above the city gates and surmounted with paper crowns. I must confess that I found this rather unedifying, but Prince Edward clapped his hands for joy, and I had not the heart to reprove him, as above all I sought in the boy a warlike spirit so lacking in his official father.

I arrived at York on 20 January, and resolved, while the Yorkists were still in disarray, as I was informed, to march on London, rescue the King, and resume all our prerogatives. My lords were in favour of this, but they pointed out that York's eldest son and heir, Edward, Earl of March, was still at large in the west, and was reputed to have accumulated an army with which to avenge his father's death. It may be recalled that I had met this youth from time to time when he had been a small boy. I had not laid eyes on him for some years, and had no wish to now, but although I had heard reports that he had grown into a tall and strong and handsome young man, I do not think I can be greatly criticised for not considering a youth of nineteen, totally inexperienced in warfare, to be a threat to my ambitions.

However, acting on the advice of my lords, I despatched part of my force under Jasper Tudor to march west and deal with the boy. The rest of us continued south, for I was more interested not only in regaining London and the person of the King, but in dealing with the last remaining Yorkist leader of any account, as I saw it: Warwick, who my spies informed me was moving north to meet me.

What is more, I learned that he had occupied that very town of St Albans where our cause had suffered its first military setback. Well, I thought, there could not be a better place for a return match. My generals, needless to say, were busy with plans and advice of how to circumnavigate Warwick and get between him and London, of how to parley with him ... I determined to ignore them. I wanted to fight.

At the same time, I was aware that I did not know sufficient of either the Earl's power, or his dispositions, and this was concerning me as we marched south, when my army received a most delightful and, as it turned out, valuable accretion to its strength. For who should come riding up at the head of a hundred men-at-arms but John Grey of Groby, and with him Bella!

It was over six months since I had last seen her beautiful face, and what a six months they had been, for me at the least! It turned out that she too had not lacked adventures. She told me of some of these as I folded her in my arms. My delight in her presence knew no bounds. My horizons had been greatly enhanced by my sojourn in Scotland, and larger than life as Mary of Guelders had been, she could never, by our very circumstances of both being queens and herself being very much in the ascendant at that time, have hoped to replace my dearest Bella in my affections. Bella, for her part, seemed every bit as overcome to be again in my arms, perhaps even more so, as during our separation her experiences had been entirely and even violently heterosexual.

This came out during our mutual reminiscences, in the course of which I naturally outlined some of my problems. 'You seek information about the Earl of Warwick, your grace?' The dear girl's eyes were alight with martial ardour. 'I shall obtain it for you.'

'You?' I cried in alarm.

She then related to me what had happened to her during our separation. She and Grey had escaped the ruination of our hopes at Northampton, and made their way home to Grafton, her mother's seat. There Bella had remained, while gallant Grey had gone off to see what could be done about our cause. Now of course it was widely known that Bella was one of my ladies-in-waiting and, indeed, that she was my favourite. Thus while some Yorkist bands were sent to Eccleshall, and others in various other directions seeking my whereabouts, it had seemed obvious to the victors to visit Grafton as well.

This visit had been carried out by no less a person than Warwick himself, eager to be the one to lay hands upon my person, and I am not speaking figuratively. Well, I was not there, but Bella was. According to her, and I entirely believe her (not only because it fits well with what later happened, but because I find it difficult to imagine any man – save perhaps my husband – having Bella as virtually a prisoner and not *acting* the man) the Earl then indulged in a little rape and pillage on his own account, seeking the comfort of those glowing white orbs which were at that moment pressed against my own.

'The foul wretch!' I cried. 'Did he achieve the ultimate?'

Bella blushed most prettily. 'What was I to do, your grace? My husband was away, my mother is aged, my sons are young . . . he was just a little fellow, after all.' I was in no way mollified, but I listened with interest as Bella continued her tale. Having had his way, several times, with the beautiful girl, Warwick departed; but that he had enjoyed himself had been evidenced by the arrival of many presents during the following six months.

Now Bella's own feelings in the matter were what one might have expected: outraged femininity that she should be forced into adultery. Above all other things she sought only the downfall of Warwick, and in this, if in nothing else, I do believe she remained constant for the rest of her life; or rather, as she is still living and prospering, of *his* life. Now she was determined to spare no effort to bring about his defeat. Her plan was a simple one. Warwick could not possibly yet know that Grey of Groby had joined my forces. He did, however, know that Grey was a Lancastrian supporter. Bella was certain that if she happened to stumble into St Albans, seeking her husband who had ridden off she knew not where, Warwick would welcome her with open arms and a warm couch ... and that she would have ample opportunity to discover his strength, his dispositions, and his intentions.

I was aghast at the risk she would be taking, but she was so enthusiastic at the prospect of playing the spy I finally agreed, while wondering if her femininity had been quite as outraged by the Earl's earlier advances as she pretended. Be that as it may, she went off, and returned several days later, tousled but triumphant. Everything had gone exactly as she had anticipated, she had spent three nights being debauched, and as many days gleaning all the information she could.

What she told me was this. Warwick was supported principally by the Duke of Norfolk, the Duke of Suffolk, and the Earl of Arundel, but by few other of the Yorkist magnates. He had a large army – Bella estimated it as perhaps thirty thousand men, which made it hardly smaller than my own since I had detached Jasper – but it was in the main composed of untried levies, and he had little artillery. She further told me that it was not his plan to sit tight and hold St Albans, as we had attempted to do so disastrously six years earlier, but on hearing of our approach he would move his people out of the town and on to the high, flat ground north of the houses, blocking the north road along which he assumed I had to advance. There he would give battle, or more likely, she told me he had said, watch me turn aside from the prospect of so sanguinary an encounter. He still considered me nothing more than a little woman and he no doubt remembered the ease with which he had gained the day at Northampton. Possibly most important of all, Bella told me that Warwick had the King with him.

My lords immediately went into a huddle, everyone as usual offering conflicting advice. I may say that seldom can there have been a more lively assembly of all the best blood in England. Consider! Standing around me were the Earls of Exeter, Somerset, Devonshire, Northumberland and Shrewsbury, not to mention Lords Clifford, Fitzhugh, Grey of Codnor, Greystoke, Roos, Welles, Willoughby as well as Grey of Groby, who was as yet not even a knight but was well known to possess military talent. Nearly all of these men had been present at Wakefield, and should thus have been filled with martial confidence, but still they shillied and shallied until I interrupted their debate and told them what we would do.

I flatter myself that my plan was as simple as Bella's, and as forthright as any of Caesar's. I may add that it was certainly as successful. Some of my generals were for meeting Warwick upon his blasted heath, others were for attempting to bypass the Yorkist army. To my untrained but intelligent mind there seemed no reason why we should not do both, and thus sow confusion in the enemy ranks. They were aghast at the prospect, but I was not to be gainsaid, and so the following day I and two-thirds of my people set off on a flank march to the west, while Somerset led the remainder, which included the ferocious Highlanders, straight down the road.

Somerset's orders were to move very slowly, while I had my men moving as fast as I could. Now, obviously we were overseen by the Yorkists, who immediately understood my manoeuvre. This had been feared by my lords, who had been afraid Warwick would seek to interpose himself between our two bodies, and defeat us separately. But I knew Warwick. I knew that not only was he an inept general whose career this far had been dependent more on luck than ability, but that he had a fatal disinclination for risking all, and especially himself, in aggressive action if there was a chance he might gain the day by defensive measures. More than anything, I knew that he had the King, who, whatever his trials, was still the sole fount of any attempt at government the Yorkists could attempt. The future King-maker was not going to risk losing possession of his ace.

In the event, he behaved exactly as I had foreseen. He could not stay where he was, or he would be attacked on two sides at once; he was afraid to advance and risk all on a single throw of the dice; so he opted to retreat into the supposed safety of St Albans. This in the face of a rampant and advancing opponent. As soon as I saw his banners streaming to the rear I knew that victory was ours. I personally could do nothing more. I pulled my horse aside, and told Clifford, commanding my half of the army, 'Cut me a path to my husband.'

He gave a great shout, bellowed, 'A-Marguerite!' – how glorious it sounded – and led the charge, while Bella and Prince Edward sat their horses beside me and watched the spectacle. My men were inspired. With our enemies in disarray as we gave them no time to reform their ranks after their retreat, my brave fellows smashed their way into the town from both north and west, and not for the first time Warwick's heart failed him at the vital moment. He can have had little doubt what would have been his fate had he been dragged a captive before me, after denouncing me as an adulteress and dismissing my son as a bastard. Within less than an hour the Yorkists were in full retreat, led by their commanders, and a body of men-at-arms had returned to my position to escort me into the town and the scene of my victory. 'His grace?' I asked anxiously, fearing that Warwick might have carried Henry off with him.

'King Henry awaits your grace,' the stout fellow told me. After all, in his fright Warwick had not even had the wit to realise that without the King he was merely a rebel outlaw.

My heart swelled fit to burst as I rode between the ranks of my cheering men and on to St Peter's street. It was now for the first time they hailed me as 'Corporal Marguerite', and why not? It had been my strategy, which has been greatly praised by military historians – although they have not always given me the credit for thinking of it – that had brought our victory.

Waiting for me in the centre of the town were several of my lords, their swords and armour bloodied, but all wearing the smiles of victory. And waiting there too was the husband I had not seen for seven months.

I am bound to say that he looked well; in fact he had put on weight through lack of exercise, and he had certainly not been starved. Equally am I bound to say that he did not reveal any great pleasure at beholding his wife, who had so gallantly come to his rescue. Or his young son. 'Why Meg,' he remarked, 'you are windswept.'

'We have gained a great victory, sire,' I told him, in case he had not noticed it.

'I am pleased,' he said. 'Pleased.'

'Many of your devoted followers performed great deeds, sire.'

'That is good news,' he said.

'Will you not knight them?'

'Why, willingly.'

'Beginning with the Prince of Wales?'

Henry regarded Edward benevolently enough, but without any display of love or even affection. Obviously during his incarceration the Yorkists had been firing their foul insinuations at him from every quarter, and no doubt he had come to believe them. But he was prepared to knight my son, and on the field of battle, which was gratifying. While the preparations were being made, I took Clifford and Somerset aside. 'Do you round up every deserving captain,' I told them. 'We must make this a great occasion. Particularly do I wish to see Grey of Groby knighted.'

They nodded and sent off their esquires to bring forward all those worthy of the honour, while Bella, who had ridden

into the town with Prince Edward and me, clapped her hands
for joy. Meanwhile, Clifford directed my attention to two
vaguely familiar men who were standing behind the King,
under guard.

'What is their crime?' I asked.

'Why, simply that they are Yorkists, who forebore to flee
with their fellows,' Clifford said. 'They are Lord Bonville,
and Sir Thomas Kyriel.'

They knelt before me. 'We were appointed by the Earl of
Warwick to guard his grace during the battle, your grace,'
Bonville explained. 'When the orders came to abandon the
town, we would have taken his grace with us. But he wished
to stay, and begged us to remain with him and continue to
guard his person. This we did, your grace, and so are now
your prisoners. But we did our duty to the King.'

Henry had by now joined us. 'They are right good fellows,
Meg,' he declared. 'I have promised them their freedom.'

With that he wandered off again, making for the nearest
church, no doubt to give thanks for his deliverance.

Now, I had no reason to hate these men, beyond the mere
fact that the were Yorkists. I have indeed some difficulty in
recalling my exact emotions at the time, as there was so
much happening, or about to happen, but I know I even had
some small idea of rewarding the pair for protecting the
King to the last. With this in mind I turned to my son, and
in my continuing high good humour, asked, 'Well, Edward,
what shall we do with these two fellows? You shall decide.'

'Cut off their heads,' Prince Edward replied, without a
moment's hesitation. I was struck dumb, for the first time
truly realising how deeply had the iron of our misfortunes
entered into that childish soul. And before I could give any
thought to my reply or to how I was going to extricate
myself from my dilemma, after having announced before the
assembled Lancastrian lords that the Prince should decide
the Yorkists' fate, I was distracted by a huge shriek of horror
from Bella, who fell to the ground in a swoon.

I saw the reason immediately. My lords, as I had

commanded, were bringing forward every one of our leaders not already a knight to receive the accolade from the King. And amongst these gallant fellows was John Grey of Groby ... but he was being carried on a litter, blood oozing from his smashed armour.

The Yorkist prisoners were forgotten as I hurried forward. Someone had thoughtfully emptied a bucket of water over Bella, and she joined me, her coiffure a dribbling golden mess, her houppeland similarly damp, her bosom heaving. To that bosom she now clutched her husband, rapidly becoming as bloody as he.

I understood immediately that Grey had not long to live; he had been struck several times with a mace, and then, when lying on the ground, had been ridden over by several horses. But I was determined that the widow Grey would be the widow Lady Grey, and had the mangled wreck of a man carried before the King, that the might receive the two taps of the sword which separate the élite from *hoi polloi*. This Henry was pleased to do, as he was always at his best when responding to distress in others. I then sent Sir John and Lady Grey apart, having first clutched Bella tearfully to my breast, that they might spend his final hours together.

This concluded, I was quite distraught. On leaving the King to discover what Prince Edward was doing, I found him where I had left him – in the main square of the town, watching the erection of a scaffold. 'Surely there is more useful work those fellows can be doing?' I demanded of Clifford, who was overseeing the proceedings.

'They are obeying the command of the Prince of Wales, your grace,' Clifford told me. 'Bonville and Kyriel are to lose their heads.'

'Oh, really, Sir John,' I snapped. 'What crime have they committed, other than being Yorkists? Did they not stay with the King, most loyally? And did he not promise them their lives?'

Clifford held my arm to lead me aside. 'His grace may have done so, your grace. But it was privily. Before our assembled army the Prince of Wales condemned them to death. It may well be that in the next few years our people will have to take all their orders from the Prince. Do you think it is fair to his authority to have his first public command contemptuously set aside?'

I bit my lip. I knew, of course, that Clifford had as much iron in his soul as Edward, and sought only to be avenged on every Yorkist he could lay hands on, just as I knew his hatred was compounded by guilt over the murder of young Rutland. On the other hand, his words had a certain dreadful truth about them. Above all else I wanted my son to be a reincarnation of Great Harry, or better yet, his mighty namesake Edward III. To reach those heights he would necessarily have to command actions which might seem cruel, or even abominable. Thus, unusually for me, I found it difficult to reach a decision. While I was still considering my position I was distracted yet again by the arrival of a messenger, all foam-flecked horse and mud-flecked clothing, who fell from his exhausted mount to his knees before me. 'Your grace,' he gasped, 'I come from the Earl of Pembroke.'

'Yes?' I demanded, while an icy hand seemed to clutch at my heart – the man did not look as if he were about to make me jump for joy. I feared to hear of Jasper Tudor's fate.

'A great misfortune has overtaken our arms, your grace,' the fellow stammered. 'The Earl, accompanied by his father, met the Yorkists at Mortimer's Cross some days ago. The Yorkists were commanded by the Earl of March, your grace, who claimed to see several suns in the sky. Thus inspired, he was irresistible.'

'We were defeated?' Clifford demanded, as if that were not now obvious.

'The Earl of Pembroke fled, with what part of his force he could save. His father, and all other nobles who were captured, were taken to Hereford and there beheaded in the market place.'

'Owen Tudor is dead?' I muttered, wondering what effect

the news of his step-father's demise would have upon Henry.

'And many others, your grace. It is said that the Earl of March, who now claims the title Duke of York as heir to his father, has declared that he will slaughter every nobleman on the Lancastrian side in payment for the deaths of his father and brother at Wakefield.'

I glanced at Clifford, who for a moment paled, and then gave a great shout of laughter. 'The boy will behead us all, will he? Well, then, we shall throw him a few heads to play with, first.'

From that moment there was no possibility of saving the lives of Bonville and Kyriel. Had I attempted to do so I might have lost the allegiance of those very lords upon whom I counted to support the throne. And thus I stood with the Prince and watched the two hapless fellows, whose only crime was that of having done their duty, marched up on to the scaffold and there beheaded.

Remarkably, this was the first time I had ever seen a man's head separated from his body.

But there were more important considerations than that of executing Yorkists. A fierce debate now raged as to what we should do next. In this, I admit it freely, I was not my usual dominant personality. I was exhausted, physically by the exertions of the past few days and mentally by the crushing blow I had received when I had counted myself utterly triumphant. Of course, I told myself, this Yorkist victory was but a pinprick, even if an expensive one; there should be little difficulty in dealing with this upstart boy. It will be understood that I still had no idea of the monster with whom I now had to contend. Nevertheless it was a daunting thought that, far from resting, I must needs be immediately undertake another campaign.

Another reason for my inability to take control of our council of war was my concern for Bella. As I had feared,

Grey died only a few hours after being knighted. Bella was utterly distraught, and I could do little to comfort her. When she begged leave to take her husband's body back to Groby for burial, I readily acceded. We hugged and kissed each other and she departed that very night, having promised to come to me at Westminster as soon as I was back in residence. How do we mortals make our plans, only for the Deity to set them at naught. I was never to be in residence in Westminster again, and I was not to see Bella again for more than ten years ... by which time our circumstances had greatly changed. One could almost say they had been reversed.

Bella gone, I went to bed and slept like a corpse. When I awoke, my brain and my body were alike refreshed. I breakfasted, dressed, and with Prince Edward set off to call upon my husband. Emerging from the house I had chosen as my quarters, I was confounded to see and hear my army packing up to move out. Well, I had not intended to hang about St Albans, to be sure, but it was my intention to march on London ... only as far as I could see my people were taking the road back whence we had come, to the north. I hastily sent squires left and right to summon my generals, who gathered quickly enough. 'Will someone be kind enough to tell me what is going on?' I demanded. 'London is that way. The Earl of Warwick went that way. The seat of government is that way. And that is the way we must go.'

Henry Somerset shook his head. 'It cannot be, your grace.'

I was confounded. 'Why not?'

'The Earl of Warwick will be back in the city by now,' Clifford explained.

I was more confounded yet. 'Then should we not hurry behind him?'

'We would never catch him now, your grace,' Wiltshire said. 'And he is very popular with the Londoners. We have not the men to fight a whole city.'

'Apprentices,' I snorted.

'Then there is the Duke of York,' someone muttered.

'I assume you are referring to the Earl of March,' I snapped. 'The Duke of York is dead, and no one has the right to call himself Duke of York until the King has agreed to it.'

'Whatever he is called, your grace,' Clifford said, 'he is marching on London with an army which is attracting men at every stop. For us to press on would be to risk finding ourselves between Warwick and his Londoners, and March and his people.'

'There is another point to be considered,' said Wiltshire. 'The Scots. There is not a man in London would not fight to keep those rascals out, especially as it is remembered that your grace promised her army the sack of the city.'

At the time I was too angry fully to grasp the import of his words, which meant, in effect, that my own oratory before the battle of Northampton had ruined my chances of ever being accepted in the capital. 'Are you gentlemen trying to tell me that this victory we have gained is meaningless?' I inquired, loading my voice with sarcasm.

'By no means, your grace,' Clifford said. 'But the whole matter must be considered. Should we withdraw to the north, we may enlarge and replenish our forces, link up perhaps with the Earl of Pembroke and his Welshmen, and seek to deal with York – I beg your pardon, your grace, with March – and Warwick when we are ready.'

'Leaving London to them,' I said.

'London is meaningless, your grace. It is but a town. It is the King who matters. We have regained possession of the King. That is the real measure of our triumph here. It means that the Yorkists are rebels in arms against their anointed lord. They will realise this soon enough. Then they will either disperse, leaving the road south open to us, or they will have to seek another battle, which will be fought at a time and a place of our choosing.'

Perhaps I was not as refreshed as I supposed. I allowed myself to be persuaded, did not even take offence at having the King spoken of as if he were some kind of inanimate trophy – because that was what he was. And so we marched north again. As we did so, I was pleased to discover that my advisers seemed to have been proved correct. I rode at the head of our army, the King at my side, and the roads were crowded with people, eager to see and cheer their monarch. Shouts of 'Henry for ever!' were interspersed with those of 'Corporal Marguerite!', and men flocked to our banner. By the time we reached Yorkshire, I commanded the largest army ever assembled beneath the banner of an English king. I myself do not know for certain how many men had drawn the sword in defence of the right, but some estimates have put it as high as sixty thousand.

Now indeed I was ready to turn about and head south again, when we received the news that the Earl of March was on his way north to give battle.

But this was not all the news I received. This nineteen-year-old boy had suddenly proved himself to have an ambition which made his father's seem modest. Having marched with his army to London, and linked up with Warwick's beaten forces, he had entered the city itself, and been received with acclamation by the inhabitants. Well, they would, wouldn't they? Thus encouraged, this juvenile delinquent had summoned a parliament, and before the assembled Lords and Commons of the Yorkist cause had laid claim not merely to the Dukedom of York, but to the entire Kingdom of England.

He marched against us now as King Edward IV.

12

My lords of course made merry of young March's preten-
sions, and I reminded myself that the youth had not been
anointed and crowned, and that the mere announcement that
Henry had been deposed had absolutely no legality whatsoever. At the same time, I am bound to confess that the
boldness of the act struck a chill to my heart. Hardly less
distressing was the publication by March of a genealogical
table setting out very clearly his superior right to the throne.
And more disturbing than all was the way the Londoners had
taken him to their bosoms – already we were hearing tales
that the young giant (who stood several inches over six feet)
had so captivated the women of the capital that their bosoms
were not all they took him to at every opportunity – and the
way they advanced him money, something they had always
refused to do for my own poor husband.

I could not help but share these apprehensions with Henry
Somerset, who appreciated my anxiety. 'Our only hope is to
fight the rascal, beat him, and kill him' he declared. 'There
is absolutely no need for thoughts of treating with him, or
clemency for him. He is a self-acknowledged traitor and
rebel, and you can have no doubt what would be the King's
fate, and that of the Prince of Wales, were he to triumph.'

And what of mine, I wondered, giving a womanly shudder
as I recalled some of the tales of this young lecher's doings.

What might be his reaction to finding so much beauty a hapless captive at his feet? I had just celebrated, if one can call it that, my thirty-first birthday, and I am bound to say that – no doubt owing to the strenuous life I had been forced to live over the past two years – I was as healthy and physically fit, and therefore as beautiful, as ever before in my life.

But I was in total accord with Somerset's point of view. Having regard to our own tremendous strength, as it appeared, the decisive battle could not take place soon enough.

That this encounter *was* going to be decisive was obvious to us all; it would be the final throw of the dice, we were determined. To making this last throw successful for us, we bent all our minds and endeavours.

We were favoured, at least as it seemed, by the headlong determination of the Yorkists to throw themselves upon our swords. Or certainly the anxiety of Warwick to avenge his defeat at St Albans by a woman, as was being loudly bruited. Our spies informed us that the Earl commanded the vanguard of the youthful 'king', whose elevation he regarded as his own personal triumph. March was following behind in a more leisurely fashion.

I established my headquarters in York, and there assembled my generals to listen to my views. I had studied the map with great care. Once again was I surrounded by the best blood in England, every one of whom had tasted victory under my banner. Thus none of them was inclined to question my dispositions. King Henry, I might add, took no part in these discussions; he preferred to pray. I assumed he was praying for our victory – I thought it best not to inquire.

I had learned a good deal from my previous encounters with the Yorkists. I had been present, and in reasonable command, at three battles. At St Albans it had been the enemy standing upon the defensive in a poor position, and I had been able to make him move and catch him while moving. But at both Blore Heath and Northampton I had been obliged to cross a stream to get at the foe, and in each case it had proved disastrous. There had been other factors involved, to be sure. But the stream had in each instance played an important part in the outcome of the battle.

Now, some ten miles south of York there was a stream, called the Aire. Immediately to the north of it there was a large moor, an ideal place on which to draw up my army. Equally was I sure that March had far more anxieties than I, as his entire fortune rested upon establishing his claim to the throne by capturing and forcing the abdication of Henry – or murdering him: it came to the same thing. 'Therefore,' I explained to my generals, 'he will seek to attack. If we hold the line of the Aire, in strength, but with our main body drawn up on the moor behind, we will face him with an insuperable problem. To attack us frontally will mean disaster. Thus he will seek to turn our position. And once he does that, we will be able to attack him at will'. I looked from face to face, and saw nothing but agreement with my plan. 'We will establish our field headquarters there,' I said, and placed my finger on the village of Towton, some eight miles south of York and on the edge of the moor.

Again, agreement with the plan. 'My lord Northumberland,' I said. 'You will command the van. My lord Somerset, you will command the main battle. Clifford, you will have the cavalry and patrol the stream.'

'And you, your grace?' they asked.

'I shall be with the Duke of Somerset.'

But at this, as usual, they demurred; and, as usual, I had to bow to their wishes. I could quite understand that for my generals to worry about my safety in the midst of a battle would be greatly to distract them from the business of beating the foe, and equally, having made my dispositions, there was little I could do about the conduct of the battle itself, at least in its early stages. However, there was a church in Towton with a conveniently high steeple, and from that vantage point I would be able to oversee the field. With a body of stout gallopers at my disposal, so that I could quickly send commands to whomever I chose, I reckoned I would be more in charge of events from such a perch than in the thick of the mêlée; being on an elevated site had worked well enough at Northampton until that damnable rain squall. And so I agreed.

I am afraid that, even after sixteen years on the throne of this benighted country, I had still not properly come to understand the vagaries of English weather. Of course, no self-respecting Continental general campaigns in winter. Uncle Charlie had always shut up shop completely between October and April, and great soldiers like Henry V, Edward III or the Black Prince had only ever descended on France in the heat of summer.

But in this war all sense of decorum had gone by the board at Wakefield, fought in December. Now there had been two battles in the February snow, and this month of March was even colder. But even so, a beastly blizzard was the last thing anyone expected, even when the skies turned dark with clouds.

On being informed of the approach of Warwick and the Yorkist van, I commanded my army to move out and take up their positions. Then I visited the King. I may say that we had not slept together since our reunion; Henry had entirely renounced the flesh and I had other things on my mind – not that I had the slightest desire ever to find myself in bed with him again, knowing all the frustrations that would ensure. However, he was the King of England, and it was his army I was commanding and intending to lead to victory. 'I believe the next few days will be decisive to your reign, sire,' I told him. 'Will you not accompany me to oversee the battle? It would greatly hearten the men.'

'Tomorrow is Saturday,' he pointed out.

'I am aware of that, sire.'

'Meg, Meg,' he remonstrated. 'What a heathen creature you are, to be sure. If tomorrow is Saturday, then the next day is Sunday.'

'Your logical deductions have always filled me with admiration, your grace.'

'What is more,' my husband continued, ignoring my sarcasm, 'it is Palm Sunday, when all good men and true, and all good women too, should be on their knees. No, no, there can be no battle this weekend, unless we can be certain of returning to York by tomorrow night.'

It was useless to argue with him, of course, or to point out that Warwick was not likely to stop advancing because of a religious festival. 'I do assure you, sire,' I told him, 'that I have every intention of being in church tomorrow, and perhaps even on Sunday.' Or at least, on top of one – but why split hairs?

I now rode out with my generals to oversee the posting of our people; word had been received that March had caught up with his cousin Warwick at Pontefract, and that there could be no doubt that they would be on us tomorrow. I had already reconnoitered the ground and chosen my position. This was on the brow of a shallow hill, facing down into the valley beneath, which meant that the Yorkists would have to come at us up the slope, to their discomfort. But the position held other advantages; it could not be turned, because my right wing was protected by a cliff, and my left by a marsh. 'We are impregnable, your grace,' Trollope told me. He of course had more reason than any of us, except myself, to require victory. His fate if he fell into the hands of the Yorkists after deserting them the previous year did not bear consideration.

But I agreed with him. By now reports were coming in that the enemy advance guard was almost at the stream; and so I despatched clifford and his horse to keep them off, and retired for the night in the best of spirits. Twenty-four more hours, one more battle, and the kingdom would again be mine, I was certain. However, as Henry Somerset, the Prince and I were dining, a galloper arrived all in a lather. 'The enemy have crossed the river, your grace,' he stammered.

'How can this be?' I inquired, refusing to share his alarm.

'They used the unguarded ford at Ferrybridge,' the man said.

'Has the main body crossed?' Somerset demanded.

'No, my lord. The ford is held by a detachment. The main body has not yet come up.'

'The boy is a fool,' I said. 'He knows not how to take advantage of temporary success. Now we must dislodge those fellows immediately.'

Somerset nodded. 'I will attend to it.'

'Begging your pardon, your grace, my lord,' the messenger said, 'my lord Clifford is on his way to Ferrybridge now. It is from him that I have come.'

Obviously Clifford and his horse would get there long before Somerset could detach sufficient men for the task, and in any event, I was against any disruption of our ranks, even if the Yorkists managed to cross in good order. So we placed our trust in Clifford. But there went the prospects of a sound night's sleep.

I was awake and dressed at first light. Bailly, being now too old for campaigning, had been left in York, but I had a couple of young girls with me. I then had a hasty breakfast, but had not yet finished the meal when another galloper arrived from Clifford. 'Great news, your grace!' he announced. 'Lord Clifford has retaken the ford. The Yorkists were asleep when he fell on them, now they are all dead.'

'Great news indeed,' I said. 'I wonder what those two scoundrels will do now?' With that the Prince and I set off for my church tower. Somerset accompanied us to Towton, to see us well posted. He was pleased with Clifford's triumph, of course, but was unhappy about the weather, for the clouds were now very low and threatening. Yet I still had no doubts about the outcome of the battle. 'If it rains, well, our artillery will be useless, but so will theirs, Henry. Be of good cheer.'

It was just as well I told him that, for as I embraced him for a last time before climbing the steps to the tower, a third galloper arrived, and one look at his face indicated catastrophe.

We had suffered a grave set-back. Far from being the military idiot I had supposed him, this young tyro Edward of March was already revealing himself as a man of immense energy and considerable genius. He had indeed seized the ford at Ferrybridge, but one might almost have supposed this was but a decoy, as he obviously knew the event would very rapidly be known to us, and no doubt he anticipated being expelled by Clifford. But apparently he also knew Clifford, and was confident that rash but careless man would rest on his laurels, because at the same time the Yorkists had seized another ford, at Castleford, three miles higher up, and this was *unbeknown* to us. Thus while Clifford celebrated his victory, he suddenly found himself assailed from behind by the rampant Yorkists. 'His men are routed, your grace,' the unhappy fellow related.

'My lord Clifford?'

'Dead, your grace. He received an arrow in the throat and was killed outright.'

I looked at Somerset in dismay; Clifford had been his best friend. But this was no time for mourning. 'What is happening now?' I asked.

'The Yorkists have retaken Ferrybridge, your grace, and the whole army is now crossing.'

Hastily I climbed the tower, Somerset with me. From the parapet we looked out across our own people, whose position was some two miles to the south, at the distant edge of the moor, which was a-bristle with pikes and banners. 'Let us join our men,' I said.

'But you were to remain here, your grace,' Henry protested.

'I will return here when the battle commences,' I promised him. 'I wish to be with my people until then.' I rested my hand on his shoulder. 'Put Clifford from your mind, Henry,' I said. 'Only vengeance remains to us.'

*

In fact I had already discerned that as the day was now well advanced, it was unlikely there would be a battle before the morrow, and thus the encounter would take place on Palm Sunday after all. That would no doubt distress my lord the King, but it could not be helped. Meanwhile it was my business to inspire my troops, and this I did as I had before Northampton: by riding among them with Prince Edward, reminding them that they were fighting for the right, exhorting them to surpass themselves, and being amply rewarded by the huzzas and shouts of 'Corporal Marguerite!'

I also of course kept an eye on the Yorkist host, which gradually assembled on the slope opposite to us, although my anticipation was proved correct, and it was nearly dark by the time they had all come up. Obviously there was the temptation to advance and attempt to fall upon them piecemeal, but both my generals and I felt that our defensive position was so strong it would be a mistake to compromise it by snatching at victory on less favourable ground. So we waited, and watched, and Somerset held my arm and pointed. 'Look yonder, your grace.'

I narrowed my eyes the better to see and made out a mounted man in sable armour, who was clearly head and shoulders taller than those around him. 'The Duke of York,' Somerset said.

I did not like his tone, which had a suggestion of awe in it. 'I am sure you mean the Earl of March,' I commented. 'So he is a large youth. He is thus the easier to hit with an arrow.'

The Earl of March was actually making his way to the front of the army, and for a moment I thought that after all he intended to do battle in the darkness, which would obviously have been total folly. However, a moment later two mounted men rode away from him and towards us; one carried a flag of truce, and a trumpet with which he blew several blasts just in case we had not seen his approach. The Prince, Somerset and I rode out in front of our people in turn, and were joined by several other of my lords.

The herald drew rein when some fifty feet from us, and unrolled a parchment. Behind us there had been a great rustle of interest, but this now died and the evening was silent, the only sound that of the breeze whipping our banners and the flag of truce.

The herald spoke in a high, clear voice. 'These are the words of his grace, Edward the Fourth, King of England, France and Ireland. Be it known that a Parliament of this land, summoned to meet at London Town, has unanimously pronounced Henry of Windsor, previously known as Henry the Sixth, unfit to rule, and he is thereby deposed. In his place, Parliament has unanimously chosen His Grace Edward of York, King of this realm.' He paused for a moment, but no man in our ranks moved.

The herald resumed. 'As of this moment, therefore, Henry of Windsor, his wife the Princess Margaret of Anjou, and her bastard son, the so-called Prince of Wales, are attainted traitors to this realm.' Now there was a rustle, but it was mostly of anger, I was happy to note.

The herald continued. 'As of this moment, therefore, any man, be he lord or villein, who attempts to defend or fight for, or who offers assistance or succour to, the said Henry of Windsor, the said Margaret of Anjou, and the said Edward of Wales, is also attainted traitor. Be it known to every man that it is the intention of his grace the King to advance with his army and seize the persons of the said Henry of Windsor, Margaret of Anjou and Edward of Wales, and place them under arrest, pending the judgement of Parliament. Be it further known that no quarter will be granted to any man who attempts to fight for these attainted traitors. Those true men who would prove their loyalty to his grace the King have but to lay down their arms and leave the field this night. No harm will befall them. Any man found on this field, under arms, and beneath the banner of the said traitors, when dawn breaks tomorrow, will be executed on the spot. This is the will of his grace, Edward the Fourth of England, France and Ireland.'

With that he wheeled his horse and rode away, returning to the Yorkist ranks somewhat faster than he had approached ours in his haste to be out of range before one of my Welshmen decided to ignore the flag of truce and send an arrow behind him.

My lords were looking quite dismayed at March's words. But I smiled at them, and said, 'Well, my lords, at least we know where we stand. Believe me, if any man is sufficiently faint-hearted to be frightened by threats, he is welcome to depart this instant.' Of course none of them had the courage to reveal himself a coward. 'Well, then, my lord of Somerset,' I said, 'I think it would be appropriate of us to make a reply.'

Our own herald was summoned and sent forth, to answer in kind: that Edward of March was a self-confessed traitor, as was Richard of Warwick and all the lords who gathered beneath his banner. As were all the common soldiers. Their only hope, our herald told them, was to abandon the White Rose, which here for the first time floated above the rebel ranks, and escape to the safety of their homes.

I am bound to admit that our threat was received with a great shout of derision, but in any event the die had now been cast. There was to be no quarter on either side, and the coming battle was to be to the death. With this in mind I slept easily, among my gallant men. I was prepared to let it all rest on the morrow.

Looking back on my life, I can say without reservation that I have been scurvily treated by the Almighty. Perhaps, as time goes by, He may see fit to atone for all His past behaviour towards me, but time is now running short. And there is a lot to atone for. I will not go into the question of the mere fact that I was unfortunate enough to be married to Henry of Windsor, when I could have been the wife of Charles of Charolais, or even James of Scotland. How different my life would have been! I had not forgotten the rain at Northampton, and could not believe that God could be so scurvy as to rain on me again at a decisive moment. Well, He was not so scurvy; He possessed a far more potent weapon which He was about to hurl, quite literally, into my face.

As I have said, I slept soundly, although during the night it turned very cold. As Prince Edward was in my arms I perhaps fared better than most, but we were both shivering when we awoke into the half-light of an uncertain winter's dawn. All around us was the hustle and bustle of my army preparing for battle. Somerset was armed and accoutred – no difficult matter as we had all slept in our clothes – and had our horses waiting. He saw me into my saddle, and I stooped to squeeze his arm and kiss his cheek, and remind him that he above all other men was my champion. I then walked my horse, the Prince at my side, along the ranks of my men, who uttered a mighty shout of loyalty and passion. It was a great moment.

But the Yorkists were obviously preparing to advance, and so Prince Edward and myself and my ladies, together with my escort, returned to Towton, and the Prince and I climbed the tower in order to oversee the battle. The morning had grown steadily colder since dawn – there was no sign of the sun – and perched as we were some sixty feet above the ground Edward and I needed to slap our hands together to maintain our circulation. But I was warmed by my anticipated victory as the Yorkists slowly advanced to within bowshot. Our position was immensely strong, given that we also clearly possessed a superiority in numbers; therefore it seemed to me that the attacking force, and the Yorkists appeared determined to be the aggressors, must suffer inordinate casualties in their endeavour to break our line.

I had reckoned without the Deity! As I have said, it was a very cold, black morning, with the clouds seeming to collide with each other as they rushed by above our heads. The wind was blowing from the south, that is, into our faces. This was inconvenient, to be sure, but not necessarily fatal; I had drawn

Somerset's attention to it, and he had agreed that our archers should wait until the Yorkists were within a hundred yards before loosing their shafts. This waiting period had now begun, my men standing patiently beneath a Yorkist barrage, for their archers had fired earlier than usual, relying on the wind to carry their shafts that much further. But they did little damage, and with easy confidence I watched the approach of the clanking mass of men and arms, quickly identifying both Edward of March and Warwick, who rode together, the one an immense figure, the other much smaller, and more quick and nervous in his movements. The gap between the two forces was rapidly narrowing, and I could see Somerset preparing to give the command for our archers to shoot . . . when it began to snow!

To begin with there were only one or two flakes, whistling across the morning; one settled on my nose, and I hastily brushed it away – I was cold enough as it was. But before I could catch my breath I was assailed by what seemed an almost solid wall of the stuff. I gasped and shivered, as did Prince Edward, while we attempted to peer into the murk. But we might as well have been a hundred miles away from the battle, instead of less than two. It was as if a white curtain had been drawn around us and we were isolated in our tower, quite unable to determine what was happening, or to affect events in any way.

What was actually happening was the grimmest and most bloody struggle ever to take place on English soil. Consider: there must have been some fierce encounters between Alfred's Saxons and the Danes, but these were small armies and brief affairs. The battle of Hastings, we are told, was fought from dawn until dusk, but it seems unlikely that there could have been more than ten thousand men on each side, and certainly not all on each side were slain. The contests between Simon de Montfort and the royal forces were mere skirmishes, as were those between the English and the Welsh and the Scots half a century later, saving perhaps Bannockburn, when compared with this famous day of 29 March 1461. The Lancastrian forces were well in excess of thirty thousand men, the Yorkists only just short of that number. On either side, this was a far higher number than any king of England had ever commanded into battle at any time in her history, again saving only the army Edward II had led to catastrophe at Bannockburn. (This mighty host, reputed by some historians to have numbered a hundred thousand men – an entirely spurious figure, to my mind – had contained but a handful of true fighting men, judging by the ease with which it had been put to flight.) Here there were two kings engaged, or so the Yorkists would have us believe, and every man in either army was a war-tested veteran.

As I have said, Bannockburn was a rout. At Towton the battle waged with the utmost fury all day while I sent off a succession of gallopers to discover what was going on, for all I could hear was a frightful din. The first returned with the ill news that the young rascal March had been revealing his talents again, and in the initial exchange of arrows, his own men having loosed their first volley just as the snow was starting, he had then not only halted the advance but ordered a retreat of a few yards, so that our reply, caught as it was in the blizzard, fell far short of his people.

This was but a temporary setback, however, although it was compounded by a more serious mishap, as my next messenger informed me that the Earl of Northumberland and Sir Anthony Trollope, in anger at what was happening, had left their defensive position and led their men forward. This was contrary to all of my instructions, and the wretches were immediately in trouble as they became encumbered amidst their own spent arrows, which were sticking up out of the ground almost like a self-inflicted *chevaux de frise*; while they were endeavouring to reform their ranks they were assailed by a second volley, which killed many men and drove them back in disarray.

Fortunately, their breach of discipline did not affect the rest of the army, and just as I was mounting my horse, determined to rally my people or die, another messenger arrived to tell me that the two hosts had finally clashed. Well, I could tell that from the din drifting through the snow-fog. But this good fellow assured me that my people were standing firm, and that the Yorkists were being held all along the line. As we still possessed a superiority in numbers, this seemed to clinch the matter. And indeed it should have. The battle raged for ten hours, while the Prince and I had to rely upon messengers coming to and fro. They told us the most lurid tales of men heaped high one upon the other, of blood running in rivulets down the hillsides to form pools in the valley, and, less pleasant to hear, of the prodigies of valour and physical prowess accomplished by the Yorkist leader. In fact it has reliably been estimated that some twenty thousand men were left dead on the field of Towton, evenly divided between both sides.

The day, if it could be so called, as the sun never did appear, began to disappear into evening gloom before the snow finally ceased. I returned to my tower – with some difficulty as my boots sank ankle-deep in the white sludge and it was intensely slippery – to gaze in a mixture of pride and horror at the continuing mêlée, now at last clearly visible before me. But still the Red Rose banner waved high in the air, and it seemed to me that my people had forced their way forward, which could only mean that the Yorkists were being forced back. Victory was absolutely within our grasp when Prince Edward clutched my arm and pointed, saying, 'What force is that, Mother?'

I narrowed my eyes to peer into the gloom. There was certainly a large body of men just crossing the river. My heart gave a bound, as I dreamed for a moment that it might be the Earl of Pembroke. Was Jasper Tudor marching to my assistance with additional forces raised in Wales? It was a brief dream. I could not make out the banners flying above the approaching host, but those nearer at hand did, and I saw several bodies of my men leaving the fray and starting to hurry towards the north. Immediately I sent a galloper to discover what was happening; he returned in half an hour, his face ashen. 'It is Lord Stanley, your grace,' he told me. 'Marching under the White Rose of York.'

I realised then that all was lost. It is an axiom of military strategy that where two approximately equal forces have been locked in combat over a considerable time, victory invariably goes to the general who can throw in the last fresh troops, however small in number. Stanley was approaching at the head of several thousand men. Here again it is possible, in the light of later events, to suppose that Edward of March had summoned Stanley to his aid and, knowing of his imminent arrival, had thus engaged us for all those bitter hours when he had seemed doomed to defeat, knowing full well that victory was bound to be his. In which case, taken in conjunction with his strategy before the battle, he must rank – at the age of nineteen, mark you – as fully the equal of Henry V or the Black Prince or even Edward III, much as it goes against the grain to say it. Even more, with the best possible respect to my French countrymen (who at Agincourt, Poitiers and Crécy were badly led and suffering from an excess of arrogance), none of those three mighty warriors ever faced an army as devoted and determined, or as well placed, as my Lancastrians at Towton.

Yet now all was finished. Men were fleeing in every direction. Prince Edward and I mounted our horses at the foot of our tower, while the people of Towton stared at us as if we were the ghosts we were very likely soon to become. Indeed, for a terrible moment I almost rode my mount towards the disintegrating battle, such was my despair. But then I recollected who I was and my responsibilities, the principal one being at my side, and so turned my horse's head and galloped for York. At least, I was determined, the Yorkists should not have the King.

As for the battle, I may as well complete the sorry tale. Some twenty thousand men lay dead on the field, and not less than an equal number were wounded. One has to turn to the massacres perpetrated by the Turks on the armies of Hungary and Serbia to find a parallel to such blood-letting. Of my nobles, several died in the battle. The Earl of Devonshire regained York, but was there captured and executed. The Earl of Wiltshire, well known for his ability to escape a lost conflict, got as far as Cockermouth, but then his luck also ran out, and off came his head.

From this it will be gathered that the Yorkists were in rampant pursuit in every direction. Principally, of course, they sought the King and me, but we were ahead of them, with the Prince, riding through the stormiest of weather, wearing out our horses, as we made for the border and the safety of Scotland. And the arms of Mary of Guelders.

Or so I believed. Certainly there was no check to our entry into Scotland, and as soon as we had identified ourselves we were directed to Linlithgow, and thence to the convent of the Black Friars in Edinburgh. I felt that this was all to the good, as on my earlier visit I had been kept out of the capital, whereas now it appeared that Mary was granting us an official welcome. I was therefore the more taken aback by the events which followed. We were assembled in the great hall of the convent to await the Queen, our entire party being present. That is to say, in addition to the King and myself, and Prince Edward, there were my ladies, including a sorely-tried Bailly, who had suffered greatly upon our precipitate journey, as well as Somerset and several lesser lords who had made their escape with us, and of course John Combe. The good nuns had also assembled to receive their monarch. But our royal party made the centrepiece, as it were.

Mary entered as was her wont, in a storm of golden hair and swirling skirts, stamping mud from her boots. Now it may be supposed that I had given a good deal of thought as to how I should approach my second encounter with this forceful woman. I had previously come to her as a suppliant, but left her with every prospect of regaining my premier position. Now I was back, again as a suppliant, in

hardly more than two months. It seemed to me that it was
necessary to regain our earlier intimacy just as quickly as
possible, and so, as she appeared, I stepped forward with a
smile, and said, 'It seems, fair cousin, that Fate refuses to
allow us to be separated.'

To my dismay the Queen of Scots did not smile in return.
'Indeed, your grace,' she replied, 'Fate and yourself do not
appear to get on at all.' Saying this, she stepped past me and
gave a brief curtsey to the King, who was as usual totally
fogged by what was going on. 'We have much to discuss,'
she remarked. 'But for the time being, you are welcome to
the shelter of this convent.' Her gaze swept the faces of the
rest of our party, and arrived at Somerset. Like me, he had
arranged his features into a smile; after all, it was hardly
more than two months since he had held all of that
voluptuous beauty naked in his arms.

But he too was the recipient of a cold stare. 'There is no
welcome for you here, my lord of Somerset,' she said. 'Your
mouth is too big.'

I was deeply disturbed by this cavalier greeting. But I also
understood right away that there was something amiss. The
Queen having departed to her own apartments, I sent for
Henry Somerset. 'There is something going on that I do not
understand,' I told him, 'but which may well be injurious to
our cause. You have offended the Queen of Scots. How? You
have not seen her since the last time I did.'

He looked thoroughly abashed. 'Well, your grace, I may
have been too proud of my prowess.'

She had said his mouth was too big. 'My God!' I cried.
'You boasted of having had the Queen?'

'In my cups, I may have claimed her, yes.'

'You are both a fool and a villain,' I snapped. 'You may
have ruined our cause.' Then a thought struck me. 'Have you
ever boasted of possessing me?'

'Never, your grace,' he protested. 'You are my Queen.'

I glared at him, not knowing whether or not to believe
him.

But it was the damage he had done to my relationship with Mary that was most concerning me at that moment. I despatched a servant to beg an audience with her, but it was twenty-four hours before I received a summons to her chamber. During this trying period Henry the King was of course perfectly happy. He was in a convent, and was only interested in its prayers and orders; he had immediately become a great favourite with the nuns.

To my relief, Mary received me alone, but fully dressed, standing before her fire; nor were we in her bedroom, but an antechamber; however, through the open inner door I could tell that the bedroom was adjacent. There was no time for niceties. 'Mary,' I said, 'that stupid boy has confessed his crime. What can I say, save that I am most terribly sorry.'

'You can get him out of Scotland,' Mary growled.

'I shall, I promise,' I said. 'But Mary ...' I went closer. 'I should hate to suppose that the indiscretion of one senseless youth should end our friendship.'

Mary sat down and gestured me to the chair opposite. 'Your paramour has ruined my reputation.'

I felt she was being a little extreme; a woman with such a voracious sexual appetite must surely have lost her reputation long ago. 'I still love you,' I ventured. Well, of course, I had never loved her, however much I had been excited by her. But now I had to use every weapon I possessed.

'Do you, Meg?' she asked, her face softening. 'Oh, to be able to believe that.'

'Oh, please believe it,' I begged, leaving my chair to kneel beside her.

She kissed me on the mouth, but her body remained stiff. 'My lords tell me you come to me only because you are desperate.'

'I will not deny that I am desperate,' I said. 'But ... if that were the only reason, would I not have gone to France and sought the aid of Uncle Charlie and my father?'

'Perhaps that is your best course,' Mary muttered.

I began to grow alarmed. 'You mean you will not help me?'

She stood up in such a swirl of skirt and body that I fell over and sat down. 'It is not so easy. Do you not know I am cousin to the Duke of Burgundy?'

'Indeed. So am I.'

'Duke Philip has been approached by the Earl of Warwick, and has agreed to support the Yorkist cause.'

Oh, that viper, I thought. But I continued to smile. 'I find this hard to believe, my sweet Mary.' I got up as well, as the floor was hard and cold. 'There was no talk of it when I was here in January?'

'It was nonetheless already in hand. The negotiations had been commenced by the late Duke of York.'

'You mean there is a formal alliance between Burgundy and the house of York?' I was aghast. 'Do you know the terms?'

'Not all of them. I do know that the Count of Charolais is betrothed to York's daughter, who is now sister to the *de facto* King of England.'

'Self-proclaimed, Mary,' I pointed out. 'No country can have two kings. And no man may be crowned king while the anointed and consecrated king still lives, unless he has abdicated. Henry has never done that.'

'Nevertheless, there is talk about the original usurpation ...' She sighed. 'Duke Philip is pressing me to abandon you. His ambassador, the Lord of Gruthuse, is here now, importuning me at every opportunity ...' Another sigh.

I put my arms round her to hug her and sniffle into her bosom. Well, what would you? I had never been more desperate in my life. 'If you abandon me, my dearest Mary, I am lost.'

'Your Uncle Charles will help you, I know,' she said, but she was embracing me in turn, and moving gradually towards the bedroom.

'I fear that if I ever leave this island, I shall never return,' I sobbed. 'I know not who I can trust, sweet Mary, saving only you. How can I be certain that even Uncle Charlie will not wish to treat with this upstart youth? As for the Dauphin . . .'

'I will tell you why your uncle will not treat with York,' Mary said, throwing me on the bed and commencing to undress. 'It is because the Dauphin has rebelled against him, and has fled to Burgundy. King Charles will naturally support any side opposed to Burgundy, even were that side not wearing the colours of his favourite niece.'

As she was by now consumed with lust, further serious conversation had to be postponed for an hour, but as was her wont, she returned to the matter as soon as her passion was sated. 'So, France it shall be,' she suggested.

'I shall appeal to Uncle Charlie for assistance,' I agreed, sitting up and attempting to untangle my hair. 'But despite your reassurance, I dare not go to him without a safe conduct. Mary, you must permit me to remain in Scotland until I hear from him.'

She got out of bed and began striding the room, a compelling sight. 'My nobles will demand a quid pro quo,' she said. 'None of them is at all anxious to cross swords with Edward of York.'

'Anything that I have,' I assured her. 'And surely you mean Edward of March.'

She ceased her perambulation, all heaving bosom, and waited for her hair to settle on her shoulders. 'Berwick!'

I gulped. 'That was to be after I had regained power in England.'

'It will have to be now, dearest Meg, or I cannot assist you.'

The fact was, this oversexed bitch was as treacherous as anyone else it was my misfortune to encounter. Well, I had no choice – but I was determined to gain what I could from the exchange. 'It shall be yours, if you will give me permission to recruit from amongst your nobles.'

She gazed at me for several seconds, her mouth twisting into a variety of shapes. Then she nodded. 'I see no reason why you should not do that, sweet Meg.'

I had thus surmounted one grave difficulty. Others were soon to press upon me. I immediately despatched Somerset to France as my emissary to Uncle Charlie. Actually, I was glad to see him go. As an army commander he had proved no more successful than his father, while as a lover he had proved a disaster. But I kissed him fondly as I bade him farewell; I needed all the loyalty I could command.

To my great relief, Mary also found it necessary to take herself off; after all, she had a country to rule, and as she had hinted, a large number of her nobles were not as enamoured of me as she was. In any event, it was one thing for me to give her Berwick; to possess it she needed to march against it.

From my point of view I needed some time to myself, for a variety of reasons. Mary was a magnificent woman but, as I have indicated, I was never in any doubt that her loyalties lay to Scotland and herself first and to anyone else, myself included, a poor second. Then, much as I found her embraces stimulating and educational, I am afraid the arms of a woman can never supplant those of a man, at least in my opinion. And thirdly, in her company, even when she was at her most generous and charming, I was always aware – and she certainly never forgot – that she was Queen of Scotland and I was a fugitive. This frame of mind does not make for true intimacy.

It may be pertinent to ask at this juncture, as I had sent Somerset across the sea, which pair of male arms was going to comfort me after the Queen of Scots departed. Actually, there were many obvious volunteers, but for the time being I had more important things on my mind.

I needed an army, and Mary had given me permission to recruit one. Thus I entertained a variety of nobles at my convent, and eventually settled on George Douglas, fourth Earl of Angus. He was fifty-one years old at this time, and just at the time of life to be captivated by a beautiful thirty-one-year-old queen, but this was not the only reason he sought to serve me, or that I accepted his advances. He came from what is known as the Red Douglas branch of his famous family. This had always been the junior branch, the senior being known as the Black Douglas. Now the Douglases had long been the lords, and the terrors, of the Borders; and being powerful, they had always been sought as allies by whoever happened to be reigning in Scotland. The second Lord Douglas, of the Black half of the family, had been an intimate of the immortal Robert the Bruce, had fought beside him at Bannockburn, and, in accordance with his King's wishes, had carried the embalmed heart of Robert to the Holy Land, where, surrounded by the Saracens, he threw the precious relic into their midst before leading his knights in a gallant charge to regain it. Not very successfully, I may add.

The point is, however, that while he and his descendants were supporting the throne, there was little hope of advancement for the Red Douglas branch. But times change, and so do people. The Black Douglases had become difficult and overbearing, the Red Douglases had risen in favour at court, and when the current Black Douglas, James of that ilk, had rebelled against Mary's husband James II, it had been George Douglas, Earl of Angus, who had been sent with a royal army to chastise the villain. This he had done, and the Black Douglas had been forced to flee the country – to the protection of Edward of March, who was now calling himself King of England, leaving his lands to be forfeited to his cousin.

George Angus, of course could not feel safe while his cousin lived and prospered, any more than I could feel safe while *my* cousin lived and usurped, and so it will be seen we had a mutual interest in bringing down the house of York. Angus thus began to raise an army, and I began to feel quite positive again. My main problem, as ever, was money, and for this I depended upon Uncle Charlie. I thus awaited some

word from Somerset with much anxiety. But when it came,
it was of the most disastrous import: Uncle Charlie was
dead!

Uncle Charlie was fifty-eight years old, which I suppose is
not an unreasonable age to die, but of course he had helped
himself on the way by his lifestyle of the past fifteen years;
even the youngest and healthiest of men would find a
programme of fornicating morning, noon and night wearing
on the constitution.

Needless to say, his death could not have come at a more
inconvenient time for me, when he was my very last hope of
raising the funds necessary to sustain my campaign. Even
worse was the prospect which now appeared before me:
Cousin Louis on the French throne as the eleventh of that
name. Even if Louis and I had ever been friends, which we
had not, the plain fact was that, engaged as he was in
constant rebellion against his father, Louis had spent most of
the past half-dozen years sheltering in Burgundy ... and
Burgundy was now apparently the firm ally of the house of
York. I all but despaired.

However, I have always taken too simplistic a view of
political matters. I have known what I wanted, and I have
been very straightforward in my attitude to those who
wished to stand in my way. Cousin Louis has always been
entirely the reverse. Over the past ten years, indeed, he has
earned himself the sobriquet of 'The Spider', and his
machinations have always been very arachnoid. My first
intimation of this was when, to my consternation but also my
relief, a Scottish bishop named Kennedy arrived hotfoot
from Paris to attend the Queen of Scots with a message from
the new King of France, to the effect that he would greatly
appreciate her continued support of the house of Lancaster!

This conundrum needs explaining, which I shall endeavour to do, in so far as anyone can properly explain the mental
processes of Cousin Louis. The fact is that Louis had taken
refuge with his Uncle Philip from necessity rather than

choice, and Philip had taken his nephew to his bosom from a desire to cause Uncle Charlie trouble rather than from affection. Louis's lengthy stay at Bruges had been fraught with differences between himself and both Philip and Cousin Charles of Charolais. He had also had ample opportunity to witness the strength and grandeur of the Burgundian state and court, and I must record that at this time there was no more resplendent principality in Europe.

Louis pondered on this. It must be recalled that in the days of Henry V, who had so very nearly conquered France as an appendage of England, and who had certainly brought a great deal of distress to the kingdom, the English successes had been made possible largely by alliance with Burgundy. That had ended with Henry's death, Philip being unable to get on with Bedford and even less with Humphrey of Gloucester, but now there was a new alliance, inspired by the house of York. Louis therefore, while determined to keep his country at peace, was equally determined to break up that dangerous partnership just as quickly as possible, and the quickest possible way to do that was to get Edward of March off the English throne, or at least keep him so preoccupied with the possibility of being removed that he would have no time for Continental adventures.

There was another factor working in our favour with Louis. Having become King of France by right of primogeniture, he found himself surrounded by younger brothers intent on making themselves a nuisance. These young men had remained in France, either at their father's side or on their estates, while Louis was an exile, and they had equipped themselves with considerable followings. Louis therefore needed all the followers he could get, and chief among these prospective allies in the event of a civil war he counted my own elder brother, John of Calabria.

John, I have to admit, had fared little better in his attempt to gain the crown of Naples than I had in my attempts to retain the crown of England, and had for the moment abandoned any idea of establishing Papa on that sultry throne. He had thus returned to the family estates in France, with a great, if perhaps exaggerated, reputation as a soldier. Louis wanted Duke John, as my brother was known, at his side rather than on the side of his enemies; and the surest way to do this, he felt, was to support – even if clandestinely – Duke John's fugitive sister.

All of this was very encouraging, but it was largely the froth which accumulates on the top of a mug of ale. Louis was encouraging Mary to continue her support of me, but he was doing so secretly; and Mary was being assailed by demands for my expulsion, not only from Burgundy but from her own nobles. Then again, while it was splendid news to learn that Brother John was back in France and an intimate of the King, Brother John suffered from the curse of the Anjous ... he had absolutely no money. But neither, apparently, did Cousin Louis. And it was money I needed most urgently.

It will therefore be seen that I spent a most unhappy year in Scotland. Mary visited me regularly, but I soon came to dread these invasions of my privacy, not only because of her unceasing lust, but because she always told me how well her armies were doing. They were certainly waging an unde-clared war with England as they sought to gain control of the fortresses I had promised them, even if they had not as yet succeeded in doing so. Then there was the business of learning how Edward of March was appropriating my husband's kingdom and, apparently, every woman in it, for himself. And above all there was the uncertainty of knowing what was going to happen next. Angus had raised a considerable force of men who said they would follow me. My spies informed me that the North of England was but waiting to rise on my behalf. But no one would lift a finger, much less a sword, unless paid.

I received no help from my entourage. Henry spent his time at prayer. Prince Edward, now coming up to his eighth birthday, was always a source of great comfort for me, but an eight-year-old boy cannot give counsel. The same applies to a fifteen-year-old page, for all of John Combe's continuing heroine-worship. Somerset was cautiously remaining in France, being unwilling to risk again placing himself in Mary's power.

Worst of all, just before Christmas, Bailly died. She had been my good and faithful servant for more years than I cared to remember, graduating from the position of my nurse to that of my principal lady of the bedchamber. But she had not been intended by nature for the constant campaigning of the past few years, and indeed she had been ill before Towton. Now I buried her with a heavy heart, which became even heavier as I contemplated the future.

I have never been one to despair, but it was difficult to know whence I was going to receive succour, until it dawned on me, not for the first time in my life, that the only person who was going to help me was myself. Thus, despite the risks involved – for Warwick's cruisers swarmed the Channel – and the discomfort of the journey, I realised it was necessary for me personally to go to Louis and put the position squarely to him: if he wanted the Yorkists to be pushed from power, he would have to do more than offer sympathy.

The decision taken, it was a matter of waiting for the weather, and this, as was usual in a Scottish winter, was invariably abominable. Mary of course was of the opinion that I was doing entirely the right thing. Like so many insatiable lovers she was also an inconstant one and, quite apart from the inconvenience of having me as her guest, she was now tiring of my company. She willingly advanced me funds to make the journey, quite sure, I feel certain, that she would never look upon my face again. She had agreed to keep Henry for the time being – I could hardly risk delivering the King of England into French hands – but she well understood that there no longer existed any conjugal relations between us.

Having made the decision to seek my own salvation, I was

in no less of a hurry to brave the elements. But it was not until the beginning of April that the gales abated sufficiently for Prince Edward and myself, and our sorely shrunken party of attendants, to embark at Kirkcudbright – exactly where I had landed some eighteen months before.

Now it may well be remarked that this was a most roundabout way to transport me to France, and I felt the same. The reasons were weather and English cruisers, but I understood immediately that I was in for a most miserable time. I had not realised this miserable time was going to turn out to be a miserable fortnight! We beat down the Irish Sea, and were blown back up again. We stayed in sight of the Welsh mountains for days, and once even approached the shore close enough for me to make out the banners flying from the battlements of Harlech Castle, where the gallant Earl of Pembroke, Jasper Tudor, was still holding out for the Red Rose. How tempted was I to order our captain to put in and allow me to cease my endless vomiting at least for twenty-four hours! I did not, for two reasons. One was I feared the captain might desert me, and the second was that I feared I would be unable to bring myself to resume so unpleasant a journey.

Thus I pressed on, and finally brought up in Roscoff in Brittany on 16 April 1462.

13

I landed in France, as may be supposed, with some trepidation. Seventeen years before I had departed these shores, never intending to return. And here I was, returning, in the worst possible circumstances. But the event itself entirely surprised me.

My coming was unannounced, of course, and the captain of Roscoff looked askance at the strange ship requesting permission to enter his harbour. No doubt he looked even more askance when he received the signal that his unexpected visitor was the Queen of England. Roscoff is a tidal harbour (which is to say it dries out at low water, and can only be entered from half-tide up) so that it took us some considerable time to moor. By the time we had done so there was a regular guard of honour drawn up to receive me. This was gratifying, but it also turned out that messengers had been sent hotfoot to inform the Duke of Brittany himself of my arrival, and it was to St Malo that I was immediately transported – a journey of several days – where the Prince and I were royally entertained by the good Francis and his lady wife.

Gallopers had been sent in every direction, and from St Malo I travelled as quickly as could be arranged to Angers. How can I possibly describe the feelings in my breast as I approached these girlhood haunts where I had spent so many happy and untroubled hours, unsuspecting the vicissitudes which lay ahead of me? Even less can I describe my emotions as I approached the city and found myself greeted by bowing pages, cavorting virgins, armoured knights and hennined ladies. The red rose was everywhere, emblazoned on every banner and strewn before my horse. I later learned that Papa had borrowed eight thousand florins to give me the welcome worthy of a queen. If only he had sent the money to me in Scotland to help me equip an army!

But to see dear Papa and Mama and my brother and sister again was a boon. Papa did not seem to have changed a whit in seventeen years. Mama had aged a great deal. John was darker and grimmer than I recalled, but then, no doubt, so was I. And Yolanda had turned into a fat housewife. Her husband was as ill-favoured as ever.

However, pleasant as was my reunion with my family – not one of whom I had ever expected to see again – the purpose of my visit to France was to confer with Cousin Louis. It was arranged that we should meet at Chinon: which is to say that he was prepared to come to me, rather than have me go to him. Actually, of course, this was not courtesy on his part. He desired to keep our meeting (indeed, he wished to keep the very fact that I was in France at all) from Burgundy and Edward of March – a vain hope – and so, out a-hunting, he happened to find himself weary and deciding to rest for the night at Chinon, where by a happy chance I also happened to be spending the night.

Cousin Louis, it may be recalled, was a mere six years older than myself, which is to say he was thirty-eight at the time of this, our first meeting in seventeen years. I am perfectly willing to accept that he had had a difficult life, but I defy anyone to claim that he, or she, had had a harder life than myself; and I am a woman, to boot. However, I will also claim that my beauty was almost entirely untarnished. There was slightly more colour to my complexion, but as a girl my only failing had been a tendency to sallowness. There was a slight heaviness to my breasts, a slight wideness to my hips, but these are but the more comforting to anyone attempting to share a woman's couch, and I will shortly produce evidence to prove that they rather increased than diminished my attractiveness. My hair was still a glorious tawny-brown, my breath sweet, my movements filled with vigour.

What then am I to say of the crumpled wreck who stooped before me, hardly able to hold himself straight, his hair both thinning and greying, his legs mere spindles, his conversation constantly interrupted by a hacking cough? I formed the conclusion that he was not long for this world. In this I was mistaken, as he is still alive as I pen these words, and in fact shows absolutely no sign of dying at any time, much less in the foreseeable future; some people seem to be born old and merely grow older, while others retain their youthful outlook on life to the bitter end. I certainly intend to.

Louis was affable enough on this occasion of our first meeting, but non-committal. He asked me a great number of questions regarding my prospects supposing Edward of March were induced to give up the throne, all of which I answered as truthfully as I could while being as optimistic as I could. I had no reason to believe that the people of England, if freed from distractions, would not welcome Henry back again as their King.

Louis departed the next day, leaving me none the wiser as to my progress. But soon he arranged to meet me again, at Tours. Here we got down to the nitty-gritty. 'What is your plan?' he asked.

'Why, to invade England, drive the Earl of March from the throne, and reinstate my husband.' I felt it best at this stage to stick to generalities, and reveal nothing of what I had in mind for the obstreperous March and his feeble cousin Warwick.

'To do this,' Louis pointed out, 'you will need both men and money.' I know, of course, that my cousin has been called one of the wisest men in Christendom, but it is a sad fact that wisdom too often manifests itself in stating the obvious. 'In this regard,' Louis continued, most dolefully, 'while I am anxious to help you, I am myself in a parlous state, being beset with difficulties.'

I waited with what patience I could muster; he would not have sent for me had he planned a flat refusal. 'Now, in these affairs,' he said, 'money is the prime factor. With money you can buy men, whereas with men you can only obtain money through victory, and victory requires bringing men on to the field, which requires money.'

I suppressed a sigh, while my heart went out to those French princes and lords who presumably had to listen to this claptrap on a daily basis; the wonder was they had not revolted before. But now at last he said something worthwhile. 'However, sweet cousin, I *might* be able to raise some funds on your behalf. From bankers, you understand,' he hastily added.

'Indeed I understand, your grace,' I said.

'The trouble with bankers is that they need security,' Louis pointed out.

'Once I regain my kingdom, they may have whatever security they wish.'

'Unfortunately, they will wish security, or at least a promise of it, before they will lend the money.'

'Would you care to be more direct, your grace?' I asked, ever the optimist.

But directness was not a part of Louis's nature. He hummed and hawed and talked at random, while I did my best both to stay awake and keep my temper, until at last he said, 'I would say what you need is the sum of twenty thousand francs.'

This at least had the effect of startling me out of my stupor. A franc, while not a generally used medium of exchange, is, as is well known, a gold coin containing sixty grams of the precious metal. Twenty thousand of these would therefore amount to something like two and a half thousand English pounds in *weight* of pure gold. That is a very large sum of money, certainly more than the King and

I had possessed in total throughout our reigns. He could tell I was interested. 'Do you think that will suffice?'

I controlled my suddenly flaring imagination. 'I think it might suffice, your grace. But who will provide such a sum?'

'You may leave that with me. As for the security, I should think Calais would be sufficient.' The penny, or should I say, the franc, dropped with a clunk which all but stunned me. Louis, as was his wont, was lying like a badly constructed sundial. The money was going to come from his own coffers, in exchange for ... Calais! All my life I, and my ministers, had been bedevilled by the misfortune of losing, or being constrained to surrender, various bits of France which the English had come to regard as inalienably theirs. Calais was the very last bit of France left in English hands. The man, or more pertinently the woman, who gave it up would most certainly be torn to pieces by the mob.

But then I reflected that mobs are but an extension of their leaders. If with the aid of Louis's francs I could regain my kingdom, I intended to dispose of all those leaders who had ever opposed me; and my memory of Suffolk's untimely end, and all those who had brought it about, was still fresh and angry. In those circumstances, I would at the same time dispose of anyone who attempted to protest against the loss of Calais ... even supposing it came about, for once I was Queen again might I not be able to find sufficient gold to repay the loan, even if I had to wring a few Yorkist necks to do so? Besides, how could one town, which possessed a sentimental rather than a strategic value if we were not again going to war with France, stand in the way of Henry's restoration – or more importantly, my own? 'I will agree on certain conditions, your grace,' I said.

He looked somewhat sceptical, presumably because he did not see what conditions I could impose in my situation. 'Of course you will understand that I cannot surrender Calais until I am back in power,' I told him. 'Until then, I consider it essential that the details of our transaction remain

a secret between you and me. The reason for this is obvious;
to succeed in England I need the support of the people, at
least *until* I am back in power. That support will be withheld
if they know Calais is the price of my victory.'

'I understand,' he said. 'But our agreement must be
legally drawn up and signed.'

'I accept this. My second condition is that I return to
England with at least a token French force, both as a
personal bodyguard and to stiffen whatever forces I may
raise.' I had no desire to be left entirely at the mercy of
Angus and his wild Scotsmen.

'Hm,' Louis said. 'Hm. I will see what can be arranged.'

With that, we agreed to meet a third time, and on this
occasion more openly, for I was to go to Rouen. The Prince
and I travelled thither in the early summer, accompanied
now by Henry Somerset who had rejoined our party – but
whom I still excluded from my bed as I had not yet forgiven
his boastful callowness which had so nearly cost me dear.
Louis was waiting for us, with a perfect army of lawyers,
and I signed this and signed that, following which the
enormous sum of money was solemnly counted out before
me. I felt quite giddy.

'Now,' my cousin said, 'as to the token force you require,
I am afraid I can offer you no royal troops. Not only would
this bring about an immediate breach between England and
France, and this I wish to avoid, but I need all my men here.
Any assistance given you by France will have to be of a
private nature. However, you will be pleased to know that
there is a gentleman who is willing and able to raise a force
of two thousand five hundred men in your cause.'

I was both surprised and overwhelmed. I could not
conceive of anyone wishing to take so expensive a risk on
my behalf, as I had even been refused by Brother John when
I had tentatively suggested he might care to lend me the use
of his strong right arm. The fact was that had he been only
my brother, he might have been interested, but as the Duke

of Calabria he did not feel he could afford to lose himself in what might turn out to be a long campaign on behalf of someone who could have not the slightest influence on his chances of gaining the Neapolitan throne. Cousin Louis was a different prospect, for he had great influence at least in northern Italy, where Sforza in particular was in his pocket. But failing Brother John . . .?

'Your champion awaits you in the antechamber,' Louis said with one of his sly smiles, and himself opened the door to admit me – into the presence of Pierre de Brezé.

My combined emotions of amazement and delight redoubled. Pierre of course immediately dropped to one knee and seized my hand to kiss it, while I turned to Louis for an explanation. But Louis had already returned through the door, closing it behind him. 'Pray rise, my lord,' I said. 'I am utterly confounded.'

He stood. 'That I should wish to serve you, your grace? Have I not intimated this often enough in the past? My only problem was obtaining the King's permission. But this has now been granted.'

In fact, as I later learned, Brezé had recently been informed that there was no prospect of his being returned to Paris in any position of authority, much less as chief minister. Sons often take this line with their father's employees on obtaining power themselves. Louis was well aware that during his quarrel with Uncle Charlie, Brezé had virtually ruled the kingdom . . . a kingdom from which *he* had been expelled.

But he had also understood that a man like Brezé, who had used his years of prosperity to enrich himself and create a vast power base, chiefly in Normandy (of which province he was Seneschal), could not merely be cast aside like a worn-out boot: Louis had sufficient enemies without adding Brezé to their number. At the same time, however, he had been aware of Brezé's undying adoration of me – it was Louis's nature to attempt to discover the secrets of all his subjects – and this had given him the answer to his problems. Let Brezé step aside from French affairs of state for a season, and dabble – entirely as a private person – in *English* affairs of state, on behalf of the woman he loved above all others. Should he not return from this unlikely crusade, well, France would mourn a hero. Should he return, Louis had every intention of by then having arranged things so that Brezé would find himself a subject being commanded by a king rather than a subject who instructed his monarch.

I have no doubt that Brezé was aware of these machinations; I know I certainly suspected them from the outset. But equally was he aware that the means he had employed to gain ascendancy over Uncle Charlie – producing a succession of beautiful women for the royal bed – was unlikely to have much prospect of success when applied to a dry stick like Louis. As for me, I cared not a jot for Cousin Louis's mental processes. After seventeen years Pierre and I were to adventure together, and we were both well aware of where that was going to lead – to our mutual delight.

It was of course necessary to preserve decorum until the appropriate moment. Having kissed my hand again, Pierre invited me and my entourage to accompany him to Caen to inspect his troops and make our arrangements for our departure back to England. I graciously accepted, and the next day – having spent a sleepless, anticipatory night – I took my leave of Cousin Louis. He smiled most graciously. 'I look forward to hearing nothing but good reports of you, Meg,' he told me. He did not specify in which regard.

It took us two days to reach Caen, a pleasant journey in which Pierre and I did no more than look at each other, while at every stop he entertained myself, the Prince and Somerset, as well as the other members of my entourage, most royally. Henry Somerset, having observed that my fortunes were now on the mend, felt that his also ought to be, at least as regards my bed, and became quite surly when I refused to accept his attentions. But I was saving myself for bigger game.

We duly arrived at Caen and, Pierre having sent ahead, were received with the usual huzzas, bowing youths, cavorting maidens, and flying rose petals. Had I not by now become somewhat more interested in substance rather than display I would have been overwhelmed. As it was, I accepted the plaudits of the mob with a smile and a wave, and allowed myself to be escorted to Pierre's castle and entertained to a very lavish banquet, at which the Seneschal and I sat together at the head of the centre table and smiled at the assembly. Prince Edward was on my right, but he was entirely interested in food, while Somerset was being attracted further down the table by some big-titted girl who had clearly been instructed to entertain him into the small hours.

This enabled Pierre and myself to enjoy a tête-à-tête. 'I trust your grace is satisfied?' he inquired.

'Thus far, certainly,' I assured him, and inadvertently dropped my napkin between us.

There was, of course, a horde of lesser nobles and their ladies waiting behind my chair to serve me, but Pierre brushed them aside and himself retrieved the square of linen. To do this he had to bend his head beneath the level of the table, so that his face was against my knee, which he kissed most prettily while slowly drawing his hand, and the napkin, up my shin, almost displacing my gown as he did so. That his face was red when he re-emerged could not be criticised, in view of his exertions.

'You take care of my every requirement, my lord,' I told him. 'Well, possibly not *every* requirement ... at least as yet.'

'Do you know for how long I have dreamed of you, your grace?' he asked in a low voice.

'At least seventeen years, my lord,' I reminded him. 'Although I will not deny it may have been longer. But queens also dream.'

He suddenly had a great deal of trouble with his codpiece, but remained strangely uncertain for such a man of the world. 'If I could believe that, your grace . . .'

I decided to take the bull by the horns, not an entirely inept simile. 'I cannot have my army commander in doubt about anything I say, my lord,' I told him. 'I would confer with you, privately, on an urgent affair of state.'

'Your grace has but to say when.' He licked his lips.

'I repeat, the matter is most urgent, my lord. I would say it cannot wait until tomorrow.'

Nor did it. It was necessary to sit out the meal, but when I explained to the assembly how weary both the Prince and I were – Edward indeed had fallen asleep into his posset – they cheered us to our chambers. Edward awoke briefly, and then again descended into slumber, while I dismissed all my ladies after they had undressed me, and waited my lord's pleasure in bed, naked as the day I had been born.

It is a strange sensation to be aware that a consummation of which one has dreamed for a very long time is about to be realised. From the occasion when I had given Pierre my scarf, I had considered, from time to time and in a passing fashion, what he might be like as a lover, while being at that time utterly ignorant of what a lover might be like. When I became more knowledgeable, I had found my thoughts returning to him fairly regularly. I could not help but consider, when in bed with Henry the King, how a man like Pierre would have handled me, in every way. Equally had I wondered how Pierre would have coped with the mad chase around my bed indulged in by Suffolk. And when Somerset had been initiating me into the French ways of love, I could not prevent my thoughts from wandering in the direction of considering how a *Frenchman* might have dealt with it. Now all was come to fruition. Pierre gave a gentle tap on my door, and came to me. He wore an undressing robe, and nothing else. The robe was very rapidly discarded.

We made little conversation beyond a few endearments. We were both too old, and had waited too long, for the poetry of love. Instead we made poetry of our own, with our lips and our fingers, our entwined tongues and mingled breaths. He kissed me from crown to toe, and his mouth lingered long enough between my legs to introduce me into that heaven I had all too seldom experienced with my other male lovers. Then I must do the same to him, with care to stop short of the ultimate – a difficult exercise in self-control, such was our mutual ardour.

And all the while I was wondering how he *would* seek the ultimate, to be taken utterly by surprise, and even by some alarm, when the moment came. For Brezé had also served in the East, in his youth, and had long abandoned the Christian way of love. Thus he made me kneel, my buttocks locked against his groin like some bitch on heat – but this I was, at that moment – while he seemed to impale me to my very stomach. All the while his hands were caressing my breasts until he took them away to grasp my hams until we shared a mutual explosion of joy – my second of the evening – in which I cried out my lubricious happiness and no doubt alarmed my ladies in the next room. But they knew what we were about.

Ah, happiness! It is a fleeting thing, to be sure. Looking back, and remembering how brief was our time together, I sometimes wish to rail against that fate which made me wait seventeen years for the one man I could ever have loved without reservation. But then I reflect that had fate conspired to bring us together when I had been fifteen, I would have lacked the knowledge to understand what was being done to me – or worse, I might so have desired a return engagement, and again and again, that all other lovers would have seemed as nothing. Equally, had we come together in my early twenties, I suspect I might have abandoned all worldly ambition, and responsibility too, to be at his beck and call.

But now I was thirty-two years old, of an age to *feel* in a fashion youth cannot even begin to understand; and yet I had great things afoot, and knew enough never to let mere sensual enjoyment stand in my way. That Pierre would share my bed, or my tent, for the entire campaign, I took for granted. That we would neither of us let our love stand in the way of our duty, we both accepted. It was the last happy time.

At the end of September we sailed from Normandy for Scotland. It was a boisterous period of the year, but with Pierre's arm round my shoulder as we faced the wind I cared naught for the weather. Our enterprise was blessed with fortune, and we did not even see an English cruiser.

Our welcome in Scotland was less enthusiastic than I might have hoped, at least from Mary, but I put this down to mere jealousy; anyone with the least powers of observation could see that I was a fully satisfied woman. However, Mary did point out that while she was giving me all the help of which she was able, I had not yet given her one of the promised border strongholds. I assured her that this lack on my part was about to be remedied.

My husband, of course, had no powers of observation at all, save for discerning when a choir was out of tune, and hardly seemed aware of Pierre's presence. But every one else was very aware of it, for my hero was a bundle of energy and determination. He had better than two thousand troops of his own, and in addition for the first time since the war had begun I possessed a full treasure chest. Thus we summoned Angus and his Highlanders to the Red Rose standard, and crossed the border.

This was of course a surprising act, to most people. We were now well into October, a time of the year – certainly in the north of England – when men hang up their armour until the wintry winds have ceased to blow. Thus our passage was the easier, militarily. Bamburgh, Dunstanburgh and Alnwick all fell to our impetuous assault, and the north was open to our arms. But to my dismay there was no popular rising in my support. The people regarded me with apathy where they did not reveal open hostility. I feel there were several reasons for this. One was certainly the inclement weather; it was cold enough to freeze the tits off a stone statue. This of course also affected the defenders of the castles we captured.

But another reason was a pervading feeling that the Red Rose was a lot cause, so rapidly and so firmly had the White Rose established itself during the eighteen months since my defeat at Towton. I hasten to say that little of this establishing had been the work of Edward of March. That over-endowed young man had been busy doing his own sort of establishing, spraying his seed in every possible direction. The kingdom was therefore governed by Warwick, who, truth forces me to confess, was making a very good job of it. Peace reigned, and no one was very keen on replacing it with anarchy, which for some reason people associated with my presence. This was very disappointing, but I refused to be put off. I had captured three of the four strong points I sought: only Berwick remained.

'It had best wait until the spring,' Pierre suggested.

'It must be captured now,' I insisted, and explained that it was a debt of honour.

He was aghast. 'You mean to turn over these fortresses that we have captured for your husband, and Berwick as well, to the Queen of Scots?'

'I have promised to do so, yes.'

He scratched his head, and seemed to realise for the first time that perhaps his services had not been offered free. 'May I ask, your grace, what terms you agreed with King Louis?'

'Calais,' I told him. 'As soon as I am again in power.'

He gulped. 'Does anyone know of this, your grace?'

'No one, save the King and myself. And now you. And no one must know of it, either.'

'I should think not. You do realise, your grace, that when these things become known, every Englishman's hand will be raised against you? Should you be taken by the Yorkists and your transactions come to light, they may well charge you with treason and send you to the block.'

'Tush, my lord,' I assured him. 'Unless you betray me, my transactions, as you call them, cannot come to light until I am in power, when I shall fear no Yorkist. As for treason, these castles and ports are the property of my husband, are they not? If, acting in his name, I make them part of an essential negotiation for his restoration to power, I can hardly be accused of treason.'

He was not reassured, and I later learned that he wrote to Cousin Louis in much the same vein. In fact Brezé, although my favourite man, like so many of my favourite men lacked true resolution, and even more, a true understanding of my goal. That was to regain my husband's throne. For this I had already risked my life more than once, and would do so again. Set against this one overwhelming aim, was I to be distracted by fears of being accused of treason? But Pierre could only understand that I was contemplating giving away parts of England's heritage to her hereditary enemies. I do believe that from that moment he became somewhat afraid of my ruthless determination to win. Certainly, from that moment he declined in ardour, both as a lover and a general.

But we were also plagued by bad luck. I have never been fortunate with the weather. Some will say I have chanced it too often, and that Pierre was right, and we should have abandoned campaigning until winter was past. But I was perhaps the only person in Europe who truly understood the nature of my enemy. Not even Warwick had his cousin properly estimated, and it was to cost him dear. It was well known that business, either financial or parliamentary, bored Edward of March stiff, and that his principal pastime was in turning that stiffness to amatory profit. But my experience at Towton had revealed to me that there was one thing this berserker enjoyed more than fucking, and that was fighting. I had no doubt at all that when he learned I was loose in the north of England, Edward would tumble himself out of bed and come to match me. I had no desire to face him again until I was completely in the ascendant, and to give him some four months in which to prepare himself seemed to me to be the height of folly. I therefore insisted that the campaign continue, late as it was.

Here I made a sad mistake: I placed Henry Somerset in charge of the already captured fortresses, with orders to defend them to the death. Well, someone had to do it, and Somerset, in addition to being hateful to me since his sexual indiscretions, had also become quite a nuisance in that he did nothing but glower at Pierre. I felt an independent command might restore some of his stature, and I assumed that he remained utterly in love with me. That done, we went off to see what could be done about Berwick. And encountered catastrophe!

Berwick is a seaport, and therefore it seemed to me, studying Mary's unsuccessful assault on it, that it needed to be assailed by both land and sea in order to be carried. This Pierre and I set out to do. The ships which had brought us from France were summoned to block the harbour, while our men moved against the walls from the land. Pierre and I joined the fleet, much as I disliked the briny, as he deemed this the most difficult part of the operation and I wished always to be at his side. We were prepared for some weather, but not for the violent tempest which now arose, shrieking out of the north, and scattering our fleet to and fro. A large number of the vessels foundered, others were driven ashore. The garrison of course observed what was happening, and ran down to the beach to take our shaken, shivering people prisoner.

My own ship was assailed like any other, driven on to her beam ends by the ferocity of the wind, her sails a tatter and her masts gone by the board. I was utterly terrified, and Pierre had to bundle me into the small boat he had launched from the lee of the hulk, which is what our proud flagship had now become. He then commanded the oarsmen to pull away. That exposed us to the full fury of the storm, and there was the Queen of England kneeling in the bottom of this

cockleshell, vomiting constantly as she used a bailing can in
an attempt to get back out some of the water which was
pouring in. 'We must make the beach,' I gasped, in between
pukes.

'And be taken by the Yorkists?' Pierre demanded.
'Never!'

Thus we kept the sea until we were well clear of the port
and our enemies. The ordeal lasted several hours, during
which I was continually soaked to the skin and frozen solid.
At least after a while I stopped being sick, simply because
there was not even any bile left to be brought up. I gave
myself up for dead, and would have welcomed the dread
messenger. Instead, we did eventually make the shore,
whereupon I was stripped of my soaked clothing and
bundled up in several blankets then placed before a roaring
fire while hot whisky was given me to drink. Food would
have been better. My last memory of that dreadful night is
of singing bawdy songs with the Scots who had rescued us,
and who were as drunk as myself.

Once again I crawled back into Scotland, a hapless fugitive,
my armies destroyed, and my credit nil. Mary did not look
particularly pleased to see me, and I could understand her
point of view, even if I did not then understand the
underlying cause. But at least we held three of the four vital
fortresses, and there was every prospect of using them as a
base for a new campaign in the spring. Imagine my feelings
therefore when, at the turn of the year, news arrived that
Henry Somerset had surrendered all three to his cousin of
March!

Consider! I had known this lout for seventeen years. We
had played together as children. Circumstances had conspired to make him my stepson, if only in common law.
Additional circumstances had conspired to bring him into
my bed. We had shared every possible adventure, even the
heady whiff of victory at St Albans. I had made him
commander of my army – at least until the coming of Brezé,

the far superior soldier – and Henry could have had no doubt that when I regained the throne he would be the premier noble in the land. And yet he had betrayed me!

What was worse, I learned that Edward of March had not chopped off his head as one might have expected him to do, but instead had welcomed him as a friend and more. Rumour even had it that on occasion they shared the same bed! Well, heaven knows, I have no prudish views to offer on how other people behave. What concerned me was that Somerset, with his known weakness of garrulity, would use his intimacy with Edward to reveal the secrets of other beds. I had never told him – I had never told anybody – the truth of Prince Edward's parentage; it might have upset him to know I had had relations with his own father. With both Edmund Somerset and Bailly now dead there was no risk of it ever coming out; and indeed, as Henry and I were no longer lovers and the Yorkists continued to denounce the Prince as a bastard in any event, it would not have mattered if it had. But Henry Somerset could tell all about his own amatory adventures with me, and *our* amatory adventures with Mary Queen of Scots. The thought made my skin crawl, and no doubt it had the same effect upon Mary, who no longer even came to see me.

But the truth of her situation was soon to be revealed to me. My dear Mary, one of the two closest female friends I ever possessed, was dying of some monstrous tumour extending from her womb.

I did not know this when, the weather improving, and Angus having gallantly raised yet another army, I once again tried my fortunes south of the border, Brezé at my side. We were even accompanied by the King! As well as, on this occasion, Prince Edward. I felt it was all or nothing. Well, I was very nearly proved right, and was certainly about to endure the most horrendous experience of my life to that time.

We recaptured the border fortresses easily enough, but once

again received no support from the local people, and very
rapidly ran right out of money. There were days when we
could not even buy a loaf of bread, and I well remember one
Sunday when I opened my purse at mass and found it quite
empty: a Scottish archer kneeling nearby lent me a penny for
the offering.

Desperately I sent off letters to Mary and to Louis begging
for financial assistance. From Louis I received reply that any
woman who could get through twenty thousand gold francs
in little more than six months was obviously a bottomless pit
where money was concerned. I was not in the mood to put
up with financial lectures from my cousin. More importantly
he also pointed out that he had problems of his own and had
given me all the aid that was possible, and that I must now
fend for myself. Worse, he hinted very strongly that I should
no longer regard France as a refuge should my affairs go
from bad to worse. How changeable are men!

From Mary I received no reply at all, but soon enough
news arrived that the Queen was receiving the last rites. That
ended the campaign, as the Scots streamed back home, led
by Angus. For the Queen's children were still very small,
and the Earl, like every Scottish nobleman, felt he had a part
to play in coming domestic events more important than
forays against England.

In these circumstances we were quite unexpectedly left
bereft of both physical or financial support, and now Edward
of March was definitely on the march against us. Before I
knew what was happening we were utterly surrounded.
Brezé went off to seek help, or so he claimed; Henry took
refuge in a neighbouring monastery, the attendants left by
Brezé to guard me fled, our remaining French troops went
off to surrender. Suddenly I found Prince Edward and
myself quite alone, while in the distance I could hear the
tramp of armed men and cries of 'York!' and 'The White
Rose!' I think I am entitled to ask was there ever a woman
more scurvily treated by Fate? But the wench was not done
with me yet.

My instincts were to arm myself – there were enough discarded weapons lying about – and ride into the midst of the foe, there to perish as gallantly as I could. But I was constrained by the responsibility of Prince Edward at my side. Poor boy, he was still only nine, and yet as warlike as I could have wished. He would cheerfully have died at my side, I knew ... but he was the future King of England, on that I was determined. I therefore did the womanly thing, and fled towards a nearby wood. How often is the womanly thing quite the reverse of the wise thing! Frankly, though, I do not see that I had a great many alternatives, and the outcome would probably have been the same no matter even had I fled towards the Yorkists.

It should be understood that the Prince and I were dismounted, as every last horse had also run off. We therefore stumbled into the trees on foot and, being intent upon putting as much distance between the Yorkists and ourselves as possible, we hastened on for some time, regardless of lowering tree or snatching branch. These made pretty work of my gown and hat, so that the one was torn to ribbons and the other lost before I had stopped to take breath, while Edward's clothes were also in tatters. Then I realised that the wood was actually a forest, that night was coming on, that I was exhausted, that Prince Edward was crying, that we were both starving as well as thirsty ... and that I had not the slightest idea where I was or in which direction we should go to seek succour.

We stumbled a little further, and to our great relief came upon a tumbling stream. This slaked our thirst and then we waded across, completing the ruination of our clothes. By now it was absolutely dark, and we were simply too weary to go any further; and so we lay down there on the banks of that stream in each other's arms, endeavouring to comfort each other against the noises of the forest, and at the same time to forget the rumblings of our empty bellies. We slept only to awake at first light, and find ourselves being regarded by several men.

My first terrified reaction was that they were Yorkist scouts. My second, as I sat up and pushed hair from my eyes, was that we might have been more fortunate if they had been – for clearly these were neither soldiers nor farmers. They were too uncouth in appearance for the one, and too well armed for the other. The outlaws seemed very pleased with their discovery. 'Here's a pretty,' one commented.

'And a pretty boy,' said another.

This brought a shout of laughter from his companions. 'You and your pretty boys, Will,' one said.

My alarm began to grow, but of course I could not show it to them. It may be recalled that I had been in a similar position before, on my journey to Eccleshall following my defeat at Northampton, but then not only had I possessed a great deal of wealth to distract my captors, but I had also had a friend. On this occasion neither wealth nor friend was available. However, I scrambled to my feet, straightened my clothes as best I was able, and inquired, 'Are you loyal servants of the King?'

'Now there's a question,' said the man called Will. 'To which king would you be referring, lass?'

'Why, the King of England,' I retorted. 'Henry the Sixth. I am his Queen. Margaret of Anjou. You assist me to your great credit, and you harm me to your great peril. Before you stands the Prince of Wales.'

I had intended to overawe them with this sudden revelation of our identities, and for a moment seemed to have gained some small success. Then one said, 'She don't look like a queen to me, Harry.'

'Never a queen, John,' Harry said. 'A lady who has taken a tumble, mind. But never a queen.'

'But he's a pretty boy,' Will commented again.

'I *am* the Queen,' I insisted, stamping my foot. 'And I need succour. A mount, a change of clothing, and above all, food.'

'What do you reckon?' Harry asked. 'She's a beauty. And who's to know, if we cut her throat after?'

'And I could have the boy,' Will said.

My blood ran cold. But again I would not reveal it. 'You would not dare,' I told them.

'Let's think on it,' John said. He was clearly both the oldest and the wisest of the three. 'She'll only improve by waiting. You come along with us, woman. Bring the boy.'

'Where?' I demanded, as imperiously as I could.

'You said you was hungry. We'll feed you.'

I was not going to argue further; I was so hungry I could not think straight, and I knew I would be more able to cope with rape on a full stomach. Prince Edward was not so pliant. 'Mother,' he asked, 'why do we not strike off their heads?'

This seemed to amuse them, for they gave another bellow of laughter. 'There is no need, Edward,' I told him. 'They are going to feed us, and help us on our way. To rejoin the King and our army, which is close by,' I added meaningfully.

This raised another shout of laughter, which indicated that they were well aware of what had happened to the King's army, but I grasped Edward by the hand and followed them into the trees. My brain was working overtime, as may be imagined, but I knew that my only course was to practise patience and fortitude, and await my opportunity to escape them – after being fed, I hoped. My resolve to protect and rescue England's future king was absolute, but I had no idea just how much fortitude was going to be demanded of me.

We did not have very far to travel before we arrived at a sudden hillside rising out of the centre of the forest. In this hillside there was a cave, and this was clearly the robber gang's lair; here there were two women, as poorly dressed and uncouth-looking as their menfolk, kneeling round a roaring fire in the very entrance of the cave. They scrambled to their feet at our approach. I found the presence of the women reassuring, for no very good reason, as they surrounded me with cackles of laughter, and began pulling and prodding at me. 'Says she's the Queen,' Harry told them, which seemed to amuse them even more.

But one came right up to me and peered into my face, then took some of my hair into her greasy fingers to hold it against her face. 'Suppose she was the Queen?' this harpy asked. 'She has the look of a queen. And she's lovely, ain't she, as the Queen is supposed to be?'

That made them think, and gather closer. 'She'd be worth a pretty penny,' the woman said.

This seemed promising. 'I *am* Queen Margaret,' I said. 'And this is the Prince of Wales.'

'She's no queen,' asserted the other woman. 'Queens wear crowns.'

I ignored such ignorance. 'But return me to his grace,' I promised, 'and you will be richly rewarded.'

Unfortunately, while they might be ignorant of what a queen should look like, they had, as I had already surmised, some knowledge of current events. 'The King is a fugitive,' Will said. 'I was at the Yorkist camp and heard this. He has no money. There'll be no reward for returning her to him. But . . .' he looked from face to face, 'I've heard it said that King Edward would pay a fortune to get his hands on this one.'

They clapped their hands with glee. 'And the boy,' Harry said.

Will looked disappointed. 'We could keep the boy.'

'He's the next King of England, maybe,' Harry said. 'The Yorkists would pay a lot for him. For the pair.'

'If she's the Queen,' said the Cassandra of the group. 'If she ain't, we'll just get our necks stretched.'

'We'll ask Dickon,' said the first one. 'When he comes in.'

All this while, concerned as I was for our safety – and Prince Edward's chastity! – my nostrils had been assailed by a most heavenly smell. Well, perhaps in other circumstances I would have found it a bit strong, but I was starving and there was certainly some kind of stew simmering in an iron pot suspended above the fire. Whatever our dangers, I had no idea how long it might be before this mysterious Dickon arrived. So I reminded them, 'You promised me food, and for the boy.'

'And food you shall have, your grace,' Harry said, words I would have found most reassuring had they not been accompanied by a lascivious grin. However, at that moment only food mattered, and a moment later Edward and I were digging into the stew, which turned out to be rabbit. True we had only the one earthenware bowl, and we were not even offered a knife or a slice of bread, so that we had to dip our fingers into the mess, but nothing had ever tasted so good. We were also regaled with drink, a species of what appeared to be home-made beer, which had my head swinging as if it had been Scotch whisky and had Prince Edward fast asleep before he had properly finished his meal. In the circumstances which were now to follow, this was just as well.

Our captors also indulged, men and women, in a good deal of laughter and bawdy talk. Next I made a mistake, but it was a mistake which had to be made. Having eaten until I could eat no more, and being also filled with this liquor, I staggered to my feet and headed for the nearest bushes. This alarmed them. 'She makes off,' John shouted, also getting up and staggering to and fro.

'It is a call of nature,' I retorted.

'You'll not leave our sight,' Harry declared.

'Nor need I,' I assured him, and merely stepped behind a bush. It was high enough to conceal me when I crouched, but low enough so that they could see my head at all times. What a situation for a queen! But worse was to follow. My movement, and the suggestion in it, had obviously aroused more than their alarm. When I returned, feeling slightly more my own self, I found them all quite animated, and conspiratorial with it, as they had been whispering together.

'Now you must pay for the meal, your grace,' Harry said, with an even more lascivious grin.

'I will have to owe you,' I told him. 'You have the word

of a queen that you will be paid.' If only by the hangman's rope, I promised myself.

'That's for the future,' John said. 'We'll have payment now.'

'You're to dance for us,' the woman I had mentally named Cassandra told me.

I gave them my most imperious stare, but it is difficult to be imperious when one is conscious that one's clothes are torn, one's coiffure does not exist, and one has had too much to drink.

'Will has his lyre,' said the first woman. 'You'll enjoy a dance, your grace.'

My reflection was brief. Perhaps a dance would soften their attitude, and it seemed a small price to pay if I could get them on my side. No doubt my judgement was affected by the alcohol swirling around my still exhausted brain. 'If that is what you wish,' I said agreeably, having ascertained that Prince Edward was still fast asleep.

Will thereupon struck up a tune and I kicked off my shoes, in any event in a sad state of disrepair, and swirled about in front of them holding my skirts and doing a good deal of stamping and even some writhing, while I tossed my hair to and fro. All of this was another sad mistake. They clapped loudly, drank some more of their home-made beer and gave me a cup as well when I stopped to catch my breath; it set my senses reeling again, and then Harry said, 'You'd do better without clothes.'

'No doubt,' I agreed carelessly.

'So get them off,' he commanded.

I am afraid I goggled at him in my consternation.

'We'll have to help her grace,' John said, and together they advanced on me.

I have ever been adept at making quick decisions. These are not always the best decisions, to be sure, but they are usually better than no decision at all. Fuddled as I was, I understood immediately that to allow them to lay hands on my body would lead to disaster. Not only would my remaining clothes be torn to shreds, but having got hold of me they were unlikely to let me go until their passion was sated. I also recognised immediately that no help was likely to be forthcoming from the women, who seemed as attracted by the idea of inspecting my most intimate charms as their menfolk. As for the likelihood that they might become even more inflamed by the sight of my body, that was once removed, as it were.

And so the Queen of England stripped herself naked and again danced for her loutish subjects. As I sobered, I wondered at the fate which had pursued me almost from the moment I had laid eyes on the Earl of Suffolk with his devilish proxy proposal of marriage! I may say that my audience was entranced, for my constant campaigning had left my body as hard and firm as that of a young girl, save that it was obviously that of a mature woman, and I doubt any of them had ever beheld its equal. Certain it is than when I at last dropped to my knees, dripping sweat and totally exhausted, the three men made a concerted move towards me, and I would have been flat on my back – or worse – in the next moment had they not been checked by a huge shout.

They turned, and I raised my head to see a man who must have emerged from the trees some minutes before, but who had been overlooked in their passion and my preoccupation. I say man because he was clearly a human male, but I had never seen anything like him before in my life; nor have I since. His huge voice was indeed the smallest thing about him, for he stood not less than seven feet tall, I swear, and had shoulders like the door of a barn. As he wore hose I could see he had thighs like a horse, while there was no codpiece in the world would have contained what lay between. Possibly my dancing, which he had clearly been watching, may have caused him to appear somewhat larger than usual in this direction. 'By God and by Hell,' this monster now declared, advancing towards us, while I gathered my hair in front of my shoulders in an effort to

cover the more compelling parts of my body. I had achieved
a certain drunken intimacy with my captors, so that I was
almost resigned to the coming rape, but I instinctively
understood that here was a far more serious crisis. 'What's
this?'

'Says she's the Queen of England, Dickon,' Will
explained, revealing much agitation in the way he was
wringing his hands. 'And that the boy is the Prince of
Wales.'

Dickon merely glanced at the Prince, who had been
awakened by the shout – he would have needed to be dead
not to be – while his eyes simply devoured me. 'And you
have had your way with her,' he remarked, his voice like the
rumble of an approaching thunderstorm.

'We but asked her to dance, Dickon,' said the woman who
had first identified me. 'And she has done so willingly. We
have not touched her.'

'Why, Mother,' Prince Edward remarked, 'you have
nothing on. That is unseemly.' He sounded just like his
titular father.

However, my situation had also begun to interest Dickon,
although I could not be sure he also would find it unseemly. He
had now come right up to me, and he laid down his weapons,
which consisted of a crossbow and a sword as well as a dagger.
That he was head of this band was very obvious, and therefore
it was equally obvious that he was the ultimate arbiter of my
fate. And that of the Prince. I was in a considerable quandary,
quite apart from being at the disadvantage any woman would
feel at being naked in the midst of four men – I could no longer
consider their women as of the least importance. But how to
react? To smile might invite instant rape; to frown might invite
instant death. However, I recognised that one fate was far
preferable to the other, and that it was almost inevitable in any
event, whereas death might just be avoided. And I had always
my responsibility to the Prince, and therefore the Crown of
England. Besides, even if I were about to suffer the very worst
of fates, I was the Queen of England. 'I find it a trifle warm,

dear heart,' I explained to my son. 'And these people are our good friends.'

Saying this I abandoned my supplicatory position and stood erect, a movement which most certainly overtook a vital part of Dickon's anatomy at the same moment. 'Goddam and by God,' he commented, thereby indicating that he had at least the instincts of a nobleman. 'You are the most beautiful thing I have ever seen.'

I did not take offence. I was in no position to and, after all, Suffolk himself had once referred to me as a creature. Instead I sought to improve my position, so I tossed hair from my eyes and met his gaze. 'I am also your Queen, Dickon.'

'A queen,' he muttered, and stretched out his hand to grasp my hair, and let it trickle through his fingers. 'I have always wondered what it would be like to lie with a queen.'

I made myself stand still, and took another decision; this giant's combination of awe and desire rewakened my hopes of survival; certainly, at his hands, failure and even death would be at least interesting. 'Then lie with a queen, Dickon,' I whispered. 'But only you. And take me to the King, after.'

His eyes seemed to be boring holes in me, as his hand slipped from my hair to my shoulder, and then to my breast. This he fondled, as he might have tested the ripeness of an apple. Yet I still refused to move, although my whole body was moving as the intensity of both heartbeat and breath quickened. 'Mother!' Prince Edward complained at this familiarity.

'Shut the brat up,' Dickon recommended, 'or I'll cut off his balls.'

I gulped. 'Edward,' I said, 'please be quiet. Mother will attend you in a little while.'

'Do you take her, Dickon,' John said. 'And we will have her after.'

'Would you share a queen?' I whispered. He frowned, still kneading away. 'If you would learn how a queen makes love, Dickon,' I told him, still keeping my voice low, 'it must be done secretly. Take me into the wood, and I will make you the happiest man alive.'

He hesitated, but I could tell that I had gained the day. 'You'll come with me, then,' he announced.

'If you will give me time to dress.'

'Dress?' he roared. 'What do you want with dress? I want you naked, woman.'

'And you shall have me, naked,' I assured him. 'In the proper place and at the proper time. What, would you forego the pleasure of watching a queen undress?' He glared at me, but I had achieved a total intellectual superiority and, as I met his gaze with equanimity, he turned aside with some muttered threats and began drinking copious quantities of their very strong brew. This suited me. I knew what I had to do, and I have never lacked determination. I pulled on my tattered clothing and knelt beside the Prince. 'We are going to leave this place,' I told him.

'Oh, Mama,' he groaned. 'My head hurts.'

'Fresh air is the answer to a headache,' I told him. 'We are to take a walk with this gentleman.'

'I do not like him,' the Prince declared. 'He has made free with you, Mother.'

The dislike was clearly mutual. 'What's the boy to do with it?' Dickon demanded.

'I cannot leave him here,' I pointed out. 'Will not that Will have his hose off in a matter of seconds?'

Dickon acknowledged the truth of that with a shout of laughter. 'Then let him come,' he agreed, 'and learn the joys of life from a master . . . and his mother. But he's to keep his mouth shut.'

The other members of the gang were by now somewhat agitated, and John was bold enough to inquire, 'And what of us, Dickon?'

That earned him a buffet on the side of the head which stretched him on the earth. 'I'll bring 'em back,' Dickon announced. 'When I'm ready.' He now picked up his weapons, as well as a flagon of beer – I would have preferred it had he secured some of that delicious rabbit stew – and seized me by the arm to drag me into the woods.

'I am coming willingly,' I protested, beckoning Edward to run behind us. I was following my instincts, which had convinced me that it would be easier to hoodwink, cajole or bewitch one man rather than three, especially where one of the other trio clearly possessed unusual tastes and we should be constantly carped at by the two women. That Dickon was likely to be more of a handful, in every possible sense, than the remainder put together did not seem an insuperable problem. But now I began to consider mere escape if he were to become any more drunk than he now was; although first there were certain preparations to be made, such as discovering my exact whereabouts. I therefore trailed obediently behind him, and Edward trailed obediently behind us both, until we regained the stream where we had first been captured. By now the morning was well advanced, and with the sun out it was almost warm. 'I must drink,' I said, and lay on the bank to scoop water into my mouth. What would my ladies have made of me?

Dickon knelt beside me. 'This is a likely spot,' he said, and rested his hand on the nape of my neck to thrust his fingers up into my hair. 'To have a queen,' he muttered, apparently just beginning truly to believe his good fortune.

I finished drinking, and also knelt. His hand left my neck and began to play with my bodice. 'Are we safe here?' I asked.

'Oh, aye. The Yorkists have marched on.' He grinned. 'They are seeking you, and the old King. How much do you think young Edward would pay for you, pretty?'

If I had had any doubts that he deserved to die before, they quite vanished. I smiled at him. 'Not so much as the French and Scots. Do you deliver me to Marshal de Brezé or the Earl of Angus, and I promise you rewards beyond your highest hopes.' It would, after all, merely entail building a larger gallows than usual.

'The Scots,' he muttered, busily laying me bare from the waist up, for it is a remarkable fact that although a man may know full well what a woman looks like, the act of stripping her greatly encourages his manhood.

'We are not far from Scotland, I know,' I said, endeavouring to keep control of myself, because equally when a woman is being stripped with lubricity in mind it is very difficult for her to concentrate upon anything else. 'Dear Edward,' I said over my shoulder, 'would you be a good boy and take yourself into the woods for half an hour?'

'Shan't,' he declared. 'That is a bad man.'

'I'll take my belt to him,' Dickon vowed.

'He is but a child,' I pointed out. 'I will take a strap to him myself, in a little while. But you cannot leave me now,' and I panted most realistically, and not entirely falsely, for he was now engaged with my nether regions. 'Edward, obey me or you will make me very angry.'

I managed to get a good deal of venom into my voice, and he slunk off. I had no idea where he was likely to go, but had no doubt I could find him again when the time was right.

'You were telling me of Scotland,' I reminded Dickon, as he laid me on my back on the fortunately sun-warmed grass to remove the last of my clothing; he even took off my shoes the better to inspect my feet, which are as beautifully formed as the rest of me.

'Scotland,' he said, and waved his hand. 'It is but a few miles to the border.'

I made a note of the direction of the wave, and then had other matters forced into my mind. Having stripped me he now commenced to strip himself, and the effect was startling. It is a sad fact that very large men are not necessarily very large where it matters most, but no possible fault could be found with Dickon. In this regard I had already deduced that he was outsize, from the bulge in his hose. Now I was face to face – if that is the correct terminology – with the real thing and I will confess that, however steeled my resolve, I felt quite faint. I am a small woman, and it occurred to me not only that I would very likely suffer a mortal injury but that, even if I survived his thrust, I was going to be crushed out of existence by his weight, which I estimated at nothing less than twenty English stones.

Naturally I had been considering ways and means of escaping him, once I knew in which direction to travel. This information having been obtained, my first determination had been that it would be best attempted when his passion had been sated and he perhaps had fallen asleep. However I now doubted that escape was going to be practical when he had had his way with me, and so fell back on what might be called Plan B – like any experienced military commander I had several alternatives ready in my mind.

During the course of my life I have observed that strong drink, while it makes a man more mentally lubricious, at the same time often inhibits performance. Thus I said, as winningly as possible, 'Should we not toast our encounter, and future happiness?'

'Now that's how I like a lass to speak,' he shouted, 'even if she is a queen. Drink!'

He held out the flagon, having removed the stopper, and I lifted it to my lips. I had of course intended merely to sip, but as I raised the jug Dickon tapped it on the bottom, so that I swallowed far more than I had intended, while an equally large amount poured down my naked shoulders. The whole thing left me staggering, and before I could recover Dickon had taken the flagon away, placed it on the ground, and was licking beer from my breasts. I was quite unwomaned; nothing like that had ever happened to me before. I considered swooning, but it would have made little difference as he laid me on the ground again in any event.

I closed my eyes so as not to become too involved in what might happen next, but in fact nothing did, so I opened them again, and found him busily gulping the remainder of the beer. There was enough alcohol in there to lay several men cold, or certainly make them impotent ... but it seemed to have no effect at all upon Dickon, who threw the jug away and proceeded to impale me. I mean this quite literally, as far from taking me in any Christian fashion, or even infidel fashion as demonstrated to me by Brezé, he merely sat down, scooped me into his arms, and still sitting, with me also sitting astride his thighs, sank into me like the veriest spear. Of course I was shocked and distressed by such treatment, while wondering why none of my previous lovers had considered such a splendid means of gaining entry to our mutual advantage. Positioned as I was, I could not prevent myself from being embedded to an extent I had never even suspected possible; while again, positioned as I was, and facing him, Dickon was enabled to make free with my body from breast to buttock, which he did most enthusiastically.

These tumultuous events drove all thoughts of escaping him from my mind; indeed, when he at last allowed me to recline beside him, I was far more enervated than I had ever hoped *he* might be from a combination of excessive passion and strong drink. In fact, my first tentative thoughts were in the direction of a continued partnership, as it were. 'Take me to the Scots, Dickon,' I said, 'and remain forever as my faithful attendant.'

'Ha ha,' he said, and up-ended the flagon. But it was quite empty.

'Does that thought not appeal to you?' I asked, sitting up.

'You are a queen,' he pointed out.

'Am I not a satisfactory queen? Have I not also proved that I am a woman?'

'As queens go,' he argued, 'I doubt there is a better. But then, you are the only one of whom I have had experience. As women go, why, you are satisfactory enough. But I *have* known better.' If looks could kill he would have dropped dead on the spot, but he was not looking at me.

'As for taking you to the Scots, why, they would undoubtedly hang me,' he continued. 'Nor do the Scots ever pay good money for anything. While even if they did, your *grace* would soon enough find a way to dispose of me once

I ceased to be useful. No, no, it were better we both remember this one set-to as a most enjoyable occasion, and go our separate ways.'

'You mean to abandon me here, with the Prince?' I asked, uncertain whether to be glad or sorry.

'Abandon my queen? Never.' He gave a guffaw of laughter. 'I shall take you to where you will receive a warm welcome. To King Edward himself, by God. Now there's where money is to be made. And I'll not have to share it with those louts. Why do you suppose I brought you out here by yourself, anyway? Ha ha.' He went down to the stream, arched his back, and began to drink the water, very noisily.

I doubt that any woman has ever been more insulted. And I *know* no queen has ever suffered such contumely. After all, while hating every moment of my ordeal, I had done my best to satisfy him. And now to be dismissed as no better than any other woman ... that rankled more than his determination to deliver me to my enemies. Either way I was faced with destruction. Up till now, my thoughts had been entirely devoted either to escape or to so beguiling this great oaf that he would become my faithful servant. I had certainly failed in my second objective, and it seemed extremely unlikely that I was going to be able to escape him, so long as he retained his size and strength as well as his ability to drink me or anyone else under the table. There was only one solution left.

Anyone who may have perused these words will by now have no doubt that beneath my shapely but essentially feminine bosom there beat the heart of a warrior. How often had I longed to lead my men into the thick of battle, and win or die at their head? I had always been dissuaded by my male advisers reminding me of my duty both to the King and to posterity in the form of my son. But unless I acted the warrior now, it seemed to me that both King and son were lost for ever, not to mention myself.

I did not hesitate. In any event, this man was a condemned felon, as robber, traitor, no doubt murderer ... and despoiler of his Queen. My anger was the more compounded by the utter contempt he obviously felt for my physical capabilities, in that he cheerfully knelt with his back to me while he slaked his thirst. I thus picked up his discarded sword, held it in both hands, and swung it with all my force on to the nape of his neck.

He uttered not a sound, but tumbled forward into the water. However, from the lack of blood I determined that he was not dead; I had not cut off his head, as I intended, but merely stunned him with the force of the blow, no doubt because I had never been trained in the use of a sword.

'Oh, well struck, Mother,' declared the Prince, revealing that he had been watching us all this while. However, now was no time for either mortification or embarrassment, and certainly he showed none as he emerged to stand beside me. 'But I doubt he is dead. Why do you not shoot him with an arrow?'

I looked at Dickon, lying on his face in the water, and then at my son. 'I do not know how to load a crossbow.'

'I do,' he said; and did so, having to lie on his back and use his legs to create the necessary tension, but presenting me with a fully-loaded weapon. 'Aim between his shoulders,' he recommended. This I did, with a gratifying result, even if the force of the discharge knocked me over: when I sat up, I discovered that the bolt had embedded itself in Dickon's back to a good half of its length, and the water around the unhappy man was discoloured with blood. 'Well aimed,' Edward declared, and took the bow from my fingers. 'You will need another shot.' And he commenced reloading.

'Are you sure he is not dead?' I asked. Apart from being disturbed by the shallow water, Dickon's body, having become wedged against a fallen branch, had not moved, and as his face was down, I was sure he must have drowned by now.

'It is best to be certain,' my precocious youngster said. I fancy he was enjoying playing with the crossbow. In any event, he made me fire twice more into the inert flesh before he was satisfied. 'And now, Mother,' he said, 'do please dress yourself. You are quite unseemly, and beside, you will catch cold.'

14

Incidents like that of Dickon the robber do a great deal to cement a relationship between mother and son. We had always been close; now we seemed like twin souls.

Of course we never confided the truth of the matter. It would, as Prince Edward would have put it, have been unseemly. When, a few months later, I related the story of my adventures to the Duchess of Bourbon, I merely told her that in our escape we had been assailed by a robber, huge of body and savage of mien, who had threatened our lives but had been won over to helping us the moment I had declared myself to be the Queen. Anyone who would believe that will believe anything; fortunately, people, especially other members of the royal clan, as well as those scribblers who hurry at their heels anxious to write down every word of wisdom or scandal that drops from their lips, are always eager to believe that the common people are at heart utterly loyal.

Dickon disposed of, the Prince and I made our way to Scotland. This is a very simple thing to say, and in fact it was a very simple thing to do, in the abstract, a mere matter of walking some fifty miles, while it alternately snowed and rained, and we were forced to steal fruit in order to stay alive, as after our experiences in the wood we dared not show ourselves to anyone. I will therefore pass over the horrid privations to which we were exposed for a period of nearly a week, and merely state that we reached our goal.

Here it may be pertinent to ask why I did not seek my husband. Well, that would have involved traipsing from abbey to abbey, and while this would have resulted in food and shelter, I could not tell whether it might also entail my betrayal to the Yorkists. As for Henry, our marriage was long over, and although it is sinful of me to admit it, as far as I was concerned the sooner he went off to join his famous forebears the better; I had at my side and in my care a far more positive prospect as King of England. In the event, I never laid eyes on my husband again. I doubt he missed me during the coming years. I know I did not miss him.

I had, of course, wondered somewhat as to what sort of reception I should receive in Scotland, but in this event fortune at last smiled on me, and almost the first people I encountered were servants of Angus. They were astounded to see me alive, the report having been spread of my demise, and when I made my wishes known, they were all eager to assist me. Clothes were provided to replace my rags, and for the Prince; we were bathed and fed, given soft beds in which to sleep, and a party was immediately assembled to escort me to Edinburgh where, I was informed, the Queen lay ill with her lords in attendance, and also Pierre de Brezé. However, I never saw Mary again either, for she was buried by the time I reached Edinburgh. But her death affected me grievously. Politically and financially, this was obvious; I could no longer count on Scotland as an ally, and indeed it was very rapidly made plain to me that the Scots would like to see the back of me. But even more, the thought of one so vital, so anxious to gain every moment out of life, subsiding at such an age – she was more than a year younger than myself – filled me once again with an overwhelming appreciation of the slender threads that bind us to this earth.

It may be supposed that my bereavement was alleviated by being reunited with Pierre. But this relationship too had soured, although neither of us would immediately admit it.

The fact was that he was unused to such total failure as had attended his efforts in the North of England, and he could not help but feel guilty at the way his abandonment of me had nearly cost my life. I say nothing of the actual cost in chastity – he did not know about that. As men will, he managed to turn this carelessness of his into my fault, and became resentful. In addition, he had a roving eye and it had roved over me sufficient times; he had been, as I have indicated, alarmed at the ends to which I was prepared to go to regain my kingdom; and he had his own way to make: to ride at the right hand of the Queen of England would have been sufficient for even his ambition, but now that this was clearly not going to happen his thoughts were drifting elsewhere.

So were mine. Clearly I had to make tracks. But where, that was the question. Pierre was quite certain: I must recross the Channel. To Louis? He thought not, and recommended Burgundy. I was aghast, but he had persuasive arguments. Not all of these were honestly concerned with me, as I later discovered. He knew, and I did not, that he had written to Cousin Louis informing him of my various pledges, and indeed stating that in his opinion I was worthy only of the block from an English point of view. Thus he was able to represent to me that Louis, who certainly knew about my pawning of Calais, as he was the broker involved, might well decide to hand me over to the Yorkists in the interests of peace.

Pierre also knew, as did I but I did not consider it of great importance, that Louis had surrounded himself with his own people, and that there was no room for the Seneschal of Normandy at court, and he further feared that his enemies (and he had many, as do all great men) might perhaps seize the opportunity of his return from a grotesquely unsuccessful campaign to accuse him of treason and thus prevent any risk of his *ever* being able to regain the royal favour.

He thus felt that we would be welcomed at Bruges, relations between Duke Philip and King Louis having declined sharply since Louis had gained the throne. When I pointed out that Duke Philip was soon to be related to Edward of March by marriage, he assured me that the Duke of Burgundy, quite apart from being far more closely related to me – he was every bit as much my uncle as he was Louis's – not only had an eye for a pretty face but was also widely accepted as the most gallant knight in Christendom, who would certainly not turn me away out of hand.

Thus to Burgundy we went.

In August I landed at Sluys, after a comparatively calm crossing – one should only ever take to the sea in summer – in a state of utter destitution. With me were Prince Edward, John Combe, and Sir John Fortescue. Having existed in some discomfort since the disaster at Northampton, Sir John had made his way to Scotland as he refused to serve Edward of March, and now volunteered to be the Prince's tutor, even though I explained to him that I had no means of paying him at the moment. Seven of my ladies were of the party, and not one of us had so much as a change of clothing. We were accompanied by Brezé, who supplied us with the bare essentials of existence from his own meagre store of money. We had no idea what the future held for us, and it must be said that my fortunes had never been at a lower ebb.

I was, however, informed by the captain of the port that if I would take myself to Bruges, I would find the Count of Charolais waiting for me. It was at this juncture, when it may well be imagined that I needed all the support I could obtain, that Pierre informed me that he must leave my service. He was embarrassed by his decision, and stood awkwardly, twisting his hat in his hands. 'The fact is, your grace,' he said, 'I have been summoned by King Louis.'

It turned out that in a sense he was speaking the truth, as Louis, understanding that his policies were leading him into a confrontation with his own brothers and nobles, had realised he needed all the loyal and talented soldiers he could find, and Brezé certainly ranked high on that list. The word had therefore been spread that the Seneschal would after all find a welcome at court. Additionally, of course, Pierre had no intention of placing himself in the power of either Charles of Charolais or his father, to be used as a pawn in the coming game against the French monarchy. However, at the time, I could only see that here was another of those base betrayals with which I had been plagued all of my life, and from the man who had talked me into surrendering myself to Burgundy in the first place. In my bitterness I used harsh words against him. Thus we parted, for ever.

That night, as I lay sleepless in my narrow bed in my equally narrow and mean bedchamber, John Combe came to me. The youth was now seventeen, and had filled out splendidly since our flight from Northampton three years before. Equally had his love for me grown, as was plain for all to see. In my loneliness, I was now able to reward him, and at the same time solace myself for the various curses I had to bear.

Then I took my weary way to Bruges; not being at all sure what the future held, I left Prince Edward with Fortescue at Sluys, and travelled with but two ladies, and of course, John. To say that I was both depressed and a little frightened would be an understatement. Consider: this prince to whom I was going a-begging had been the first ever proposed as my husband, and had been refused by my family; he was now betrothed to the sister of my most bitter enemy; his father had once been a close friend and ally of my husband's family, but had now gone in quite the opposite direction. And I had placed myself entirely at his mercy.

Never was a woman more pleasantly surprised. In addition to all my other fears, I was aware that Cousin Charles had earned himself the sobriquet of the Rash, because of his hasty temper. However, I determined to do the best I could, dressed myself in a new gown I had managed to procure in Sluys, and swept into the Count's presence, wondering as I did so if I would be able to keep from scratching out the eyes of Margaret of York, supposing she sat at her fiancé's side.

Fortunately, she did not, and no one could have been kinder than Charles. He rose from his chair to take and kiss my hand, addressed me as your grace, and indeed treated me with all the honours due to a queen, while at the same time not forgetting those due to a beautiful woman. Not for the first time I cursed that fortune which had ended our early romance before I had even set eyes on him – for he was a handsome man – and before I was old enough to understand what it was all about.

However, as he was at the moment separated from his betrothed – she had in fact not yet been delivered to Burgundy by the canny Yorkists, who were busily making sure every i in the marriage contract was dotted and every t crossed, and she was a girl even younger than I when I had been wed to Henry – and as Charles, or his father, were the very last hopes I had in the world, I reckoned that it might be to advantage to consider that the twenty-five odd years that had elapsed since our abortive betrothal had never been.

In reasoning thus I was at least partly correct, and this was gratifying, for, as I have said, Charles was a handsome man, and a vigorous one, to boot. Indeed, but a year earlier I would have felt he was too vigorous; but after an afternoon spent in the company of Dickon the robber all other men seemed as mere boys, and I flatter myself that I left him exhausted rather than the other way around. John Combe was a little put out by this event, but I explained to him that it was all part and parcel of international diplomacy, and that I was not about to suffer from the jealousy of a seventeen-year-old page – while acknowledging that seventeen-year-olds are more likely to be unreasonably jealous than their elders.

Unfortunately, enjoyable as was my set-to with Cousin Charles, it produced very little in the way of concrete results. Charles was at this time entirely the servant of his father, and although he did persuade Uncle Philip to receive me, it was

a most unsatisfactory business. Uncle Philip was, I think
fairly, adjudged the greatest knight and the most opulent
prince in Christendom. But let us be honest: knightly
manners and behaviour, as well as ostentatious opulence, are
all for show. They indicate nothing of the man who lies
beneath the glittering exterior, and even less of the means he
may employ to continue such extravagance. Duke Philip
wished to receive me, and perhaps he even wished to help
me, but his great days were in the past; he had become a
nervous man who was constantly wringing his hands, and he
was more anxious not to excite his two powerful neighbours
and relatives, Edward of March and Louis of France. Thus
I was forced to travel in disguise, in the back of a tinker's
cart, if you please, from Bruges to St Pol, in order that no
one might know the Duke of Burgundy was receiving the
Queen of England.

When we did get together he was all charm, and despite
his great age – he was sixty-seven – I could tell that he was
not immune to my charms, either. But alas, men, as they
grow older, become more interested in affairs of state than
affairs and he forced me to sit through an analysis of my
situation, at the end of which I was compelled to agree with
him – although I did not say so – that my cause and that of
my husband was hopeless, and that my only prospect was a
retirement into private life.

It may well be imagined with what grief this realisation
crept over me. It was now that I poured out my heart to
Philip's sister, the Duchess of Bourbon, and related to her
the major part of my misadventures of the past ten years.
However, as I have indicated above, I retained enough sense
not to let her into the truth as regards Prince Edward's
parentage (I told her that Henry had had a sudden rush of
conjugal passion, eight years after our marriage!), my true
relations with their niece Mary of Guelders (I claimed we
had been merely the best and closest of friends!) and even
more, what had passed between myself and Dickon the
robber. I saw no reason to dissemble regarding my affair

with Brezé, as after all a woman in my position, with my looks and breeding, would have seemed unnatural had she never had a lover at all.

The Duchess was aghast at what I had been forced to undergo; I have no idea what she would have made of the truth.

But at the end of it all I was left to face the sober fact that all my hopes had come crashing to the ground, and that I was yet again a penniless refugee. Uncle Philip determined to alleviate my condition, and made me a present of two thousand crowns, having done which he indicated that the sooner I left Burgundian territory the happier he would be.

So back I traipsed to Bruges, where I took a tearful farewell of Cousin Charles, and had a last romp with him. How I wished his father would drop dead so that he could succeed; I felt sure I could persuade him to lend me his strong right arm, as well as the other, hardly less important, parts of his body he had already bestowed on me. I may have been over optimistic here; Charles was already making his plans for the confrontation with Louis which he knew was bound to come the moment his father's grip on the reins could be loosed.

From Bruges, attended by my sorely attenuated court, I went to St Michel-en-Barrois where Papa had set up a home for me, supported by an income of six thousand crowns a year. I recognised that this was all he could spare from his own limited resources, but it was barely sufficient for my expenses; there was nothing left even for paying spies and agents, much less raising armies. In vain did I again apply to Louis, to be met by stony refusals of assistance. Equally did I apply to my brother, but Duke John was firmly in Louis's camp, and regarded my cause as but an irrelevance compared with securing the French monarchy.

Thus picture me, chafing in my exile throughout that winter and into the following year, with only John Combe as solace. Chafing the more because I was surrounded by great

events in which I could not share. Not least of these was the
news that my husband had somehow managed to escape into
Scotland, and was being given assistance, affairs in that wild
kingdom having now settled down as the regents for the boy
king, James III, elected to resume their age-old antagonism
to England. Henry gave the Scots a guarantee of special
trading privileges with England once he regained his throne,
they again determined to support him and sent him into
England with an army. There, believe it or not, he was joined
by Henry Somerset, turning his coat for the second time.

Naturally, when this news reached me at St Michel I was
all martial ardour, anxious only to recross the Channel and
join my loved ones in their endeavours. To my disgust I was
forbidden to go, not only by Louis, but by Papa himself. I
reacted strongly. I pointed out that they had no jurisdiction
over me, as I was a queen in my own right and was in every
way their equal. They did not dispute this, but pointed out in
turn that they had two very useful weapons at their disposal
in order to make me comply with their wishes: Louis had me
in his power, as I was residing on French soil, and Papa had
control of my purse strings. In fact, as I soon became aware,
Louis was negotiating with Warwick, who was more than
ever the *de facto* King of England, to marry Edward of
March to a French princess in order to cement a vast Western
European alliance. While he was unable to prevent Henry
the King and Henry Somerset from causing trouble, he *could*
prevent me from joining in – and had every intention of
doing so.

He was the more agitated, because his protégée's was not
the only cap in the marriage ring. Also being offered as a
bride for March was the Infanta Isabella of Castile. Imagination boggles at what might have resulted had this match
come to fruition. In recent years this Isabella has achieved a
remarkable reputation as a woman of great strength of
character as well as unusual chastity, whereas March's
reputation, both for strength of character and lubricity, has
grown. At this time she was of course only thirteen years of

age, but as the half-sister of a totally incompetent king she was already a rallying point for the disaffected Castilian nobility, and her various uncles were desperate to get her out of the country. In the event, they failed, and her marriage to Ferdinand of Aragon has made the pair of them two of the most powerful rulers in Western Europe.

Some women have all the luck.

As it turned out, the delay while I wrote angry letters and received non-committal replies and strode the battlements of my castle in high dudgeon proved a fortunate one. It was the old story. Although Henry did succeed in rousing the north in his favour – oh, if only they had supported me, two years before! – on 25 April Somerset was defeated at Hedgeley Moor, and on 15 May again at Hexham. Henry was thus again left a fugitive, now, like myself, no longer welcome in Scotland, while Somerset, captured after Hexham, at last met the fate he so richly deserved, and was beheaded.

If therefore I had reason to rejoice that I had not been a part of this latest disastrous campaign, I was deeply saddened by the other events of this year. For Louis finally went to war with his brothers, who were supported by Burgundy; Uncle Philip had at last sunk into his dotage, and Cousin Charles was all martial ardour. The ensuing campaign was of no great interest to anyone. Given Cousin Louis's nature, this is not surprising, as he far preferred to indulge in truces and intrigues, plans and counter-plans, rather than risk a straightforward meeting on the battlefield, which, after all, is what wars are all about. However, he finally found himself in a position where he had to fight, or lose control of Paris. The battle took place within sight of the capital, and resulted in a royal victory. But among the slain, fighting for the King, was Pierre de Brezé.

Long as our mutual desire had lasted, tumultuous as it had been when eventually consummated, I cannot pretend that I still loved Pierre. But nonetheless, I wept at the news of his death. More and more I conceived that I was becoming

totally isolated; all the friends and supporters of my youth
dead, and no new support for the future at all to be perceived.
John Combe was a great comfort to me in the privacy of my
bedchamber, but I could not pretend that he had at his
disposal either wealth or men or even talent, and these were
what I needed most.

Indeed, it was at Michaelmas in this year of 1464 that I
had news of the crowning blow, but this was so ridiculous
that instead of weeping I had to laugh, even if it was bitter
laughter. I have mentioned that one reason Cousin Louis was
no longer prepared to support me was that he had been
approached by Warwick with a plan to secure yet another
Anglo-French rapprochement by the time-honoured means,
the marriage of Edward so-called the Fourth of England to
a French princess. This idea had appealed greatly to Louis,
not only because he was desperate to have peace on his
borders while he dealt with the various factions within his
kingdom, but because he had a healthy respect for the
abilities of Edward of March as a soldier. The thought of this
reincarnation of Edward III, the Black Prince and Henry V
rolled into one ever landing in France at the head of an army
gave him nightmares. Thus all summer the negotiations had
proceeded, hindered only by an apparent reluctance on the
part of King Edward to tie the knot. This seemed strange to
everyone, given the known lubricity of Edward's character,
and to a suspicious mind like Louis's it could only mean that
the young King was indeed bent on war, now that he had
apparently settled his domestic problems, even if, at this
time, King Henry was still at large.

But at Michaelmas the awful truth became known:
Edward could not marry a French princess, even if he had
wanted to, because he was already married, and had been
since May. His bride? A certain widow Grey, the wife of a
Lancastrian soldier killed at the second battle of St Albans,
known to her intimates as Bella!

The truth of this amazing event came out slowly, and took

even longer to be believed: I do not suppose anyone in the
entire world save Bella could successfully have carried out
such a coup.

It may be recalled that after the second battle at St Albans,
when Grey of Groby had died of his wounds, I had given
Bella permission to take her husband back to his home to be
buried, anticipating that when her duty was done she would
return to my side and my arms. However, by the time Grey
was interred, there was a whole Yorkist army between the
two of us. By the time my dearest friend had worked out how
to circumvent the enemy, my own fortunes had gone
tumbling at Towton and I was again a fugitive. Bella had, no
doubt wisely, opted once again to flee to the sanctuary of her
mother's home at Grafton, where she could feel that the
worst fate she was likely to suffer was another bollocking
from the Earl of Warwick. With her of course went her two
sons, and here she might well have remained for the rest of
her life, although this is unlikely. Bella was only twenty-
seven years old, and as she had grown even more beautiful
with the years it seems certain that a new husband would
sooner or later have beaten a path to her door.

In fact it has been suggested that she did not lack suitors,
but turned them all down. Was she in fact already planning
her masterstroke? I would not put it past her. For she knew
as well as anyone that once his great victory at Towton had
shattered the Lancastrian cause, as it seemed, permanently,
Edward of March had willingly turned over the kingdom to
his cousin Warwick and set about enjoying the pleasures of
being young, handsome, vigorous, lecherous ... and the
King! Now, like most vigorous men, Edward had only three
passions: fighting, hunting, and fucking. In Edward's case,
I have listed them in reverse order. As fighting was for the
moment finished, only the other two were left, and in
between tumbling every available woman he would ride
behind the hounds with great gusto. One of his favourite
hunts took him to the neighbourhood of Grafton, and Bella
must often have watched him pass by, and indeed, stop for

a stirrup cup from time to time, from the hands of the fading
but still attractive Duchess Jaquetta. Soon enough, therefore,
on one of his visits, he found himself regarding an extra-
ordinarily lovely young woman, with flowing yellow hair, a
comely face and a figure to match, seated beneath an oak tree
in her mother's garden while her two young sons played at
her feet.

His reaction was instantaneous and predictable: the
gorgeous creature was summoned to his bed. But here Bella
revealed both her determination and her courage: she
refused to go! Her motives have been variously represented.
The Yorkists naturally say that she was too chaste and
modest a matron ever to consider becoming any man's
mistress, even the King's. Well of course I knew better than
to accept that rubbish. This leaves three possible alternatives. The first is that Edward did not interest her
sufficiently, but this too is impossible to believe in view of
the young man's good looks, not to mention his position.
The second is that she remained my own faithful Bella who
would not contemplate a liaison with my most bitter foe. I
would very much like to believe this, but alas, I know Bella
too well. The third possibility is the obvious one: she had her
eye on the main chance and was prepared to risk losing all
to obtain it. The gamble was an immense one. Not only did
Edward have the pick of every woman in England, and in
addition, virtually every princess in Europe, but Bella was
five years the older of the pair. Most men think twice about
marrying a woman five years their senior; princes may
occasionally do it, but this is for reasons of state; there was
nothing stately about Bella Grey. Nor can I believe that
March's intentions towards her were at all honourable in the
beginning; he wanted only to get to grips with those
magnificent breasts and get between those not less magnificent thighs. Yet so besotted did he become with the
realisation of this ambition that when it was made plain to
him that the only way he was going to reach his objectives
was by means of a golden band . . . he actually agreed.

One must presume that he enjoyed his wedding night, for it was to cost a heavy fee.

As I have said, my reaction to the news was a bitter laugh. Dear little Bella, my companion of so many happy hours, was now calling herself Queen Elizabeth of England! But others were not so amused, and it was for this reason that Edward of March had kept his marriage secret for six months.

I do not think there can be any doubt that at this early stage of his career Edward was a little afraid of his imperious cousin, who, after all, had earned himself a great – if, as we have seen, entirely spurious – reputation as a soldier, and was undoubtedly the *de facto* ruler of the country. All Edward wanted was to be left alone to enjoy his bride, and he knew Warwick would carp, to put it mildly. However, when the Earl began to bring up the subject of the French marriage time and again, asking for – nay, demanding – a decision, Edward at last felt constrained to tell him the truth. I can only judge Warwick's reaction from his feelings about it when next we met, and that was some years off. But even in 1470 he was viciously angry at what his protégé had done, and at all who had been involved. We may suppose jealousy had something to do with this, remembering as we do how Bella and Warwick had had a couple of romps in the past, and there can be no doubt that Warwick knew how, on the occasion of their last amatory tussle, Bella had been playing the spy on my behalf, and had utterly hoodwinked him. But there it was. If Edward was King of England, as Warwick would have the world believe ... then Elizabeth Grey, née Woodville, was Queen, and the proud Earl could do nothing less than drop to his bended knee whenever they met.

I naturally had no idea at this time that this remarkable turn of events could possibly have any bearing on my personal fortunes. They had never seemed at a lower ebb, the more so as Bella very rapidly began to produce children for her new husband. The first were all girls but, given the remarkable fecundity of her mother, it seemed certain that before long heirs to the throne would be appearing to perpetuate the Yorkist line. And there was nothing that I could do about it, lacking as I did arms and money and men. However, I did possess what Bella and Edward did not as yet: my own heir to the throne, and in *my* Edward I rested all my hopes. Over the next few years, therefore, aided by the faithful Fortescue, my efforts were concentrated upon bringing Edward to manhood, in the right frame of mind to be King.

In this regard I have been criticised by those who should have known better for encouraging the more warlike aspects of my son's character. But consider. All my misfortunes seemed to stem from the fact that my husband had been entirely *un*warlike. Had he been but one tenth the warrior his father had been, and one tenth as strong and ruthless when need be, I would have been residing in comfort at Westminster, Queen of England in fact as well as name, with Salisbury and Warwick, and York and his son, either kept well to heel or executed for treason ... and Bella as my treasured companion and playmate. Instead I was a fugitive. I don't think I can be blamed for planning a future in which revenge and my own security and comfort, and power, were closely linked.

My confidence in that future grew with every day as I watched the Prince grow into a strong and athletic young man. I sought no marriage alliances at this time. Since the death of Mary of Guelders, the arrangement whereby the Prince would marry a Scottish princess had been quietly dropped. I was in no hurry to raise it again, or indeed to make any arrangement with anyone else. I was very conscious that I might be rebuffed as Papa had been, when in his impoverished state he had sought a husband for me as a young girl. But, even more, I wished no distractions to interfere with Prince Edward's determination to obtain his heritage. Indeed, I did not even offer him a mistress, nor did he wish one. His only studies were past campaigns, his only toys his weapons and armour, his only friends the few soldiers I was able to employ.

I watched this, I admit it freely, with equanimity. I was well on the way to achieving my goal. I had no doubt that when the time came, a marriage alliance would be found – although even I never in my wildest dreams had an inkling of where and with whom it would actually arise.

Meanwhile, I watched events in England. The following year my fortunes, already low, seemed to sink out of sight. To begin with, in May, Elizabeth was crowned. She has already, as I have recounted, taken upon herself the fame of declaring open my college at Cambridge, which had at last been completed. And then, the following month, King Henry was finally captured, lurking in one of his northern abbeys. From the reports which reached me, it seemed that he was no longer treated with the least respect, but tied to a horse and in this humiliating state led the length of England and through the streets of London before being incarcerated in the Tower like a common criminal.

Now, it may be asked, why did Edward of March and Warwick not immediately see to it that their royal captive joined his ancestors? But they were in a difficult position. Keeping Henry alive, as a captive, and as an anointed king, was an expensive and controversial business; they might claim he had abdicated – probably truthfully, as Henry would have signed any piece of paper thrust before him – but having two kings is hardly acceptable. Richard II had abdicated the throne to Henry IV in a blaze of publicity about which no man had argued, yet my grandfather-in-law had still considered it necessary to have him go to an early grave. Additionally, it might be supposed that the mere fact that Henry was alive and well and living in London would act as a continual spur to his supporters to attempt his restoration to the throne.

Against these arguments, however, there were others. Henry had been publicly captured. For him now to die, suddenly, having lived for so long, recently in the worst of circumstances, would have raised eyebrows: the world at large was just a little bit more sophisticated in 1465 than in 1397. The second argument, however, was far the most potent. Henry alive could be persuaded to disavow any action I might take, or alliance I might form, thus confusing his adherents. But with Henry dead, neither March nor Warwick could doubt that I would immediately have my son proclaimed King Edward IV, which would have led to even more confusion, as March was already claiming that name. Worse yet, from their point of view, anyone who wished to oppose England would then support me, and in place of a feeble and decrepit and prematurely aged man, they would be faced with a rampant youth supported by a no less rampant mother, and by no one could guess what other forces.

Thus they opted to let Henry live – for the time being, at least.

I was well aware of their machinations, but I am bound to say at that time I could see little future for either Prince Edward or myself. We had heard how displeased Warwick was with the King's choice of bride, but we did not suppose he could do anything about it; or at least, anything which would in any way benefit our cause. In all England we held but a single castle, impregnable Harlech, from where the gallant Earl of Pembroke, Jasper Tudor, was still defying the world. He wrote to me to say that he was sure he could raise a Welsh army for me, could he but find the money to pay for it.

There was the rub. Yet it is strange how, no matter how low one's fortunes may appear to be, one should never totally despair, because the rest of the world is busily pursuing its own affairs all the while, and one can never tell when other people's affairs may suddenly turn out to one's advantage.

The principal cause of a change in my situation was Bella

herself. I do not suppose she can altogether be blamed. She may have had royal blood in her veins, but she had never experienced any of the great pleasures of that inheritance, except at second hand, as it were, during her sojourn with me. Her mother and father were, by the standards of royalty, impoverished, their situation not assisted by their enormous progeny. Now on a sudden she was Queen of England, and wife of a man who could refuse her nothing. It can hardly be wondered at that she set out to enjoy her position as much as Edward of March was enjoying his, and as adultery by a queen is treason whereas by a king it is a national sport, her enjoyment had to follow somewhat more narrow channels. Which rapidly came down to one: the pursuit of wealth.

Perhaps had she indulged in a totally selfish manner it would have been accepted. But Bella was ever a loyal daughter and sister. She had her father created Earl Rivers. This too might have been acceptable. But over the next couple of years England was swamped by a deluge of Rivers. Rivers, male and female, were married to the highest in the land. One of Bella's brothers, a lad of not yet twenty, was wedded to a dowager countess of over eighty, to obtain her portion. This was scandalous behaviour. It was also dangerous, because it offended Warwick, who found himself being replaced in the King's Council by this horde of ultra-handsome, forceful, watery in-laws. Even more did it offend March's brothers. Actually, it only offended one brother: George, Duke of Clarence. Richard, Duke of Gloucester, was at this time still in his teens, and in any event had already begun to show that total loyalty to his brother the King which is the sole redeeming feature of his character. But Clarence commenced to brood. It was another case of deferred heirdom. Until Edward married and begot, legitimately, Clarence was heir to the throne, and Warwick was content; Clarence was as weak as butter, and would easily be ruled by a personality as strong as that of the Kingmaker. But neither Warwick nor Clarence could sit back with equanimity and watch the King's Council and the King's counsel being entirely taken over by these grasping Rivers, who were not men to be browbeaten, and who were bidding fair to have secured every worthwhile position in the kingdom before their brother-in-law died; and if he did die young there could be no doubt that the guardianship of the heir apparent, whenever he appeared, would rest with the Rivers family.

It may seem strange to harp on the possible death of the King, when that young man was himself not yet thirty, and was agreed by all to be the largest – he stood several inches over six feet – strongest, healthiest man in the kingdom. But men do die young, even when they are not assisted, and in the case of kings it is always wisest to look to the future, if it can be done without treason. Or even with treason. The facts are shrouded in mystery, and I can only recount them as observed from my retreat at St Michel.

In 1467 Duke Philip died, and was succeeded by Cousin Charles. Naturally I knew I could hope for nothing from this, in view of his betrothal to the Yorkist princess, but in fact events now began to run in my favour. Cousin Louis, it may be recalled, when he had quarrelled with his father, had taken refuge at the Burgundian court, and between himself and Uncle Philip there had sprung up a certain intimacy, and mutual trust, even if they had never actually liked each other. Louis had not been happy at the gradual rapprochement between Burgundy and the Yorkist faction, but had always felt that Uncle Philip would never let it get out of hand, and that he was right is evidenced by the Duke's kind reception of me.

But Cousin Charles was a different kettle of fish. He and Louis cordially loathed each other, and as we have seen had already fought a pitched battle outside the gates of Paris, when poor Brezé lost his life. There was no longer any guarantee that Burgundy and England would not return to that alliance which had cost France so dear in the days of my father-in-law Henry V, and this disturbed Louis greatly.

The immediate fruit of this, from my point of view, was

the sudden and unexpected arrival of Louis at St Michel. It was a courtesy call and nothing more; we discussed no affairs of state. Indeed, he rather rudely terminated all my efforts to introduce the subject. On the other hand, he was well aware that his visit would be widely reported in England, and should give Edward of March pause for thought. From my point of view, the word 'fruit' has to be used rather loosely. As I have mentioned before, entertaining a king and his court is a costly business, and I was endeavouring to get by on a strict budget, while I disliked being used as a pawn in a game being played by other people.

However, there were straws in the wind. Before the end of the year I was visited by gallant Jasper, who informed me that he had been able to borrow some money in France, and persuaded me to allow him to chance his arm. I would have liked to accompany him back to Harlech, but he was against this. 'I shall send for you when I have gained a victory, sister,' he promised.

Most interesting to me was his companion on this visit: Edmund, Duke of Somerset, younger brother of the infamous Henry, and now head of the house of Beaufort. Edmund was a couple of years younger than Henry, and I had not seen a lot of him in recent years as he had been rather kept in the background by his brother. He was very like the father after whom he had been named, but while he appealed to me for this reason, and on account of his good looks, he at the same time rather frightened me; he possessed a wildness of character and an instability of temper which were disturbing. However, I did not take long to discern a distinct military talent, far greater than either father's or brother's, and, I am afraid to say, than that of Jasper. I marked him down as of future value, could he but be controlled.

He in turn swore eternal allegiance to the Red Rose. I do not know if he hoped to supplant his father and his brother

in *every* way, but for the time being I encouraged him to lend
Jasper all the support in his power, and this he was happy to
do, for how better to beat a way to a lady's . . . well, I doubt
he was actually interested in my heart, than over the dead
bodies of her enemies. So off they went. Of course they did
not gain a victory. Jasper's untrained host was shattered by
a Yorkist army commanded by Lord Herbert, and he was
forced to flee back to impregnable Harlech, while Edward of
March added insult to injury by depriving him of the
earldom of Pembroke and awarding it to Herbert instead.

None of this did much to lift my spirits, even if I was
amused to learn that March remained so concerned that I
might cross the Channel that he had his brother-in-law
(Anthony Woodville, whom he had made Lord Scales) keep
the sea after escorting Princess Margaret to Burgundy for the
long awaited marriage to Cousin Charles, just to make sure
I did not attempt to return to England.

It was the following year that the subterranean rumblings
that had been apparently simmering for some time broke
into public view. This was the year, 1469, incidentally, in
which Isabella the Catholic finally married her cousin
Ferdinand of Aragon. That event of course had no bearing on
English circumstances. But early in this year Louis paid me
another visit; this time he actually invited me to leave St
Michel for a season, and visit Honfleur. He suggested it
would be proper for a queen like myself, even in exile, to
maintain a proper regiment of guards, which he would be
happy to finance. He knew, he told me, that I would rather
have Englishmen about me than Frenchmen; and Honfleur,
being a seaport, was the place to find a great number of
itinerant Englishmen who would surely be happy to serve
the Red Rose.

Of course this was utter nonsense. My visit to Honfleur
was duly reported in England as a recruiting venture for an
invasion, and stirred things up no end. How much of a plot
there was, and how much of a hand Cousin Louis had in it,

I am unable to say for certain. The facts are that while I was still at Honfleur there was a Lancastrian uprising in the north led by one Robin of Redesdale, a bandit about whom many fanciful tales have been told, as he has often been confused with an even more fanciful bandit who is reputed to have lived during the reign of Richard the Lion-Heart.

This Robin was, by all accounts, an utter scoundrel, but at the same time an able soldier. Edward of March, enjoying the fleshpots as ever – in fact it has been asserted that he was unable to take the field owing to an attack of the clap – despatched Herbert, the new Earl of Pembroke, together with his father-in-law, to deal with the matter. The two armies met at Edgcote on 26 July, and to the general surprise of everyone Herbert and Rivers were routed. Taken prisoner, they were promptly executed.

It may be imagined with what delight I received this news, even if I was saddened to hear of the sudden demise of Bella's dad, who was also Jacquetta's husband, of course. But it was the upshot of this revolt that caused most consternation in the courts of Europe. Edward of March – having apparently regained control of his genitals – duly mobilised his army, and with Warwick and Clarence marched north. Robin of Redesdale was duly defeated and disappeared. So what was new? Simply that word reached the Continent that March was himself a prisoner, in the hands of his brother and his cousin. Indeed, there was a rumour that Robin's revolt had not after all been inspired by the Red Rose, but by Warwick himself, to draw Edward away from the capital where he was so popular; and that the execution of Rivers had not been an act of Lancastrian vengeance for the way his family had turned its coat, but had been decreed by the Earl simply to get rid of one of the most obnoxious of Edward's supporters. To confirm this rumour, and perhaps most sinister of all – from Edward of March's point of view – the Duke of Clarence had married Warwick's daughter, Isabelle.

This was sensational stuff, but it hardly affected our

position, as I was still mistaken enough to suppose that
Warwick was a more dangerous foe than March. In any
event, March proved more than a match for his two
adversaries, even the great Warwick, and soon regained both
his freedom and his powers, although the kingdom remained
unsettled. Indeed I was more sorry than pleased to learn that
in the wake of these tumults a rising in the Lancastrian cause
had taken place in Lincolnshire, led by Sir Robert Welles.
This was rapidly and easily crushed, and Welles lost his head
along with several other good fellows.

However, this also had its repercussions. Apparently
Edward extracted from Welles, before his execution, an
accusation of treason against both Clarence and Warwick.
This from a man, mind you, who had officially revolted in
my name, but who appeared to know a great deal more about
what was happening in England than about me or my plans.
The immediate outcome was that Warwick and Clarence
were denounced as traitors, and had to flee the realm. This
was at the end of March, 1470. There seemed no doubt but
that they would come to France, as obviously they could not
go to Burgundy. In fact rumour soon reached me at St
Michel that they were anchored off the mouth of the Seine,
having been refused entry even to Calais, of which Warwick
still held the captaincy.

I reflected that he was receiving his just deserts at last, and
was only sorry that obviously Cousin Louis would give him
shelter, simply to have a card to play against Edward of
March should he ever consider an invasion of France. Again,
of benefit to myself and my son I saw absolutely nothing in
these events.

I was therefore the more utterly surprised when a galloper
arrived from King Louis, summoning Prince Edward and
myself to Amboise . . . to discuss the restoration of the house
of Lancaster!

15

My immediate reaction was one of pique that I should have been summoned like some vassal to attend her lord and master. But when I reflected on the rest of the message, I had no doubt that I must go.

It should be remembered that we were now in June, 1470. Three months earlier I had celebrated, if one can possibly use such a word for such an event, my fortieth birthday! Is there a woman alive who can contemplate being forty years of age with equanimity? I had found the concept of being thirty unpleasant enough. It was not that I felt anything less of a woman, that my passions had waned; perhaps indeed they had deepened. John Combe was now twenty-four years of age and in every sense had been, over the past six years, more of a husband to me than ever anyone before him.

Nor had my beauty in any way diminished. I can say it without fear of being accused of false vanity. I will admit to a slight sag of the breasts, a slight thickening of the waist, a slight plumpness to the thighs, but these things were scarce to be noticed save in bed. Equally the odd grey hair which had appeared was only to be discovered when I was naked, and in any event I plucked each one quickly enough. For the rest, I still hunted with all the vigour of my youth, and ate and drank in equal quantity. But where thirty brings with it a definite end to youth, forty brings with it a definite

introduction to old age. The future suddenly seems no longer
limitless. What must be done, must be done as rapidly as
possible. And where there is no prospect of anything being
done, one is forced into passive resignation. This had been
my lot for the past six years, with every birthday seeming to
sink me further into a bottomless bog from which there
appeared no possibility of escape. No, my fortieth birthday
had been an occasion for tears rather than celebration.

But now there came this strange, exciting, enthralling
summons. What could it mean? I attended the King with a
pounding heart, while trying all the while to throw off the
weight of years and misery which had accumulated on my
shoulders. I would be again the girl who had set Europe by
the ears.

Perchance I succeeded a trifle too well. Cousin Louis was
definitely taken aback when I swept into his presence
wearing my finest gown and headdress, and all the jewellery
I had been able to accumulate during the recent years to
replace that I had lost in the Wars. Indeed, his new wife
Charlotte of Savoy – she had only recently filled the position
once held by the unfortunate Scots girl Margaret – who was
heavy with child, seemed likely to have a miscarriage on the
spot, as we had not previously met. However, Louis
managed to overcome his surprise at seeing me so ready for
the fray, as it were, and even complimented me upon my
obviously radiant good health, while he could not help but
admire Edward, now sixteen years of age, the very picture
of Plantagenet manhood with his red-yellow hair and his
broad shoulders, his open face and determined demeanour –
here was every inch a future king. Louis's son Charles was
a puling babe, already showing signs of deformity.

Then we got down to business and I was quite fascinated
by what he had to say, even if he said it in his usual tortuous
fashion. 'This fellow King Edward is an upstart. I am sure
you'll agree, sweet Meg.'

'I imagine you are speaking of the Earl of March, cousin,'
I pointed out. 'I know of no King Edward.'

'Oh, quite. Absolutely. A slip of the tongue. I am going to be frank with you, Meg. He is causing me a great deal of trouble. Almost as much trouble as he has caused you, eh? Ha ha.' Hearing Louis laugh was a privilege confined to a very limited number of human beings – certainly I had not enjoyed it before – and so I understood that my cousin was nervous. Which made our tête-à-tête even more interesting. I could think offhand of no reason for the reigning King of France to be afraid of the exiled Queen of England. 'I am informed that he is concluding an alliance with Burgundy,' Louis went on. 'Now, who can that be directed against, if not me?'

'No one,' I assured him. 'And so you wish me to resume the war.'

'Well, is that not what you wish as well? There will be conditions, mind.'

'I was sure of it.'

'I wish to conclude a thirty-year treaty of amity with the house of Lancaster, in return for which I will provide you with men and money to undertake an invasion of England. Does that sound fair?'

I understood that he was actually about to employ a woman to fight a war for him, but as that was what I most fervently desired to do, I was happy to agree. 'Very fair, cousin.'

'Thus there only remains the question of your army commander.'

I waved my hand. 'Whoever you wish, provided he is an able soldier.' Edmund Somerset was certainly too young, although I intended to give him a command as soon as possible.

Louis did a great deal of throat-clearing, which indicated that he was more nervous yet. My mystification grew. 'I will offer you the most skilful general in Europe, Meg,' he said at last.

But that was surely March himself. 'Pray tell me this paragon's name,' I suggested.

This time the throat-clearing sounded like a rumble of thunder, but when Louis spoke it was in such a soft voice I could not quite grasp what he said. What I did grasp seemed nothing better than a silly joke. 'Would you repeat that?' I asked.

He leapt to his feet, as if expecting an immediate assault on his person. 'I said, the Earl of Warwick.'

I leapt to my feet also, and Louis hastily removed himself behind his chair. 'I do not find that the least funny,' I informed him.

'It is not meant to be funny, Meg. The Earl of Warwick has offered to command your armies to assist your husband in regaining his throne.'

'Are you deliberately trying to insult me?' I demanded, keeping my temper with a considerable effort.

'Of course I am not, sweet Meg.'

'Then you are mad. Stark, raving mad.' Well, given his ancestry, this was certainly possible.

'Meg, if you would but listen . . .'

'Listen?' I shouted. 'I have listened. I have listened to that . . . that crawling thing describing me as a murderess and an adulteress, a witch and a harlot. I have listened to him denouncing my son as a bastard. I have seen the evidence of his savagery on my own most faithful followers. I will tell you this, Louis: the next time I behold the Earl of Warwick, he shall be on his knees, before the block. I do not intend to look upon his face before then.' I sat down again, suddenly exhausted, as much by the realisation that all my hopes had been false as by the vigour of my declamation.

His courage restored, Louis returned round the chair and also sat down. 'I had thought you were a stateswoman, Meg.' I glared at him, for the moment out of breath. 'You have devoted your entire life to the cause of the Red Rose,' the scoundrel said winningly. 'But the odds against you have always been too great, simply because York and Warwick combined were too powerful. Think about it, Meg. Think about your battles. You lost the first St Albans because they

were combined against you; you won the second because
only Warwick was in the field. We can discount Northampton, because of Grey of Ruthin's treachery, and Blore
Heath, because of Audley's incompetence.' This proved that
he had followed my career much more closely than I had
imagined. 'But you won at Wakefield because only York was
in the field, and you lost at Towton because March and
Warwick were combined. Do you honestly suppose you
could possibly have lost that battle had Warwick been
fighting on your side? Why, you would be sitting in
Westminster now.'

I began to understand why this scoundrel had always been
more successful in the negotiating chamber than on the field.
Every point he made was like a hammer blow in its absolute
truth. 'Now he offers you the support of at least half the
kingdom,' he went on. 'Where Warwick plants his banner,
there will men throng to serve. This is well known.'

'The concept is utterly distasteful to me,' I grumbled.
'What would people say?'

'Why, Meg, they will say that here is a truly dedicated
woman, determined to let nothing stand in the way of the
restoration of her husband, and her son, to their proper
rights.'

There was another telling blow. But I was not entirely
simple. 'And the Earl's reward?'

'Why, to stand at your right hand.'

'Oh, yes?'

'Well, of course there would have to be certain safeguards, on both sides. We are thinking of a marriage
alliance.' He hurried on before I could speak. 'The Earl's
younger daughter, Anne, to the Prince Edward.'

'Now I know you are mad. That would make Warwick
father-in-law of a future king.'

'Is that so unthinkable? His aunt Cicely is mother of the
man who at present sits on the throne of England.'

That was true enough. 'How old is this person?' I asked.

'The Lady Anne? I believe she is ten years old. The

consummation would have to be postponed for a year or two.'

'Yes,' I said thoughtfully. A great deal can happen in a year or two. Then a thought struck me. 'But what does Clarence say to all this?' Because if my Edward was marrying the Lady Anne, as part of a plan to regain the throne for my husband, then there could be no possibility of Clarence succeeding his brother as King.

Louis merely smiled. 'I doubt he will like it. But then, he is not considered of great account.'

I rose again, to his evident alarm, but he was somewhat relieved when he realised I was merely wishing to walk to and fro while I thought. There was certainly a great deal to be thought about. I could not pretend ever to do anything but loathe and abhor Warwick, and the thought of his daughter as my daughter-in-law, and the mother of my grandchildren, filled me with disgust. On the other hand, spending the rest of my life in exile at St Michel, with my son a king without a country, was even more disturbing. And if there was one man in the world with the ability, as I and everyone else supposed, to overthrow Edward of March, it was Richard Neville. Then of course he would seek to control the kingdom. But times were changing. Warwick was actually older than I, whereas my Edward was just coming to manhood, and Edmund Somerset was already there. Here were two very worthy and strong right arms with which to deal with Warwick when the time came – he was handicapped by having only daughters.

Perchance Louis, with all of that cunning observation which was his greatest strength, had noticed something about my expression to make him calculate the time had come for his *pièce de résistance*. 'You remarked just now, sweet Meg, that the next time you laid eyes on Warwick, he would have to be on his knees. Well, I can tell you that he is prepared to grant you that desire, and to beg your forgiveness for all the ill that he has ever done you, if you will agree to this alliance so advantageous to you both.'

*

The things that men will do to reach a desired goal! I do not believe Warwick had any such subservience in mind when he and Louis had first discussed the project. Undoubtedly Louis twisted his arm. In any event, on 15 July he came to Angers where I had been joined by my father and Louis and there went on bended knee before me, placed his hands between mine, begged my forgiveness – which I was graciously pleased to grant – and swore to be my liegeman for the rest of his life. This probably was the only oath he ever took which he faithfully kept, simply because he never had the opportunity to break it.

But of course I had to swear too, to honour him above all other men, saving only my husband and son. To make sure we both understood what we were about, Louis had produced a fragment of the True Cross he had managed to discover and appropriate, and we swore our oaths on this sacred, if remarkably convenient, relic. At the same time Prince Edward was betrothed to the Lady Anne, a pretty child.

Clarence was not present at this ceremony. We gathered that, like Achilles, he was sulking in his tent. I foresaw trouble here, and strongly recommended that the Duke be placed in protective custody in France until after our expedition had achieved its objective. Warwick, however, assured me that Clarence was his man, simply because in view of his treachery, he dared not be Edward of March's man despite being his brother, and that his presence would be of great value to our cause, as showing the English people that even the house of York favoured a restoration of Henry VI.

Not for the first time in my life I accepted the judgement of others over my own instincts. I, of course, had learned the hard way that the surest way to disaster is to trust others. But with the English, trusting their peers or betters is a national disease. We were about to witness some more examples of it.

For the moment, however, everything went according to an apparently very well-laid plan. The signal having been given, there was promptly a fresh uprising in the north of England, led by Lord Fitzhurst, one of Warwick's innumerable cousins. As was expected, Edward of March promptly sallied forth to deal with it. Here was example number one, for in command of the Yorkist army in the North was Lord Montague, Warwick's brother, and he had been retained in this position despite the falling-out between his brother and his cousin. March, galloping north with only his household guards for company, apparently did not think twice about placing himself in the centre of Montague's army to deal with Fitzhurst ... whereupon Montague promptly declared for his brother and placed March under arrest.

Had I been present, that would have been that; this youth had plagued me long enough. But in my absence there was the usual shilly-shallying, and Edward of March managed to escape. Don't ask me how, but I suspect there was some more absurd trusting involved. However, his cause seemed to be lost, as he galloped to the coast and took ship for Burgundy, where he threw himself on the charity of his sister's husband; the marriage between his sister Margaret and Charles of Burgundy had been concluded in 1468. So great was his haste that he even had to abandon Bella and her brood. And brood it already was, as she displayed to the world that she was indeed Jacquetta's daughter. Thus far they remained all girls, but she was at this moment again big with child. In the circumstances, she prudently removed herself from the Tower, where she had been left in her husband's absence, to the sanctuary of Westminster Abbey.

Again, had I been present, I should have done everything in my power to draw her out. Not that I meant Bella any harm. But she would have been a useful asset in the coming manoeuvres. However, I was not present. The moment news was received that Warwick's plan to lure March to the North and there arrest him had worked, the Earl set off. I had assumed that the Prince and I would accompany him. But

Louis said no. It would be safest, he told us, for the Prince and me to remain in France until the business was settled.

I understood immediately that, for all the bits of the True Cross which might be lying around, my rascally cousin trusted neither Warwick nor me. He wanted to have his bird in the hand as well as his birds in the bush. Thus he received me in great state at Amboise, and entertained me royally as the Queen of England, while Warwick pressed on.

I was uneasy. And yet everything continued to go entirely as we had hoped. Warwick duly landed in Kent, accompanied by Clarence. The people duly flocked to their support. London duly opened its gates to them. And Henry was duly released from the Tower, fed his first square meal in years, and placed upon the throne to the plaudits of the multitude. It was now that Warwick began to be hailed as the Kingmaker. This was quite fair, as he had first of all raised Edward of March to the throne, and now had displaced him with another. The question was whether the Kingmaker could also acquire the title of Kingkeeper!

These stirring successes having been achieved, I naturally wished to be at the side of my husband. But once again Louis demurred. Ranting and raving, shouting and screaming, weeping and wailing, cajoling and cursing – and I tried a bit of all of these – had no effect whatsoever on that cold brain: it is of course pointless to refer to the heart when speaking of Cousin Louis. Instead of letting me go to England he took me to Paris, where I was again royally entertained, and enjoyed not a moment of it; my thoughts were elsewhere. It was not until February 1471 that we received a peremptory summons from King Henry that he wished his wife and son at his side, and Louis agreed to let me go.

Now obviously Louis was not about to be browbeaten by Henry. His decision was influenced by certain facts of which he was in possession, and we were not, as yet. His fears had entirely been based on the possibility that Warwick, having set off with a good deal of French money in his purse, might do another volte-face, and present the kingdom back to

Edward, for making war on France. Now, the information he
had received, and of which as I have said we were then
ignorant, precluded such a turn of events, and it became
necessary for the Lancastrian cause to summon all its
resources and brace itself for the trials ahead – and obviously
the principal one of its resources was myself.

Knowing nothing of what was going on, I was merely
relieved and happy, refusing even to be downcast at the
prospect of a Channel crossing in the dead of winter. Thus
I hurried down to Honfleur, accompanied by my ladies, who
included the Countess of Warwick, and by the Prince and
Princess of Wales, as well as by a goodly number of
Lancastrian lords who had rallied from every direction.
Among them, to my astonishment but also my gratification,
was old Sir John Wenlock – he was old indeed, past seventy
– who now again offered his sword in my cause. I wept as
I embraced him. I was also joined, from Brittany where they
had been sheltering, by Margaret Beaufort and her son by
Edmund Tudor, Henry; he was known as Henry of Richmond, although he had never been confirmed in his right to
his father's title. It was some years since I had seen this boy,
then fourteen, but I was struck by his resemblance to his
poor father. Physically, that is. He had none of his father's
outgoing personality, but appeared rather withdrawn and
frightened by it all. Well, seeing that he had been a fugitive
since he could remember, this was hardly surprising. But I
hugged him most tenderly. He was quite a close relative, in
a roundabout sort of way: as Edmund's son he was my step-
nephew, as he was equally as Margaret's son. More
importantly, I saw in him a future support for my own
Edward when he ascended the throne.

We embarked on 24 March, the day after my forty-first
birthday, despite lowering skies. But outside the harbour the
wind was in the north, and we could make no progress. My
stomach was a good deal stronger now than it had been
twenty-six years before, and I was prepared to brave even a

storm to regain English soil; but no ship can sail into the wind, and thus we were forced back. Over the next three weeks we put out twice more, and still the wind persisted from the north-east. The skies were clear and a most brilliant blue, the sun shone ... and we could not move. It was most galling.

And became more so when word arrived that Edward of March, financed by his brother-in-law Charles of Burgundy, had made a landing on the north-east English coast. That wind which was restraining us had actually assisted him, as he had made the crossing from the Low Countries. The news that March had managed to enlist the help of Burgundy was what had determined Louis to send me as well to England, as there was no longer any chance of Warwick again changing sides; March was clearly bent on revenge.

The news of March's manoeuvres was of course worrying, but if we could not sail north, ships could certainly sail south. Soon a messenger arrived from Warwick assuring me that he had the business well in hand, and intended to leave London and march northward to deal with the invader. Fool that I was, I still believed this was possible.

At last we managed to put to sea, on Easter Sunday, 13 April. The last news I had heard had arrived several days previously, stating that Warwick was leaving London to unite his army with that of Clarence in order to give battle to March, who it was known was coming south and gathering support as he did so. It was therefore entirely probable that the two armies would have met by now, and in fact they did encounter each other on this very day.

But I was ignorant of it. The wind had gone from northeast to east, and so it was on our beam, as the sailors say. This meant that any attempt to gain the Solent and thus Portsmouth was out of the question. We clung as close to the north as was possible, but yet could only make port at a fishing village in the West Country, situated at the mouth of the River Wey, and called for this reason Weymouth. This

place is a good distance from London, but we were happy
just to be ashore.

Naturally the Prince and I were anxious to gain London as
soon as was possible. Horses were requisitioned from the
neighbouring farms, and off we set, not pausing before
nightfall when we halted at Carne Abbey. We were exhausted and retired after a hasty supper, but not before
Edward and I had walked out into the night to look at the
twinkling stars and inhale the fresh smell of England in
spring. 'I shall rule this land,' my son said, 'with you at my
side, dearest Mother.'

We embraced. A lifetime of endeavour had it seemed
come to an end. Indeed it had.

Next morning we rode on as far as Beaulieu, where we
stopped for a meal. We were preparing to mount up and
resume our journey when we heard the drumming of hooves.
We stared at the low hills fronting us in a mixture of
emotions, but I will confess my heart gave a great lurch as
I recognised not only Edmund Somerset, but his younger
brother John Beaufort as well as several other Lancastrian
lords, all clearly in a great bother – obviously, had Warwick
gained a victory and captured March, it would have only
been necessary to send a simple messenger with glad tidings.
But now: 'We are lost!' John Beaufort shrieked, throwing
himself from the saddle at my feet.

I endeavoured to maintain my composure. 'How can this
be?' I inquired.

'Clarence!' the young man moaned. 'He deserted us for
his brother.' Well, I could have told them that would
happen.

Edmund had also dismounted. He was the picture of
misery. 'That would have mattered naught. It was the fog,'
he muttered. 'It led to friend and foe being unable to
determine which was which. We gained the day on the right,
but the Yorkists had the advantage on the left. It might still
have turned out well, but when the Yorkists swung round

and came in upon our rear, there was a shout of treachery, and our people fled.'

'And Warwick?'

'Warwick is dead, your grace.'

At these dread words the morning suddenly grew dark and I became giddy. I lost my balance, and had to be held by my ladies. This was the first, and last, time in my life that I had ever fainted. And it only lasted a short time, although when I got my eyes open I wondered why I did not immediately close them again as I gazed at the gloomy faces around me. The Princess of Wales was in tears, as was her mother. They could not be blamed; after all, the man had been their father and husband. But . . . 'How did the Earl die?' I inquired.

'He had dismounted, to fight on foot,' Edmund explained. A necessary precaution, I supposed, to convince his people he would not run away and desert them, as he had at St Albans.

'Then when the battle was seen to be lost,' Edmund continued, 'and he was urged to save himself, he could not find his horse, and was cut down in the mêlée.'

'Where did all of this take place?' asked the Prince.

'At High Barnet, north of London,' Edmund replied. 'March is in the city by now. Your grace, you must flee. Are your ships still waiting?'

But I had recovered from the blow, and I was realising that it was what I had always half-expected to happen; at the vital moment Warwick had proved a broken reed. On the other hand, he had only ever been going to be a millstone round my neck. As for that other millstone . . . 'And King Henry?' I asked.

'Taken by the Yorkists, your grace. Your grace, you must flee!'

This time, surely, they would put the poor old sod to death. But I remained alive. As did my son. 'How many men can we muster?' I looked past the lords at the banners on the hilltop.

'Why, we have some two thousand men with us, your grace, but the Earl of March has at least twice that number.'

'But he is in London, and we are here,' I pointed out. 'Is not Jasper Tudor, the Earl of Pembroke, in Wales, raising an army?'

'He is, your grace, but Wales is several marches away.'

I smiled at the pun. 'It is yet nearer to us than it is to March.'

They were astonished. 'You mean to fight again, your grace?'

'I have come here to fight,' I reminded them.

'But without Warwick—'

'My lord of Warwick has played his part right well,' I told them. 'He has delayed our enemy, and killed a good number of his people. And he has died on the field of battle. We could not ask more of him. Now it is up to us to take advantage of his prowess. We will return to the West Country, raise our standard and then march north for the Severn and Wales. Edmund, you will send gallopers ahead to command Jasper Tudor to join us with all haste.'

He tugged his beard and looked at his fellows.

'It might work,' the Earl of Devonshire muttered.

'If King Edward stands still,' John Somerset said.

'King Edward?' I demanded. 'There is no King Edward on the throne of England, unless you are trying to tell me that my husband is dead. In which case, King Edward stands before you.'

They stammered their apologies, and I brushed them aside. 'We will make the Earl of March stand still,' I told them. 'By occupying his mind. Edmund, I appoint you commander-in-chief of my army.' He swelled with pride.

'You will therefore, firstly, carry out my orders as regards Jasper Tudor. Secondly, you will despatch a small force of men to march on London, with as much noise and publicity as possible, so that they will everywhere be taken for our advance guard. And thirdly, our main body will move to the West Country, recruiting as we go; the moment we are sure of March's dispositions, we shall swing north for Bristol and then Gloucester and the bridges into Wales. Is this understood?'

They exchanged glances; none of them had ever seen me, or any woman, in full martial ardour – saving only old Wenlock, who drew himself up. 'We understand, your grace. I would crave a command.'

He was seventy, but he was probably the best man amongst them. 'You shall have your command, Sir John,' I promised. 'But first, there are domestic matters to be attended to. Prince Edward must be escorted back to Weymouth, and put on a ship for France.'

'Mother!' the Prince protested. 'I came here to fight.'

'My darling boy,' I said, 'it is extremely likely that by now your father has indeed been done to death. Therefore you are King of England. Therefore your life is our most precious possession.'

'My lords!' Edward appealed. It was the first time he had ever defied me. 'Did not the Black Prince win his spurs at sixteen? Have I not the right to fight for my kingdom?' My heart went out to him. If only my husband had been such a man!

'The Prince is right, your grace,' Somerset said. 'He has the right, nay, the duty, to fight for his kingdom. Equally will our people fight the more heartily, knowing of his presence, than in his absence.'

I knew they were right; and indeed that I had been wrong to suggest flight.

'But that you should withdraw, Mother, is entirely proper,' the Prince said.

'And abandon you, and the cause! Never,' I declared. 'Where the Red Rose fights, there do I.' Indeed, if only I had been present at Barnet.

My lords cheered my courage. Margaret Beaufort and her young son had no such inhibitions; they fled for the coast and safety.

*

My commands were obeyed and we set off, heading first of all for Exeter, where we were joined by the remnants of Warwick's army, and then north for Bristol. I was somewhat disappointed in the reactions of the local gentry, few of whom rallied to our cause, but I remained confident; if I could but unite with Jasper I would have a formidable force. As yet we had no word of any move from March – there was always the chance that he had lost himself in the fleshpots of London.

Bristol opened its gates to us, and we requisitioned not only men and arms but even some artillery we found there. Thence it was on to Gloucester, and the bridge across the Severn.

It was now that messengers arrived, bringing two very different pieces of news. One was from Jasper, reassuring me that he had mustered an army of some size, and that he would await my arrival on the north bank of the Severn. This was most encouraging. The other was that Edward of March had not been deceived by our feelers towards London, but was instead hurrying day and night to catch up with us before we could cross the river. Well, of course, he had no hope of that. Or he should have had none; we were at least forty-eight hours ahead of him, and virtually in sight of the bridge at Gloucester. We therefore directed ourselves to this, congratulating ourselves that, strategically at the least, we had had the better of the argument so far.

Alas, I doubt anyone has ever had the better of any argument with Edward of March. Once he had realised that I was moving north, he knew exactly what I was up to, just as he knew that to allow me to unite with Jasper would be a grave mistake. Thus when we arrived at Gloucester, we found the gates closed, and the walls lined with determined men. A galloper from March had got there only hours before us, commanding the governor of the city, a lout called Richard Beauchamp, to refuse us entry, and thus access to the bridge. I was furious. Was this upstart rogue to wreck all my hopes? But neither threats nor the offers of bribes had any effect upon this disgusting man; indeed, his archers fired upon me while I endeavoured to talk some sense into his stupid head.

Thus was I faced with a considerable dilemma. The next available ford was some three marches away to the north, and all the while the Yorkist army was advancing from the east. 'We are lost,' Edmund Somerset muttered. He was, in almost every way, an exact replica of his father.

'Never,' I declared, as I looked over the ranks of my people. 'Look at old Sir John! He breathes fire.'

'He has little choice,' Edmund pointed out. 'From the Yorkist point of view, he is a turncoat. If he is taken, he loses his head.'

'Dear Edmund,' I said, 'if *any* of us are taken we lose our heads.'

He gulped, as if he had not previously considered that fact. 'There is yet time to make the coast, and escape.'

'And desert all these gallant men? *They* cannot escape. Nor are we yet defeated. We will march north.'

'Your grace, it is forty-eight hours to the next ford. In forty-eight hours the Yorkists will be upon us.'

'Well, then, we shall just have to cover the distance in thirty-six hours,' I said. 'Certainly we do no good standing here arguing. Move out your men, my lord of Somerset. We have all to gain. Haste, haste, and may the devil take the hindmost.'

I rode among my men myself, as I had before Northampton and Towton. 'Once across the river,' I told them, 'and victory is within our grasp. Once we are united with the Welsh, we will outnumber our enemy by two to one. Once across the river!'

They gave a great halloo and set off, on perhaps the most desperate race against time in military history. All through that day and the following night we struggled on. There were stragglers, and undoubtedly there were deserters. That scoundrel Beauchamp sallied forth from his lair in Gloucester and harried our rear; he even managed to make off with some of our cannon. But the main part of my force kept up and kept marching, drooping with exhaustion. I may say that no one was more exhausted than myself, for I did not rest either, but spent the entire day and night walking my horse up and down our column, encouraging and exhorting, letting the men see the beauty they were fighting for, sustaining myself with a morsel of food and a glass of wine from time to time. I thought only of Jasper and his Welsh legions.

And so we came within distance of Tewkesbury and the ford. It was again evening, but the town was only a few miles further on, and although we had marched non-stop for thirty-six hours and could scarce put one foot in front of the other, I was determined to press on, even if it meant crossing the river in the darkness. But as I waited for the rearguard to come up, for I was determined not to be checked at this town, which lacked the fortifications of Bristol, my scouts came riding in with the grimmest news: Edward of March's advance guard had seized the ford, and his main body was close at hand.

'How can this be?' Edmund cried. 'No army can have marched as we have done.'

'The Yorkists appear to have managed it,' I said quietly, even though sick despair was lapping at my stomach.

'What's to be done?' Devonshire asked.

'We have no choice,' I told them. 'We must fight.'

They exchanged glances.

'We are outnumbered,' Edmund reminded me. 'And exhausted.'

'The Yorkists cannot be less exhausted,' I said. As for being outnumbered, we will have to choose our position. They will certainly seek to come to us.'

I immediately rode out to inspect the ground where we should have to fight, while my people sank to the ground where they stood, only glad to be resting instead of marching. My first task was to send a messenger to Jasper telling him it was no longer possible for him to wait on me, but that I was now waiting on him. I begged him to come to my aid with as much publicity as possible; obviously he could not hope to arrive in time for the morrow, but the very news of his coming might give March pause for thought, while in the event of a drawn battle, I would have reinforcements closer at hand.

And indeed I could see no reason why we should not be able to withstand the assault of even such a soldier as Edward of March. The ground was well broken, save immediately in front of the position I selected as our own. This I told Somerset to have entrenched; to either side there were numerous hedges and sunken lanes, which would surely preclude the possibility of a flank attack, and which would conceal our own flankers. Behind our position was the abbey I had made my headquarters.

'What are your dispositions, your grace?' Somerset asked.

'We will form up in three divisions,' I told him. 'You and your brother John will command the first. The Prince of Wales will command the second. The Earl of Devonshire will command the third.'

Edward clapped his hands for joy, but Somerset frowned. 'With the deepest respect, your grace ... the Prince has never fought a battle before.'

'That is not important,' I told him. 'I will be at his side.'

'You, your grace?'

'You, Mother?' echoed Edward.

Here we went again. But all my chieftains were aghast at the idea of my fighting at the side of my son. As usual I allowed myself to be overborne, conscious as I was that I could play no actual part in the hurly-burly, and that once battle was joined, if I were in the hurly-burly, I would be quite unable to exercise any command. 'Very well,' I agreed. 'Then do you, Sir John Wenlock, be my son's guide and mentor in this affair.'

I knew I could not look for a better man for such a post,

and indeed the old fellow was overcome with gratitude.

By now the day was well advanced, and we were
informed that there was a meal waiting for us in the abbey.
We had just turned our horses when we heard a whisper of
sound seeping across the valley. It was made up of many
things, from the clink of armour to the neighing of horses,
but principally was it the tramp of marching feet. 'The
Yorkists,' John Beaufort muttered. He was in a state of high
agitation.

'We knew they were coming,' I reminded him. 'All that
remains is for us to defeat them tomorrow.'

I at least ate a hearty meal; unlike most of my commanders
I was an experienced campaigner. Indeed, I surveyed them
with very mixed feelings. On the one hand my heart could
not help but swell with pride, as I saw these young lions,
almost all of whom were young enough to have been my
sons, gathered around me in this most decisive moment of
my life. At the other extreme of course was John Wenlock,
but here again was a cause for pride: that a man old enough
to be my father should so willingly take up my cause once
again. But, on the other hand, I could not help but feel a
sensation of approaching doom as I reflected on their
inexperience, when they were about to be confronted by the
most fearsome warrior of the age. There could be no
question about that, now that Warwick was in the dust –
there had actually been none while Warwick was alive! I
could only tell myself that their glory, and mine, would be
the greater after our victory.

Yet sleep was slow to come. I went out on to the terrace
of the abbey to look through the darkness at the campfires
of my people and, in the distance, the glow which marked
the fires of the Yorkists. There, I found my son seated, also
staring at the night. 'You should rest,' I told him. 'Tomorrow
will be a very long day.'

'At the end of which I may be resting for ever,' he
remarked.

I rested my hand on his shoulder. 'At the end of it, you and I will be marching on London, and your heritage.'

For sixteen years, since he had been a babe at my breast, had I spoken to him of that heritage, reminded him of his great forebears, beseeched him to emulate the Edwards who had gone before. I had sought to make him a ruler and a soldier as much as a man. There were times when, as after the second battle of St Albans, I had feared I had put too much iron and not enough love into his soul. There had been times, indeed, during our exile at St Michel, when I had doubted he loved even me, so rigidly had I set his face towards the future and the strength that would be needed both to achieve and maintain that future.

Now he took me by surprise. My hand still rested on his shoulder, and his came up to grasp my fingers. 'I will be a good king, Mother,' he said. ' I swear it by all that I hold sacred. I will be just, and strong, and make England great again.'

There were tears in my eyes. 'I believe you, Edward,' I replied. I believe him still.

Our forces were astir at dawn, listening to the bugle calls of the Yorkists scarce a mile away. My men tramped to their positions and I stood on the terrace of the abbey beside Somerset, who was in full armour. I could not help but reflect on his elder brother and his father, both of whom had sallied forth to do battle for my cause, and found themselves dead at the end of it. But perhaps third time was indeed lucky. 'You must withdraw, your grace,' he said.

'Not until I have spoken with the men,' I told him, and summoned my palfrey.

My commanders were agitated as I rode down to the Lancastrian ranks, for they could make out a forward movement among the Yorkists. To the front was the Boar's Head banner of Richard of York, who had been created Duke of Gloucester by his brother March. I had never met this youth, who was a year older than my Edward, but I had

heard that he was a soldier inferior only to his brother. My
people were obviously alarmed at the possibility that I might
still be within range, when this impetuous boy launched his
assault.

However, I was in no mood to be frightened by anyone
young enough to be my own son, and rode slowly through
the ranks of my men while I reminded them of many things.
This time I really let myself go, as I had nothing to lose. I
told them that they were fighting to end an usurpation and
release their rightful king, the good and honest Henry, from
a vile and iniquitous imprisonment. I told them that victory
would gain them the highest awards, and again suggested
that the traitorous London merchants would be required to
meet our demands.

I commanded them always to look to the Prince of Wales,
who was standing among them, determined to conquer or to
die, and who would never forget those who stood at his
shoulder this day. Once again I promised them rewards, as
I told them that every man should share in the distribution
of the Yorkist estates and the Yorkist wealth. But above all
I reminded them that this field would be immortal, as would
all those who fought and died, and won, here.

Never had I received such a roar of loyal applause as from
these, my last few lions. Swords were held aloft to catch the
morning sunlight, and a huge paean of promised victory rose
from their throats. This certainly stirred the Yorkists and
with a great shout their first battle swarmed towards us,
while with a boom their artillery also loosed off a cannon-
ade. 'You *must* withdraw, your grace,' Somerset begged.

I nodded, gave Edward a last clasp of the hand, received
another cheer from my men, and then rode my palfrey back
up the slope to the abbey and my ladies. From this vantage
point I overlooked the field and could see Gloucester's men
tramping forward, pausing from time to time to loose off
their crossbows. They made slow progress, owing to the
broken nature of the terrain; when they came to the slope on
which my army was posted they were greeted with a hail of

arrows. They checked their advance, and then insensibly began to move to the rear.

My ladies clapped their hands, and I too felt a glow of confidence. Alas, for my hopes. All was going well, and more important, was going according to plan. That plan was, it may be recalled, to hold the Yorkists and make them exhaust themselves in attacking our very strong position. Above all we had to keep the ground, in the certain hope that Jasper and his Welshmen were marching to our succour. Every hour, nay, every minute we occupied the Yorkist host while still maintaining our position could be regarded as a victory. No one in my camp had once raised the question of carrying the fight to March, where our lack of numbers was sure to tell.

Yet now Somerset proved himself to be a true son and brother, at once headstrong and incompetent. Seeing Gloucester's men retreating, he seems to have completely lost control of himself, forgotten our strategy, forgotten our plans, forgotten the strength of our position, forgotten that we were outnumbered by perhaps two to one, forgotten that only a third of March's army had thus far been engaged . . . Uttering a great halloo, he led his division, the largest in my army, forward in a great rush. I clapped my hands to my cheeks in consternation. 'My God!' I said. 'The fool! We are utterly undone!'

Somerset's mad charge would probably have cost us the battle in any event. But March had actually taken steps to counter an advance on our part, and sent two hundred mounted men-at-arms into the woods on our left. Now, as soon as it was seen that Somerset's division had left its entrenchments, Gloucester halted his own men and faced about, the rest of March's troops moved forward, and as Somerset's people closed with Gloucester's, the two hundred horsemen emerged from the wood and struck them in the flank. I stared at the scene beneath me, quite unable to believe my eyes, while my ladies screamed their terror. And yet, my other two divisions remained, for Wenlock had refused to permit Prince Edward to follow his crazy half-brother, and Devonshire's third battle remained in reserve. Perhaps I even yet had some hopes of withdrawing in good order, to remain confident of Jasper's coming.

Vain hope! Even as I watched, Somerset's division broke and ran in every direction. My son's division stood firm, but to my horror I saw Somerset, who lacked the courage to stand and die with the men he had led to disaster, come galloping back. Waving his arms and his battleaxe, he confronted Wenlock, who stood at Edward's side, clearly demanding why Wenlock had not supported his advance. I do not know what reply the old knight made, but it was apparently not good enough. Before our stricken gaze Somerset swung his axe around his head and brought it down on Wenlock's bald pate, the old man having discarded his helmet the better to argue. I will swear Wenlock was split down to his neck.

Witnessing this catastrophe, Wenlock's men gave a great shout; instead of attacking Somerset, which would have made some sense, they turned and fled. Their rout carried along Devonshire's division, and in a matter of moments my army had ceased to exist.

My sole concern was for the Prince, and I would have gone to him, even had it meant facing the Yorkists single-handed, and dying. But I was not even allowed that privilege. I was virtually kidnapped by my ladies, who forced me from the field, found our mounts, and galloped away for their lives – or at least their collective virtue – until we reached a nearby convent, where they begged sanctuary. John Combe gallantly volunteered to ride into the mêlée and bring Edward to me, and off he went. I was never to see him again.

I was incapable of thought. Life became a matter of mere awareness: that I lived and breathed but that my cause, and that of Henry and my son, was irretrievably lost. My only concern was for the Prince. Action was beyond me.

Not that it would have availed me. One or two of my

ladies spoke of flight, of attempting to reach the south coast, and a ship for France. They were soon dissuaded as they learned of Yorkist patrols scouring the country in every direction. In any event, I would not have gone without certain news of the Prince. Thus we languished for three days, three days in which I did not wash or change my clothing, in which my only sustenance was an occasional glass of wine, and in which I spent every waking moment on my knees like a true wife to my husband, praying. To no avail. On the third day the Yorkists came.

They stood before me, great mailed monsters, while my ladies trembled in a huddle of terrified femininity.

But I faced them as defiantly as ever. To my surprise, they treated me with the deference due to my rank, although their words were sinister enough. 'His grace the King wishes to receive you, your grace,' they said. 'He will be here in an hour. Will you not prepare yourself?"

I flushed at the reference to my state of *déshabillé*, and summoned my ladies. An hour later I was back at my best, and face to face with the villain who had brought me to bay. I found him every bit as overwhelming as had been suggested by report. He wore full armour, although he had removed his helmet, and was quite the tallest and broadest man I had ever seen; I had to bend my neck to look up at him. His features were quite magnificent, bold and strong, handsome and ruddy, and crowned with a thatch of red-gold hair. Only at second glance were some evidences of dissipation to be seen.

At his side, his brother Richard of Gloucester seemed almost like a changeling, being a good head shorter, dark-complexioned, and inclined to walk with a slight stoop.

Both brothers were obviously exhilarated at their crowning victory, but they greeted me gravely enough. 'Your grace,' March said, 'it is too many years since we last met.'

I did not lower my gaze, even if he was about to order my execution. 'Fate has seen fit to give you the victory, my lord.'

Gloucester snorted in anger that I had not addressed his brother as king, but Edward did not appear to take offence. 'And no man, or woman, can go against Fate, your grace,' he agreed easily. 'Now I must ask you to accompany me to London.'

'For what purpose, sir?'

He smiled. Again, it was an easy smile, but there was neither softness nor pity in his eyes. 'Why, madam,' he said, 'for whatever purpose it may please me to decide.'

We stared at each other, but both of us knew who was the master. 'Am I allowed to ask after my son?'

'Alas, madam, your son is dead.'

It was some seconds before I could speak. Then I asked, 'How did he die?'

Edward and his brother exchanged a quick glance. 'He died most gallantly, madam,' Edward told me. 'Cut down while trying to rally his troops.' I wished to believe him. I wish to believe him still. But since that day I have heard rumours that my son was in fact taken prisoner and led before March and his brother, and there answered them with contempt, and was murdered for it. Thus I do not know what to believe, and I remember that conspiratorial exchange of glances.

In these circumstances it seemed pointless to inquire after the fate of John Combe.

Certainly there could be no question of Edward of March's ruthlessness. Both Somerset and his brother had certainly been murdered, after taking sanctuary in a church. Even this age-old custom had not saved them, as they had been dragged out, some said by Edward himself, and butchered. I set out on my melancholy journey to London but Gloucester had ridden on ahead; and by the time I reached the capital, my husband was dead. Of course it was given out that Henry had died from sheer despair at learning of the final ending of all his hopes and the death of his son. But the fact is that the Yorkists had always refused to accept that the Prince of Wales *was* Henry's son, while, with him dead and me a captive, they had no reason to keep the poor old man alive. Even more conclusive in its delineation of Edward's character is the execution, more recently, of his own brother, George of Clarence, never forgiven for having allied himself with Warwick, even temporarily.

Then what of me? In Yorkist eyes I was the most guilty as well as the most formidable of their foes. But as I have mentioned earlier, the English do not make war upon noble ladies; perhaps it would have been better if they did. I was treated with the greatest of courtesy ... but I was forced to ride in a cart, bumped and jolted on the uneven roads, until my rump became so sore I could scarce sit. Every hour of every day I was exposed to the stares of the unwashed. Some of these hooted and jeered, and were only prevented from pelting me with mud and missiles by my guards; more stood silently – but all knew they were watching a deposed and captive queen.

And so to London. It may well be imagined that it was this final part of my journey which concerned me most. Quite apart from the well-known hostility of the Londoners to my person, I had no doubt that it would be the most utter humiliation. In the event, it was not in the least as I had feared. The Londoners seemed in awe of me. They stared and pointed and whispered as I rumbled by. The Queen of Lions was chained at last.

I think my worst moment came after I had left the public gaze, and was in my cell in the Tower, and Bella came to visit me. I stood at her entry, and indeed all but curtsied. Tall and beautiful, more voluptuous than usual as she was still feeding the son to whom she had given birth the previous November, she was wearing the finest clothes and jewels, and looked every inch a queen. I had nothing save travel-worn garments and naked fingers.

We gazed at each other, and I looked for some sign of the love we had once shared. Perhaps I even hoped for an embrace. But she made no move towards me. 'I am sorry for the death of your son,' she said.

'Thank you.'

'It is sad to see you come to this, Meg,' Bella said at last. 'But my husband has given me his word that you shall not be harmed.'

'Then what is to become of me?'

'Well . . . you must understand that the King cannot just let you go, without adequate safeguards. I will send you some books to while away the hours.'

This she did and I was most appreciative, even, if I understood there were going to be a great number of hours to be whiled away. In fact, I have neither the time nor the energy to calculate how many hours there are in six years, but I can assure you it is a very long time to be kept in captivity.

Bella was as good as her word, and I suffered no physical ill-treatment beyond the inconvenience of being moved from castle to castle, and custodian to custodian. Edward apparently feared that if I remained in one place for too long plans might be set afoot for my rescue, or that I might seduce my gaolers and escape. For a while, indeed, I was placed in the custody of old Alice Suffolk, who treated me most kindly. But when she died in April 1475 it was back to my perambulations. For a spirit like mine to be a captive, to have no share in the great events around me, to realise that my life of endeavour was behind me, was a severe punishment. Equally severe was it to watch my beauty begin to fade, wrinkles to appear on my marvellous neck, grey streaks in my hair.

Worst of all, however, was the uncertainty as to how long I was going to be kept in this brutish incarceration.

In fact, I was released within a few months of Alice's death. Papa had been labouring long to raise the ransom demanded by Edward of March, and in the end this was only accomplished by the sale of his favourite demesne, the County of Provence, to Cousin Louis, for fifty thousand crowns. Oh, if Papa had been able to bring himself to make such a sale during my heyday, what could I not have accomplished with such a sum?

Naturally I was not kept informed of what was happening, and thus it was with some surprise that in November of that year I received a visit from Richard of Gloucester. I have to confess I received him with a certain alarmed flutter at my heart, for rumour had it that this dark-visaged boy had disposed of my husband with his own two hands, and had carried out various other secret executions for his brother. Had he now come to dispose of me?

Nor were my feelings immediately relieved when he presented me with a sheet of parchment, which read as follows:

I, Margaret, formerly in England married, renounce all that I could pretend to in England by the conditions of my marriage, with all other things there to Edward now King of England.

This document I signed. I had nothing left to fight for, or with. Or so it seemed at the time.

That done I was escorted to Portsmouth, and once again crossed the Channel. I had hoped to be greeted by Papa, but he was not there, and in his place were stern-faced lawyers representing Cousin Louis. These produced another document for me to sign, this one renouncing all my rights to any titles ever held, or claimed, by the house of Anjou, in return for a pittance of a pension. This too, in my depressed state, I signed.

I was then escorted to the manor of Reculée, which Louis had graciously assigned to me. I remained there for some years, before being removed to the castle of Dampierre, where I pen these words. Dampierre is, of course, close to Saumur and, although I am not allowed to venture into the town, it is nonetheless of some gratification to me to be once again in the land where I spent my girlhood, and to be able to overlook that River Loire, where I was wont to bathe so carelessly.

How long ago that seems! How many wild adventures, and wild adventurers ago! Sadly, they are no more. Indeed, I hate to see those of my old followers who from time to time come to Dampierre. They are broken men, lacking money and sometimes even clothes. And I, in my straitened circumstances, can do little more than offer them a meal.

I grow old, and am confronted with the failure of my life. Edward of March ... but I suppose that now I must grant him the title he seized and call him Edward IV of England, is acclaimed the most successful monarch of his day. Having announced his determination to invade France, it took all of Cousin Louis's treasury to buy him off, which merely left him more successful than before. His line is also secure, as Bella has now given birth to two young princes, both handsome – as they should be with such magnificent parents – and healthy.

As for the rest of my old sparring partners: well, Cousin Charles of Burgundy has managed to get himself killed by the Swiss pikemen, and Cousin Louis continues to rule France – and sadly, me – with all of his usual duplicity.

Is there no future for the Red Rose? I must be honest and admit that there is not. People dream, but it is cheap to dream. This week I am to receive a visit from Margaret Beaufort's son by Edmund Tudor. This Henry of Richmond is now twenty-two years of age, but has changed little from the youth I remember hurrying away from any involvement in the fight at Tewkesbury. Yet amazingly he is the last Lancastrian prince, supposing we can possibly acknowledge that the son of a bastard has any such right.

Ostensibly, he is coming to celebrate my fiftieth birthday. I do not wish to celebrate my fiftieth birthday. I can think of nothing more detestable. My hair is grey and my complexion is fading. My beauty is only a memory, and I am so very tired all the time. But he will come. And he will dream aloud, of one day ... It has always been, one day. That day will never come. The idea of frightened little red-headed Henry of Richmond ever confronting the bold, bad and beautiful Edward of York is ludicrous. What a pair *we* would have made, had he looked kindly on me, instead of Bella!

Dampierre, 18 March, 1480.

Postscript

Margaret of Anjou died on 25 August 1482. She was fifty-one years and five months old, worn out by her years of effort on behalf of the Red Rose.

She was, as usual, wrong in her judgements of both people and the future. Less than a year later, Edward IV followed her to the grave, struck down – probably by appendicitis – in the very prime of life, and after his brother Richard of Gloucester had seized the throne from Bella's sons, Henry of Richmond did indeed regain the crown for the house of Lancaster, and by his marriage with Bella's daughter ended the dynastic quarrel and founded the house of Tudor.

Henry VII and his mother-in-law did not get on, and Bella fell on hard times, as had Margaret before her.

Cousin Louis died on 30 August 1483, almost exactly a year after Margaret.

OTTOMAN

Alan Savage

In 1448 an English master-gunner, John Hawkwood,
arrives in the fabled city of Constantinople. He intends to
enter the service of the Byzantine emperor, whose capital
is this astonishing meeting-place of East and West – now
in dire threat from the Ottoman Turks.

But even gun-powder cannot prevail and, in 1453,
Constantinople falls to the foe. By fate the Hawkwoods
have already changed allegiance, and now serve the
conquerors in their victorious surge across eastern Europe
and the Mediterranean shores.

Though showered with wealth and privilege, they need
every ounce of political cunning to survive the swirling
intrigues and bloody massacres which dominate the
Ottoman realm. For four generations the Hawkwood men
are military leaders and envoys, while their women are
beautiful captives or dutiful concubines trained in the arts
of sensual pleasure.

But always the grim spectres of betrayal and sudden
death, of ravishment and torture lurk behind the gilded
pillars of their palaces and harems . . .

QUEEN OF NIGHT

Alan Savage

Queen Joanna I of Naples was the most beautiful and accomplished woman of her times. She is also remembered as a cold-blooded murderess and a woman of the most questionable morals.

Queen of Night is her story, told through the eyes of her devoted companion Richilde Benoit – an Englishwoman whose own life parallels Joanna's in its astonishing range of intrigue, romance, warfare, rape, betrayal and sheer adventure.

Set against the rich tapestry of mediaeval Italy, with all its colour and passion, brutality and splendour, *Queen of Night* is an enthralling account of a truly remarkable woman.

☐	Ottoman	Alan Savage	£4.99
☐	Moghul	Alan Savage	£4.99
☐	The Eight Banners	Alan Savage	£4.99
☐	Queen of Night	Alan Savage	£4.99
☐	The Last Bannerman	Alan Savage	£4.99

Warner Books now offers an exciting range of quality titles by both established and new authors. All of the books in this series are available from:

    Little, Brown and Company (UK) Limited,
    P.O. Box 11,
    Falmouth,
    Cornwall TR10 9EN.

Alternatively you may fax your order to the above address. Fax No. 0326 376423.

Payments can be made as follows: cheque, postal order (payable to Little, Brown and Company) or by credit cards, Visa/Access. Do not send cash or currency. UK customers and B.F.P.O. please allow £1.00 for postage and packing for the first book, plus 50p for the second book, plus 30p for each additional book up to a maximum charge of £3.00 (7 books plus).

Overseas customers including Ireland, please allow £2.00 for the first book plus £1.00 for the second book, plus 50p for each additional book.

NAME (Block Letters) ....

....

ADDRESS ....

....

....

☐ I enclose my remittance for _____

☐ I wish to pay by Access/Visa Card

Number ☐☐☐☐☐☐☐☐☐☐☐☐☐☐☐☐

Card Expiry Date ☐☐☐☐